FAERIE DESTINY

THE FAE CHRONICLES

VALIA LIND

SKAZKA PRESS

MARKED BY FAE

THE FAE CHRONICLES PREQUEL

CHAPTER 1

$\mathcal{P}$retty sure I'm cursed. And not the fun kind.

Although, people would probably argue with me about there being a fun kind. I guess it all depends on your definition of a curse.

I, for one, think that moving schools at the start of senior year is the worst kind of curse. Not only that, but I'm starting at Thunderbird Academy. The school that's now legend. Last year, one of the students and her friends here stopped a pretty powerful Ancient from getting her hands on some magic. There was also a very big threat of this Ancient killing half the students and turning others to the dark side. But good prevailed and now this place is a fortress.

With everything going on in our world, with the Ancients rising and wreaking havoc, my parents thought this would be the safest place for me. Considering it's the hot spot for the most powerful spells and enchantments, they might be right. If the school had a reputation before, it has an even bigger one now. Everyone wants to send their kids here. My parents had to pull some strings.

It's not that I don't want to be here. It's just the human part of me is rearing its head, the part that's not exactly a fan of being thrust into the middle of a tight knit community, all by my lonesome. I had to leave my family and friends behind. But my parents thought it would be best, and I'm in no position to argue. With everything that's been going on, if this gives them even some small peace of mind, I'll do it.

"Hello!" A cheery woman with curly burgundy hair greets me as I walk into the reception area. "I'm Miss Cindy! You must be Avery."

"I am."

"Don't look so surprised, I make it my business to know who comes into this school. I'm Headmaster Marković's personal assistant. I have your class schedule and room assignment right here."

"Thank you." I smile, her energy making it easy to like her. She might have some hospitality spell in this room to make it easier for newcomers, but I kind of think this is just her personality.

"I know it must be hard being away from your family and friends, but this school is like one big family. You'll fit right in." She pats my hand, and I soak up the small gesture like a thirsty flower soaking up water. Miss Cindy is the perfect person to greet newcomers. She put me right at ease. "Do you need help finding your room? I can get one of the helpers." She motions toward a group of students talking right outside the door, but I shake my head.

"I'll be fine on my own. Thank you."

With that, I take the materials she offered and head for the door. My old school wasn't nearly this impressive. Magical, yes. But kind of boring. It was housed in an old human school building, so it was modern. Mostly. This place is like stepping inside of a gothic novel. Everything is baroque and dramatic. But still inviting somehow.

If that makes sense? Did it make sense? Clearly, I'm on top of my mental capacity right now.

Sighing, I glance down at the map and head toward the stairs. There are groups of students everywhere. Suddenly, a burst of wind rushes through the hallway, slamming my hair into my face. I push it back before I walk into a guy talking to his friends. Everyone is laughing, but thankfully, not at me. They seem to know each other well, and that's probably the case. Most people don't wait until their senior year to start at a new place. But that's just how my life turned out.

Good thing I was raised resilient. Most of my friends panicked more than I did when they found out I'd be leaving.

"That sucks so much. How will you ever have a fun year with all those strangers?"

I heard that more than once. But I've learned we're not given anything we can't handle. If this keeps me and my family safe, I can work on my antisocial tendencies and make a few friends. Maybe.

Truth be told, I'm not here to make friends. I'm here to learn about my magic and hopefully, check a few things off my graduation list. I could've been sent to worse schools. This one brings a lot of potential to my future. It's just that I'm being uncharacteristically emotional about the whole thing at the moment.

Either way, it's going to be an interesting year.

* * *

MY ROOMMATE ISN'T there when I finally reach my room. Her stuff is on one side of the room though, so I drop my backpack on the other. Everything else has already been magically transferred. When I pull the top drawer of the dresser out, I find my favorite sweatpants and sweatshirt right there. The sight brings a smile to my face because I'm sure that was mom's doing.

I sit down on my bed, hugging the sweatshirt to me. I know why my parents thought this was a perfect place for me, but I'm still sad I couldn't figure out my magic at home.

The truth that matters a whole lot to my hometown and doesn't really matter to this school is that I'm half witch, half shifter. Back home, it's not a widely known fact, simply because people have a difficult time with the unusual right now. Well, I guess they've always had a difficult time with it, or I wouldn't have had the childhood I did.

But I'm not complaining. Not really. I have a wonderful family and great friends. But now that I'm graduating, I need to figure out where I fit in the world. That's why I'm at Thunderbird Academy.

I have plans for my future. Becoming part of the Watcher Council is all I've thought about for the last five years. I like facts, I like structure, and I like being able to do the impossible with my magic. In truth, my magic is already a little bit impossible, coming from both sides of the tracks, which is why Thunderbird Academy is such a good choice for me. But there is still so much left to discover.

Since the Ancients began waking up and sending the magical and non-magical community into full on panic, many things have changed for us. Most didn't even believe the Ancients were anything but a scary story told around the campfire. They're the oldest and the strongest of supernatural creatures. After they exhausted their magic warring with each other, they decided it was time for a nap. Apparently, nap time is over.

So here we are.

This school was in the middle of a war with one of these Ancients just last year. One of the students comes from one of the strongest families of witches, the Hawthorne's. Not only that, she discovered she was a story spell caster. Ah, I can't even imagine it.

Lying back on my bed, I look up at the ceiling, my mind spinning. If... no, *when* I become a Watcher, I can meet all of these amazing witches and shifters and work directly with them. I'll be the one responsible for preserving our history and recording it for generations to come. I'll be on the front lines of decision making, instead of a grunt doing all the dirty work.

There are opportunities here at this school, and I have to be open to the possibilities. Maybe that's why I wasn't as sad as my friends about leaving. The only people I truly miss are my parents. We're close. I know my friends still think it's strange that I tell my parents everything. It's more than just keeping my lineage a secret though. I truly respect my mom and dad, and I know this decision to send me away wasn't easy on them. It might've been even harder on them than on me. But I'll make them proud. Because I'm determined to do whatever it takes to reach my goals.

Turning my head to the left, I look over at the empty bed of my roommate. The one thing I'm not really good at is making friends. I keep to myself more often than not and find the company of a dimly lit library or a science lab more my speed. But maybe I'll luck out, and my roommate and I can be friends.

Looking back up at the ceiling, I bring my right hand in front of my face, turning it over. My magic has been a little wacky lately. It's what started the whole idea of me coming here in the first place. Closing my eyes, I concentrate on calling it forward. I can feel it waking up. It's never completely asleep, but lately, it's been more dormant than not.

When I open my eyes, my fingers pinch together and a flame bursts from the top. Letting my fingers dance around, I watch as the flame moves over each one, as if it's happy to be let free. There's no unnatural queasiness rising in the pit of my stomach like there was last time, and that makes me smile. Just when I think I'm in control, my magic gets a little bigger. I sit up hurriedly, trying to keep it contained.

"No, no, no, you stay where you are," I say, looking at the flame. Suddenly, a burst of water appears in my palm, extinguishing the flame entirely. I jump up, looking around to see where the water magic could have come from, but nobody's there. My own magic is still here, awake and present, but it feels different. Wiping my right hand with my left, I feel the moisture on both before it evaporates.

Well, I guess I won't be showing off my magic to anyone any time soon. First order of business is figuring out what's going on with it.

Before I can do anything, three rings sound over the announcement system, and a voice calls the students down to the lawn for a meeting. Pulling my magic back, I straighten my clothes and head for the door. I'm hoping I don't have to do some initiation ritual and prove I belong here, because my magic is not up for a performance.

"*H*ello, students. To those of you who are new, welcome! To returning students, welcome back."

I glance around at the Headmaster's words, trying to gauge who's new and who's returning. It's hard to tell, but a few look as unsure as I feel, so at least I know I'm not the only one. Typically, the newer students arrive later in the week. I'm one of the few who came with the returning students. Many have duties and jobs at the school, which is why they come early. I stick out like a sore thumb being a newbie.

"Last year was an interesting year, and as you all know, the threat is not eliminated. But it has been diminished. This place is the safest place for you, and that is why most of you were sent here. However, it is also a place of great learning. I hope you take every opportunity to do just that. Make friends, study hard, and enjoy yourselves."

The Headmaster pauses, and it seems like he studies each of us in turn before he finally speaks up again.

"Your class schedules are on your bed. If you have any questions, please do not hesitate to come see any of us teachers. More first year and transfer students will be arriving in the next few days. Please make sure to welcome them with open arms, like I know you will. Here is to a great year everyone!"

With that, he waves a hand, and a ball of magic explodes in color over our heads. It seems to light up the area in hues of the rainbow. It's beautiful.

"I think they're trying a little too hard, don't you?" A girl's voice reaches me while I'm staring at the sky. Looking over, I think she's talking to me, but her attention is on a boy next to her. Except I'm not sure I'd call him a boy. He's so big, he stands a head taller than anyone here.

"I think it's nice," he replies, shrugging a little.

"You would, Owen." The girl huffs and then pushes her way through the crowd. She nearly barrels into me, growling a little as I jump out of the way. She's gorgeous with long dark hair and a confidence that would make anyone stop and stare. Which is what I'm doing apparently. And the guy doesn't miss it.

"Don't mind Nat," the guy, Owen, says when our eyes meet. "She's salty about everything."

"I wasn't going to say anything," I reply, not sure what else I can say.

"I'm Owen." He puts out his hand for a handshake. I stare at it as if I've never seen a hand before. It takes me a second too long, but then I place my own into his and shake.

"I'm Avery." And apparently a shy mess all of a sudden.

"Didn't mean for the handshake to unsettle you." Owen gives me a small smile. "It's how my papa raised me."

"No, it's okay. It's just not something people do anymore."

He gives me another smile and then falls in step with me as we turn back toward the school.

I'm still pretty amazed at the grandeur of it all. The buildings in my town are mostly one and two stories. When I was little, we lived in a big city. But then Mom got a new job and we moved to the smaller town. I love it though. I never thought I would.

But this place, it's bigger than I imagined it. And so intriguing. The different architectural designs should make it look like a mess, but it actually looks well put together.

"So, you're a transfer or a freshman?" Owen adds the last part hurriedly.

"A transfer." I reply with a smile. "I'm a senior this year."

"Oh, that must be tough. I can't imagine leaving here and going somewhere else."

"And you are?"

"Junior."

"So, you were here last year, during all the..." I'm not sure how to ask the question politely, but I guess I don't have to because Owen knows what I mean.

"Yes. My Alpha was directly involved. His girl was the center of it all."

That makes me freeze in my tracks.

"You know Madison Hawthorne?"

I know I sound in awe, but she's a legend. No one story spell casts like she can. Not for centuries now.

"I do. And look at that, you're about to as well."

"Wait, what?"

I glance at the guy beside me and he smiles, nodding to the left. When I turn, my eyes land on a girl and a boy walking toward us, hand in hand. Right away, I know exactly who they are. I would have known even if we weren't just talking about them.

"Hi, I'm Maddie," the girl says the moment they stop in front of us. She's beautiful with her long brown hair and piercing eyes that carry a lot of knowledge behind them. Her smile is genuine, and I'm instantly at ease.

"Maddie, this is Avery. She's a senior."

"Oh, an upperclassman transfer. We don't get many of those."

"Sometimes you have to do what you have to do," I reply with my own smile.

"Don't we know it," the boy next to her says, giving Maddie a squeeze around the waist. He's so beautiful, it's a little blinding. I can also feel the air of Alpha around him. My shifter side isn't dominant enough for him to pick up on it, but I can always tell when there's a leader of a pack around. "I'm Aiden, by the way."

"Not to be a huge fan girl, but I've heard all about you two. It's amazing what you did."

"It's what we had to do," Maddie says, looking up at Aiden. There's so much chemistry between the two of them, I'd be blind not to see it. They both radiate with it, and it brings a warm feeling to my chest. Soulmates used to be a myth as well, but looking at these two, even without all the proof from the last two years, I'd believe in that kind of magic.

"But I'm glad you're here, Avery." Maddie smiles, looking from Aiden to me, "This school is a great place. Even with all the crazy."

We share another smile. The nerves I was feeling earlier subside. Sure, I don't have any friends here, but that doesn't mean I won't make some. All I have to remember to do is be open to the possibilities.

* * *

WE GO our separate ways after that because the pack has a meeting. Even though I'm part shifter, I don't actually have a pack. And I wouldn't even know where I'd fit, since I've never shifted. I've heard that some with mixed blood never shift and others only find out their animal when they finally do. My mom is a wolf, but that doesn't mean I would be.

It doesn't matter anyway. That's not the side of my magic I'm focusing on. When I get back to my room, there's a packet on my bed. My roommate is still missing in action, but I don't mind it. I like getting my bearings first.

When I pull out my schedule, a small post-it note is attached at the top. Glancing at it, I grin.

"Yes!"

Putting my stuff down, I quickly turn and rush back out of the room. Without getting lost once, I find myself in the Headmaster's waiting room once more.

"Back so soon, sweetie?" Miss Cindy asks. I nod.

"Headmaster Marković wanted to see me about a work study program."

"Ah, of course. Go right in."

It may seem so silly to be excited about a job, but I'm a hands-on learner. If I want to graduate and be allowed in the Watchers council, I need all the experience I can get. Which is why when I heard about this opportunity, well, more like overheard my dad discussing it, I jumped on it. If this works out, my resume is going to look just as good as my graduation diploma.

"Hello, Miss Kincaid, come on in." The headmaster's voice reaches out to me when I step into his office. He motions to a seat in front of his desk and I take it. His office is any bookworm's dream with shelves lining the walls that are all filled to the max.

"Let me properly introduce myself. I am Headmaster Marković. It is very nice to welcome you to Thunderbird Academy."

"Thank you, I'm very excited to be here," I reply honestly. I study the man in front of me, amazed at how young he looks for all his years of wisdom. One of my friends would call him a silver fox. He appears to be in his fifties, clean shaven, and wearing a dark suit. But I know for a fact he's much older than that.

"I could tell by your enthusiastic application you are very ready for the apprentice position."

Somehow, it doesn't sound like he's mocking me. There's an air of regality to him, but it's not as intimidating as I would have thought. As old as he is, he's very approachable. Which is why he's the headmaster, I suppose.

"I am, sir. Very ready and eager to learn."

"Your father said you are looking to work for the council upon graduation?"

"Yes, sir. I would love to attend the Watchers college first."

"Smart girl. Your credentials are excellent. You do not shy away from hard work."

"No, sir. I believe hard work is important."

He nods at that, and somehow, I think I've impressed him. There's no lying here, I actually do love working hard. It makes me feel accomplished in a special kind of a way. I know what I want in life, and I'm not afraid to go after it.

"Sir, Headmaster Marković, I understand that I'm technically an outsider and that there may be someone else who has a place in line ahead of me. But before you make your decision, I want to say that I have worked myself into the ground learning everything required of me when it comes to being a Watcher. I have spent countless sleepless nights taking every available position in the coven just to learn. I believe, with every part of me, including my magic, that this is what I'm supposed to do. If you give me this opportunity, I will not be a disappointment."

A little out of breath, I stop speaking and look at the man in front of me. He watches me carefully, and silently, and it takes much of my self-restraint to not fidget. Keeping my back straight, I sit as still as possible, allowing Headmaster Marković to finish his thought process.

"That was quite the speech, Miss Kincaid."

At first, I think he's going to reprimand me, but then his lips twitch just a tad. He turns before I can see the smile that is absolutely on his face now.

"But I do have to say that I already made my decision before you stepped foot inside of this office."

My heart sinks at his words, and I can do nothing but watch him walk around his desk and stop in front of his chair. He doesn't speak up right away, but when he does, he meets my gaze straight on.

"Such an opportunity is given to those who have already proved themselves. It is not an easy decision because it requires a large commitment."

The more he talks, the further my heart sinks. Only years of practice keeps my face void of emotions.

"Which is why we believe you are a great candidate for such a program. You have been assigned to Miss Hannah."

At first, I don't think I hear him correctly. But then he gives me just a glimpse of a smile, and my own lips split in a grin.

"Thank you so much, Headmaster Marković!" I nearly jump off the chair with excitement, but I manage to hold myself in my most professional pose. "You will not be disappointed."

"I do not think I will, Miss Kincaid." He sits at his desk then, folding his hands in front of him. "You are to report to Miss Hannah at the library first thing in the morning. She has been sent to us specifically for such an apprenticeship. She is also working on various projects for the council. I believe you will learn much from her."

"Thank you," I say again, because those are the only words I can string together at the moment. Headmaster Marković dismisses me. I stand like the proper lady I am and walk out of that office like a professional. I make it all the way to my room and shut the door before all sense of poise leaves me. Then I jump up and down like a crazy person.

"I'm going to be an apprentice," I say out loud, just to hear it in the air around me. This is the best thing that has ever happened to me.

CHAPTER 3

*S*ince classes don't start for a couple of days, I'm more than eager to get to the library. I like structure and keeping to a schedule. My parents are complete opposites, and they always say they don't know where I got it from. But honestly, they're just being modest. Each has their own drive.

Grabbing my notebook, and a few pens, I glance at the other side of the room on the way out. At this point, I wonder if my roommate is even coming. But I guess we shall see.

Everyone, apparently, decided on an early start, because the halls are already busy with activity. Others are still arriving, and more transfers and new students will be here in the next few days. I came with the others because of the job. My feet are quick and sure as I make my way to the dining room. Last night, I memorized the layout of the school so I don't have to look so out of place.

The tables are filled with groups, and there's a low buzz of conversation in the room when I step inside. Quickly, I make my way to the buffet and grab a bagel, cream cheese, and a banana. After I fill my cup with coffee, for which I am very thankful, I'm out the door. Taking a sip, I focus on centering myself in the moment. This is it. I'm finally closer to reaching my goals.

Being back home, it felt like the council was an unreachable dream. But here, with Headmaster Marković's help and the weight of the school behind my diploma, I might actually stand a chance. That's all I've ever wanted. It makes leaving everything behind so much easier. I guess I would've been doing this at the end of the year anyway. While most of my friends were going to stay in our hometown, I wasn't going to be one of those people. This is just a head start on my exit strategy.

"Good morning," I say, walking up to the front desk of the library. It's set up a bit unusual in that the help desk is outside the doors, which sit on either side of it. The guy behind the desk doesn't look at all like a mentor.

"Hey, how can I help you?" he asks with a friendly smile. He's cute. I'm not immune to the charm, but I don't encourage it, even when he leans a little closer.

"I'm here for an apprenticeship. I was told to report here first thing?"

"Ah, yes. I saw the note. I was wondering who was brave enough to study under Miss Hannah."

"What do you mean?"

"You're new?"

"Well, yes."

"I don't want to scare you."

"I don't scare easily." I raise my chin a little, looking him straight in the eye. He grins, clearly enjoying this. My own lips want to follow suit. The charm seems to pour off him.

"No, I don't think you do."

"Well?" I prompt when he doesn't continue. He cocks his head to the side, studying me for a moment before speaking up.

"Miss Hannah is a little intimidating to most. That's all."

Well that doesn't sound as scary as he made it out to seem. But she could be even scarier. I can't really get a read on him, but his smile seems to unnerve me. It didn't at the beginning, but here we are.

"I think I can handle her."

"I think you can." He nods, leaning forward again, which makes me take the tiniest step back. However, he doesn't miss the move, and chuckles. "You seem plenty capable of taking care of yourself."

Before I can ask exactly what he meant by that, he hands me a piece of paper.

"Here, go to this aisle. She'll meet you there. Good luck."

"Thanks." I finally return the smile, although mine is much less enthusiastic. I'm mostly apprehensive. Being from a smaller town, I don't meet many strangers. So that interaction was... interesting to say the least.

Glancing at the numbers and letters on the post-it note, I hurry into the library. The moment I step inside, I realize it's much bigger than I imagined. It's actually a few stories high. In my head, I try to remember if there's an area outside that matches this interior. I don't think there is. A few students are seated around tables on the first floor, and this time, I do smile genuinely. This has always been me. I'm prepping for school before it even starts. It doesn't matter what others think, I like to be prepared.

Moving past the stacks of books, it takes some willpower not to stop and dilly dally. That's one of my Mom's favorite words. Grandma used to say it all the time. But I do pause long enough to run a hand over the spines. Thunderbird Academy doesn't seem so intimidating now.

"There you are." A voice reaches me right as I step into the correct aisle. "In the future, it's good to be on time."

I glance at the watch I'm wearing and narrow my eyes.

"I'm seventeen minutes early," I say, still not seeing where the voice is coming from. Maybe it's not best to talk back to a teacher right off the bat, but I've never been good at being accused of things I'm not guilty of.

"Ah, a girl with a tongue. How predictable."

"A woman who knows her own mind will be unstoppable," I reply, raising my chin for the second time this morning. One thing I've never done is back down from a confrontation. Especially if I'm in the right.

"I suppose you are right." The voice is much closer, and then, it's like she materializes right out of the stack of books. She's wearing a red maxi gown, all the way to the ground. Her hair is blonde and loose around her shoulders. I can't say I expected her to be old and raggedy, but I didn't expect her to look like an older sister either. For a second, I don't know what to say.

"Are you Avery?"

"Yes ma'am." I recover quickly, taking a few steps toward her. "Avery Kincaid. Headmaster Marković sent me."

"He mentioned you come highly recommended. I guess we'll see about that."

With that, she turns to walk the opposite direction down the aisle.

"Well come on," she says over her shoulder, and I hurry behind her. This is definitely not what I pictured.

* * *

ONCE WE'RE at the end of the aisle, Miss Hannah stops in front of the wall and waves her hand. A door materializes in front of her. She turns the knob, pushing it open. It starts to shut before we're all the way through, so I hurry to keep up. Inside is a large room, with high ceilings and bookshelves lining the walls. They seem to have one decorator for the whole building. Not that I mind. There are a few tables set up with piles of herbs on one and books on the other. The farther table has a few test tubes and liquids on it as well.

That's when I realize we're not alone. A guy is reclining on one of the chairs farthest from the door. His leg is draping over the arm of the chair, a book in his hands.

"Liam, I thought I told you to stay out."

"I can't help it. You've got so many lovely books in here." The guy looks up, smiling at Miss Hannah before his eyes transfer to me. "You must be the new apprentice."

"Did they send out a memo?" I mumble, which earns me a side eye from Miss Hannah, and a chuckle from the guy.

"Good news travels fast," he replies before closing the book and jumping to his feet. "I'm Liam. Hannah here is my sister."

"At least three times removed," Miss Hannah replies, walking past us and farther into the room. Liam stops in front of me, that smile still on his face.

"Sorry, I'm Avery. What does *three times removed* mean?"

"Only that we fae have a problem keeping it in our pants. Most of the time. I'm very loyal by nature, but that's because I'm only half fae," Liam replies.

"You're a fae?" I turn to watch Miss Hannah take a seat in the chair opposite the one Liam was just in.

"Didn't they tell you anything?" She sighs, running a hand over her hair.

"No, they definitely did not."

"Don't worry, Avery." Liam brings my attention back to him. "Hannah here has been sworn to play nice. Even if you break the fae rules around her, she can't use it against you."

"Good to know." I'm still a little in shock. I mean, I knew there were fae here, but I wasn't mentally prepared for meeting any just yet. Especially since I heard all the stories of what this school went through last year being in the fae realm.

"How many of you are there?" I ask before realizing what I've just done. "My bad. Ignore that rude curiosity." But Liam just laughs it off.

"No worries. You remind me of my best friend. She has a tendency to say things she shouldn't. Especially around fae."

"That could be dangerous."

"You have no idea. Sometimes I think Maddie is a magnet for dangerous."

The moment he says her name, it clicks.

"You're *that* Liam?"

"Oh look, you have a fan base. How cute." Miss Hannah speaks up from her place on the chair. When I glance over, I find that she's sprawled out like a queen on a throne. This is supposed to be my mentor?

"How do you know of me?"

"Well, I heard Maddie had a friend who's a fae. And I met your brother. Briefly. Nolan and Krista came to our town to update the coven."

"How is lovely Nolan? Still foxy?" Miss Hannah pauses and then starts laughing as if she said the funniest thing in the world. Confused, I glance at Liam, who rolls his eyes.

"Nolan is a fox shifter. Hannah thinks she's funny."

"What I am is *hilarious*," she replies and then goes back to playing with her hair. I really don't know what to make of her. She seemed so intimidating when it was just her voice floating toward me, but now she seems like she's here for a good time and nothing else.

"Don't let her demeanor fool you," Liam says up, keeping his voice low. "She's powerful, smart, and you will learn much from her."

"You're so sweet!" Miss Hannah gushes, but even I can tell her tone is sarcastic. "But he's right you know. You lucked out in your choice of teachers."

"Didn't exactly have a choice."

That makes Liam laugh.

"You've got spirit. I think you'll be able to handle Hannah just fine." He walks over to what looks like a drink station I didn't notice before and pours himself a glass of water. "And to answer your earlier question, there are quite a few of us here. I'm sure you've met at least one already."

"What do you mean?"

"Stewart. The kid at the front desk. He's fae."

"Oh, that explains things."

"What do you mean?"

"He kept smiling at me, like nonstop. I found it a bit weird."

Liam pauses with the glass to his lips and even Miss Hannah sits up.

"What? What did I say?"

"He was trying to glamour you. That stinker. He knows the rules," Miss Hannah says, and now it's her turn to roll her eyes. Wow, I can see where she and Liam are related. They carry themselves kind of similarly. Or maybe it's a fae thing.

"But it didn't work," Liam comments, still studying me.

"I guess he wasn't really trying hard enough," I shrug, because now I'm uncomfortable. Ever since I was little, certain magical things didn't work on me. But outside of my family, not a lot of people know that. Just like the whole shifter and witch thing is a secret. Mostly.

"You are an interesting one, Avery," Liam finally says, finishing up the rest of his water. "I will leave you in my sister's capable hands. I'm going to pop in and say hello to the gang and then I have to be going back."

"Back?"

"To Faery, of course." Liam flashes me a grin. "There are many things afoot."

With that, he waves a little and then leaves out the door I came in. Slowly, I turn toward Miss Hannah, not knowing what to do next.

"Oh fine," she huffs, getting to her feet. "I suppose I should teach you something."

CHAPTER 4

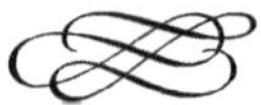

"You know, most kids your age are out there, living their lives to the fullest. And your idea of fun is being stuck here with me? Not that I'm not fun," Miss Hannah hurries to add as she walks over to the table filled with herbs. I move toward it as well, reaching for my notebook when my stomach growls. "And you didn't even bother to eat?"

"I grabbed food. I just didn't eat it yet."

Miss Hannah sighs, she really likes expressing herself in puffs of air. She motions to the chair Liam vacated.

"Take a seat and eat your food while I go over a few things."

I'm not about to argue. I eat the banana first before I grab the cream cheese and spread it on the bagel. Miss Hannah takes a seat in the other chair, rearranging her dress around her before she speaks up.

"First, none of that *miss* stuff. Here, I'm Hannah. Understand?"

"Yes ma—"

"No *ma'am* either." She looks at me pointedly.

"Yes, Hannah."

She smirks at that, leaning back in her chair.

"I know I seem like someone who shouldn't be in such a high position, but I earned my place. I want you to know that right now. Also, I won't be nice to you, and I won't be your bestie. But I will be fair. Always."

From what I know of fae, I know they can't lie. But Liam said the rules don't apply to her.

"When Liam mentioned the rules not applying—"

"Oh, of course you caught that." She smirks. That seems to be her standard expression. "No, I still can't lie. But if you thank me, you won't be attached to years of servitude. It's a bit muddled around here, but I don't like liars, so I won't be one."

I nod at that, taking another bite of my bagel. She cocks her head to the side, giving me a once over before speaking again.

"You're a pretty girl. Is there a cute significant other to take up your free time?"

"No," I reply with a small smile. "I'm here to study, not flirt."

"Oh, come on, Avery. You should always have time to flirt. Liam there is a nice-looking fella. I'm sure he'll let you practice on him."

"I think I'll be okay," I reply, this time suppressing the smile. I'm not sure what Hannah is trying to do, but I'm starting to like her. There's a kind of no-nonsense attitude about her that I appreciate.

"Fine. I guess you'll be the studious kind." With that, she stands, throwing her hair over one shoulder. "As you can see, I have divided the work for different magics."

I swallow the rest of my bagel and hurry to my feet as she walks over to the herbs table. My notebook and pen are at the ready.

"We'll start with herbal magic. You may know most of it, but with our connection to nature, this is the most powerful foundation there can be. The foundation must always be strong or everything tumbles down. But that's not something I need to teach you, I'm sure you already understand."

I nod, still writing everything down. She sees the movement, and this time, her smile is less mocking.

"The science table is a bit of a mess right now. I was trying to work up some potions the council requested, but honestly, it's so boring. Anyone could do them. Not sure why I have to. But whatever the council wants the council gets." She does her hair flip again and rolls her eyes. I'm really not sure if I'm allowed to smile at her comments, but I want to.

"As you can also see, I like to color code my books. Please make sure it stays that way." She waves her hands at the shelves. This time, I do smile. Each shelf is adorned with spines of the same color. There's a red, green, yellow, blue, and purple area. There are also brown and black spines in the shelves between. It looks pretty neat.

"I think today we'll see how well your magic responds to regular herbal work and then go from there."

I nod as she motions toward the table. Placing my notebook and pen at the side, I take the chair while she stands on the other side of the table.

"The Council uses teas in their meetings to enhance interrogation at times. Have you ever created a psychic tea?"

"No, but I've studied the method."

"Oh, a girl who's prepared. I like it. Show me what you got, and talk me through it."

I glance at the supplies on the table and find I have everything I need. Not that I expected Hannah to trick me. Well, maybe a little. She is fae after all.

"First, I'll take six rose petals and four tablespoons of thyme." I reach for the ingredients and then pull a mortar and pestle toward me. I place the ingredients in the mortar and begin to crush them. "Then, I'll add four tablespoons of yarrow root along with two table-spoons of cinnamon."

I continue to move the pestle in slow circular motions as I add the other ingredients. The aroma of herbs is already filling the air. It makes me more relaxed. I feel comfortable doing this, using the knowledge I've learned and applying it with my hands.

"Last but not least, I'll add two tablespoons of cloves." With that, the aroma is even stronger. It makes me miss home for just a second. This is something Dad and I would do together.

"After everything is crushed, it's ready to be steeped." I glance at Hannah, and she gives me a slight nod. I jump down from the chair and walk over to the drinking cart. After pouring water into a mug, I carry it back to the station. This is the tricky part because my magic has been so out of whack. But with the way Hannah is looking at me, I know she's aware I should be able to heat this cup with no problem.

Wrapping my hands around it, I concentrate on the water within. Mentally, I'm begging my magic to work, to be nice to me for this one moment. It opens up, reaching for the liquid inside, and then it's bubbling. I smile, exhaling a little with relief.

I place the mixture into the water, stirring it before I look up at Hannah. She's watching me with concentration. I see why they picked her as my mentor. She knows what she's doing.

"Not bad, Avery," Hannah says, "Not bad at all."

* * *

THE NEXT DAY, I'm at the library even before the sun is up. Yesterday was such a full day. There is so much information to go through, and we haven't even covered one percent of it yet. My skin is buzzing with excitement and so is my magic. I can tell it's just as happy to be part of this as I am.

But then again, me and my magic are one.

That's something that isn't taught as much anymore, at least from what I've overheard in the last few months. Some of the council members have been arguing that magic is a separate entity, and it chooses a vessel. But my father has always believed that magic is who we are. It's a part of us, like our souls. That's what I choose to believe as well.

When I reach the library, Stewart isn't at the desk. Thankfully. I don't think I can deal with the fae this early in the morning. The lights are still off, so I flip the switch for the lower floor and make my way to the table.

I know I can't get inside Hannah's workroom without her, and I won't even try. Instead, I take a seat, pulling out my notebook and some pens. Then, I pull out a journal, this one clean. After a sip of water from my water bottle—I would love some coffee—I get to work.

Some may think transcribing from one notebook to another is a waste of time, but this is how I learn. The notebook I carry with me is messy, with scribbles and drawings and random diagrams. But when I copy the information over to the clean journal, I do so carefully. All the while I organize my thoughts and ideas clearly. I leave room at the front of the book, to create my own table of contents. If it ever came time for me to have an apprentice, I want to be able to teach them to the best of my ability. That means everything I learn must be learned right.

A noise reaches me, breaking me out of my concentration. I'm not sure how long I've been here. When I glance at my watch, I see that an hour has passed. The school will be waking up soon but not yet.

Setting my pen in the spine of the journal to hold my place, I do a quick scan of my surroundings. Most of the shelves are still in shadows because I only turned on the lights over a few tables. Even so, I don't see anything out of the ordinary. It must've been the building settling. Or maybe someone woke up somewhere and is moving around.

Satisfied that no one is out there, I settle back in and start writing. It's another few minutes before I hear it again. There's definitely someone moving around in the room. I just can't tell where.

This time, I do my study a bit more discreetly. That's when I realize I only checked the downstairs. There are plenty of places on the upper floors that someone may be. I try to focus on the task at hand, but now my curiosity is piqued. Who could be here this early? And in the dark? Since I didn't turn any of the lights on up there.

I close the journal as quietly as possible before I get to my feet. Keeping my movements as slow and sure as I can, I move over to the aisle and head to one of the staircases. It takes me but a minute to reach the next landing. It feels like everything I do is too loud. Even my breathing has become louder, and not just from walking up the steep steps.

Once I'm on the second floor, I do a quick survey, but I can't see anything in the near darkness. Unfortunately, I didn't inherit supernatural vision with my shifter genes. That would've been helpful more than once at this point in my life. Still, I walk forward, keeping to the railing. The floors above the main one are set up in a circle around the middle area on the first floor that has all the chairs set up. There are rows of books going in from the center toward the wall, and each has its own light. All of them are off right now, so someone could be standing right beyond the shadow, and I wouldn't know.

I'd be lying if I said this didn't unnerve me.

Yet, I continue moving forward, knowing I won't be able to get back to work unless I figure out where the noise is coming from. It still feels like a person moving around, but that seems more impossible now that I'm up here. Quickly, I reach the next staircase and make my way to the third landing. Here, the darkness is thicker. I can't even see a few feet in front of me. Maybe this isn't the smartest move.

Just as I turn to head back down the stairs, the noise comes again. It's closer now. I squint, trying to find the source. It sounds almost like someone closed a book. I can't imagine anyone actually being able to read in the dark, but there are all kinds of magic in the world.

I move slowly toward where I think the noise is coming from. Again, the book is opened and then closed. The little thud of the pages falling together sounds again, this time to my right. Now, I move quickly, rushing to where I think it's at. But when I reach the aisle, no one is there. No one I can see, at least. If they're leaning against the far wall, I wouldn't know. I walk forward a few steps, now completely surrounded by the stacks of books. There's not even a sliver of light. A part of me is tempted to call up my fire, but since my little mess up in the room, I haven't tried my magic beyond using it to heat up the water yesterday. I wouldn't want to set the books on fire if it doesn't act like it should.

I can walk until I hit the wall, or whoever is hiding at the end of the aisle, but I'm done with this. Heading downstairs is my best bet. I'm ready in case I get jumped from the back, but I don't feel any danger around me. Just as I'm about to leave the aisle, a thud louder than any I've heard before sounds right behind me. I turn to find a book on the floor. I didn't think I bumped anything, but maybe I did.

Kneeling down, I pick it up. The moment my fingers touch the cover, a buzz goes up my arm. Curious, I lift the cover, but I can't make out much of what's on the front or the inside pages.

When I'm back on the first floor, I find my table just how I left it. I sit down, pushing my notebooks to the side and placing the book in front of me. The cover is leather with some kind of forest design carved on the front. I run my finger over the bumps and indentations, feeling that rush of magic once again. Because I know that's what it was. I could feel my own magic answer in kind.

Opening to the first page, I begin leafing through it. I quickly realize it's in a language I've never seen before. It's beautiful though. I can see that at a glance. The words weren't printed on the page, they were written and drawn. I pause when I come across an illustration. It's a full page of a forest with vines and flowers growing every which way. Tentatively I run my finger over a vine. For a second, I think I feel its silky texture. Leaning forward, I try to see if my eyes are playing tricks on me or if the leaves are actually moving. It's like they're blowing in the wind.

Suddenly, the room lights up with brightness, making me jump back from the page. Looking around, I see someone has turned on the lights. A moment later, there's a sound of heels on the marble floor.

"Avery. Why am I not even surprised?" Hannah asks, coming into the library from her room. I'm tempted to ask if she actually sleeps in there, but since there's no bed inside, I doubt it. However, she got here before me. Or snuck past me. Somehow.

"Well?" She says, turning and walking back toward her room. "Let's go. I got us coffee."

That's all I need to hear.

CHAPTER 5

"*I* know I said be here earlier, but you didn't have to be here at the crack of dawn," Hannah says once we're inside the room. I can smell the unmistakable aroma of coffee and watch as she makes her way to the drink cart. It now carries a coffee pot.

"Don't think this is only for you. I forgot how much I liked coffee until you brought your cup in yesterday," she says, when she notices my look. I try and suppress a smile because clearly, she got it for me.

"How did you know I was here?" I ask as I pour myself a cup of coffee and head for the chair I occupied yesterday. Hannah is once again dressed like she's going to *Litha*. Or the human equivalent, prom. The color is blush pink with sequins adorning it top to bottom. The plunging V-neckline and the open back leaves little to the imagination. The fitted empire waist and A-line skirt make the whole dress beautiful, yet effortless. And Hannah carries herself as such. I'm a bit in shock she can wear something so revealing.

"I guessed."

She half reclines in her chair, the dress spread out around her, the sequins reflecting the candles and lamps in the room.

"Do you like it?" Hannah asks when she notices me staring.

"Yes. I could never wear something like that." The words leave my

29

mouth before I can stop them. But she doesn't look offended or take it the wrong way. Her laugh rings out as she leans forward.

"Oh honey, you could pull this off, no problem. Believing it is half the battle."

My face heats up with the idea, but I want to. I really want to. I've never been much for dresses, especially sparkly ones, but the idea is officially appealing. If only I was as confident about my looks as I am about books.

Speaking of which, I completely forgot what I found. Setting the coffee on the table, I grab my bag and pull out the book. Immediately, Hannah sits forward.

"Where did you get that?"

"In the library. There was a noise on the third floor. When I went up there, I found this on the floor. Do you know what it is? The designs are beautiful. But I can't read it."

"You wouldn't be able to." Hannah reaches over, and I surrender the book to her. There's a note of reverence in her voice and on her face as she studies the cover. Her own fingers do a similar study of the grooves on the leather. For some reason, I get the feeling there's more to this than meets the eye.

"Why wouldn't I?" I ask after a few minutes of silence. Hannah seems to come out of a fog at my question, glancing up for a second.

"It's an ancient fae language. I didn't think Thunderbird Academy carried any of these books. Most are kept under lock and key."

"What do you mean?"

Hannah smiles, but there's no humor in her eyes. She looks down at the book again before slowly opening it up. She doesn't go to the front page but somewhere in the middle. I think I'll have to prompt her again, but then she speaks up.

"There are stories told about these kinds of books. They say they were written by the Ancients themselves. Creatures who lived even before the fae."

"I thought the fae have lived for thousands of years."

"We have. And yet, there is always a beginning to these kinds of things. These writings came from those beginnings."

"So why keep them under lock?"

"Because if you could read this, it would break all the rules of Faery."

"I don't understand."

Hannah stands, the book still cradled in her arms. She holds it open, studying the pages as if they're the most amazing thing she has ever come across.

"When I was a child, my aunt would tell me stories of the Ancients. They're not as unheard of in Faery as they are in this realm. She told me of their conquests and their wars and the powers they possessed. They could reshape worlds if they only chose to do so. Their connection to the earth is stronger even than of a fae. Not something that's a popular truth to spread about." She smiles then, and I understand what she means. The fae like to appear the most powerful.

"She also told me of the books written by the Ancients, ones that hold much of their history. No one knows how many there are, but we have a few. The language they are written in is a forgotten one. But the stories talk of a magic that can understand it and can wield it. Much like the now famous story spell casting, whoever can read these spells can move mountains with a word and grow whole forests with a flick of the hand. It's how much of Faery was born, back when the Ancients destroyed and rebuilt on a whim."

Hannah's gaze focuses somewhere in the distance, as if she's seeing the history play out right in front of her. I've never heard of such power, but then, with the Ancients waking up, many of the stories we believed to be fairytales are becoming realities. What Maddie can do, tell a story with her spell and then make that story happen? It hasn't been seen in centuries. When it was around, it was feared beyond all.

"Whoever wields that kind of a power, they will be a hot commodity. Wanted by every court, feared by every family."

And fae—they are not kind to things they want. They take without permission, that much I know.

"What do you think the book is doing here?"

My voice once again brings Hannah back to the present. She looks over at me before glancing at the book still in her hands.

"I'm not sure, Avery. But it did find you. So, it must be up to you to figure it out."

* * *

"I DON'T SEE how an ancient book would have anything to do with me," I reply, narrowing my eyes a little. Sure, I felt an urge to go figure out what that noise I kept hearing was, but it doesn't have anything to do with the book. Does it?

Hannah hands over the book, almost reluctantly, and then struts over to the drinking cart. She pours herself something that's definitely not coffee and takes a long drink. I do nothing but wait for her to say something else. I have too many questions, I don't even know where to begin.

"If that book ended up at Thunderbird, specifically found by you in a dark library, I'd say it's all you, honey." Hannah turns, throwing a wink my way.

"And what am I supposed to do with that?"

"That's up to you. But I would be very careful with who you show that book to." She gives it a long look, almost like she wants to take it from me. My hand curls over the spine automatically. The move doesn't go unnoticed. This time, Hannah grins when she meets my eye. "See. You're already protective."

"Great," I mumble, glancing down at the cover. It would be nice if there was a manual somewhere for dealing with rare magical findings. I can't even do any research because I can't read it.

"I have to mention that I'm obligated to report the book's finding to the Queen."

That puts me on high alert. If Hannah is obligated, it means magically. Fae don't really like being locked into anything or have anyone tell them what to do. Such an obligation must've come from the queen herself. That's when I realize Hannah has walked to the opposite side of the room where one of the bookshelves houses only green books.

"Try not to start any fires while I'm gone."

"Wait, what?"

With that, she waves her hand. The green books appear to ripple, as if she's thrown a stone into a pond. Then, there's an opening and the noises of the forest trickle through the room. Quickly jumping to my feet, I try to peer in, but she's blocking most of the view.

"Now?" I ask, and she turns to give me one of her signature smiles.

"I'll be back before you know it." And then she steps through the opening. It closes behind her immediately and I'm left standing alone in her room. A room she specifically told me I could never be alone in.

This is much more mind boggling than I originally imagined.

Plopping back down in the chair, I don't know what to think. The book feels heavy on my lap, and my fingers seemed to have attached themselves to it. I feel the protectiveness over these pages, and it makes my head spin. Now, more than before, I don't think I found it by accident. But who would bring this to me? And why.

Knowing I have no other choice, I take the book to the herb table where I sat taking notes yesterday. Pulling out my notebook and pen, I open it to a blank page, my hand at the ready. Typically when I do research, I'll write out the name of the book, the author, and any important information found in the opening pages. Since I can't read any of it, I have no idea what to write. Putting the pen down, I sigh and then pull the book toward me. I'll have to go through it page by page and see if anything jumps out at me.

The prospect is not all together unappealing. It's the meticulous part of research that I actually enjoy.

Turning to the cover page, I once again stare at the beautiful handwriting. If what Hannah said is true, and I don't have any reason to believe otherwise, then this was written by an Ancient. I couldn't even begin to guess who or what he or she was. I know from recent sightings, the Ancients can take any form. Some were shifters, some were witches. The first of the supernatural creatures. I know for a fact Maddie's sister met one that looked like a handsome man. There's no way of telling with them.

I flip to the next page, my eyes taking it all in. The words seem to glow on the page. I can't tell if it's actually happening or if my mind is playing tricks on me. Trying not to get distracted by the beauty, I keep flipping until I find something that jumps out at me. When I come to a full-page drawing, I stop.

This one isn't a forest but maybe a courtyard of some sort. I can see the forest behind it, but the front area has cobblestones. The tree on the left is half hiding a bench. This definitely looks like an area in some castle, most likely in Faery. I've never been there myself, but I've heard plenty of stories and seen enough research to make an educated guess.

The one thing I notice right away, the same as the forest painting I saw earlier, there are flowers everywhere. They grow from the very bark of the tree. And they're fully blooming, so this must be the Spring or Summer court. I wonder if I showed the picture to Hannah if she'd maybe recognize the place. Immediately, I don't like that thought. Shaking off the unwanted feelings, I frown. Why am I so protective of the book, even from Hannah?

It must be the whole, her having to report the findings. That's the only reason I can come up with, even though it still leaves a weird taste in my mouth. I'll have to ask my parents about this. Maybe they'll have more information. They have many more resources with the council.

I flip to the next page and freeze.

There, in the middle of the page, right between two paragraphs, is an indented block of words.

And I can read them.

Quickly, I shut my eyes and then open them again. But no, the words are still there, and I can still read them. My mind races with possibilities. If I can read this, does it mean anything? Or does this book just have a random part written in modern language? But how would that be possible? None of this makes sense.

I get to my feet, walking over to the door and then back to the table. There has to be a rational explanation. Sure, I found the book because of some weird noises. Yes, I'm getting a little protective over it, but I get protective over any research I do. Since I'm the one doing the work. But no, this is different. It feels different. Maybe it's enchanted.

Yes, that must be it.

Stopping near the book, I close my eyes for a second, centering myself and my magic. Then slowly, I open my eyes and place my hand, palm down, over the open pages. I call on my magic, asking it to come forward and feel my surroundings. If there's an enchantment, my magic will be able to tell. But when I feel it rising, it's not pausing to find a culprit. It reaches right for the book, as if it's been waiting for it. My powers are almost giddy with excitement. I snatch my hand back before I cause damage. I'm afraid to do anything with it, since it's been going haywire. But I especially don't want to hurt the book.

Glancing down at my hand, I frown. This is getting stranger by the minute. Taking a few steps forward I resign myself to what must be done. I have to read everything that's written on the page. That's the only way to figure out if this is an enchantment or if I can read this ancient book. Goosebumps race over my spine as I take a deep breath.

Slowly, I move my eyes down the page until they land on the paragraph in the middle. The words are as clear as day.

"Many centuries have gone by since the rise and fall of the magical kingdom. But there is none who has answered the call of the forest."

MY MIND PROCESSES the first two lines quickly, and it doesn't feel strange in any way. It feels almost natural. However, the words make no sense. It's like I'm coming into the middle of a story. I move my eyes farther down to read the other three lines. As I do, it's like something inside of me clicks.

"There are those who will want to steal the power for themselves. There are those who are eagerly waiting for the door to open. Yet, there are those who possess the skill and steadfastness of a real knight."

A BIG RUSH of power surges through me, nearly knocking me off my feet. I grip the table for support. The magic inside me dances in glee, twisting and turning with such happiness it takes my breath away. Gasping, I try to reel it in. It won't listen. It won't be tamed. It's answering a call I can't hear, and it's more excited than I've ever felt it to be before. And it makes me happy. It makes me laugh.

Just as quickly as the feeling comes, it leaves. I'm bent over, gasping to force air into my lungs. My body feels exhausted, but my skin buzzes with power. Also, I feel more balanced than I have in months. None of this makes sense.

I stand up slowly, checking on my magic and feel it nice and settled. It seems satisfied somehow. I'm definitely going to have to ask Dad about this. He's told me before that our magic can do weird things, but it's never been this strange before.

When I finally look over at the book, I stumble away, hitting my back against the other table. There's no way I'm seeing what I'm seeing. Once again, I close my eyes and count to ten before opening them back up. Tentatively, I take a few steps forward, as if I'm sneaking up on an injured animal. But when my gaze lands on the book, it's the same.

Instead of being able to read the middle paragraph, I can now read the whole page. Both pages actually. The words are no longer foreign.

Shaking my head, all I can do is stare. There's no way this makes sense. Before I can do or think anything else, there's a banging on the outer door. The Headmaster's voice reaches for me.

"Miss Hannah, open this door immediately."

* * *

MY MIND GOES blank for exactly one second and then I spring into action. For some reason, maybe it's because of Hannah's warnings, I can't let Headmaster Marković know that I have this book. Not yet at least. I need more information first. Quickly, I close it up and place it on one of the bookshelves. Since no one can get in without Hannah's invitation, it'll be safe until I figure out what to do. Then, I give the area a sweep with my eyes and head for the door.

"Headmaster Marković, good morning," I greet him with a small smile on my face. He's surprised to see me but recovers immediately.

"Where is Miss Hannah?"

Here is a dilemma I didn't think about when I hid the book. The only reason he's here is because he felt me use the magic. When

Hannah returns, she won't be able to lie to him. So, I have to stick as close to the truth as possible.

"She's in Faery."

"Why?"

"I came across an ancient book in the library this morning," I say, keeping my gaze steady and my breathing regular. "She said she was obligated to tell the queen."

Headmaster Marković is good at hiding his emotions, but for a split second, I think I see worry in his gaze. He looks back over the room, doing his own sweep. I try my hardest not to glance away from him or in the direction I've hidden the book.

"Where is the book?"

"She took it with her, sir." I say. This makes him pause. He studies me carefully, as if deciding what to do about me.

"Grab your stuff, Miss Kincaid. You need to come with me."

"Did I do something?"

"I believe you did."

My bravado deflates at his words because of course he knows. He can probably sense the magic on me. That's also how he knew to come here. No one can practice magic on campus without him knowing about it. That was one of the first rules I read in the handbook. He watches me, and I realize he's waiting for me to move. I rush over to where I discarded my bag and quickly put my notebook and pen inside. Without a backward look, I leave the room with Headmaster Marković on my heels.

There are people in the library now, though not many. They all look up anyway. Of course it's noticeable when the headmaster is escorting a student. Stewart is at the front desk, and I swear he's working at not meeting my eye. There are more students out and about as we make our way to the headmaster's office. I see Owen in the corridor. He gives me an encouraging smile, which makes me wonder if I look as guilty as I feel. I'm not typically one to keep things from my elders. But everything in me is screaming to do just that.

When we reach the headmaster's office, Miss Cindy is there with a smile. Even that feels a little strained. Great, now everyone has seen my walk of shame. I don't understand why I'm being subjected to it. Once the door closes behind me, all I want to do is bombard Headmaster Marković with a bunch of questions. But I'm smart enough to know that if I speak first, I'm guilty. Of something.

"Please take a seat, Miss Kincaid," Headmaster Marković motions to the chair in front of his desk, the same one I occupied when I was given this apprenticeship. I follow his instructions, setting my bag at my feet. But I still don't speak. "I am sure you know why you are here."

"I don't," I reply honestly, because I know things he doesn't, so it can't be for the same reasons I think. He studies me carefully, as if trying to gauge how truthful I am. But in this case, it's one hundred percent.

"The school experienced a wave of magic that originated from Miss Hannah's office. There is a very large trace of it all around you. Tell me what happened."

It's not really a request.

For a moment, I think about lying. But I already decided to stick mostly to the truth. Besides, if I'm to trust anyone at this school, it should probably be the headmaster. So, I tell him about the book, how I found it, and how Hannah had to report it.

"Did you read from the book, Miss Kincaid?" Somehow, Headmaster Marković caught on to my one omission. Not that I'm really surprised.

"Only a few words," I reply. This time he's not quick enough to cover up the worry and a bit of wonder in his expression.

"I knew it, the magic, I felt it," he mumbles to himself. I strain to hear the rest, but it's lost to me. "Where is the book, Miss Kincaid?"

"Miss Hannah has it."

He does that quiet study again. I realize he's using his magic to assess my truthfulness. Since the book is in her office, what I said is true.

"This school has a tendency to attract the most powerful people," Headmaster Marković comments. I'm not sure I was meant to hear that. "We must get to the bottom of this before there are any other magical incidents."

"Incidents?"

He ignores my question and stands. "I need to inform the Elders, and we must speak with your parents. Please stay here for the time being."

Headmaster Marković doesn't give me a chance to respond. Instead of heading for the door we came through, he walks to the doorway on the left, one situated between his bookshelves. When he opens it, I see that it leads somewhere else. Apparently, this school is just filled with magical portals. Right before he walks through, he waves a hand. I feel the magic do a sweep around me before the entry door clicks shut. I jump to my feet and race toward it. When I pull, nothing happens. Headmaster Marković is gone, and he locked me inside his office.

I spin in a circle, trying to figure out my next move. My mind is going over every possibility. None of them turn out all that great for me. What did Hannah say about someone with the power to read these books? They would be a hot commodity. That won't play out well. And there's nothing I can do. I don't really have friends here to help me. My parents are far away.

My parents. They must know something about it.

Hurrying over to Headmaster Marković's desk, I grab for his phone. When I pick it up, it has a normal dial tone. I just hope it works regularly. Communication is something that's protected on campus too, but since I'm in the headmaster's office, maybe this will work in my favor. When I dial my home number, it goes through.

Exhaling, I grip the phone, mentally begging for someone to be there to pick up. *Please pick up.*

"Hello?"

"Mom," I breathe out, all the relief I feel in that one word coursing through me.

"Avery, what's wrong?" She knows, right away. Of course she does. She's my mom.

"Mom, something happened. I—" I realize I don't know how much

I can say on this line without it getting to someone else. "I read something I wasn't supposed to," I say instead of blurting out all the details. "It's not from our realm, and it's not new."

There's a moment of silence on the other line and then I hear Mom call for Dad. His voice comes on the phone next and tears spring up into my eyes.

"Avery, what happened?"

"I found a book I wasn't supposed to, and I read from it. Only, I didn't know I could."

I hope that's enough information because I'm scared to say more. But my dad doesn't need more. He's a smart man. He's learned in the ways of the Ancients. Since the books exist and the fae know about them, so would my dad.

"Oh, Avery." That comes from my mom. A tear slips down my cheek at her tone. I wipe it away quickly, trying to keep myself from losing it completely.

"What do I do?"

"Where are you?"

"In the headmaster's office. He went to speak with the Elders."

"That makes sense. They'll be calling me shortly." I can hear Dad's voice talking in his thinking tone. I can almost see the wheels turning as he formulates a plan. I got my thinking skills from him. "You need to find a way to leave."

"What?" My mom and I ask at the same time.

"If this is what I think it is, then you need to find a way to get out. There's no telling what they will do when they find you."

"Dad, you're scaring me."

"Good. You should be scared. Let that fuel your survival skills. Think of every single thing I've ever taught you, Avery. Whatever it takes, Avery. Do you hear me?"

"Yes, Daddy," I manage through the fear gripping me. I've never heard him like this before, so harsh and straight to the point. I never want to again.

"Avery,"

"Yes, Mama?"

"We love you; you know that. We'll figure this out. But until then, don't trust anyone."

"Understood. I love you too."

There's a commotion on their end. I hear someone's voice and then Mom is on the phone again.

"They called your father in. We have to go."

The phone disconnects before I can say anything else. I stare at the receiver for another moment before replacing it on the hook.

This is way worse than I could've ever imagined it to be. I have all the questions and not enough answers. I can't even begin to imagine what will happen next. My only thought is that they'll take me to the council. Or to Faery. Those are the only two options. And neither one will end well for me.

* * *

"Cool, cool, cool." My mind is spinning with possibilities and what this could mean for my future. If I'm lucky, I'll only be enslaved. If I'm unlucky, I'll be a lab rat. There are no good choices here. None at all.

Unless I run. Like my dad said.

That's it. I have to run. Sure, it's not the best idea, but it's the best I got at the moment. Do I even have time to go back to my room? *Is there a way I can get away?* Thunderbird Academy is pretty protected. If they really wanted to, they could track me. Especially if I use my magic. There has to be a way to get out without my magic.

My eyes zero in on the window, and I march to it immediately. I could get it open. We're on the bottom floor. I could slip out before Headmaster Marković comes back and then I could find some kind of transportation or something. Maybe I could sneak away in one of the cars coming in to drop off the students. I'll just have to hide until then.

I reach for the latch holding the window locked. A voice stops me the moment I touch the lock.

"I wouldn't do that if I were you." The voice sends goosebumps down my spine. I drop my hand.

Spinning around, my eyes land on the guy who has just stepped into the office. The office that was locked a second ago. But that's forgotten when I get a good look at him. He's a few feet taller than me, and he looks sturdy somehow. My eyes are immediately drawn to his face. It takes me a second to process what I'm seeing. Skin as clear as a newborn baby with a hint of a glow that could be blinding if I looked at it too long. Chiseled jaw, strong nose, lips made for kissing.

Quickly, I push that thought away and move my study to his eyes. The moment ours meet, everything in me stops for just a second. His are the lightest blue I have ever seen, framed by long dark eyelashes. I don't even know what to compare it to, but I already know I won't be forgetting them. Ever. His hair is dark as well, falling in soft waves around his head, barely past his ears.

He's beautiful, like a painting in a museum that's been admired for centuries. No matter what your taste may be, you still can't look away. And yet, somehow, I do.

"Interesting."

That voice again. I would really appreciate my skin not reacting every time he speaks.

"Can I help you with something?" I snap because I officially don't have time for whatever this is.

"Hmm," is his only reply as he steps farther into the room. "I am here to help you. You are to come with me."

"Excuse me, I don't know you. I don't travel with strangers." I cross my arms in front of me, almost daring him to take me on. He does that slow survey of me again. It takes all my focus not to fidget.

"You're different than I expected."

Well, I think I'm going to take offense at that.

"What exactly did you expect?"

"Someone stronger."

"Okay, mister. I don't know who you are, but I'm plenty strong. And I can take you on if need be."

Apparently, I've resorted to the tough bravado persona, but I'll take it. I'm wasting precious time standing here talking to him. I need to go.

"The fire in you will serve you well."

That makes me pause for a second because it almost sounded like a compliment. But I shake that off too.

"Okay, great. You may go now."

"Only when you come with me."

"I don't understand."

"You, Avery Kincaid, possess a rare sight. I have been instructed to bring you back with me."

"Back where?"

"To Faery, of course."

Of course. It all makes sense. The beauty, the way my body is reacting to him. He's trying to glamour me. And it's not working. Because it won't. But he can't know that, can he? Maybe I can use it to my advantage. I just don't know how.

"If I come with you, will I be safe?"

"You will be taken care of."

Ah, the fae trick. They can't lie, so they don't answer directly. Being taken care of can mean a plethora of things. None of which may include safety.

"And if I don't come?"

"I'm afraid you don't have a choice."

Just like that, I know what I have to do. There's only one way I can get out of this, and it won't be pretty. Because this guy, this fae, he's bigger and stronger than me. For all I know, he's got magic more powerful than I've ever seen. My only advantage is to take him by surprise.

"Well, I'm sorry to tell you that I'm all about free will."

No sooner do the words leave my mouth than I raise my magic, blasting it right at him. The surprise worked. He's not prepared, and it sends him flying across the room. But he's quick. Even before I can decide my next move, he's up on his feet. He throws his own magic at me, a wind so powerful I'm nearly swept off my feet. I throw a shield up just enough to minimize it.

"This is foolish," he says, dropping his arms as we stare at each other.

"Are you afraid you'll lose?" I ask, my eyes flashing. Whatever this is, it feels like a life and death battle to me.

"I do not lose." I believe that. But I also believe I have more at stake. "There's a first time for everything."

My magic flares up again. This time, I don't hold back. Raising both of my hands, I push the fire at him. He throws up his own defenses, but I'm not done. My dad has taught me that as powerful as my magic can be, personal contact can do the job just as well. Before I think too much of it, I rush at him, throwing my whole body on top of his. My move takes him by surprise as we tumble to the floor. He's quick on his feet. Before we've rolled once, he's already getting up. I swipe my leg around, taking his from under him. He drops fast. I send another wave of fire at him, pushing him straight across the room.

Then, I don't hesitate to turn. I throw another blast at the window, shattering it into pieces.

Before I can think too much of it, I'm jumping through, landing hard on the ground. I remember to roll at the last moment, but the impact still rattles my bones. I guess the drop was farther than I thought. But it doesn't matter. He'll be on me in seconds if I don't figure out what to do next.

So, I do the only thing I can come up with. I run.

CHAPTER 8

I have no idea where I'm going, so I head for the woods surrounding the school. The moment I rush into the them, I realize how stupid I am. I have no supplies, no direction. I could get lost in these woods and never be found.

All I know is that I have to get away from the fae. I'm not about to become anybody's science project. My body is still buzzing from all of my power. I surprised myself a little in there, throwing so much of it at him. With all the weird frizzing lately, I'm shocked it worked at all. But maybe whatever happened with that book righted my crooked magic somehow.

The forest is not quiet around me, but I try to move as quickly and quietly as possible. Every time I look behind me, I expect the fae to be there. I can still see his eyes. It's like they're embedded in my brain, and I try to push them away.

Suddenly, a noise reaches me. I freeze, doing a quick turn to see where it's coming from. It sounded like a twig snapping, which could be anything. When I turn, I gasp.

"Oh, Avery, what have you gotten yourself into?" Hannah steps around a tree, still wearing one of her prom-looking dresses, her arms behind her back.

"You have to let me go," I say, my hand at my side, ready with battle magic. I don't want to fight her, but I will if necessary.

"I wasn't going to stop you." That takes all the wind out of my sails.

"What?"

"The fae want you, Avery. They want you badly. The Summer and Winter courts are about to go to war over what you can do. It's not a place for my apprentice."

"You know what happened." It's not a question, but she answers anyway.

"The fae felt a power surge. I knew it came from you. I saw potential in you the moment I saw you."

"So, what now?"

"Now you leave. I'll get you through a portal."

That stops me. It can't be that easy.

"Why are you helping me?" I ask because there isn't a scenario where this would be in Hannah's best interest. She gives me a sharp look, as if she can read my mind.

"Because I want to."

"That can't be it," I argue.

"Don't you people have a saying about not looking a gift horse in the mouth?"

"I never liked that saying. I like to have my bases covered."

"Fine. I want you to be able to decide for yourself."

"What do you mean?"

"If you go to Faery right now, all your choices will be taken from you. You're a powerful tool, and they won't hesitate to do whatever it takes. You don't know this power. You don't know how much you can handle. You won't know how to protect yourself. You need to learn that first. And then, if you decide to go to Faery and help, then it will be your choice. No one else's."

"Help?"

"Your power, it can help Faery. Or it can destroy it."

I let that sink in. It feels like I'm about to get all emotional again, but I push it down. Now is not the time.

"You'll give me that choice?"

"Yes, I'm such a softy." She rolls her eyes, but I've already figured out that's just a defense mechanism. There's something in her words that makes me think she speaks from personal experience. I don't know what choices may have been taken from her, but she seems to understand. Then, she does her customary flip of the hair before she continues. "I've been around you humans for far too long."

I know thanking her is dangerous, but I do so anyway.

"Thank you."

Her eyes flash, but she doesn't comment on my slip.

"Now, get going. Once I open the passageway, you'll have two minutes tops to disappear. You think you can do that?"

I glance at Thunderbird Academy, barely visible through the trees. It shouldn't matter, but I'm already mourning a future that will never be. It's not like they were going to let me stay here anyway. Everything changed the moment I opened that stupid book and read the words.

"I'll do what needs to be done," I say, nodding my head firmly. Hannah's lips curl up at the sides.

"That, I can absolutely believe," she replies before waving her hand. A ripple shatters the empty air between the two trees and then it opens like a veil.

"Oh, and one more thing." I glance at her. She pulls her other arm around, the one holding the book. I stare at it in shock, but my hands are already itching to hold it. "I thought you'd need this."

I nod as I take it because I don't have words for her generosity.

"Go, Avery."

"I won't forget this," I say before I step through the portal.

* * *

TRAVELING by portal is a tricky concept, and one I haven't mastered. When it spits me out on the other side, I land on my knees, gripping the book to my stomach. Looking back, I watch the portal close over before I get to my feet. I'm in an alley in what looks to be a big city. If the skyscrapers I glimpse are any indication.

There's no time to waste, so I move before that fae shows up on my tail. Oddly, I don't feel tired after all the magic I used. I feel energized. I keep the book close to my side as I step out into the busy street. From what I can see and know of big cities, this looks like Chicago. The train is visible from where I'm at, so I walk over to the station.

I'll have to figure out money and food. I'll have to find a place to stay. Thankfully, I know all about most of the magical communities around the world. After all, I was going to be a council member.

With a wave of my hand, I'm through the toll booth and on the train. I'll have to be very careful about using my magic, but for now, that was a necessity. When I sit down, it feels like the weight of the world is on my shoulders.

Everything I have ever outlined for my life, all the hours I've spent studying and planning, it all has been swept away.

One book, one spell, and everything has changed.

I glance down at the leather-bound volume on my lap and feel that strange pull toward it once again. Somehow, maybe, this is what destiny feels like. I made plans, but the powers that be had different ideas. I may not understand it, but it's my life now.

It's time to make different plans.

I'll find a job. I'll find a place to settle. And I'll learn what I can about this strange magic and how to wield it. Of that, I am sure. After all, I am my parents' daughter, and they didn't raise a failure.

My mind shifts back to the fae and his blue eyes, but I push the thought away. That's over and done with. I'll make sure he never finds me. I'll make sure no one finds me until I'm ready.

And I'll be ready.

SHADOW OF THE FAE

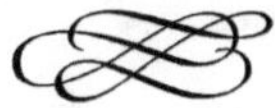

THE FAE CHRONICLES #1

When the night is dark,
And the pain is deep,
There's a spark inside,
That will carry you still.

When the day grows long,
And the week's a year,
You will find your home,
In the now and here.

Trusting in yourself,
Learning what is true,
Reaching for the next,
Being true to you.

Storms will come again,
Rain will fall like tears,
But the pow'r in you,
That will never fail—nor it'll disappear.

CHAPTER 1

"If you want to keep your tail attached to the rest of your body, I suggest you drop the necklace. Right now."

The tip of my knife is securely lodged in the indent of the troll's tail as he whimpers in fear. The jewelry he's clutching drops from his fingers while he continues to eye me.

"Push it toward me." I nod at the necklace, and the troll takes a deep breath before blowing at the metal. It slides, stopping against my foot. "Now, was that so hard?"

I smile but also don't remove my knife. Not yet.

"You tell your thieving friends if I catch them—and I will catch them if they cross me—you all will be walking around minus a tail. Capeesh?"

The troll nods. After a moment more, I let go of the tail.

"Witch," he mumbles before scurrying off into the darkness.

I squat to grab the necklace but keep my awareness locked on my surroundings. It would do me no good being jumped from behind. Once my bounty is secured, I stand. I notice the troll dropped something else on the way out. Walking over, I pick up the discarded vial, studying it in the dim light. It might be worth something on the black market. Well, the magical black market. Not a place I ever would've imagined going.

The last month of my life has molded me into someone I don't really recognize. But that's life. You do what you have to in order to survive.

That's all it's been about recently.

Survival.

Survival.

Survival.

This is definitely not where I thought my life would take me.

Tucking the items away inside my inner pocket, I sheath my knife and head out of the alley. Right before I hit the main street, a prickle at the back of my neck makes me pause. Scanning the rooftops in front of me, I then turn and do a quick study of the rest of my surroundings. There's nothing. The prickle doesn't go away, but I don't sense any immediate danger. I'm not particularly sure what I sensed, but it unnerves me.

This is how my life is now. I have to be on constant guard, moving more than standing still. At least years of perfecting my research skills provided me with a nice job. I can find pretty much anything on any wish list when it comes to magical items. Not exactly the glamorous life I planned for myself, but it's getting me through.

It takes me about a block and a half to recognize that I'm being followed. The same prickle of awareness is there, but it's been growing as I walk. It could be the troll and his friends, but I doubt it. This feels... more somehow.

More magical.

More dangerous.

More unnerving.

Keeping my pace steady, I run through my options. There's no way I'm taking whoever is following me anywhere near the market or my apartment. Which means I'll have to shake them off. Without causing a scene. Everyone is always up in arms about magical battles in public. The last thing I need is to draw attention to myself.

Turning into the next alleyway, I give it a second before I take off running. The feeling of being watched doesn't diminish, so whoever or whatever is out there must be keeping pace with me. And for me to still be able to sense them, it means they're more powerful than the average troll. If I could, I'd throw a shield or two of protection around me, but I'm not really that skilled. I could've been if I stayed at Thunderbird Academy. But I chose staying alive over education.

Now, I'm rethinking that choice.

I've had magic since before I could walk, but what happened at the school—no, I can't think of that right now. First, I have to get to safety.

The steady beat of my feet against the pavement syncs with the rhythm of my heart. I have to stay calm and in control. Wouldn't want my magic going haywire and alerting the Council. Or worse, the fae.

When I round yet another corner, I pause. Slowing my pace to match those around me, I step into the crowd. A game must've just gotten out. There are people everywhere. That awareness of being watched doesn't go away, but I still don't see any immediate danger. They won't attack in public. It's an unspoken, and sometimes spoken, rule of the magical community. It'll have to do for now.

I have a meeting to keep.

* * *

IT TAKES me twenty minutes and a ride on the light rail before I reach my desired neighborhood. The magical market is a typical hidden entity that moves its entrance when it chooses to. This week, it's across the river in Tempe. At the Tempe Mission Palms hotel to be exact. The buildings are structured in a square shape with an outside sitting area in the middle. There's also a large pool area where guests can be found on a regular basis. There are always people present since the hotel is used for conferences year-round.

This is a perfect place to hide a magical black market. No one notices a few extra people coming in and out. The sun has gone down by the time I reach the designated door, which opens up to a regular mop closet. Not very original, but I think many enjoy playing on the stereotypes.

I place my palm against the far wall and the air around me ripples. That is really all it takes. Any magical being can enter. If they know it's here, of course. The wall seems to faze in and out, and I don't hesitate to step through.

Instantly, there's noise all around me. The market is straight out of some fairytale book. We're in a forest, naturally, with stands arranged in between the trees. All kinds of magical beings fill the space, bartering for the best deal. I weave in and out of the crowd without stopping to look at the tables. I know exactly where I'm going.

A group of nymphs dance near the fountain, and a few stop to watch, mesmerized. The first time I came here, I was mesmerized as well. Nymphs have that effect on people. Most of those who come through here are witches and shifters. It takes some maneuvering to make sure I'm not seen by anyone I know. With my parents being on the Council, I've met a great number of witches growing up. That's why I stick to bartering with the shifters and the sprites. Although, even the latter isn't what I imagined.

When I was younger, I thought sprites were tiny spirits, the size of a sunflower at most. But the woman who greets me when I reach her is nothing like that. She's a little taller than me and beautiful beyond words. Her hair is braided in places and falls way past her back. She wears a dress full of layers that makes me think of spring, with it pastel colors and flowery scent. I haven't asked her too many questions, even though I'm fascinated.

"Greetings, Avery. You have something for me?" Lucinda says when I reach her.

"Just like I promised," I reply. She motions for me to follow her into her tent. Most of those selling at the market also live here, whether it's a tent, a tree house, or simply a tree, each makes it their own.

Stepping into Lucinda's tent, I'm always fascinated by how it opens up into a much bigger area. There is even a separate room for bathing and a small kitchen.

When I first found the market, Lucinda was kind enough to show me the ropes. Well, maybe kind isn't the right word. I made a deal with her. She keeps my secret and teaches me how to survive. In turn, I become her personal errand girl. That often means I have to be an enforcer too.

Not that I told her my situation easily. She can sense a lot of what goes on inside a person's mind, and I came to the market completely unprotected from such invasions. She zeroed in on my pain immediately. I would never confuse her for a friend.

"Let's see it." She reaches out her hand as she takes a seat at the table. I sit opposite of her before I pull out the necklace. "Was there trouble?"

"Nothing I couldn't handle." I shrug. I can never tell if she's actually concerned or if it's just a trick. I've only ever demanded one answer from her. And that was whether or not she's a fae. Since they can't lie, when she told me no, I realized I was somewhat safe. Not that I carry an illusion it will stay that way.

"What's on your mind?" Lucinda asks when I don't offer up any more information.

"I thought I was being followed. Maybe it's time for me to leave Phoenix."

It's not like I'm really asking her for advice. I've learned not to ask anyone of anything. It's safer that way. But I'm still hoping she gives me something to go off of.

"Have you been practicing your magic?" she asks instead. I sigh.

Even before I started at Thunderbird Academy, my magic has been on the fritz. But when I arrived at the school to begin my senior year, everything snowballed. My crazy magic, the magical book I found, and the fae that's been sent to retrieve me. I can still picture his blue eyes studying me from across the room. That happened right before I blasted him with my magic and jumped out a window.

"I've tried," I reply, pushing all thoughts of the tall, dark, and dangerous man out of my mind. "It's still being weird. Most of the time. It's as if it doesn't know what it's supposed to be. But also, it's not safe for me to use it, so I'm a little stuck."

"Sounds like growing pains to me." Lucinda shrugs, making the gesture elegant somehow. She stands, walking over to the small kitchen area and pouring out two cups of tea. Typically, I try to stay away from eating or drinking anything while I'm at the market, but I've broken my own rule at times. Right now, I just want a warm cup of tea and a nap. So, I accept the mug gratefully.

"What do you mean by growing pains?" I say, taking a small sip of the tea. Chamomile with a hint of honey and lavender. My lips curl up in a small smile. After years of study, I'm happy to know my senses are still attuned.

"It seems your magic is trying to figure itself out."

"Shouldn't it have done so when I was, I don't know, six and first coming into my powers?" Although, granted, I came into my powers before then. She doesn't need to know that.

"Maybe. Maybe not."

I narrow my eyes at her tone, something about it almost familiar. She's not done, however.

"I don't know your story, Avery, and I don't want to. I chose this life to be away from the drama and the heartache. But I can feel the magic brewing inside of you. Something is happening, or something is coming. Either way, you're in the middle of it."

"Great. Because I need that reminder."

I down the rest of my tea and stand. I don't want to be part of this conversation anymore. I'm tired, and I want my bed. But then I remember the little vial.

"Is this of any use to you?" I ask, pulling it out. Lucinda eyes the vial, her eyes lighting up. She takes it from me, giving it a little sniff and a shake.

"Where did you get it? It looks like troll juice."

"Okay, first of all, ew. And second of all, good nose because that's who dropped it."

She grins at me again, clearly very happy with this extra find. I don't even care to ask what she's going to use it for.

"I will take my leave now," I say without a thank you. I've learned that those two words are dangerous in these parts, and I won't utter them. "Let me know when you have another errand for me to run."

Lucinda walks back over, handing me a wad of cash. Much bigger than I was expecting. That juice must cost a pretty penny. Even though I'm curious to know where she gets the cash, I don't ask. We have an arrangement, and I need to stick with it. It's the only way I've been surviving on my own. I nod my thanks and then I'm out of there.

Today has been much like all the other days since I ran from Thunderbird Academy.

Except, that nagging feeling hasn't gone away. I must be tired. I just need rest.

CHAPTER 2

When I finally reach my apartment, the day has caught up with me. My limbs feel heavy and my head is pounding. I've been awake for over twenty-eight hours.

Finding the trolls who had the necklace Lucinda wanted ended up being more of a hassle than I let on. It's not like I can look up troll residences in an online search. So, after doing some research and finding out where troll activity has happened in the past, I had myself a stakeout. Then there was the matter of finding the right troll. All in all, it took a lot longer than I expected.

I lock the door behind me, switching on the light right away. My eyes instantly go to the crystals I placed above the doorframe. The three stones sit in a row, undisturbed. Black tourmaline, jet stone, and red jasper. Each is a stone that focuses on protection from negativity and unwanted energy. I may not be a witch who graduated high school, but I am a witch who studied her butt off to always be prepared.

Giving my small room a quick scan, I let out a sigh of relief when I don't sense anything off. My apartment is very basic, a studio size with a bed, dresser, and a television. All three of the items were already in here when I moved in. The small kitchen area has a refrigerator and a microwave. Which reminds me, I need to get groceries.

I head for the bathroom first, shedding my clothes and stepping under the shower. The water feels refreshing against my skin, but it also calls to my water magic. I have to keep my magic closely guarded in order to stay under radar. But when I'm in the shower, the call of the water is too loud to ignore. I let the magic come out to play. I only use it for a few seconds, just long enough to make the water droplets dance in a pattern in front of my face, before I drop them back down. The funny thing is, five months ago, I didn't even have water magic. My element has always been fire. But here I am, in a completely different magical column. I can't explain it. And I've tried.

Since I ran away from Thunderbird Academy, my magic has been slightly more stable. I can't truly experiment with it, but it feels steadier. More balanced between the fire and the water. One of these days, I'll get to play and then I'll know for sure. But having my magic traced would be the worst kind of happening. I do everything in my power not to let that become reality.

When I finally climb into bed, it seems like I've been awake for days. Living with this constant dread really puts extra pressure on the mind and body. I always think it'll take me forever to fall asleep, but then I'm out like a light.

Hands and claws reach for me, tearing at my clothes and skin. Blood splatters, marring the space around me. Monsters descend, hungry for my flesh. I open my mouth to scream, but no sound comes out. Just the noise of the creatures around me.

It's not like any dream I've had before.

Somehow, I know it's a dream. And yet, it feels real. The pain clouds my thoughts, tears leaking out of my eyes unbidden. I try to get away, to break free, but the creatures have their grip on me. When I finally do pull away, my arm is raw.

I stumble away, pushing through the trees that block my path. The branches are just as merciless as the creatures were. Glancing back, I worry they're behind me, but what I find freezes me in my tracks.

Everywhere my blood dripped on the ground, a bush has sprung up, blocking the creatures' path to me. I raise my arm and watch as another drop falls. The moment it's in the dirt, it becomes a bush. Flowers begin to form at the tops, blooming immediately. I jump back as not to be scratched by its branches. Before I can think too much of it, I reach out to one of the leaves, and then, I wake up.

The pain is sharp and pointed as I jerk into a sitting position. Looking at my arms, I expect to see scratches and blood, but there's nothing there. Just a lingering sensation of the pain. My body is covered in sweat, and I push the hair out of my face. Glancing at the clock, I see it's seven in the morning. I slept longer than I thought.

Keeping busy is my only defense against losing my mind. So, while lying in bed all day sounds nice, I have a job to do. There are three individuals looking for a magical bounty hunter, and I'm determined to score at least one of those jobs.

Pushing all thoughts of the dream away, I head for the bathroom. It doesn't matter that dreams are omens. It makes no difference that I need to sit down and dissect what I saw. That's not my life anymore. I have to keep moving. It's the only way I'll stay alive.

* * *

MY LIFE HAS BECOME a monotony of daily chores. I get up, I eat, I go in search of odd jobs. And I try to figure out how not to get killed. I never thought I'd find myself here. But life has a way of taking the wind out of our sails every now and then. With me, it decided to sink the whole ship.

After grabbing a bagel, I head out. The feeling of being watched hits me the moment I am on the sheet. Phoenix isn't like other big cities I stayed in. When I first went on the run, I moved every few days.

I didn't really have a choice.

It seemed that no matter where I went, there was someone right on my heels. I lasted in Boston for a whole week before I split. I figured since Phoenix wasn't even on my list of choices, I could buy myself a little time.

But now, it seems the time is running out.

Keeping my pace steady, I head for downtown. This city isn't as filled with pedestrians, so it's a little harder to lose oneself in the crowd. But downtown is still my best option.

There's an event going on today, some kind of a conference. When I finally reach the flow of people, I find them dressed up as various types of creatures. Now it makes sense. I've heard of these cons before. It's interesting to see, that's for sure. As I walk past a warlock and a werewolf, I try not to laugh. We definitely don't dress like that. And as far as I know, werewolves aren't real. They're just a take on who shifters are. A movement catches my attention. I shift my gaze a bit to try and figure out what distracted me from my amusement.

My eyes latch onto one of the conference goers, a hood over his head. There's something about the way he moves, so I go to follow. When he steps into one of building's indents, I am right behind him. I round the corner fast enough to watch him step *into* the wall. A smile spreads across my face as I follow.

When I'm on the other side, I find myself in a bar. I know he's behind me, even before he fully materializes. Twisting around, I reach for my knife. When he steps out of the shadows, I'm ready.

"I really can't get a drop on you, can I?" Julian says, chuckling. I narrow my eyes, studying his handsome face. My knife still at his jugular.

"Were you following me yesterday?"

"Absolutely not." I'm watching him closely, and only when I know he's telling the truth, do I step back.

"Trouble?"

"Nothing I couldn't handle." Sheathing the weapon, I turn back toward the room. In the past month, I've learned these magically cloaked bars exist in every city. And every realm, for that matter. When I first started going to the black market, Julian was there too. We ended up fighting for the same job, and the nymph decided to hire both of us. It's the only time I've worked with anyone else, but I don't regret it. He's become as close to a friend as I can get right now.

"I know you can handle anything," Julian comments as we head for the bar. "But if you ever need a second set of hands..."

To that, I only roll my eyes. He's smooth all over, but I won't bite. And he knows it. He chuckles at my response and calls to the bartender for some drinks.

"What brings you in today?" Julian asks once we grab our sodas. I could use some coffee, but I'll settle on Dr. Pepper for now. The caffeine should do the trick.

"I was following a suspicious individual in the crowd." I smirk, taking a seat against the wall at one of the tables. My eyes continue scanning the room, always on alert.

Technically, these types of bars are neutral ground. There are creatures all over the room who are in an all-out war outside these walls. But in here, they are drinking buddies. Yet, that doesn't mean I'm not set to my highest alert setting. I can't afford lowering my guard.

"How is it you can always tell when one of us is around?" Julian leans forward, and I turn my attention to him.

"It's a gift." I shrug, but honestly, I'm not sure what it is. There's something about the aura of a supernatural that calls to me. It hasn't always been like that. I can't tell what kind of creature is in front of me, but it's like I can feel the magic on them. No matter if they're disguised as a human.

"It's a gift anyone in here would covet," Julian comments, lowering his voice further. I glance at him sharply, trying to decipher if it's actual danger he's feeling or just precaution. While I can sense supernatural, he can sense impending doom. I'm not sure which one is more impressive. I could use his gift as much as mine right now.

"Do you know something I don't?"

"Only that there have been a few strangers in the area."

I sit up at attention, trying to keep my apprehension down. Julian doesn't know my story any more than I know his. I don't even know what type of magical creature he is, and I'm not about to ask. If I don't ask, he won't ask. The less we actually know about each other, the better.

"Just passing through or looking for something?" I try to keep my tone nonchalant, but I think he can tell it's more than mild curiosity.

"Not too sure. I think one was asking questions, but they always do when coming through here."

I nod, letting that information sink in.

Yesterday, I thought someone was following me. Today I find out there are strangers in the neighborhood. Maybe it's time for me to move on. Except I have no idea where I would go.

"Avery." Julian's voice brings my attention back to him. "I wouldn't make any sudden moves just yet."

"I don't know what you mean."

"We all have secrets," he narrows his eyes at me. I really can't expect him to not realize I'm hiding from something or someone. "But it would be better to have all the cards on the table before making any big decisions."

I nod again, this time agreeing with him. He seems satisfied with that, but it really doesn't make me feel better. Something is brewing, and I have to be ready.

*J*ulian and I leave the bar behind a few minutes later. I no longer feel protected in the supposed safe environment, and Julian doesn't question me. He keeps pace with me as we move to get lost in the crowd, no one commenting on our lack of costumes.

"If I asked you what has you spooked, will you give me an honest answer?" Julian asks after a few moments of silently walking through the room.

"No."

"I expected as much."

"And yet, you still asked."

That remark also comes with another glare, to which he just chuckles in response.

"Why are you even still here?" I ask as we head into the main floor of the convention center. Here, vendors are set up across the whole room, selling all kinds of things I've never even thought of buying. Replicas of creatures from various shows and movies, books and trading cards, as well as costumes. People really go all out for this stuff.

"I thought you'd be interested in a job."

That perks me up immediately. I look over at Julian and find him grinning down at me.

"You could've led with that."

"I could've."

Before he continues, I spot something that catches my eye. Without waiting to see if he follows, I beeline for the stand, mesmerized by the work in front of me. There are tiny dragons made from some shiny material perching on various areas at the stand. Of course, once I'm in front of them, I see they're not even remotely real. But they are beautiful. The man selling them is showing a customer how the dragon can perch on their wrist, wrapping the tail around the forearm.

"Is it as weird for you as it is for me to see real creatures reduced to this?" Julian says, over my shoulder. I turn my head just slightly to the right, his presence directly at my back. It goes without saying. The human world has a tendency to romanticize aspects of our world I wish they didn't. But sometimes, they create something this beautiful, and I can't help but admire it.

"What's the job?" I ask, running a finger gently over the dragon's scales. I'm not worried about discussing such matters here. It feels like these people would just assume we're playing a part.

"There's an event at the theater. Some of the Council members will be present. And they'll be bringing a crystal ball with them."

I twist around, shock plainly displayed on my face.

"You want to steal from the Council?"

Julian reaches for my wrist, tugging me out of the crowd. We find a quiet spot against the wall before I extract myself.

"Are you out of your mind?"

"I'm perfectly in my mind, thank you very much," he comments while I shake my head.

"You told me yourself that you like to keep a low profile. How is stealing from them going to accomplish that?" I'm not sure if I'm more concerned with him or me right now, but I definitely don't like this.

"You don't think I know what I'm doing?"

"You definitely don't know what you're doing."

Julian chuckles like he really doesn't have a care in the world.

"Stop that," I say, smacking him in the shoulder. "Be serious for a second."

"I am serious," he replies, sobering up. "This score will set me for years. I can disappear for real. I can travel without the fear of discovery because I won't have to rely on my magic. I could actually afford a plane ticket. Don't you want to be able to say the same?"

I can't deny the offer is tempting. And he wouldn't be mentioning it if he didn't need my help. But I can't shake the fact that if I go through with this, I'm putting myself directly in the path of the Council.

"I'm not entirely convinced," I finally say, "But," I raise my hand, "I'm not entirely opposed."

"Yes!" Julian exclaims, wrapping his arms around my middle and lifting me off my feet.

"I didn't say yes." I swat at him to put me down.

"But you also didn't say no."

Shaking my head, I get lowered to the floor. Julian is grinning like an idiot. I would be lying if I said it wasn't contagious. What have I become? I sober up right away. Being on the run has really messed with my morals. Two months ago, I wouldn't be caught near such an idea. Yet here I am. Actually considering it.

Just then, the feeling of being watched returns. I don't hesitate to spin around to see if I can spot the source. Facing it head on might be my best option, instead of this constant tiptoeing around danger.

"What is it?" Julian asks, clearly picking up on the tension.

"Not sure. But we need to move."

He doesn't hesitate to follow my lead, and for that I am thankful. I wish I knew what I was looking for. This is really getting on my nerves.

* * *

WE HEAD BACK into the crowd, weaving in and out of the conference goers. At first, I think maybe it's just my paranoia. There are a lot of people here, and we're not exactly dressed to be part of the fun. Regular clothes are a little more noticeable than not. Although, others here are in t-shirts and jeans as well, so that logic doesn't work like I want it to.

The more we move, the more I feel like something is following us. It would be nice if I could do a searching or a protection spell to get a feel for my surroundings, but that would be kind of like wearing a beacon for all magical beings to see. The fact that my magic has been acting weird, and I haven't been using it has been working in my favor so far.

"Are you going to tell me what's going on?" Julian asks, easily keeping pace with me. It helps to have long legs, unlike my shorter ones. Not that I'm that short. Five-five is pretty average. But Julian is at least six-two, so he has a slight advantage.

"If I knew, I would. I told you someone was following me yesterday. The same feeling has returned."

Julian takes my words at face value and does his own study of our surroundings. Since I don't know what kind of magic he possesses, I have no idea what that entails. But I'm hoping it will be helpful. If I was truly in danger, he should be able to tell with his special talent. I hope. Because whatever is out there? It's getting closer.

"I can't tell if anything is directed at you," Julian comments. I glance at him in confusion. Before I can ask what that means, double doors open up, and a fresh flood of people rush into the corridor. Julian and I get separated, but I don't pause to look for him. Now I'm feeling watched and claustrophobic. I need to get out.

When I push through the doors leading to the outside, I'm met with the constant Arizona heat. There's nothing like hiding in the hottest oven of the States. No one would actually think I moved here willingly.

"Avery!"

Twisting around, I spot Julian coming out of another set of doors and pivot toward him.

"Anything?" I ask when I'm closer.

"Nope. But come on. Better safe than sorry."

That's the smartest statement I've heard all day, so I don't hesitate to follow him as he heads away from the convention center. We're about a block away when I finally feel like I can slow down and reassess my situation.

"Stopping?"

"I need to think. I can't exactly keep running around the whole city, hoping whatever is out there doesn't find me."

"Any idea who it may be?"

"Absolutely not."

That last part is a lie of sorts. It has to be someone from the Council. Or someone from Faery. Or actually, it could be the Ancients themselves coming to claim me. All three parties would benefit to have me on their side right now. I would put my money on the second option though, if I had any to spare. Waiting on someone from their realm to find me has been my constant fear for the last month. They're too powerful, and I'm too inexperienced to hide for long. But I'm learning. Like making alliances, for example. Which is why I turn to Julian.

"I'll help you steal from the Council," I say, already knowing I'm going to regret this. "If you help me evade whoever is after me."

The guy in front of me studies me for a very long thirty or so seconds before he finally nods. I have no idea what he's thinking, and I'm not sure I want to. We made a deal, so I put my hand out for a shake. His fingers wrap around my own with no hesitation. The small gesture brings back a memory of the last time I shook hands with someone. It was back at Thunderbird Academy where the gesture took me by surprise.

I pull back, pushing back the thoughts of my life before as well. That's how I have to think about it. The before and the after. I'm living in the after now.

After I found that ancient book.

After I read the forbidden words no one has been able to read for generations.

After I had to leave everything behind and run.

It does me no good focusing on the before. I have to focus on the after.

"I think we need to find an advantage." Julian's words pull me from my thoughts. He clearly has a destination in mind, so I follow. I'm not too excited to be trusting anyone with my wellbeing right now, but this is the best option I have. He seems to know what he's doing. He at least seems to be sure of himself. I can use a little bit of that right now. I haven't been sure of myself even before this whole book fiasco happened.

"What exactly are we doing?" I finally ask as Julian heads into an alley between a building and an empty lot.

"Finding higher ground. I can do some magic," he wiggles his fingers, "And see if I can find any specific danger."

"Magic?" I ask, wiggling my own fingers in a similar matter.

"I do have it, you know."

"I wouldn't. But carry on."

I motion him with a shooing motion, and he throws a smirk my way before jumping up and grabbing one of the fire escape ladders. It pulls down with a resounding clang, and Julian doesn't hesitate to climb it. Shaking my head, I follow as well. We reach the roof of the five-story building in no time.

Up here, I can see how big the conference actually is. People are spread out in front of the convention center, which actually occupies more than one building. More groups are heading toward the food areas in downtown while others lodge in various spots around the closed off streets.

"They really go all out," I comment, watching a couple of dressed up vampires walk by.

"They're fascinated. You can't really blame them."

Of course I can't. But I do envy them. Maybe my life would be easier without magic. But then again, maybe not. I'm just being a big baby. I really need to suck it up.

Julian walks over to the edge of the room, placing his hands on the minuscule railing. When I join him, I see that he has closed his eyes, his face full of concentration. I don't interrupt, instead watching the crowds below. Then, something catches my eye.

"What?" Julian asks, and I realize I must've gasped out loud. I find his eyes, full of concern on me, but I'm not sure I want to put to words what I thought I saw. "Avery?"

"I think I saw someone." I nearly whisper. My heart is beating a mile a second. When I finally tear my gaze away from Julian and look down, there's no one there. Except, I can't deny it. He was here.

The fae who was sent to capture me at Thunderbird Academy was here.

CHAPTER 4

"You're not going to tell me?" Julian asks as we descend from the roof down the ladder. I look up at him where he's perched a few steps above me and shake my head. Saying it out loud will just make it more real. I know what I saw, and I know what it means. I have to go. When my feet hit the pavement, I try to do just that.

"Hey now." Julian catches up with me before I've taken any steps, pulling me to a stop. "I thought you were going to let me help."

"We made a deal, Julian. But now, that's off. Because I have to go. That's actually my only option."

"I don't believe that."

I realize he still has his hand on my upper arm. I retract it carefully, taking a step back. I know this isn't fair to him. He's been my only friend since all of this began. But that's precisely why I have to leave. It would be foolish of me to put more people in danger.

"Look, I appreciate everything you've done for me. You've had my back a few times. But this is my problem. The best thing I can do for you is disappear."

He stares at me like he's never seen me before. There's emotion in his eyes which I can't quite understand, or maybe I just don't want to.

I don't need anyone attaching themselves to me. And I certainly can't risk the same.

"I think your friend will surely disagree."

A deep voice comes from behind Julian. I don't need to see to know who it is. Julian turns swiftly, coming face to face with my fae pursuer. The two guys stare at each other, as if sizing the other up. Neither says a word. I hope they're distracted enough for me to have a head start. But when I start inching away, the fae's gaze shifts immediately to me.

"We meet again," he says, the simple words spoken by that delicious voice travel over my body. I suppress a shudder, refusing to give him the satisfaction.

"Wish we hadn't."

His lips curl up in a smile that carries no humor as he continues to track my every move. There's a part of me, maybe the magic itself, that reacts to his proximity. But I have no idea what to do with that information, and I refuse to just lay down and give in.

Whatever opportunity I may have had to go unnoticed is over now. He found me, and I have to figure out a way to get out of this. Which actually seems more impossible than moving the sun and the moon with my magic.

Julian hasn't moved from his spot, slightly in front of me and to the right. If I was to run, I could run behind him. That would put him in fae's way. At least for a second. But I'm also having a difficult time being okay with putting Julian in danger.

"Not that I'm not enjoying this stimulating conversation," the fae breaks the silence once again, "but if you and... your friend here want to keep all your organs intact, I suggest we move."

"Are you threatening me?" Julian half growls, taking a step toward the fae.

"No, I'm merely stating a fact. The danger isn't coming from me but from those sent to take Miss Kincaid by any means necessary. And from what I know, they like the rough option."

"*You* were sent for me!" I snap, anger overpowering the fear. "You are the reason I ran in the first place. If there is any danger here, it's you."

The fae watches me for a tense moment before he smirks once more.

"You are correct. I am dangerous. But I think the humans have a saying for that sort of a thing. Better the devil you know?"

Coming from his lips, the phrase takes on a dozen different meanings, and really, none of them are anything good for me.

"You don't have to trust me," he says. "But I would rather not cause a scene. We should get moving."

Julian has placed himself directly in front of me now, and I can feel his body heat reaching out to mine. He's tense, more tense than I've ever seen him. I'm not sure if that comforts me or makes me that much more nervous.

But before I can make a decision, something comes into my peripheral vision. All three of us twist to watch three huge men step into the alley.

"There goes that plan," the fae mumbles. The statement and the way he delivers it is so human I almost become curious. But only for a split second.

Turning, I start to move in the other direction when three more drop from somewhere above.

"Are they who I think they are?" Julian asks. I stare at him in confusion.

"Yes," is the fae's one-word response. They exchange a look I don't understand but absolutely hate. I don't need them on the same side. Well, maybe right now I do? I have no idea what's happening.

"We can't take them," Julian comments as the men move closer. There's something about them that I can't quite put my finger on. They look... not right somehow.

"We could. But it wouldn't be pretty."

"Guys, I need some information here. What are they?" I ask.

"Werewolves."

I snap my gaze to Julian, already shaking my head.

"Werewolves aren't real. They're just a take on shifters. They..."

"I can assure you they are very real, and they are very vicious, and they are about to pounce on us, so I suggest you move."

With those words, the fae reaches for me, wrapping his arms around my torso and sweeping me right off my feet. In the same moment, he twists his body, draping it over mine. As he moves, the loudest growl I've ever heard resounds all around me. It goes through me, filling up my head. My back presses against a wall as the fae covers me from the front.

I try to reach forward with my hands, but the fae pins my arms down. The desire to move toward the werewolves slams into me, making my body squirm.

"Don't focus on the sound. Don't give them an entrance. Avery!"

It's my name that breaks through the fog. I glance up to find the fae's face inches from mine.

"Better," he says before he drops his arms. He stands, spinning around in the same motion. The werewolves attack the same moment the boys move. The sound of them clashing isn't like any I've heard before.

Getting to my feet, I reach for my knife and my magic. The fire is there, but at such a small capacity, it's almost useless. Just then, one of the werewolf men reaches me. My quick reflexes dodge his grab.

Dropping to the ground, I twist my body. I push off his legs and slam my feet into the backs of his knees. He falls forward, bashing his face into the wall. It stuns him for a moment. It's enough time for me to jump to my feet and onto his back. Wrapping my legs around his middle, I wrap my arms around his throat.

He shakes his body to try and drop me, but I'm holding on for all I'm worth. The sound of clashing bodies and magic reaches me. I look over to find both Julian and the fae with swords drawn, battling it out with the creatures. When Julian pierces one of the werewolves through the heart, I almost release my grip. But I realize it's kill or be killed, and these creature didn't come to play.

With my knife securely in my hand, I wind back and stab the creature in the neck. He drops to his knees immediately. I jump off his back to watch him crumble to the ground. Blood gushes over the asphalt, drying into a stain almost immediately in the heat of the day.

Pushing away the horror of what I've just done, I turn to face the boys. The moment of distraction costs me as huge arms wrap around me from behind. I scream as I am lifted off my feet, the knife clattering to the ground.

"Let me go!" I try to twist, to reach for my magic or some kind of footing, but the werewolf is too strong. He's moving backwards as I thrash, the energy leaving my body in waves.

All of a sudden, a blast of magic goes straight through me. I fall forward out of his arms. The fae is there in the blink of an eye, catching me before I face plant. His arms wrap around my shoulders. I glance over my shoulder to find the creature blasted against the wall, dead.

I look up at the fae, breathing heavily. I don't know what I would've done right there, but then Julian catches eye.

"No!" I scream, pushing off the soles of my feet. But the fae's arms are still around me. I watch as a creature stabs Julian right in the torso. Julian drops to his knees, blood pouring out of his middle as I fight to go to him. He finds my eyes and utters one word.

"Go."

* * *

THE FAE DOESN'T HESITATE, grabbing my arm and yanking me to my feet. I try to stay upright, but all strength has left me. Not only have I just killed someone, I've also watched the only person whom I could call a friend get murdered in front of me.

"Avery!" the fae snaps. I drop down to my knees, tears leaking out of my eyes without me even realize it until they're tickling my neck.

"Avery." He's crouching right in front of me, his hand hovering near my face. The other hand pushes a wave of magic toward the remaining werewolves, keeping them in place. But only barely. "I need you to come back. I understand this is difficult, but if you don't work with me right here and right now, we're both done for."

I look up at him, his piercing eyes staring straight into my soul. Somehow, I get up. He nods, a glimmer of pride in his gaze before he's reaching for my hand once more. This time, my feet work a little better just by the sheer determination that I will not become a blabbering mess. Not that what happened to me is anything I've been trained for. I'm not sure anyone can truly prepare for it without experiencing it first. But I can do this. I can keep myself together a little while longer. Then, in the darkness of a room, I'll allow myself to feel whatever I need to feel.

Shut it down.

Shut it down.

Shut it down.

The fae and I race through the alley before coming out onto the busy street. The conference goers are on this end as well, happily heading toward whatever is next on their agenda.

"Come on." The fae doesn't hesitate, pulling me into the crowd. Glancing behind me, I try to find the werewolves, but I can't see them. They must abide by the same rules as the rest of us: no showing ourselves to the human world. Right now, that's to our advantage.

For some reason, I don't hesitate to keep pace with the fae. Technically, he's still my enemy. But at least he hasn't tried to cut me to pieces. Yet. I'm not about to trust that he won't do it.

Just like with Julian, he seems to know where he's going as well. I guess I'm the only one who didn't learn the city inside and out. But then I realize where we are.

"Are you taking me home?"

"To your apartment, yes. Although I wouldn't call it home."

That stops me right in my tracks. Since he still has hold of my hand, he pauses as well.

"You knew where I was this whole time?" I ask, my voice sounding small, even to my own ears. The fae doesn't answer right away. There's a momentary pause and then a nod.

"Not the whole time. Only the last few days. You've done a good job at hiding."

"Clearly, not good enough."

There's that smirk again and then he's pulling me behind him. I would extract my hand but holding onto something feels right somehow. I soak up this moment of weakness. It's the only one I'm willing to allow myself to have.

It takes us twice as long to reach my apartment as it should've. I realize it's because he's been taking weird alleys and doubling back. I'm so tired I could lay down and sleep on the ground. Taking a life really drains a person, I suppose.

"Any protection?" the fae asks, and I see that we have arrived at my door. I shake my head and step forward to unlock it. Without my active magic, I can only do crystals and herbs. Which I'm sure he knows, but he's being polite. Not something I expected him to be.

When we step inside, nothing seems disturbed. My crystals are still positioned over the door frame. The fae locks the door behind us and then waves his hand over the frame. I don't have to see what he's doing to feel it. He has no problem using his magic.

"So, what now? You kidnap me, take me to your queen?" I ask, folding my arms in front of me as I stare him down. It feels strange having him in my space. He seems to fill it just by standing there. He's probably at least six-three, taller than Julian.

A sharp pain slams into my heart at the thought of him. It's my fault he's dead. I'll have to carry that with me forever.

"I was thinking you should take a shower and get some rest."

That extinguishes whatever snarky remark I had ready.

"Why are you being... nice?"

"I'm not. And don't get used to it. It's my job to make sure you stay alive, that's all."

I roll my eyes at that, dropping my arms to my sides.

"That sounds more like it."

Twisting on my heels, I head for the bathroom. When I step into the small room, I realize he's right behind me.

"Don't worry. I don't have a window to escape through. Nor will I jump off a fourth story balcony. That's out there." I point to the living room. The fae does a quick study of the bathroom before nodding.

"I'll be right out here."

"Yes, sir. Prison Master."

Before he can reply, I shut the door in his face.

82

CHAPTER 5

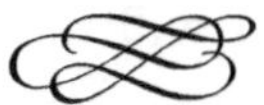

I give myself time in the shower, but I refuse to cry. I'm not about to give him the satisfaction. He's already seen me weak. I won't let that happen again.

When I found that book in the library at Thunderbird Academy, I was only curious. But it called to me. It enticed me. It knew my magic would be able to read it.

Growing up, we are taught many fairytales. Since I wanted to work for the Council, I learned more than what I was taught in school. I asked questions. I read everything I could get my hands on. That turned out to be a terrible idea. It brought me right into a war I want no part of. For the last two years, we've been fighting. Ever since the Ancients, the first supernatural creatures, started waking up. They've been roaming the realms again, taking and killing and leaving behind nothing but destruction. I wanted to help the Council figure out a way to stop them.

Instead, I'm on the run from the Faery realm and the Ancients because of one book and the magic it holds.

Now, the only friend I made since going on the run is dead, and it's my fault.

I can't get around that.

He's dead.

Glancing down, I notice my hands, stained with red. Grabbing for my soap, I scrub at the evidence aggressively. Needing it off my skin. The panic starts to set in, but I won't let it. I have to stay in control.

Focus and breathe.

Focus and breathe.

Focus and breathe.

Shutting my eyes tightly, I will the tears away. No more crying. Not until I'm out of this predicament and safe.

I know I'm not safe with the fae.

Stepping out of the shower, I reach for the spare pajamas I keep in the bathroom, thankful for my preparedness. When I walk out of the bathroom, there's a split second where I think he's gone. But then I see him by the glass door, looking out at the city.

"Oh, you're still here," I comment, heading for the kitchen. He doesn't leave his post, but he does face me. I can't tell in the near darkness, but I think he might've smiled at my tone. Not that it matters.

"We can stay here tonight, but we need to find a better place tomorrow."

"Excuse me, there is nothing wrong with my apartment."

"I didn't say there was." His tone is nonchalant once again, missing any of the mild warmth he exhibited earlier. "But you've been here for a month. Your magic is all over this building."

"I haven't been using it," I reply, surprised. I think back to the few times I let the water dance around in the shower. That could hardly count as spreading it across the whole building.

"Magic is part of you. It leaves traces of your essence behind whether you like it or not."

"So, what you're saying is no matter how much I hid, you would've found me eventually."

We have that stare down we're becoming familiar with and then I'm the first to look away. He doesn't have to answer my statement. I'm a quick learner. I have gathered the needed information.

"Tomorrow, we can find another place to lay low for a little bit before we move again. That's the trick. Never settle in one spot for long."

"I like how you just assume I'm going to go along with everything you're planning. Don't I get a say?"

"Look who has found her courage."

I don't appreciate that comment. If a glare could hurt, he'd be in pain right now. Walking around the counter, I come to stand in the middle of the room, my eyes on him.

"I may have lost it there for a moment, but in case you didn't notice, my friend died, and I killed one of those creatures with my bare hands. These hands." I raise them in front of me, showing off the raw skin left over from my scrubbing. "I had to wash blood off them. Do you think that's normal for me? So, excuse me for expressing some basic emotion!"

My voice rises with each word and then I'm gasping, trying to rein in my outburst. If I get any more worked up, I'll set something on fire. Probably him. Which honestly doesn't sound so bad right now.

"I'm not trying to tell you what to feel," he says, turning my attention back to him.

"Maybe not, but you're making fun of me, and that's not okay either. Maybe it's some sort of new torture technique you guys have in Faery. In which case, good for you. It's working."

That's probably not the best thing to admit, but I'm tired. Mentally and physically and emotionally. Nothing coming out of my mouth right now is going to make much sense.

"I'm not torturing you."

"Could've fooled me." I sit down on my bed, staring at the floor for a minute before I look up at him again. "Are you going to murder me in my sleep?"

That question seems to actually shock him. He opens his mouth to speak before closing it again.

"I'm not going to murder you," he finally says. I chuckle at that without humor.

"Not in my sleep at least, right?"

I scoot up on the bed, my limbs weighing a ton. I let the yawn come.

"I got you out of there, remember?" the fae asks as he watches me climb under the covers. I don't even care to think of where he's going to sleep or if he does.

"You saved me—" I mumble into the pillow.

"That's right. I did. Believe it or not, I am on your side."

"Hmm. I don't believe it."

"Why not?"

It takes me a full minute to reply, my brain slow in processing as my eyes close.

"Because I don't even know your name." I finally reply. Not sure why that's the first place my thoughts go. But how am I supposed to trust him if I know nothing about him? Not even the basics. Sleep almost overtakes me, but then at the last moment, I hear his reply.

"My name is Derek."

* * *

WAKING UP THE NEXT MORNING, I have no idea what to expect. There's a moment right before I'm fully awake that I remember everything that has happened. Thankfully, I didn't dream. But that will come with time, I know it. My mind will need to work through what happened and dreams will be the easiest way.

When I do finally sit up, I scan my studio apartment, zeroing in on the fae.

Derek.

I remember him saying that right before I drifted off. He's standing behind the counter, pouring himself a cup of coffee. That's what woke me, the smell. I can't believe I slept so hard with him here.

"I thought you'd sleep the day away." he says, taking a sip.

"If you wanted me awake earlier, you could've woken me up," I reply, walking straight past him and into the bathroom. He already doesn't bring out the best qualities in me, but I'm especially snarky in the mornings. Because mornings are the worst. I wash my face and brush my teeth before I feel well enough to face him.

"You need to pack a few essentials, and we need to go," he says the moment I step out, which causes me to roll my eyes.

"Okay, *Derek*, I'm going to need you to chill with the orders and let me have some coffee first." I push past him, grabbing a mug. Only after I've poured the coffee do I look up. He's watching me with that unwavering gaze of his as I narrow my eyes in response. "What?"

"Nothing."

He turns, walking across the room to the window once more. I'm thankful for the distance. I still have no idea what part of me is reacting to him, but it needs to stop. I need my head clear.

"So, since you *didn't* murder me in my sleep, I suppose you have a different plan for me?" I ask, taking another sip. He doesn't reply right away, as is his custom. It's a very annoying tactic that the Council uses as well. Especially when they don't want to divulge all their information at once. Most people want to fill the silence with something, so they'll keep talking instead of waiting for an answer. Often, they'll reveal something about themselves or a situation that they were trying to keep hidden. But I know the trick, so I don't speak. I wait him out. His brow twitches just slightly. I can't tell if it's in approval or annoyance.

"I want to help you."

That sends my eyebrows sky high.

"You're kidding."

"Fae don't kid."

"They're not supposed to lie either, but that's your only other option."

"No, the only other option is that I'm telling the truth."

"Why?" I place the mug down, leaning forward on my hands. He has to see me as capable, or he won't ever take me seriously. I can't change how I acted last night, but I can move forward from there. This is me trying.

"Let's just say my life isn't all it's cracked out to be."

"What a human thing to say."

His eyes flash, but I'm not backing down. I should be scared of him and a part of me is. But I'm more curious than anything. Which is how I get into all my troubles: curiosity.

"If we go back to Faery now, you'll become a pawn. Like me. Faery is in trouble and your power can help. If used properly. Not everything is so black and white for me. There has to be another way. At least, I'm willing to try and find it."

"You know, you're the second fae I've met who doesn't like how things work in that realm of yours." I pick up the mug again, taking a sip. But I'm still watching him, and this time his lips twitched for sure. I'm getting to him. At least slightly.

"I have my reasons. Right now, it's in your best interest to follow my lead."

"Do people usually just follow whatever you say?"

That stops him from whatever else he was going to say. I can't deny there's a ruthlessness about him. He's chiseled jaw and sharp edges all over. But there's also something else below the surface, and he's letting me see those glimpses. It's making me more intrigued.

"Right now, our interests align," Derek finally says. I suppress a smile at his dodging the question. "If we work together, we might be able to reach our individual goals."

"Oh, you mean where I don't become an eternal slave?"

"Precisely."

I was kidding, kind of, but his tone takes the wind out of my sails. Because he's right of course. This is what I've been running from. I'm just not sure trusting the one man who was sent to capture me has my best interests at heart either.

However, I don't know if I have a choice.

CHAPTER 6

$\mathcal{E}$ven though I don't particularly want to, I know leaving with Derek is my best bet right now. He's definitely not telling me the whole story, but for some reason, he wants to help. Or something like that.

And yes, my curiosity is piqued.

There are so many layers to him, I want to unravel them all. My analytical mind is creating graphs and tables, trying to organize everything that has happened. Putting the events into their designated slots allows me to process, without becoming overwhelmed. Which is honestly a constant battle.

There is a possibility that this is a trap. I'm not naïve enough to rule that out just because a pretty fae is telling me he's on my side.

Only... I have no idea what he would gain from saving me, watching over me while I sleep, and then kidnapping me. He could've taken me to Faery in my sleep, and I wouldn't have known.

I realize I've been silent for a long time. When I look up at Derek, he hasn't moved. He also hasn't ordered me to get going. He looks like someone who would order people around and they would listen to him, no questions asked.

All of this is turning out different than I expected.

"What should I bring?" I ask, only as a courtesy. I already have a to-go bag ready. It's what you do when you're on the run. I learned that in the first apartment I stayed in. There, I thought I could settle, so I actually bought a few things for the place. A mistake I won't be making again.

"Whatever is in your bag is fine." Derek's words take me by surprise, and I narrow my eyes at him.

"You went through my stuff?"

"I didn't have to. It's right there." He points to the backpack near the door, and I feel slightly less annoyed. Walking back around the counter and into the kitchen once more, I grab my two left over bagels and head for the bathroom, stopping only long enough to pull out an outfit from my closet.

"If we're about to be fugitives to who knows where, you better have a plan to feed me at least three times a day."

With that, I shut the door. I keep doing that. But I have to admit that I'm enjoying having the last word.

Munching on the bagels, I dress quickly, pulling my hair into a loose ponytail. It'd be better to braid it, but I don't have time. I can feel him growing restless on the other side of the door.

When I step out, he's by the front, the backpack in one hand.

"Really?"

"We have to go."

There's just enough urgency in his tone that I don't question it. Since I've been low on magic, I can't sense any impending doom. Plus, that was Julian's superpower. Then, my mind is back in that alley—

No, lock it away, Avery. Not right now.

Derek looks powerful enough to sense what's happening two states over, so I guess I don't have to do any sensing of my own. For now, I'll let his magic lead the way.

I grab my backup knife from under my pillow, the usual place for it, and slide it into the sheath at the base of my back. Derek watches my movements with interest, probably wondering why I even need such a puny weapon. But he should know magic is tracked. This is the best I can do. Walking around with a huge sword will draw some attention, after all. I've heard fae can conjure certain weapons, and since Derek had a sword yesterday and doesn't have one now, I'm assuming that's true. Something to ponder at a later time.

He opens the door, swinging my backpack onto his shoulder as I give my apartment one last look. There's not much of mine here, but I've been here long enough that it makes me a bit sad to be leaving. But that's the definition of survival: I have to do what I have to do.

Right now, that involves trusting the very fae that's been hunting me for weeks. Let's see how this turns out.

* * *

"I can take that," I say, reaching for the backpack, but Derek doesn't relinquish it.

"There's nothing else in the apartment that you want to take with you?" he asks instead, and I know exactly what he means.

The book.

The cursed book I found at Thunderbird Academy that got me into this mess in the first place.

"If you mean the book, it's not there." I raise my hand before he can speak. "And if you're going to ask me where it is, don't bother."

It's the only bargaining chip I have left, and I know it. The Faery realm needs that book, and they need someone who can read it. Right now, that's precisely one person: me. Since Derek has found me, I can't exactly bargain with my whereabouts. I have to bargain with the book's.

"If that's how you're going to play it."

"Duh," I reply, pushing past him and down the stairs. I'm more than okay with him carrying my stuff. But I really don't want to be having this conversation so early in the morning. Well, early for me.

"You got a magical carriage for us, or what?" I ask when we leave my apartment building behind.

"Yes, this way," Derek says and then leads me to a bus stop. I'm not sure what kind of things I keep expecting from him, but it's not this. Public transportation seems so far below him, but here we are.

We don't talk as the bus pulls up and we get on. We don't talk as he takes a seat beside me. We don't talk for the first fifteen minutes of the ride as it makes stops and more people get on.

Every part of me wants to break the silence and ask questions. But I know better than that. If I break now, it'll be easier to break later. Instead, I swallow my questions and look out the window.

My thoughts return to the book and everything it has brought my way. I thought going to study at Thunderbird Academy my senior year would be the highlight of my academic career. Well, at least until I went to college and began working for the Council.

In the few days that I was at the school, I met some amazing people, including a witch with a very rare power. I thought everything was going great when the headmaster accepted me into the internship program that gave me a chance to work under one of the Council leaders.

And then I found the book. Or maybe the book found me.

"Did you read any of it?" Derek's question filters in through my thoughts. I turn to glance over at him. At first, I think he's reading my mind somehow but no. He's thinking about the book, just like I am.

"Only what brought me here."

That gets his attention. He turns his body, so he's facing me a little more, narrowing his eyes at me.

"You didn't see what else you can learn? Not even a few pages?"

"Why is that so hard to believe?"

"Because you love school!" That comes out a little louder than he intended, and a few people turn to glance our way. He lowers his voice again before continuing. "You're all about research and data. You didn't have any interest in learning more?"

"First of all, how do you even know that? And second of all, of course I'm curious. But the one thing I've been told about that book is that it can make a lot of very bad things happen. I don't know what I'm allowed to read and what's off limits. I don't even know if it still counts as reading if I don't do it out loud. I have more questions than answers, and that book wouldn't bring forth any."

"I suppose you are correct."

I open my mouth with more protests, but I realize he agreed with me.

"Than—" I begin, before I catch myself. There's a sparkle in his eye as he meets mine. He knows I was about to thank him. Even though I have no idea if the rules apply the same here, I'm not about to make myself succumb to his fae wiles. I have to be very careful in what I say around him. I haven't been thinking this before now, but I should be conscious of this. Continuously.

He's different than I would imagine fae to be. Granted, my experience with them is very limited, but he doesn't seem as stuck up as everyone always makes them out to be. There's something almost human about him, which is a dangerous thought to have. It makes me forget to put the extra walls up. I decide to change tactics and keep both of us distracted.

"What is it you do, on a normal basis? When you're not chasing down unwilling participants?"

That earns me another look from a sitting neighbor, and I make a mental note to phrase things better.

"I'm an ambassador of sort," Derek replies, keeping his voice barely above a whisper. "I travel. A lot."

That makes sense actually. It's probably why he's so much more relaxed in the human world than I would've imagined. Even his t-shirt and jeans combo fits right in. He probably has better ways to blend in than even I. Most of my life has been spent in my small town. I only ever traveled when I went on trips with Dad.

The thought of my parents brings a sadness so strong I almost gasp out loud. I have always had a really strong relationship with them. Not being able to talk to them for a month now has made things difficult. There are so many things they could explain to me. But I know if I talk to them, it's putting them in danger. And I can't do that.

Even now with Derek beside me, I can't contact them. Not until I know for sure what his endgame is. I glance over at him from the corner of my eye as he keeps his eyes to the front. It would be foolish to deny how attractive he is. People getting on the bus immediately look at him because they can't help it.

But I know how the fae are. They're cunning and manipulative, and they will do whatever it takes to put themselves first. I have to remember that. No matter what.

CHAPTER 7

"Why are we at the airport?" I ask when I see where he led us. We disembark with the rest of the passengers, most of whom have luggage. Derek is still carrying my backpack. He walks a few steps away from the crowd before he answers.

"Because we need to get lost. A plane is the perfect way to do so."

I understand this, of course. Magic leaves traces for others to follow. If we're in the sky, it's much harder for those to manifest. But I guess a part of me still expects him to open up a portal to Faery and push me through it.

"What's our destination?" I ask, instead of voicing my concerns.

"Flagstaff."

That stops me in my tracks. It's another two steps before Derek turns around and gives me a look.

"Problem?"

"Flagstaff is about two and a half hours north of here. Driving. What's the point of getting on a plane?" I'm not a huge fan of them, if I'm being honest. I definitely would rather drive.

"The point," Derek replies, coming to stand right in front of me, "is that it gets us into an airport and makes those after you think you left the area. Northern part of this state is a good place to hide."

He's standing much too close for this conversation, and I can't stop thinking about the proximity. He towers over me, which means I have to lean back to look into his eyes. I can feel the magic on him, the way my own seems to wake up at his nearness. But there is also a magnetism about him that has nothing to do with his magic. It's only him, and the way his eyes shine against his perfect skin and the way his hair falls over his forehead. The stories about fae don't lie. They are beautiful creatures.

The feelings are unexpected. It takes me a second to get my bearings before I find my voice again.

"How are we getting through security? I don't think the spell I used last time will work this time."

It was a onetime deal. Without tapping into more of my magic, I wouldn't be able to pull it off. That would negate the whole point of us flying. We're trying to keep magic to a minimum.

"Follow my lead."

He doesn't say more, stepping back and heading for the doors. I have no choice but to follow. The airport isn't as full as the last time I was in one, which I guess works in our favor. Instead of heading for the ticketing area, Derek leads the way straight to security. Taking the pre-check line, he weaves in and out of warded off lanes, his steps sure. There's no one in front of us when we reach the guard. Before I can say or do anything, Derek's hand finds my own.

The feel of his skin against mine sends a million sparks up my nervous system. The sensation is unlike anything I've experienced before. I have no idea what to think about it. Instead of reacting, I stay still, waiting for Derek to do whatever it is he's going to do. I also pushing the thoughts of his hand on mine into the far reaches of my brain. For later. I'm sure I'll be thinking about it later.

And not only because it's the first somewhat human contact I've experienced in weeks. Well, when he was dragging me away from the werewolves doesn't count. This feels...different.

"Good morning," the guard says, with no inflection in his voice. He looks as thrilled to be here as I am. Derek doesn't reply. Instead, he stares at the man, in complete silence. Something shifts in the air around us, some kind of an undercurrent. But I don't move or say anything, somehow aware that I might break whatever spell Derek is putting on the guard. And the rest of the people in the area. Derek looks around, seemingly meeting the eyes of every person present, and then, he just walks through.

Past the security.

Past the scanners.

Right into the terminal, tugging me beside him.

Once we're past all the people, I turn to look behind me. But it's as if no one noticed. I expect someone to turn and realize we're past security when we shouldn't be, but no one bats an eye. I look up at Derek, at his hard profile. My mouth asks the question before I'm done processing it.

"Did you glamour the whole airport?"

Derek looks down at me, giving me a ghost of a smile.

"Only a small part of it."

It takes me a second to process, and that's when I remember he's still holding my hand. Extracting it carefully, I flex it out by my side. He doesn't miss the gesture, but he doesn't comment.

"I thought the whole point of being here is to not use magic."

"My glamour won't read the same way your powers would. Plus, that's why we're getting on an airplane, remember?"

"I remember."

We continue to make our way toward whatever gate is assigned to our plane. I'm no longer asking questions. Clearly, he'll have no problem getting us on the plane, even without tickets. I'm even more intrigued about his powers now, but making conversation seems too much like making friends.

And with every little thing he does, I trust him less instead of more. There's a plan in every move he makes. I have no idea where my place is in all of it. He said the northern part of the state is a good place to hide. Maybe it's a good place for me to get lost.

* * *

SOMEHOW, our flight leaves in the next thirty minutes. People are already boarding when we get there. I'm not sure I understand how Derek has this all planned out to a T, but I appreciate his skills. This is the kind of planning I strive to achieve.

We settle into our seats, right in front of the first-class barrier. I'm at the window. Derek is in the middle seat, which puts his body in close proximity to mine. I really need to stop noticing such insignificant things, but it's getting more difficult the more time I spend with him. Never mind that I'm planning an escape in the back of my mind. Apparently, I can multitask like a pro.

Derek stows my backpack overhead before settling back down. I try not to stare at the way his shirt rides up over his stomach, but I think I have a problem. It's the only thing I can think about now. Turning to stare out the window, I focus on counting the seconds in my breaths. Inhale. Exhale.

Get a grip, Avery.

I'm all over the place, to be honest, and I have no idea what to do about it. Julian would say I need a release.

The moment I think of him, I sober up. His death is on my hands. I will never not think that, and I will never not feel responsible. He befriended me when I had no one. He let me practice my self-defense skills on him, enough to be able to hold my own for a month on the streets. And what did I do to repay him? I got him killed.

"Whatever you are thinking, stop." Derek's voice penetrates my thoughts, and I turn to find his face close to mine. My eyes zero in on his lips before snapping up to see his expression. There's a mischievous gleam in his eye that is so staple for fae that it reminds me to put my guard back up before I lose myself. Even though his glamour seems to have no effect on me, I'm not about to broadcast that to him. Not yet at least. It's another one of my superpowers. But he'll probably find out soon enough.

"I can think whatever I want to think," I say, going on the defensive. Because this is easier. This keeps us in our corners. He exhales. I think it might be something close to a laugh, but the sound doesn't come.

"You should be careful not to think too much."

"I always think too much," I snap, rising to the challenge.

When I first went to Thunderbird Academy, I was unsure of myself. That's typical for any teenager changing schools their senior year. Or any teenager, ever. It's our job to be unsure and then find ourselves. At least, that's what I've always thought.

But finding that book and running for my life has taught me the only person I can trust in this life is myself. It's useless for me to doubt who I am, forget the fact that I barely know who that is. The magic is new, but also my own powers are on a sabbatical of sorts. I've taken risks. I've fought hand to hand, and I've threatened magical creatures with a knife. If anyone asked where I saw myself my senior year, it wouldn't be here. But I adjusted and I learned.

So, if that makes me harsh or too different than who everyone expects me to be, then too bad.

I can't keep cowering.

I can't keep pretending.

Derek gets to see the new and improved Avery.

I make that decision here and now.

"That will get you in trouble one day," he says. At first, I think he means my realization. Then I realize he's talking about my *thinking too much* statement. I smirk.

"It already has and look how that turned out."

This time, I'm almost positive he chuckles, but the sound is swallowed by the loudspeaker before I can truly enjoy it. Ugh, I shouldn't be enjoying anything about him.

Brain, get in line. Or better yet, take first place.

"Ladies and gentlemen, welcome to our cabin. We are pleased to have you fly with us this afternoon."

As the flight attendant makes the necessary announcements, I turn back to the window and tune him out. The only part I hear is when he says the flight is about an hour long.

Sitting back more comfortably, I decide to ignore the fae next to me for the duration of the flight. Already, he occupies much more of my head space than he should.

Instead, I create a mental list of all the questions I need answered if this partnership we have is going to work. If the opportunity presents itself, I'm still going to run. But as it stands, I don't think I'll have an opportunity anytime soon. Instead, I have to figure out how to make this work. To my advantage and to my advantage only.

Maybe I'm a little bit all over the place, but this is life. My life. I have to figure out how to make sure I stay alive.

CHAPTER 8

The plane lands with no issues. After disembarking, we head straight for a car rental. I would ask him how he knows where everything is, but that would just waste time. He seems to be giving me the silent treatment, just like I've been giving him.

It doesn't take long for Derek to glamour us a car. I feel a bit guilty since we keep taking advantage of these places and not paying a dime. I wonder if there's a way for me to pay them and the airline back for our free ride. Not that I actually see a way of doing so, but it's a nice thought.

When the attendant takes us to our car, I smile. It's a Toyota 4Runner, a four door SUV. It's something I would totally get myself if I was living in the human world permanently. I like the way it looks and the way it rides. I took one across three states when I was on my way to Arizona. This one is dark red, almost maroon color, and I'm a fan.

"You like it?" Derek asks when we're inside the vehicle. Not wanting to give him the satisfaction, I shrug. He doesn't comment further, turning the car on and pulling out.

This area is so different from the city. It looks like we've traveled to a completely different part of the country instead of an hour north.

The trees here cover the majority of the land, standing tall and strong. There are mostly evergreens with a few other varieties blending in.

It looks more like the area where I grew up, a small town surrounded by a vast forest. Magical communities are often in places like these. Because our magic is so strongly connected to nature, it helps to be near it. Even though my own powers have been weird lately, I can feel them waking up, as if they're finally where they want to be.

That isn't to say there aren't witches and shifters and all kinds of supernatural creatures in big cities. I mean, I just came from a city that was full of them. But my magic is happier here. I can already tell.

We get on the freeway, heading north. Derek hasn't spoken again, and I'm okay with it. I glance at him out of the corner of my eye, his gaze focused on the road in front of him. Sometimes when I look at him, I see a teenage boy, not much older than myself. But other times, it's like he's a century old. Which wouldn't surprise me. Fae can live for generations.

"How old are you?" I ask before I can stop myself. He glances at me with that very fae expression, and I almost take the words back.

"Does it matter?" he replies, turning back to the road.

"I would like to know."

"Not as old as you would think," he says, and then falls silent again. I give him a few minutes to figure out if he's going to say anything else. When he doesn't, I roll my eyes.

"We can't exactly get to the middle ground if I'm the only one trying."

That gets his attention again, briefly, and I swear the corner of his lip turns up in amusement.

"I don't remember you being this feisty before."

"You only met me briefly, and if my memory serves right, I blasted you across the room and kicked you in the stomach before I jumped out of a window. Not feisty enough for you?"

This time he does chuckle, and I refuse to admit that I like the sound. Absolutely refuse it.

"You really have come into yourself over the last few weeks," he states, disarming me with that simple statement. He doesn't get to know this about me. That's something personal, something that I should realize about myself and no one else. Maybe besides my parents. But not him. Not when he's still my enemy.

"A girl's got to do what a girl's got to do," I say, turning to stare at the window. There are a few beats of silence before he speaks up again.

"What did I say?"

Typically, there would be a tone of *something* in that question. But there's no emotion behind Derek's. He's just asking, like he would ask anything else. Maybe fae simply don't understand simple emotion. Or maybe he's just really good at hiding any trace of his.

"Nothing."

"I've been told that word doesn't mean the same to you as it would to me."

At that, I laugh. A full laugh that I feel all the way in my belly. Derek's head turns toward me. As he watches me, I see something unreadable in his eyes.

"Who taught you that? And give them a pat on the back for me." I'm still laughing because this right here is the most human thing I've heard him say. It makes him much more real to me.

Stop that. Immediately.

I can't think like that. Why do I have to keep reminding myself that I can't think like that? It's as if no matter how many walls I put up, he keeps breaking them down. And he does it without even truly trying. I have to find better defenses.

"Will you tell me then?" This time his voice is softer somehow, as if maybe, he actually wants to know. But I'm not sharing. I hit him with a question of my own.

"Where are we going? When you said you weren't kidnapping me to Faery, I didn't think you'd be kidnapping me anyway."

"You didn't?"

"Fine, I did. But I still want to know."

"That's your default, isn't it?" he asks as he turns the blinker on and merges onto another freeway. The small city grows distant behind us as he speeds, still going mostly north. I'm trying to stay aware of my surroundings as much as I can. It's only because I studied maps of the whole state that I actually know where we are.

"I like being informed." I shrug.

"It's a good quality to have."

"So I've been told."

I don't actually dislike my need for information. But it did kind of get me into this mess. There's no going around that one. I don't offer up anymore, and we grow quiet once again. Those seem to be our two settings: constant bickering or complete silence. Not sure which one I prefer more.

"We're going to a cabin. There are a few places around here that are good and isolated." Derek breaks the silences a few minutes later.

"How do you know of it?"

"There are a few in every state. If the fae ever need a place to get away, there is always a spot open."

"Wait, this is one of your places?" All my internal alarms are going off. If he's taking me somewhere the fae reside, I might be in trouble. I know he said he wasn't handing me over, but that doesn't mean they can't come pick me up.

"Don't worry. No one knows about this particular one. It... has precise barriers in place."

I would question that further, but I'm freaking out a little. My eyes land on the car door handle. I wonder if I jumped, would I survive the fall? Not likely. We're going at least ninety.

"Avery." The way he says my name instantly makes me turn toward him. "I'm not going to let anything happen to you."

The look we share is intense and heated and then he's looking at the road again. I remember to inhale, trying to wrap my mind around my emotions. I need to center myself. I already decided to be on my guard. This doesn't change anything.

But his statement? Somehow, it burrows into my heart, making me all kinds of confused.

I trust it. Unlike anything else about him, I trust those words.

* * *

WHEN DEREK SAID the cabin was isolated, he meant the cabin was *very* isolated. It takes us about forty-five minutes to reach a mountain and then we drive up it. The road is winding but beautiful. It feels like we're driving through a tunnel with walls created out of trees. They're so tall, I almost can't see the sky. For a moment, I get lost in the beauty of it. My life doesn't seem so bad being in this space of time.

Then, I remember who's driving.

When we finally reach the cabin, it's just as enchanting as I would expect a cabin in the woods to be. A large porch wraps around most of it, wooden and accented. It looks like something straight out of a good-feel movie. Charming. And inviting.

The trees surround it on every side. Once we park, I step out of the vehicle to inhale the rich woody smell. Closing my eyes briefly, I let my magic stretch out around me, giving it the much needed relief from being bottled up. It would be amazing to let it loose right here and now, but I'm not about to do any of that and put us back on the map. Reluctantly, I pull the magic back. After a brief hesitation, it curls back up, albeit a little more content now.

"Come on," Derek says, leading the way inside. We pass two rocking chairs. If those aren't a staple of a cozy cabin, I don't know what is. The inside is just as cute as the outside. The floor plan is pretty open. There are stairs on the left leading up to a loft above. There is a large wall of windows up there with another set at the back of the house, past the kitchen.

"Wait, there's a lake here?" I make a beeline straight for the back. Pushing the double doors open, I step out onto another porch. Or the same one. It seems to wrap around the whole way.

The lake is beautiful, maybe fifteen yards away. It's confusing too.

"I don't understand. How is there a lake here? There are no lakes in this area."

"Not any known to humans, at least."

Derek has followed me outside, now standing just two steps behind me. I turn, glancing at him over my shoulder. The smile on his face is the most genuine one I've seen. He's not looking at me. He's looking out at the water. Narrowing my eyes, I turn back to the view, perplexed by his attitude. It's almost as if he personally knows this place.

"You said this is one of yours? You meant personally?"

"Yes."

The whispered word ruffles the back of my head, but I don't turn. I didn't expect him to bring me somewhere that actually means something to him. But then again, this is how he would know it's safe. Maybe I can be safe here too, at least for the time being.

I want to ask another dozen questions about the lake, but for some reason, I decide against it. Maybe I want the magic of not knowing. It's not often I ask for that, but it can be beautiful. Like it is at this moment.

"Any other surprises?" I decide to ask instead, turning and walking past him back into the house. Now that I'm looking at it with fresh eyes, it seems to fit him somehow. Not sure why I'm thinking that. I don't actually know this fae. Not in any way that matters, and not enough for me to see him in a house.

"Maybe just one."

I meet his gaze then, and he gives me a small smile.

"You can practice magic here. We're, what's the phrase, off the grid?"

"Wait." It doesn't register right away. "Are you serious?"

"I am."

I'm not too sure what to do with that information, but the magic inside of me is instantly happy. It's what we've been waiting for. A place where I can let it loose and maybe figure out what's going on with it. Granted, that will be showing some vulnerability in front of Derek, but I don't care. My magic and I both need it.

"Next question," I say, feeling slightly lighter somehow. "What's for lunch?"

CHAPTER 9

*I*t's so dark, I can hardly see. I raise my hand in front of me, but it's lost in the shadows. Turning in a full circle, I try to figure out where I am and how I got here.

The last thing I remember...

What is the last thing I remember?

My mind seems blank, as if I'm unable to access the storage.

A part of me wants to call out, to see if anyone is beyond my line of sight. But I'm smarter than that. If anyone is there, they're not friendly. Keeping quiet and still gives me at least some kind of advantage. But not much. If I'm in a place full of supernatural creatures, at least half of them can probably see in the dark.

Still.

Think, Avery. Think.

Take the problem and break it down into manageable sections.

I don't know where I am, but I do know I can't keep standing in one spot. That means I need to move. Slowly, I begin to do exactly that. Arm outstretched, I take small, measured steps, feeling out the space in front of me and below me. When my hand hits a wall, I'm not prepared.

For some reason, the space feels bigger than this, but I've only walked a few feet before running into a barrier.

Okay, next manageable section is what?

It's finding the other corners. Unless this is a wall that runs parallel to something else, it'll have a corner. Keeping my right hand on the wall, I outstretch the left one in front of me and begin making my way forward once more. After about a dozen steps, I hit the wall.

With my hand, I feel out for the next corner. Finding it makes me think I'm in a room. Obviously, the only way to find out is to repeat the process I just went through. For some reason, that idea leaves me feeling even more uneasy than the darkness. Not that I have a choice. I can't just stand in one place and hope for a good outcome.

It takes me way less time than I anticipated to find all four walls. I am in a room. About ten feet by ten feet, if my calculations are correct.

And there is no door.

I ran my hand over the surface the whole time. I've also found no windows or any indents indicating there was once anything here. I'm locked in a pitch black, inescapable room. And I have no idea how I got here.

Plan.

I need a plan.

My mind is working overtime, trying to come up with a logical solution. My first instinct is to reach for my magic, but when I do, nothing happens.

The panic slams into me fast and hard. I'm left gasping.

Where is my magic?

I think I speak the words out loud, but there's no response. There's nothing but the stillness of the room, all around me. I reach for my magic again. This time, the absence of it is like physical pain.

"No, no, no. Come on."

Tears well up in my eyes, but I refuse to let them spill. I can handle this. I can find a way out.

I can.

I can.

I can.

"You won't."

The voice seems to come from all around me. I jerk at the volume of it. It surrounds me, plastering itself all over my skin. Unconsciously, I try to wipe it off. But it's still there, deep in my mind. Mocking me.

"You won't get out. You won't succeed. You are a failure."

The words repeat over and over, louder and louder. I drop to my knees, hands over my ears, but it seems to overpower everything. My body shakes, sending my head spinning as I try to hold onto my sanity.

That's when I start screaming.

* * *

I COME BACK TO MYSELF, my screams echoing all around me as I fight off my attacker.

"Avery! Wake up!"

The voice is different... a voice I know. I focus on the sound and then I'm me again.

Derek hovers over me, his hands pinning my arms to the bed. His body is less than an inch away from mine, his knee between my legs. He was clearly trying to restrain me. For a moment, I don't think about it at all. I just let my body react, sinking into the contact and taking his presence as comfort, before I shut it all down.

"Let me up," I say. He moves back instantly, pulling me in the same motion to a sitting position. I'm covered in sweat and breathing heavily. That last part might have something to do with Derek's proximity, but that's not important now.

"What happened?" he asks when it's clear I'm not going to be the first to speak. I don't answer right away. He gets up, leaving the room. I stare at the open doorway in confusion, while I also try to get my thoughts in order. Finally, he returns with a glass of water, handing it to me. I gulp it down gratefully. The small gesture seems to ground me.

"I was in a room. No doors, no windows, and no magic. I couldn't get out."

Derek watches me as I talk. Because I've been spending all this time with him, I'm learning he has slight tells. Mostly around his eyes. Only I'm not sure if it's worry he's feeling or confusion. I decide to tell him everything.

"I didn't know I was dreaming. Not until you shook me awake."

His flash of alarm is unmistakable. I narrow my own eyes, waiting for him to explain. I also know he won't unless I prompt him. We're really coming into a pattern here.

"What? Why do you look like that?"

"Like what?"

"Like you're about to pack us up again and move us to some forsaken cave dwelling."

He chuckles at that. It's only the second time I've heard that sound. This time, it sounds even more like an actual laugh. I like it. Not that I would tell him that.

"We're not moving. Yet. But if you didn't know you were dreaming, that means someone didn't want you to."

At that, I sit up even more fully, the covers tumbling off my lap. I'm wearing shorts, but I still feel exposed when Derek glances down at my legs. My body heats instantly. I really need to learn how to control my freaking hormones. This is not the time for me to have a sexual awakening. Or whatever.

"You're telling me dreams can be controlled?" Thankfully, my curious nature seems to be overtaking my... very human one. "I've heard of spells being put on dreams. But nothing like this."

"There are many secrets the fae hold dear. But even this realm has stories of dream walkers."

"Wait, those are real? I thought that was a made-up human story."

"All of these stories find their beginnings in something truthful. In this case, the old tales speak of fae who could enter dreams and cast magic inside of them. Some humans experience what is called lucid dreaming, where they become aware of their dreams, and can even control them. Often, those are just leftovers from a fae or a spell."

"But no one was in my dream. I didn't feel a presence." Just the voice. But that seemed more like it was coming from inside of me, instead of in the room.

"They're looking for you. They might be using dreamland as a way to find you."

"By putting me in a box and making me scream myself raw? How fun."

"No, by putting you in a box and taking away your magic. The more you would've tried in there, the more you would've manifested out here. It's like sending up a beacon."

That stops me because of course I didn't think of that. There is so much I don't know about the ways of magic. It makes me sad to think I won't learn as much as I could've if this whole book ordeal hadn't happened. Plus, I'm being hunted. That's a bummer too.

"Get some rest now," Derek says, standing up from where he's been sitting on the bed. Almost automatically, I open my mouth to tell him to stay. He sees the indecision in me and gives me one of his barely-there smiles. "I'll watch over you, Avery."

The way he says that... I feel it all the way down in my toes. I watch as he takes a chair in the corner, facing me. Seeing no other choice, I lay back down and pull the covers to my chest. I wonder how I'm going to fall asleep with him looking at me the way he is. We hold each other's gaze for what seems like hours before I finally, finally drift off.

This time, there are no dark rooms waiting for me.

The next morning, I'm up with the sun, but I still don't beat Derek to the kitchen. Yesterday, we ate dinner, he showed me to my room, and then I was waking up from the nightmare. I didn't think I was that tired at all, but apparently, my body needed rest. Once Derek came to watch over me, I slept better than I have in weeks.

Not that I will be admitting that out loud.

"Are those bagels?" I ask as I reach to pour myself a cup of coffee.

"Take your pick," Derek replies, motioning to a few choices. My heart gets ridiculously happy around bagels, and these look like the fancy kind.

"Where did you get them?" I ask, selecting one covered in cheese.

"I picked them up a few days ago."

That makes me pause mid-bite, and I stare at him for a moment.

"A few days ago?"

He must realize what he said. I can see him trying to backtrack, but no dice.

"You knew where I was for more than a few days, didn't you?"

"Not the whole time. But the last week, yes."

"So, you prepped for your mini kidnapping. How would you know

I liked bagels if you haven't been stalking me? I can't believe this." I turn away, not sure how I'm feeling about this realization. Having him watch over me while I slept really messed with my reality of him. I have to get back to the one where I protect myself at all times.

"You can't actually tell me that it comes as a surprise."

He's right, of course. It doesn't. I already figured as much. But that was the whole point of me being in hiding. To keep him from finding me. Yet the fact that he knew where I was, and he didn't drag me directly to Faery should make me feel better, not worse. For some reason, it's making me feel worse.

Then, it hits me. I'm not mad at him. I'm mad at myself. I was getting too comfortable in Phoenix. I let my guard down enough so that when I was being stalked for a week, I didn't know. Unbelievable. It's a wonder I've survived this long.

"I'm not mad at you," I finally state, reaching for the cream cheese, so I can finish spreading it on the bagel before I eat it all as is.

"You're mad at yourself."

"Yes. But I'd like you not to point that out." Grabbing my coffee and plate, I head to the dining table. Before I can sit down, I change my mind and push the double doors open to the back porch. Sitting on one of the cozy chairs, I tuck my legs beneath me and take a bite of my now topped off with cream cheese bagel.

The fact that Derek watched me this closely and then went out of his way to get me my favorite breakfast should make me feel better. Or safer. But I really don't know what to feel. Everything is so unbalanced for me. One moment, I'm on the run. Then I'm on the run with the person who's been hunting me.

Now I'm in a perfectly secluded place where I can work on my magic but with the very fae I should be trying to escape. If anyone could explain me to me, that would be great. I'm not sure what I'm becoming at this point.

Derek follows me out, taking a seat on the other chair. We stay like that for a while, watching the sun come over the water, sipping on our drinks. It's such a strange tranquil moment. For a second, I forget everything about my life and enjoy myself.

"So, what do we do now, Derek?" I ask, breaking the silence. It really feels like I could stay out here like this forever. With him around, it seems as if I don't have to worry about a thing. I'm smart enough to know it's deceiving, but for a second, I want to lie to myself.

"You're not going to like it."

That gets my attention immediately. I sit up, turning to him fully. My eyebrow is raised as I wait for him to go on. He smirks at my expression but not unkindly. I'm learning to decipher his moods and mannerisms. It seems like a useful skill.

"I think we should figure out what's going on with your magic."

"What do you mean?" I shift uncomfortably because we haven't really talked about this. I don't want him knowing I can't protect myself.

"Avery, I can feel the imbalance in you. I could from the first moment I saw you."

I jump to my feet, placing the mug and plate on the table in front of me. His words don't sit well with me. I hate that he can see it.

"Avery—"

"No," I say before bouncing down the stairs and toward the water.

It's like he can see all of my insecurities before even I can. I can't win this if I'm always in the unknown. Feeling my magic... it's intimate. He invaded that part of me, and I'm mad... but also hurt.

"I didn't mean to hurt you," he says, following me down the stairs toward the bank. I don't turn, continuing my march. Soon, my feet are in the water, and I feel better.

"You can't keep doing that." I turn, facing him once more. "I don't need you to splash all of my inadequacies all over the place. I know I'm messed up, okay?"

He looks taken back by my outburst because of course he is. I don't even know what I'm saying anymore. Only that I'm feeling everything at once. Suddenly and completely.

"I didn't say it to make you feel bad. I said it because I think I can help."

"Can you?" It's an accusation more than a question, but he's not fazed.

"I can."

"How?"

"By setting you free."

* * *

"What does that even mean?" I ask, after the initial shock of his statement wears off. I'm still ankle deep in water. The barely present waves have a soothing effect on me. I wade through, side to side, while Derek stays at the bank.

"It means that you've been bottling it up for weeks. Maybe even before that. This place? It's safe for you to let it out, give it the chance to roam."

"I don't think you understand how my magic works. It doesn't roam."

"Or does it? Have you ever tried to give it space to explore?"

That stops me. My dad always taught me that magic is part of us, an equal part. Not something that needed to be suppressed and controlled but something that could work in tandem. I never thought of it otherwise, but I know people who do. But what Derek is saying takes it to a whole new level.

"Are you saying I keep my magic prisoner?"

"Not specifically. You are connected at all times. But you also keep it controlled. You had to in order for you to live in the human world. But magic likes to play just like children do. The freer it is, the better your relationship with it becomes. Because it's built on trust, on a relationship. You give and take equally, so you stay balanced."

It makes sense, what he's saying. It's similar to what my dad has instilled in me. But it's also not natural for me. I've always had to keep a close watch on my magic. I've had to do it even more so since the magic itself started exhibiting unusual patterns.

"What is it that you're afraid of?" Derek's voice is almost gentle as he asks. My eyes fly up to meet his. A huge part of me wants to keep this to myself. But if he can help, maybe it's worth telling him the truth. Or at least enough of it for us to figure out what's going on. I still have absolutely no idea what kind of agenda he has, but shouldn't I use it to my advantage for as long as I can? That would be the logical thing to do.

Truly, it won't matter if I tell him. Magic or no magic, he could take me to Faery right now and I wouldn't be able to lift a finger. So using him for his knowledge is smart. That's what I'll keep telling myself.

"My magic," I begin, not sure how to put it into words. "My magic seems confused."

"How so?" He's patient with me, waiting me out and giving me the chance to find my words. I pause before speaking up again.

"I'm supposed to have fire magic."

"You don't?"

"I do, but," this is going to sound crazy when I say it, "but I also have water? Somehow."

Derek watches me for a long silent minute before he nods.

"What?" I snap, because I can't read his expression. "What's with the nodding? What does it mean?"

"It means," there's that calming voice again, "that you are more powerful than you even thought."

"That's not a thing. I can't just develop another elemental power."

"Really? You also can't read ancient unreadable text?"

He got me there. I step out of the water, bringing our bodies close together. He doesn't retreat, and I hold my ground.

"What's next then?" I ask when he seems content on waiting for me to make that move.

"Now, we see what you can do."

I narrow my eyes as he steps around me and faces the water once more. I watch him as he motions for me to stand beside him. Seeing no other choice, I do.

"Much like with your fire magic, you ask for it to come forth, correct?"

"Yes, it's instinctual."

"Good. Now, use those same instincts to move the water back a few feet."

"What?" I bristle immediately because it seems crazy to me. "I can barely make the water dance in the shower."

"So, you have practiced. Even better. It should come more naturally."

He falls silent then, waiting for me to do as he asked. A part of me doesn't want to because I'm scared. I'm not too proud to admit that. I know myself. And this... messing around with magic is scary. But I also need to know if I can actually wield multiple elements or if it's a fluke.

Closing my eyes, I center myself. My bare feet barely touch the water, but it's enough that I know it's there. I call on my magic, asking for its help, for it to come out and play. I feel it waking up, stretching and unfolding, as if it's been waiting for this. In part, I'm sure it has. I've been keeping it at a minimum for weeks.

My arms outstretch in front of me as I focus the points of the magic at the water. Letting myself feel for it, for the small molecules that make up the whole. There's a bit of science behind magic, which has always made my academic heart a little happy. I push my awareness into the magic and then into the water, asking it to push back, to retreat.

I feel the magic all around me and in me for the first time in what seems like forever. It's happy to be out, and it's happy to be with me. It doesn't hate me for keeping it dormant. It's happy I've kept it protected. When I open my eyes, I'm not sure what to expect.

"It's not working," I say, staring at the water still at my feet.

"Avery, look."

I glance up at Derek before I turn to follow the direction he's pointing. A few hundred drops as small as dew drops hover above the surface of the lake. The whole place looks like it's full of diamonds, sparkling in the morning sun. The view that was beautiful before is breathtaking now.

"Am I doing that?"

"You are."

The moment his words leave his lips, the water drops creating a ripple affect across the whole lake.

"I don't know how I did that," I say, still staring at the aftermath.

"We'll figure it out," Derek replies.

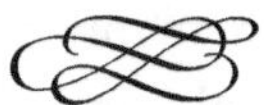

e practice me moving the water a few more times. While it responds, it's not responding like my fire magic usually does. It still has a mind of its own, somehow. If I ask it to move, it becomes floating droplets. If I ask it to come forward, it becomes crashing waves.

"Why can't I control it?" I sigh later that day as Derek and I sit on the couch inside the living room near the fireplace. I've been at it for a few hours, and my body feels the exhaustion. It's not that it's draining me per se. It's more of a physical exhaustion. Like working out.

"I thought you knew everything."

"Not this."

We fall silent again, as is our custom. Truth be told, I don't find it uncomfortable. I never did. There's something about Derek that almost speaks to a part of myself. I'm just not sure which part.

Even back home with my friends, we were never comfortable to sit and be silent. I've always been one of those people, and I've spent evenings like that with my parents. They would be reading, and I would be doing the same. Or they'd be talking while I sat in the room with them, doodling. I've never had that same experience with anyone else. Until now.

Now that I started thinking about my parents, I can't stop. They're worried about me, of that I am sure. But I also know they trust me to take care of myself. It's how I was raised. Doesn't mean I wouldn't love having one of our talks right about now.

"Can I ask what you are thinking?" Derek asks. I look up to find him watching me curiously. "You have an almost sad expression on your face."

I guess I let my guard down more than I thought for Derek to notice. I shrug a little before replying.

"I'm thinking about my parents."

"Oh."

That one word. It's full of... something. It has my curiosity piqued.

"Are you close to your parents?"

He jerks at my question, as if he's never been asked that before. I have no idea how the fae world works or if fae even have parents like we do. I suppose it could be different there.

"You don't have to answer. I just didn't—"

"No, it's okay. It's fair for you to know about my life."

"Does that mean you'll tell me more if I ask?"

"Depends on the question."

I can never get a true read on him. Right now, he seems almost playful. A moment ago, he seemed standoffish. I really do have to be my best when I'm around him. He constantly keeps me guessing.

"Let's start with parents then." I smile.

Derek grunts a little, as if it's his least favorite subject. But then he replies, "My parents do not care much about me. Well, my mother does not. I am not sure which one of her suitors is my father. We never talk of it."

There's no sadness or emotion in his words. He says them matter of fact. I've noticed he becomes more formal when he talks of his homeland. I wonder why that is.

"You never asked?"

"Fae do not bother with such minuscule things. They take many lovers throughout their lifetime. It is a long time to be alone."

"They?" I don't miss his choice of pronoun on that one. He meets my eye as if he's surprised.

"I have not."

I have no idea how to feel about that statement or if I find it entirely true. Fae have ways to trick the language to suit them. He could've said he has not ever or recently or in the last century and all of those statements would be truth. It makes me think of when I was at the academy. The fae there couldn't hold others to their standard Faery rules. They couldn't enslave me for a simple *thank you* or glamour me into submission. I wonder where Derek stands on that. I've been careful around him until this point, but maybe we've finally reached a place where I can ask.

I have nothing to lose.

"Do you lie?"

It's such a straightforward question, but I know there are many interpretations of it in his world. I'm really hoping he sticks to the human world's definition and doesn't play games.

"I do not."

He doesn't flinch when he says the words, nor does he break eye contact with me. Once again, he answered the question, but there are undercurrents in his words. I decide to push forward.

"Do you abide by the same rules of bargains as they do in Faery?"

"I do."

Once again, no hesitation on his part. But I'm growing more and more nervous. My mind spins, trying to pinpoint every conversation we had. Have I said something that would've attached me to him? Before I remembered to be careful, did I do something that would put me in jeopardy?

"Have I entered into a bargain?" I finally ask. If he can't lie, then he would have to tell me. I hold my breath as I wait for him to reply. He studies me slowly, his eyes roaming over my face like a caress before he replies.

"You have not."

I exhale a sigh of relief, at the same time vowing to be more careful. I don't understand why I have to keep reminding myself of that fact. I shouldn't trust him, but I'm beginning to.

Maybe it's my magic. It likes him. Probably because he taught me how to let it come out and play. But it could be something else. Whatever this pull I feel toward him, it makes it difficult to keep a clear mind. Maybe that's as much glamour as I can get from him.

"Is it true you are constantly using glamour?"

"Yes and no. We use bits of it on ourselves, to keep us looking how we want to be perceived in the human world. But we don't go around glamouring everyone all the time."

"What do you mean, on yourselves?"

Derek shifts to the side, exposing his right side to me. Then, he moves the hair that barely covers the top of his ear aside. Right before my eyes, it's like the rest of it grows upward. Before I can blink, he has a pointy ear.

"Wow!" I move forward automatically, my hand raised to touch it before I catch myself. "That's interesting," I say instead, curling my hand into a fist.

"It's okay. You can touch if you want."

The invitation is whispered, but I don't hesitate to switch places. We're sharing the couch now. Derek doesn't move forward or away, letting me guide my movements. Before I can think too much about it, I'm reaching for the tip of his ear. The moment my finger connects, his body jerks a little.

"I—"

"You're not hurting me. It's just not something anyone does."

My finger traces down to where his ear begins before making its way back up and over. I'm only inches away from his face. The whole thing feels more intimate than I can explain. Even to myself.

I drop my hand. He turns his face, putting our noses barely three inches apart. I stare at his eyes because I'm incapable of looking away. The tension we constantly carry between us sparks to new proportions, and it would take no movement at all to close the distance between us.

Suddenly, I want to. I want to so much that I almost make the move.

But then, I stop.

He is still the enemy.

He is still the enemy.

He is still the enemy.

The words repeat in my mind and then I can think more clearly. Sitting back, I give him a slight smile.

"Learn something new every day," I say, thankful my voice comes out normal.

"That we do," he replies, his eyes on me.

It takes much of my self-control not to squirm under that look, but I manage to keep my body still. Something is happening between us, and I have no idea what to do about it.

* * *

THE NEXT FEW days go by in much the same fashion. Thankfully, there are no more disturbing dreams, but the rest of the days stay the same. Giving my magic the time it needs to adjust is helping more than I imagined. Even when I was little and first learning how to harness my powers, it wasn't like this. Maybe simply because everything I was told to do was watched. Here, I don't have that problem. I can do whatever I want with it, and it knows it.

Derek is a quiet companion during most training sessions. He's not really teaching or talking me through it. He's mostly standing by for observation. I find his presence calming, so I don't mind.

This morning, I wake up restless. I can't tell if something happened in my dream. I can't remember it. Or maybe it's something else. But I have a lot of nervous energy inside of me, and I know just what to do about it.

Bouncing down the stairs I find Derek in the kitchen, as usual, making coffee. When I round the corner, his eyes are already on me.

"You seem happy?"

"Parallel to happy?" I reply. I think he doesn't quite understand human emotions, so he has to ask. He probably understands more than a lot of fae, considering he spends a lot of time in this realm.

"What's parallel to happy?"

"Hmm. Eager?"

"We're just going to play twenty questions this morning?"

I grab a mug. After I pour myself some coffee and take a sip, I reply.

"First, that is a very human expression, and I'm proud of you for picking it up. Second of all, no. We're going to spar."

"What?"

"Spar. You know…" I place my cup on the counter and do a few jabs. "Exercise where we fight each other for fun."

"I know what it means," he grumbles, another very human reaction. "And we're not doing it."

"Why?"

He doesn't reply, just heads for the double doors leading to the back porch.

"Derek. Derek. Derek." I stay right on his heels, using my most annoying tone of voice. It's not the best course of action, but I suddenly want to know what he would do if I revert to how I got my way when I was four. My parents didn't go along with it for long, but at first it was cute enough that it worked.

"That's not going to work on me."

"Are you sure?" I sit down right next to him on the bench instead of heading to my own chair like I usually do. My lips split into a grin as I lean forward. "Pretty please. I'm not very good at self-defense. I think it would be great if I had more practice."

I need this. I won't tell him how much though. I've already shown many of my cards. But if this will help with the restlessness I'm feeling, then I need it.

Derek is silent for another few moments before he finally nods.

"Yay!" I jump up immediately, grabbing for my mug. "I'll be ready in ten."

I gulp down my coffee as I make my way back to the house to grab water and shoes. I'm already dressed in a leggings and t-shirt combo because I came downstairs prepared. After I finished my coffee and laced up my tennis shoes, I look up to find Derek leaning against the doorway.

"You sure about this?"

"Yes," I reply immediately, placing my hands on my hips. "I've learned a few new techniques since I've been in Arizona. If I get better, I'll be handy in a fight."

And maybe the next time, no one will die because of me. But I don't add that last part. Derek gives me a long look before leading the way outside. Once he finds a spot for us, I start doing stretches. He watches me for a moment before speaking.

"What are you doing?"

"Stretches?"

"Why?"

At first, I don't understand the question. This is how everyone starts their workouts. But then I realize the fae are entirely different. This is something Derek hasn't come into contact with before.

"To help my muscles be more flexible. And to help with soreness."

He nods at that, but the concept is probably still foreign. I've never heard of fae complaining about muscle aches, or anything really. They're not a very expressive species.

As I stretch, my mind goes back to that list of questions I keep wanting to ask. I've been doing that a little at a time, so as to not over-whelm myself or Derek. He's been pretty patient with explaining things to me, but there's still so much unknown.

"The Ancients," I say now, capturing his full attention with two words, "They want the books too, right?"

"They do."

"Why?"

When I ran, I ran from the fae because the book is written in regards to them. It's their realm which would be in trouble if someone started messing with those spells. But I also ran from the Ancients. They are a little more unknown to me.

For all my life, and for generations before me, the Ancients were just a fairytale. Monsters who didn't exist in the real world but who made the stories scary enough that they had to be conquered by a hero. But then, these Ancients decided it was time to wake up and take the world for their own. On top of everything else that is going on in our world right now, they are a huge problem, like a cherry on top.

"The Ancients have been asleep for a long time," Derek replies, still standing a few feet in front of me as I continue with my stretches. "Their power is different now than it was before they went on their extended slumber vacation. The creatures they originally created have become generations of magical beings. They need the knowledge in those books as much as we do."

It's been a few days since Derek referenced himself as one of the fae. It takes me by surprise now, but I don't let it show. Of course he's one of them. Why is it so hard for me to remember that?

"The Ancients don't seem to be doing much of anything though," I say because it's partially true. There was that whole fiasco last year at Thunderbird Academy, but that has been conquered. I know different towns, including one of the Council's hubs, Hawthorne, had face to face contact with the Ancients. But other than that, the world continues to turn as is.

"They are getting ready for something," Derek states, reverting to his more proper tone of voice. "They are at the borders of various Faery kingdoms, waiting in the wings. They watch over every town that interests them while their strength replenishes."

"How do you know this?"

"I have my ways. I like to stay informed."

"I bet you do."

It's crazy to think I'm involved in all of that. The last week and a half, especially since we've been here, has made my life seem so different than what it was. I've felt more balanced here, more myself. Sometimes, I forget I'm in hiding, guarding this huge secret.

When Derek attacks, I'm a split second too late to react. He sweeps me off my feet and I land hard on my back, dust blowing everywhere.

"Classy," I mumble as I get to my feet.

"You wanted to spar."

I roll my eyes. "Fine, let's go."

CHAPTER 12

I land on my back again, this time feeling the impact all over. Apparently, I'm a lot rustier than I thought. I can't land a punch.

"What am I doing wrong?" I ask as I get to my feet once more.

"You telegraph your moves too much," Derek replies. He looks so sure of himself in his t-shirt and sweats. There's not a drop of sweat on him while I'm covered in buckets of it.

"What do you mean?"

"Just that. You have the skills, but you're thinking too much before you move. Hand to hand combat is much like battle magic. It's an instinct. You can use battle magic, right?"

"Well, yes. But I've had about seventeen years of practice. I manifested my powers almost the day I turned one."

"That's not usual, is it?"

"Not really. Most come into their powers around the age of six. But I've always been an overachiever." I shrug at that, unperturbed.

"Interesting."

"Sure, sure. Tell me how to stop being predictable."

I think Derek almost chuckles, but then he doesn't. I've been trying to make him laugh since the last time because I like the sound. And it makes me think he's opening up to me. Not exactly sure when that last fact became important, but here we are.

"Instead of planning out your next move, go for it first."

"But how is that going to help if the move is wrong?"

"It will only be wrong if you stop moving. Hand to hand combat is much like a dance. It has fluidity and rhythm. The more you move, the better chance you have at making the right jab at the right time. If you stand still, you become an easy target."

He lunges at me then, but I'm ready this time. I sidestep to the right. He follows, so I do what he said and keep moving. I dodge to the left then right again before I twist around, putting my body behind his. In the same movement, I jam my elbow into his side. I'm happy to have finally landed a hit, but I don't see him fall into my movement. He grabs me around the waist at the same moment he spins. However, instead of fighting, I go limp. It takes him by surprise. We both fall, and he twists his body at the last moment, so I land right on top of him.

"How's that?" I ask, raising my head to look down at him. Once again, we're only inches apart. I'm acutely aware of his body below mine. He seems to be frozen in time, as if afraid to breathe lest he ruins the moment.

I don't give him a chance.

Emboldened by I don't know what, I reach out a hand, pushing the hair off his forehead. He inhales sharply, clearly not as unaffected as he pretends to be. I grin, enjoying his small outburst. Maybe this is foolish, but for some reason, I can't resist playing this game.

I lean just a fraction closer.

Then, the world goes black.

I scream at the sudden darkness, but the sound only echoes around me with no response. Derek is gone as if he were never there. I stumble to my feet, looking all around me. I still appear to be at the cabin. Except everything is barely visible through the black curtain that has fallen over the area.

"Hello?" I call out, fear eating at my heels. "Derek, where are you?"

There's no answer, no noise at all. It's as if all the bugs and crea-tures in the area have disappeared as well.

"Derek!" I scream, filling the air with my voice and nothing else.

"Derek isn't here."

The words come from behind me. I twist to find a large shadowy shape a few feet behind me. It seems to float five feet off the ground, or maybe it's actually that tall. I can't tell. What I can tell is that it's terrifying. I push my chin up, determined not to show fear, but I'm sure I reek of it.

"Where is he?" I ask, managing to keep my voice mostly normal. The creature doesn't answer right away. I can't even tell if it's human or something else. The large robe it wears covers most of its body with a hood pulled low over the face.

"I have come to offer a deal." the thing says, instead of answering my question.

"What kind of deal?"

My mind races with possibilities, looking for a way out of this. Every direction only offers me pitch darkness. I could fight it. When I reach for my magic, it is there. That brings me a small ounce of comfort.

"The book is ours, and we want it back. Bring it to us, and you live. Bring it to them, and you die."

I don't have to ask who "them" is. The Ancients have a reason to fear the fae. They have been around long enough to give the Ancients a run for their money. But I made the choice already. I chose not to give it to either one. I chose to run.

"You will no longer be able to stay neutral." The voice continues, as if it can read my mind. "You will have to choose. If you choose them, you will die, as will your parents and your whole town. Everyone you have ever come into contact with will perish. Everyone."

The horror that fills me takes all the breath out of my lungs. I'm not stupid enough to think that if I made this deal, I would come out alive. Or if any of those I love would. The thing continues to watch me. I think maybe it is reading my mind. So, I fill it with every little thing I can think of.

"What is the meaning of this?" It asks after a few seconds. I realize I was right. My mind recites equations I memorized before it turns to song lyrics and then it turns to geography names. "You are foolish to try and evade us."

"Thanks, but no thanks. Get out of my head!"

"You will regret this."

"I already do. Now. Get. Out. Of. My. Head!"

I scream the words as I push all my battle magic at it. There's no hesitation when I call on it. My magic and I have a good relationship now. The creature doesn't make a sound, but then just as suddenly as it went dark, there's light again.

Somehow, I'm on the ground with Derek's face over mine. When I meet his eyes, they're full of panic. An emotion I never thought I'd see on him.

"Avery?"

"I'm here," I say, pushing myself to my elbows. "What happened?"

"You collapsed, and I couldn't reach you." His arms are still around me as he helps me sit up. I squeeze his forearm in assurance. For him and myself. That was an out of body experience I don't want to experience again.

"Well, I can tell you why."

* * *

DEREK HAS BEEN STANDING COMPLETELY STILL in front of the fireplace for the last three minutes. I gave him a rundown of what the vision guy told me, and he went stoic. He carried me to the couch while I was unconscious, for which I am thankful because my body feels like it's been run over by a truck.

It's different than when I use my magic. There's a bit of exhaustion present too, but it's more exhilarating. Like muscles that are sore from working out. It feels like building stamina.

This? It feels like I've been drained of everything that I am. Magic and body.

I'm tired. More tired than I've been in ages.

And Derek is clearly... freaking out? I can't really tell by his lack of expression. I also don't think fae freak out. They just burn some villages down or something.

"They shouldn't have been able to reach you here. Not like that." He finally speaks, jerking me out of my random thoughts.

"How would you predict that though?" I ask, pushing back against the cushions so I'm sitting straighter. "It's not like the Ancients are that predictable."

"You are right. Their magic is stronger than we planned."

He's reverted back to his more proper talk. I'm finding he does that when he's stressed. I suppose even magical creatures have that particular emotion. I know what I need to say next. I also know he's not going to like it. But I truly don't see a way around it.

"This means I have no choice but to go to Faery with you."

There's a moment of stillness and then Derek is beside me so fast I didn't see him move. His eyes are full of concern as he stares into mine. For one split second, I have an undeniable urge to pull him into my arms. Instead, I curl my hands into fists on my lap and try to keep my head clear.

"You cannot be serious."

"I am one hundred percent serious. We don't have a choice."

"There is always a choice."

"Yes, between me saving myself or a whole lot of people."

"I understand how the loss of your parents could—"

"It's not just my parents. They'll destroy the whole town if they don't get me."

"It is one town verses the rest of the world." His calm words push my exhaustion straight to anger.

"Don't pull your fae crap on me. My town is full of innocent people. I can't see them burn because I was a coward. I can't have more innocent deaths on my hands." He knows exactly who I mean. I see the realization in his eyes.

"Avery, Julian—"

"No." I don't need Derek's pity, or whatever the coinciding fae emotion may be. I'm thinking logically. I have to stay objective. "It's decided."

Derek stands again, this time to pace the length of the couch. I've never seen him this unbalanced before. It's as if he knows more than he's saying. Which wouldn't surprise me. I'm constantly aware that he's keeping secrets from me. It's the way it is for them. Especially since they can't lie.

"You have spent all this time hiding from them, and you are giving all of that away."

"I understand the risks," I say, pushing myself to the edge of the couch. I'm still not strong enough to stand, but I need Derek to understand this. "You have told me yourself, I can be taught to use the book. If I can learn how to wield this power, I can save them."

"You really think the fae will allow you to use the power for yourself?"

"You really need to stop underestimating me," I snap, but I can see this is difficult for him. I'm not sure which part of it is driving him, but he's looking out for me. And he underlines that fact with his next words.

"And what if this is a trick?"

Of course I thought of that. That was the first scenario that came to my mind. But like I mentioned, there isn't a choice here. We can pretend there is, but we both know what needs to be done. I can't learn this magic on my own.

"Then," I reply, catching his arm as he paces in front of me. It stops his progress. "We will deal with that if it comes up. But I can't keep sitting on the sidelines, Derek. There's too much at stake."

"And what about you?" He drops to his knees in front of me, peering into my eyes, my hand on his arm. "You are going to throw yourself into the lion's den without a second thought."

I watch him for a long minute, memorizing every angle of his face. In the past week and a half, he has become the closest thing I have to a friend. True, it may be that he doesn't see me as anything but a job or a way to get out from under the thumb of his heritage. Even so, the concern on his face, it's real. He takes one of my hands in his, as if he needs the contact as much as I do. My gaze drops to where our skin touches, and I smile a sad smile before I reply.

"If that's what it takes to save my people, I will walk into the lion's den with my head held high."

A big part of me wants to demand Derek open up a portal and take me to Faery immediately. But the other logical part knows I need a plan first. Which is what I've been working on for the past hour. Derek fetched me a notebook and a pen, and I've been scribbling down different ideas.

I haven't written down anything that can be used against me. Like the location of the book for example. But it helps me see my thoughts written in front of me. I use a mind map to keep it all visual. It helps me organize my ideas better. It's how I've studied for exams my whole life. The normalcy of the habit grounds me, giving me the space I need to come up with a plan of action.

"Hungry?"

Derek comes back into the living room, a plate of mac and cheese in his hands. We've been cooking very basic meals since we've been here since neither one of us is proficient. Mac and cheese is the only thing Derek can cook well. He's added grilled chicken to it, and the smell makes my stomach rumble.

"I'll take that as a yes." He smiles, handing over the plate. I nod my head in thanks, as has become our custom. I still haven't uttered those two words at him, keeping that last barrier up. Maybe it's dumb at this point, considering I've trusted him with so much. But spending all this time cooped up together has brought us to a whole new level. No longer just two strangers on parallel journeys. We're now walking the same road.

Yet, I still can't bring myself to thank him. Maybe it's for the best.

"What did you figure out?" Derek asks after settling onto the seat opposite of me with his own plate of food. He digs in right away, as if he hasn't had food all day. It's such a typical boy thing to do, it makes me forget for a second that he's anything but. Shaking my head, I focus on his question.

"I think I need to contact my parents. I know," I raise my hand to ward off his protests, "that it's dangerous. Which is why we should drive into town where I can call them. I need to know they're okay. I have questions only they can answer."

I'm thinking specifically of my dad, who has more knowledge in his pinky than most of the people I met combined. It's why I wanted to become a Watcher so badly. He taught me how to love knowledge before I even understood what that meant.

"If we contact them, we'll have to be ready to go basically right away. They'll be on our heels."

"The Ancients?"

"And those the Faery sent to find you when I didn't return."

That makes me pause for a moment. I chew my food first before I ask the next question.

"Are you going to get in trouble for helping me?"

"Most likely."

"Why do it then?"

"I have my reasons."

I wait for him to continue, but he's done. There are so many other things I can say here, but what's the use? I know where the two of us stand, and I know what needs to be done next. My body feels more rested, and there's no use waiting for tomorrow.

"We should go as soon as we eat."

"Are you sure?"

"You really need to stop asking me that. If I say it, I mean it. It's always been like that."

"I've noticed."

We fall silent again as we stare at each other across the coffee table. It's as if we're both waiting for the other person to say something else, but neither one of us is brave enough. The desire to thank him for everything he's done almost overwhelms me. I squelch it down. I've already decided that's one aspect of this I'm not giving up. But the desire keeps growing, as if something is pushing me toward it.

Breaking the eye contact, I take another bite of my food, the desire diminishing. A thought hits me like a ton of bricks. Derek is doing it. He's trying to make me thank him, but for what? For a bargain? So I owe him? My mind spins with possibilities as we eat in silence. He doesn't know he can't glamour me, unless he's tried and failed. But this feels different than a glamour.

And what would he do with it if he received my thanks? But even as I ask the question, I get the answer. He could use my debt as a way to keep me out of Faery. I glance up at him briefly and find his gaze has turned to the fireplace. He looks far away, as if he too is working out a problem.

But my defenses are back up. I already told myself I can't break down every barrier. Now, I need to build a few back up. Derek has always had an agenda, one he wasn't quick to share with me. It seems that the thought of going back to Faery is just as disconcerting to him as it is me. So he's pulling out some of his tricks. I'll have to watch him more closely.

"Are you ready to go?" I ask, breaking the silence. Derek turns to look at me as I stand. For a second, I think he's going to mention what he's been trying to do. But then, it's like he thinks better of it.

"Let's go."

* * *

WE DRIVE down from our mountain retreat until we find a gas station with a payphone. I didn't think those existed anymore, but maybe in smaller towns they're more common. Derek has been silent the whole way down. I didn't feel like saying anything either. Mostly because I'm still a little peeved at him for trying to manipulate me. Not that I'm surprised. But I'm definitely annoyed.

Thankfully, the payphone is functioning. I grab a handful of coins from inside before dialing my parents. Derek stands by the gas pump, giving me a sense of privacy. Although, I have a feeling he can hear better than he lets on.

"Hello?" My mother's voice comes over the line, and I breathe a huge sigh of relief.

"Mom?"

"Oh, my goodness, Avery, baby, are you okay?" Her voice brings tears to my eyes.

"I'm okay, Mommy. Safe, for now."

"We've been so worried."

"Avery?" My dad's voice comes over the phone next. The tears I've been holding back spill down my cheeks. "Why are you calling?"

Always the protective father. I can hear the panic in his voice at the fact that I dialed their number.

"The jig is up, Daddy. The Ancients know I have the book, and they want it. I'm going to Faery."

There's a collective hush on the other line and then I hear a sharp sound. A hiccup. I know it's my mother crying.

"Baby, you can't. You can't go there."

"I can't keep hiding either." My own tears stain my shirt, and I wipe at my cheeks roughly. "The fae can teach me how to use it, right Dad?"

"Avery, it's too dangerous for you to go there."

"And it's too dangerous for you if I stay," I snap. I have only raised my voice at my parents a few times in my life. Now, it only shows them how determined I am. "I'm sorry. I'm sorry I couldn't stay hidden. I'm sorry I'm putting you through this. But I need you to trust me."

"Of course we trust you, baby girl," Dad says. Mom continues to cry in the background. My parents are the strongest people I know, and here, with few words, I have broken them. "But the fae are more dangerous and cunning than you can ever imagine. I didn't prepare you well enough for them, and for that I am sorry. You should know they will use tricks you have never heard of before, they will push you beyond your limits, and they will break you to a point where you won't know which way is up or down."

I know he's trying to scare me. It's working. But a part of me also thinks that he's speaking from personal experience. Which I don't understand. Maybe in his dealings with the Council he has seen things, but it doesn't actually matter. Nothing will sway me.

"Daddy, tell me I can do this. I can learn from them how to use my power, and I can use it to stop the Ancients."

There's a pause as my dad realizes exactly what I'm asking. I didn't call them for permission. I called them for reassurance. He can try and protect me from them, but he won't lie to me if I ask him what I need to know directly.

"Daniel, no," I hear my mom whisper before my dad speaks up again.

"Avery, listen carefully. They are the only ones who truly understand the kind of power you possess. They can and will teach you how to wield it. But you have to be careful. You have to protect yourself at all times. Glamour won't work on you, and that is a dangerous power all on its own. Once they figure that out, they'll use other ways to keep your spirit broken. Don't let them get into your head. Play your part well. You are a smart girl, and you are resourceful. No matter what you hear or what you learn, know where you come from. You are our daughter. Know the kind of strength you carry within yourself. It cannot be taken from you. No matter what they say or do."

I know he's trying to tell me something beyond the words he's actually speaking, so I try to hold on to each one, for further examination later. But he's given me what I asked for. Going to Faery is truly my only choice.

"I love you both so much," I say, my voice thick with emotion. I have no idea if I'll ever be able to speak to them again. But I rather that be my fate than to have them killed. "You are the best parents a girl could ever ask for. Thank you for raising me to be who I am."

My mother sobs, the sound forever imprinted in my mind. I hear Dad take a sharp breath, and I know he's crying too.

"We are so proud of you, baby girl."

The phone beeps then, and the connection ends. I fumble for more coins, but it's too late. They're gone, and I'm left holding the receiver as my heart breaks. Tears blur my vision. The next moment, the receiver is being taken out of my hand as Derek pulls me into his arms. I cling to him with everything I'm worth, as if he can take away the heartache I'm feeling. He feels solid and sure and unlike anything else in this world that keeps spinning around me. I may not know my own strength, but I know my parents have raised me to do my best. I won't fail them.

I will save them. Even if it means sacrificing myself.

I will save them.

I will save them.

I will save them.

CHAPTER 14

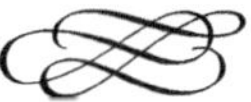

It takes me a good ten minutes to get a grip on my emotions. I didn't expect to lose it like that, but I have been carrying around a lot of pent up feelings for over a month now. It was bound to happen sometime.

"Better?" Derek asks when I finally make myself untangle my arms from around him and step back. His gaze is so full of concern, it almost sends me into another fit. The expression is so raw and more real than I've ever seen on his face before. I must've really freaked him out losing it like that.

"Better."

I take another step back, putting more distance between us. My dad's words echo in my mind about the ways of fae and how cunning they are. Except when I look at Derek, I don't see any of that. I just see a guy who has been there for me this past week. Apparently, my mind doesn't care to remember who he was before all this started.

"We should get going. It'll be best for us to put some distance between here and where we cross, as soon as possible."

I nod, following Derek back to the rental car. I feel tired again, but this time, it's an emotional exhaustion. What comes next will be the greatest test of my character. I need to be ready. But for this one moment, I let myself be tired.

We get into the car and start driving south. It didn't fully occur to me that we wouldn't be going back to the cabin. Somehow, it feels worse knowing that momentary safe haven is no longer attainable. I'm not sure why it makes me sad, but maybe it's because I'm already high on emotions.

When the car starts to spin, I'm not prepared for it.

"Derek!"

"Hold on!"

Derek's quick reflexes do what I wouldn't be able to. He turns the wheel into the spin, keeping a tight grip on it as we move. My hands slam against the ceiling. I hold them there, to keep myself steady in my seat.

We're at a stretch of the freeway with no one around. I'm thankful for that small favor. The car rights itself as suddenly as it began spinning. In that same moment, three men appear in the middle of the road. Derek slams down on the gas, but the car does the opposite. We come to an abrupt stop, about ten feet between us and the men. There's nothing particularly striking about them, but when they move, they move in complete unison. They lift their left arms over their heads before they push them forward, palms first.

"Get out!" Derek yells, but I'm already moving. Pushing the car door open, I jump, tumbling onto the side of the freeway. I roll a few times into a bush. The car makes a screeching noise as it gets pushed backward and into the same ditch I'm currently lying in. Except a dozen yards back.

My attention snaps to were Derek landed. I see he's already getting to his feet. I've never seen him use his magic fully before, but I can see it building up in the space around him. It's as if his whole aura is becoming alight with it.

The three men continue to walk toward him silently, each step the exact same. They raise their arms again, pushing another wave of magic. This time, it's directed at Derek. The panic I feel threatens to overwhelm me. Scrambling on all fours, I try to reach the freeway before they can do any damage.

Suddenly, someone appears behind me, wrapping their arms around my middle and yanking me backward. I yell, breaking Derek's concentration. The magic hits him square in the chest. He flies back, slamming into the asphalt before rolling a few times. I struggle against my attacker, but he seems so much bigger than me.

Thinking back to what I was taught, I go slack, sending the attacker off balance. That moment of hesitation is all I need. I yank my body forward, reaching for the ground. In the same motion, I reach backward between my legs. I grab my attacker's ankle and yank it forward. He slams down onto his back at the last moment, grabbing me and dragging me down with him. I hold onto his foot, wrapping my whole body around it and pulling it toward me as I kick out with my own legs. There's a scream as my foot connects with his face and my arms yank on his leg. I roll out of the way as he jumps up, this time a bit slower.

He comes at me, but I'm ready. Twisting around, I bring my battle magic to my fingertips, and I slam it right into him. He screams again, but this time the momentum carries him backward. I hear a crunch as his body's momentum is stopped by a tree. From what I can see, he doesn't look like one of the three who are fighting Derek. That works in my favor. I spin again, trying to find where he went. I see him once again on the ground, his face and body bruised from repeatedly slamming into it.

I can taste the men's magic at the tips of my tongue. It tastes strong and wrong somehow. I see them revving up once more, their arms raised. They're only a few feet away from Derek. There's no way I can reach him in time. I stumble up the side of the road. They snap their palms forward again. I scream.

I thrust my hands out, still on my knees as the sound rips out of my throat. Magic bursts out of my hands. Sudden wind pushes my hair back as I pour all of my power into this one motion. My mind goes blank, then clears in a matter of a split second. Wind and magic dance around me in a whirlpool as I bleed myself dry. Pure power pours out of me, one hundred percent focused on the three men.

Once it reaches them, there is nothing to be done.

Disappear.

Disappear.

Disappear.

They disintegrate in front of my eyes.

The moment they're gone, I pull back. My magic snaps into me like a rubber band. I drop to all fours, breathing heavily as I try to understand what just happened. That felt nothing like my battle magic, yet somehow, I know it was. My body feels tired yet alive.

I raise my head, my eyes finding Derek. Pushing myself forward, I reach him just as he's reaching for me. He looks like he's been through a battle, bruises and cuts and torn clothes.

"Are you okay?" I ask, my fingers roaming the sides of his face carefully.

"I'll live." He coughs and then looks up at me once again.

"Avery—"

"What?" I ask, alarmed immediately. But he's not staring behind me. He's staring at me. More importantly, at my hair. He reaches up, pulling a strand forward. I can't believe what I'm seeing.

"Your hair is green."

* * *

I GET Derek back to the car, which surprisingly still works. Then I drive us back to the cabin. Neither one of us is ready to face anyone in Faery looking the way we do. I'm bruised, but I'm much better off than Derek. He took the brunt of the attack, giving me the time to deal with my assailant. He looks exhausted and more human than I've ever seen him. Even his glamour has flickered a few times, and I've seen the ears pop out again.

There isn't much I can do for him, except clean his cuts and let him rest. Fae heal faster than witches, although not as fast as shifters. My own body is already in recovery mode, one perk of having a wolf shifter for a mother. Even though I have no shifter powers and have never shifted, I do have the slightly accelerated healing gene. It has come in handy since all of this started.

"We're here," I say, when I finally pull up at the cabin. It shows how out of it Derek is because he visibly jerks awake at my words.

"It's probably not the safest move," he manages as I help him out of the car.

"We'll be safe for tonight," I state, believing every word. I hope that adds to the magic of this place.

When we make it inside, Derek stumbles enough that I place his arm over my shoulder and guide him to the bathroom. He's not a water fae, but since the water comes from the lake, it'll be a solid connection to the nature around us. I've never seen anyone so beat up by magic before, but that's the only description I can come up with. Whoever those men were, they carry with them an incredible amount of power.

"Hey, I need to get these cleaned," I say, depositing Derek onto the toilet. The cuts on his face and arms are still bleeding a little. I have no idea how his body would react to infection or even if he can get regular people infection. But he doesn't protest, so I do the only thing I know to do. I reach for one of the smaller towels and soap and begin cleaning his cuts. We have no medicine in the house because why would we? But this gives me a sense of peace, as if I'm actually making a difference.

Derek leans his head back against the wall, as I lean over him to wipe at the blood on his face. His eyes open, catching mine. Suddenly, I can't seem to think. He's so close, my legs straddling one of his, my face inches away from him. His guard is down. There is so much pain in his eyes, it grips my heart.

"Thank you," he mumbles, disarming me completely. Fae don't thank. They would never utter such words without consequence. But he does, and he directs them at me.

"Hmm," I reply because I have no idea what to say. Then, Derek's hands fall on my hips. I freeze, wondering what I'm supposed to be feeling here. I understand the array of emotions going through me. I can't act on them, but I understand them. My mind races with possibilities. But he doesn't do anything, just holds himself upright as I finish working on his face.

"Let's get you in the shower," I say next, stepping back. He nods, but when he reaches for his shirt, I see it's a struggle. Carefully, I step back into his personal space and pull it gently over his head. His chest is magnificent, even with bruises. I try not to stare. I have to be professional about this. When I reach for his pants, his hand closes over mine.

"You don't have to," he mumbles. I'm not sure if he's protecting me or himself, but I'm grateful. We've already crossed too many boundaries. Instead, I wrap his arm around my shoulders again, helping him stand. Then, we step into the shower. Turning the water on, I don't have to wait for it to be the perfect temperature. He leans forward, his head against the tiles, gripping the top of the shower. I leave him be. There's something vulnerable in that pose, and I feel like I'm intruding.

Going to my own room, I get into the shower. I'm much better off than Derek. The cuts are mostly superficial. While I'm dirty, I'm not as hurt as he is. My heart hurts thinking of how much damage his body sustained. For him to be this hurt, the magic those men displayed had to have been astronomical.

Once I'm clean and dressed in my t-shirt and leggings combo, I take a moment to study my hair. There are green strands throughout, brighter than I've ever seen. I've colored my hair before in purples and rose gold, just to see. I would think this is my magic messing with what's already there, but it looks different. Bright and right, somehow.

Leaving my hair to air dry, I head downstairs and curl up on the couch. There is nothing for me to do but wait. After about ten minutes, I get up and make tea, bringing it with me to the couch when done. A part of me wants to go check on him, but I hear some movement and let him be. There's not much I can do anyway. He might not even come down. Maybe he needs time to himself. But then that thought is shattered when I hear footsteps on the stairs.

Turning, I see him make his way to me. He changed. His hair is still damp from the shower, but he looks a little better. He takes a seat opposite of me without a word. After a few seconds, I jump up and head to the kitchen. I return with a fresh mug of tea. He accepts it with a simple nod.

We stay like that for a while, sharing the same couch on two opposite ends of the "L" shape. I don't bombard him with questions, and he doesn't provide any information. We sip our tea and watch the flames dance. Somehow, it's exactly what we both need.

"I couldn't use my magic."

At first, I don't think I hear him right. When I glance up, his eyes are still on the fire.

"I couldn't do anything. It was as if they sucked my powers dry, and I was only left this... shell."

The desire to go to him is strong, but I don't think he'd welcome it right now. He's a powerful being who was made to feel powerless. He doesn't need my pity. So, I don't offer it.

He doesn't speak again, and I don't push him. I let him know with my presence that I'm here for him.

For right now, it's enough.

CHAPTER 15

There's a feeling of claustrophobia that surrounds me, except, when I look around, I'm in a forest. Once again, I have no idea how I got here. That automatically makes me remember that's how my dreams have been. When I reach out to touch the bark on the tree to my right, it feels too real to be in my head.

The confusion intensifies as I try to search for any direction or sign in the darkness. Much like the last time I found myself in this predicament, there is nothing but the fear that eats up at me from every direction. I can't tell if it's the Ancients doing this or the fae. It's as if they have created a personal torture chamber for me, and they keep dumping me in it any time they please.

My body hums with anticipation as I try to prepare myself for whatever may come next. Assuming this is a dream is dangerous, but I have nothing else to go on. There's always a possibility they have finally dragged me to wherever they are, and now I'm getting punished for taking so long. Or tortured for information.

I call on my magic to see if it's there. It flickers a few times and then goes dormant. The panic intensifies, making it hard for me to breathe. I try to find a way to focus, but the trees seem to be closing in, making it near impossible.

Then, a pain, sharp and precise hits me in my back.

I stumble forward, barely catching myself so I don't face-plant against a tree. Something warm runs down my back. When my fingers find it, I realize it's blood. Another hit comes from the right, sending me to the ground. My whole side is torn now, blood gushing everywhere.

Holding the shirt tightly around my torso, I try to stop the blood flow as I scoot backward. The darkness feels heavier somehow, as if there is someone standing right on the other side of it, pressing down on me.

I will not die here.

I will not die here.

I will not die here.

The repetition in my mind helps to focus me. At least, somewhat. I have to think.

Think instead of react.

My back hits the base of the tree, and I lean against it gratefully. Looking down at my torso, I try to see if I can stop the blood or if I can tell the extent of the injury, but it's too dark. That's when I realize I can see something.

Glancing up, I watch as the path I made with my blood once again turns into plants, this time it's flowers blooming. They're large, the size of watermelons at least, and glowing. I stare at them, completely mesmerized. How can something so beautiful come from something so horrible?

The pain in my body intensifies, snapping me out of my daze. Can you die in a dream?

But I don't even know if it is a dream. It feels real. Everything about it feels real, including the blood leaving my body.

I force my legs to obey me as I push against the tree to stand. Then I drop back down at the agony I feel.

That was stupid. I have to be smart. I have to—

I *have* to be *smart*. I have to be logical.

But then, another sharp pain goes through me. I slump down, unable to do much but force my lungs to take in air. The ground I lay on is soaked through with my blood and covered in flowers. If this is how I die, at least it looks beautiful.

No.

Whatever this torture is, it's not real. I am in control of my life. I am in control of my decisions. I decide that I will not die here.

I will not die here.

I will not die here.

I will not die here.

I look for a focus point I can reach for, putting all my attention on it. Then, I pull myself from the dream.

I sit up, covered in sweat, my heart's beating fills my ear. My body is in agony. I run my hands over my skin but come away with no blood. Rubbing my face, I push away my hair that has stuck to my damp skin. My heart is still pounding. I'm still terrified. But I got out. That's all that matters.

Glancing up, I'm not surprised to find Derek's outline in the doorway. Light from the moon makes him look like he's glowing. We stare at each other, him bruised and me broken, two unlikely people thrust into an unimaginable situation.

After a few moments, I scoot to one side of the bed before pulling the blanket up on the other. I lay down, watching Derek. I can see the second he makes the decision. Walking over to the bed, he lays down beside me with only a few inches of space between us. I tug my part of the blanket under my chin, studying his profile as he stares at the ceiling.

We don't speak because words aren't necessary. I'll tell him about my dream tomorrow, and we'll figure it out then. Right now, we both need this—whatever this is. Maybe we just both need to not feel so alone.

With that thought on my mind, I close my eyes and finally sleep.

* * *

SOMETIME IN THE NIGHT, his hand has found mine. Our fingers are entwined, my hand is resting on his chest, held closely to his heart.

I don't move just yet, giving myself this moment of tranquility. Without a doubt, my life is about to take another huge tumble into the unknown. I steal another peek at Derek, at the way his whole body is relaxed for the first time since I've met him. He looks younger, like most people do when they're not carrying the fate of their realm on their shoulders.

Sometimes I feel like that's how Derek thinks. That if something would happen, it would be his fault.

I feel like that too.

Needing to put some distance between us, I go to extract my hand. He stops me. It's just a gentle squeeze, as if to keep me in place. I look up to see if he's awake, but his breathing hasn't changed. He did so in his sleep, and that brings a strange feeling to my chest. I move to scoot over when a sharp pain resonates at my back.

"Avery?" Derek's eyes are open and on me as I retrieve my hand. I run it over my side.

"Strange pain, that's all," I say, but then the dream comes back full force, and I wonder if something is wrong.

"May I?" he asks, and I nod.

Turning to the side, I let Derek pull my shirt up. I know the moment he sees something. There's a stillness and then his fingertips run gently over my skin. I shudder at the touch, goosebumps racing over my skin as he explores carefully.

"There are marks, like claw marks," he finally says. My mind is once again in the dream with the blood gushing out. I'm screaming in pain. My mind is filled with the sound of my pain, and my chest squeezes in response.

"Hey, Avery. It's okay. You're okay."

I'm hyperventilating, I can tell because I've read about it. Derek doesn't try anything, but sits besides me, repeating the phrase over and over. I force my mind to find its center, focusing on his soft voice. After a few minutes, I'm me again.

"It was the dream, wasn't it?"

"It doesn't look like much of dream though," I say, pushing past him so I can get off the bed. Heading straight for the bathroom, I turn the light on and pull up my shirt to see the damage. Just like in my dream, the mark I can see starts right below my armpit and goes down to my hips. When I turn slightly, I can see the ending of another mark that feels like it goes across my whole back.

"What did this?" I ask, meeting Derek's gaze in the mirror. He followed me into the bathroom.

"I don't know. A dream wraith would be my top guess. They can be enchanted to hurt those whose dreams they occupy."

"But it can also be other things," I say, knowing full well there are a lot of options for evil in the world. It doesn't matter what it is. I couldn't fight it either way.

"We need to get going," I say, dropping my shirt to my waist and turning to face Derek. I can see he doesn't like that, but he's not about to protest. His eyes shift up to my hair and the strands of green that now occupy about half of it. Then, after a firm nod, he turns and walks out of the bathroom.

With him gone, I grab my clothes and shut the door to change. The pain from the cuts is fading, but it does make me wonder what else I'll be encountering in my dreams. And if these will stop when I'm in Faery. With jeans and a t-shirt on, I brush my hair, braiding it down my back. Interestingly enough, I like the green. It matches my eyes and suits me somehow.

We grab a cup of coffee and breakfast in silence and then we're off.

There is a possibility that this is the worst idea of my whole entire life. Derek doesn't like it, and that's putting it mildly. He's been in a mood since I told him my decision is final. Granted, he could refuse to take me. But I think we both know that won't actually stop me.

I would find another way. And he would like that even less. After the events of yesterday, we've been put into a tight spot. Both of us.

It's not as if I'm enjoying this either. I'm willingly surrendering myself to the very creatures I've been running from. That feels like failure to me.

But this is not about me. I've been selfish for way too long already. If the fae can teach me how to use this power, then they are my best chance at survival.

"You're still set on this?" Derek asks as we make our way the car. He won't portal out of here because he wants to keep this place a secret. But it's like he's giving me every opportunity to back out. I can't tell if he's nervous for me or for himself. We've spent this whole time together, and I still don't know where he truly stands. I only know that he risked his life to save me.

I glance back at the cabin as I reach the car. I'd be lying if I said I'm not going to miss it. This place gave me a sense of normalcy I so desperately needed. It was like a calm before the storm. The moment I get into the car, everything changes.

"Let's get going," I say, pulling the passenger door open.

Derek gets behind the wheel, and in silence, steers the car down to the rental place. Seems as good of a place as any to ruin my life.

Okay, maybe I'm being a tad dramatic, but I think I'm allowed under the circumstances. Never much appreciated myself when I'm emotional, and I've been emotional a lot lately.

It's time to put my game face one. Truth be known, I have no idea what to expect.

I have to be ready for anything.

CHAPTER 16

hen we step through the portal, I have no expectations. The portal itself was much like the last time I went through it. Simple and fast. But what meets us on the other side is surprising.

We come to in a courtyard straight out of some fairytale. The large trees, bigger than I've ever seen, stand at each corner of the yard. They look like they are a thousand years old at least. The green of the leaves is the brightest I've ever seen. There are flowers everywhere.

The tree itself holds flowers, but they also cover most of the area around the walkways. The air feels fresher somehow, more so than even in the mountains near home.

"Where are we?" I ask, turning to look at Derek. He's rigid, his whole body tense. "Derek?"

"Summer Court," he replies, his voice clipped. Something is wrong, and I have no idea what it could be. I open my mouth to ask, but we're no longer alone.

A woman who looks to be in her mid-thirties has joined us. She's dressed in the most beautiful of gowns, light green and translucent. It sparkles as she walks. The vines that grow on the skirt look almost real. I would be more surprised if they weren't.

"I see you have finally decided to come," she says, her voice like a freshly blooming flower. She gives Derek a brief glance before turning her attention back to me. "Welcome to Summer, Avery Kincaid."

I stare at her blankly. She is not appreciative of my lack of manners. I must've left those in the human realm, alongside the beat-up car we returned to the rental place. I'm experiencing very hostile emotions toward her, and I don't understand why. I was determined to come in here with an open mind, but it feels like I already know her. And I don't like her.

"May I introduce," Derek is quick to jump in as the woman and I eye each other, "Queen Svetlana of the Summer Court of Faery."

The queen raises her chin at me, and I only continue to stare. I'm not sure when I decided to be this defiant, but it was probably somewhere between getting attacked and being cut to pieces in my dream. I am not in a good mood.

"She is a difficult one, Derek." The queen addresses my companion, finally looking at him again. "You look unacceptable. Better get changed. Off you go."

Derek is dressed in dark blue jeans and a dark t-shirt. If he doesn't look acceptable, then I'm sure she's even less pleased with me. I'm waiting for him to say something, maybe tell her he'll stay with me, but he does no such thing. With a polite nod at her, he leaves without a backward glance at me.

Now I'm angry and confused.

"You have caused quite an uproar, Miss Kincaid."

I've always enjoyed people calling me Miss Kincaid, but apparently, not in this case. Her words seem to grate on me, and it's difficult to keep the full hostility out of my gaze. I need to get a grip.

"It wasn't intentional," I reply, finally speaking, if only to hear my voice in this magical place. It sounds clearer somehow, just like the colors look brighter.

Queen Svetlana studies me. I know she doesn't miss a thing. Not the scratches on my arm, nor the green streaks in my hair. She's waiting for me to say something else, but I have nothing for her. I'm here. That's what she wanted, isn't it?

"No, I suppose fighting Derek and running away was not a planned out move. Teenagers can be so spontaneous."

Oh, I don't like the way she talks to me. I'm about to spontaneously punch her in the face.

What is wrong with me?

Stay calm, stay focused.

Stay calm, stay focused.

Stay calm, stay focused.

There is a definite imbalance here. I'm just not sure what's causing it. The emotions within me are boiling to the surface, and it's like I have no control over them. My magic sits comfortably inside of me, completely unbothered. It's a strange combination.

"Hmm, you are going to be something, Miss Kincaid. Very well. If this is how you want to play this, so shall it be. We have prepared a room for you. Nora will see you there. Make sure to dress more appropriately from now on."

Just then, a girl about my edge steps out from the shadows, inclining her head in greeting. She's also dressed in a gown, although hers is much less extravagant than the one the queen wears. I suppose I can't expect anything else. The queen must present herself above everyone else.

"You are not to wander the halls alone. I would not suggest you try," she adds, probably reading my defiant expression. "Stay in your room until I decide what to do with you."

"What to do with me?" I ask as the queen turns away. She pauses, as if not used to someone questioning her commands. Which I'm sure is the case and not something I'm about to do.

"Yes. You may possess a strong power, Miss Kincaid, but we are in a middle of a war. You are of no use to me until that power can be harnessed. Until then, off you go."

With that, she turns and leaves me standing in the middle of the courtyard, a million thoughts in my head.

Derek has abandoned me.

Apparently, my clothes are unacceptable.

And I am for sure a prisoner.

"Lead the way." I motion to the other girl.

Great, just great.

* * *

WE DON'T GO FAR. When Nora pushes the doors open, I'm met with one of the most amazing rooms I've ever seen. The bed sits to the right, huge in comparison to anything I've seen. The walls are covered in flowered wallpaper, but it doesn't look tacky at all. The trim of the room is made up of gold and silver. There's a window straight in front of me. I walk over to it so I can see the Faery forest stretching out beyond the palace walls.

There's a door opposite the bed, near the window. When I peek in, I find a very modern bathroom, even including a shower.

"I thought iron and metal in general was a no go for you guys," I say, glancing back at the girl.

"That may have been the case before, but we have adapted. We kind of had to if we wanted to survive in the other realms. Plus, showers are so much nicer than medieval baths," Nora says, walking over to lean against the bed. She seems more relaxed now that the queen isn't present. But even though she looks to be about my age, I doubt we could be friends. It wasn't like we were introduced organically. She's been assigned to me, which means she's a spy. Or a babysitter. Either one doesn't look good for me.

"You'll find everything here is pretty close to what you're used to. Sure, our clothes may seem outdated to you, but the amenities are all top notch."

The last phrase makes me curious. I turn to give her a questioning look.

"What? I don't spend all my time here. I graduated three years ago from a human school."

"Which one?"

"Thunderbird Academy. I'm sure you've heard of it." She says it like she doesn't actually know my history, so I decide to be honest. Not sure why, maybe simply because it's been a while since I've talked to a girl close to my age.

"I was supposed to graduate from there this year," I say, taking a seat on one of the chairs situated in front of a fireplace. Not sure why it's necessary, considering it's always warm in Summer Court. I do know my seasons, at least.

"No way! Is that where you found that book?" She sounds like any other girl I've ever talked to, and it makes it easier to answer her.

"Yes. Does everyone know about that?"

"Oh absolutely." She jumps up, landing on the bed and stretching out her legs in front of her. The light pink of her dress makes her look like she belongs in this room, matching the decor perfectly. "We felt a pretty big magic wave and then all the big names started freaking out. Those of us in the palace knew almost immediately because no one around here can actually keep a secret. I mean, some can. But most don't."

Not exactly sure how that's supposed to benefit the government system here, but oh well. Not my problem. Nora seems eager to talk. Maybe she's starved for companionship too. Or she just might be that good of an actress.

"You graduated and then what? Came here?"

"Yep. I thought I wanted to be an ambassador, but it turns out I'm really not that interested in politics. I'm more of a garden nymph."

"Is that what you are?"

I really can't tell the difference between nymphs and fairies. Besides the ears. But I can't see Nora's with the way her curls fall over her shoulders.

"No, silly. I'm a royal fae from the house of Summer. There are a few of us running around. Fae really can't keep it in their pants."

"So, the queen is your mother?"

"Aunt, by name and blood only. She treats me more like a servant than anything else. They thought you'd adjust better if you had someone your own age around, and I'm the closest. Plus, the whole Thunderbird Academy thing. You know, things in common."

She's getting more bubbly as she talks. I wonder if she was nervous in the beginning too. I'm not about to spill my secrets, but I do feel slightly better with her here.

"Does that mean you've been assigned to watch my every move?"

Her laugh rings out, filling the space around us. I can't help but smile. She seems carefree and happy. I'm not sure why I expected only bad things by being here. Oh wait, it's because there are plenty to go around. One fae doesn't change that for the whole realm.

"I have, kind of. I'm supposed to help you learn the etiquette of the court. As you saw, auntie was not pleased with your outfit. But no worries, there is a great selection in your closet."

I point to the armoire near the door, and she nods eagerly. Pushing to my feet, I head for it, pulling it open. I realize it's not a standing closet but a cleverly disguised doorway to a walk-in closet.

Stepping inside, I find dresses of every color and shape hanging in the space around me. There are also shoes and nightgowns. That last one is a little weird but okay.

"Aren't they gorgeous?" Nora sighs from behind me. She's leaning against the doorway, gazing up at the dresses.

"They are. I'm just not a very big dress person." Mostly, because I never think I can pull them off.

"Well, you're about to be. It's a sign of respect and nobility to be dressed in these. Others will have to be reminded of your status while you're here and dressing the part will help."

"My status?"

"You are not to be touched, by the order of the queen."

I'm not sure how to deal with that information, so I ignore it for now. Instead, I turn to the dresses.

"I suppose you'd like to help me pick one out?"

 ora takes her job very seriously. She pulls out three top choices before she sets me in front of a vanity, which is also in my walk-in closet. Then, she starts on my hair.

"It's so long, and I love the green," she comments, brushing it out so she can curl it.

"The green is pretty new," I say, mesmerized by her movements. Since there are no heating tools here, I'm incredibly curious about how she's going to curl. She takes a strand of my hair, winding it gently around her finger. When she lets it free, it bounces up and down in a fresh curl.

"You're curling my hair magically?"

"Well, of course. How else would I curl it? Those heating things humans use are so damaging to the hair." She huffs and continues to make her way across my head. Her own hair falls down her back in large curls, blonde and shiny, even in this dim light.

Once my head is fully curled, she rearranges more than half to one side, pinning a section above my ear with a silver clip. With just a few moves, my neck seems longer and more elegant. She really is good at this.

"Next, just a touch of paint." She turns my chair toward her and leans over my face. "Close."

I follow her direction, closing my eyes, wondering why I'm trusting her to do whatever she wants. She could be painting me to look like a clown. Would I know? Or does my glamour radar work here as well? I'll have to test it out somehow.

Maybe I won't have to. The queen, or someone on her staff, will probably try glamouring the book's location out of me soon enough. Then my secret will be out. But at least I'll know for sure.

"Open."

I do, turning to look at the mirror.

"Wow."

Nora has added just a touch of pink to my eyelids, enough to make my eyes pop without over doing it. My lashes look longer and fuller somehow, but I don't see mascara in her hands. Even my lips have a bit of shine to them.

"I call it a natural glow," Nora says as I meet her eyes in the mirror. "You don't need any help, but a bit of sparkle never hurt anyone."

She smiles at me, and I can't help but return it. Next, she does a little twirl and heads for the bedroom. I follow her more slowly and find her standing in front of the bed, contemplating the three dresses she picked out. I would offer my opinion, but I have a feeling it won't help. She's set on this, so I let her have it.

After a few moments, she nods. "Yes, this one!" She explains it like she's picking a winning lottery ticket. The dress she chooses is exactly the one I liked the best. It has open shoulders, with small ruffles at the edge of the neck. The white flowers that cover the green fabric look lively and simplistic.

"Well, what are you waiting for?"

"Here?" I ask, because she's watching me expectably.

"Don't be so modest. Unless you want to? But like, I'll have to help you put the dress on, so."

"It's okay."

I'm not exactly comfortable, but she's right. I won't be able to dress myself, so I probably shouldn't be this uncomfortable. But I am. I know fae have no problem showing off their bodies, but that was never the case where I'm from. We kept to the norms. Or something like it.

When Nora pulls the dress over my shoulders, it feels like it's made for me. The material is softer than I expected it to be, and the bodice hugs my curves just right.

"What do you think?"

I step in front of the mirror, hardly recognizing myself. I look like a princess straight from those popular fairytales. My hair looks fuller and shinier, my neck long and elegant. Even my shoulders look like a model's. The dress comes in at my waist, accenting my figure. The skirt is just full enough to give me a bit more shape, without over-doing it. The skirt shifts against my legs, falling just above the floor.

"I love it." I open my mouth to thank her and then stop. I have to be extra careful about it. She grins at me anyway, clearly pleased with herself.

"Now, I'm supposed to take you to dinner."

"What?"

"Word of advice, eat small portions. Faery food is so addicting. Don't receive anything from anyone besides the servants. They'll put the food and drink in front of you, that's it. The council members will be present, and they will try playing games with you. They do it to anyone. While you're protected, they can still mess with you, so be on guard."

"Why are you telling me all of this?" I ask, turning to face her straight on. She sighs, cocking her head to the side as she watches me.

"Because I like you, and I haven't liked anyone in a while. It's not fun when people try to make you do things you don't want. While you're here, I have your back. My cousin says she learned about being a softy from me."

I narrow my eyes at that because it sounds familiar, but then a knock at the door makes me jump.

"That will be our cue. I'll be at the dinner with you but staying quiet is your best bet."

"And if I'm asked a question?"

I'm still not sure if I can trust her intel or not, but so far, she hasn't really said anything I wouldn't already be doing.

"Answer as specific as you can and then don't divulge any other information."

Sounds about right. I'm not exactly sure what I'm walking into, but it's going to be interesting. And bad. It'll probably be bad.

* * *

WHEN WE REACH the main dining area, there are already people seated around the large table. They all turn as one at our entrance, eyes narrowed in suspicion or indifference. I'm a walking contradiction, that much I know. They don't know what to do with me any more than I know what to do with myself.

"Finally. Take a seat." Queen Svetlana calls out. Another fae, one of the servers, comes up to guide me to my seat. It's on the left of the queen, near the head of the table. Once I sit, I realize a familiar face is right across the way. Derek.

He looks entirely different than the boy I've spent the past two weeks with. His hair is slicked back away from his face, a small band across it, maybe to keep it in place? He's wearing a suit jacket, open at the front with the collar up against his neck. His chest is bare. He looks regal somehow. That's when I notice his clothes carry the same shine as the queen's. Glancing between the two of them, a piece of the puzzle seems to fall into place.

"That is much better," the queen comments, looking me up and down, but I can't seem to look away from Derek. His eyes are on me as well, his expression distant. It's as if we're complete strangers. I don't understand the attitude.

"The clothes really do make the man, or the woman in this case." As the queen continues, the rest of the table chuckles politely. Tearing my gaze away from Derek, I finally look at her. She turns her attention to me as well, a glass of wine poised at her lips. There's a smirk on her as she studies me before she leans her elbow on the table and takes a sip.

"My son has done a good job of convincing you to play along," she comments. I know she's waiting for the shock of that truth to bring forth a reaction. But I already figured it out. The band around his head is a crown, albeit a very cheap version, as not to upstage the queen. I still haven't spoken, and I can tell it's making the queen annoyed at me.

"You do not think he was a good choice for you?" She finally asks a question, and one I can answer readily.

"I think he did his job well."

The queen's laugh rings out again, as if she found that statement the funniest joke on the planet. Derek's eyes are once more on me. This time when I meet them, I match his expression. I keep expecting him to be a friend, but that's my fault. He has never been my friend, not for a second. Just a son, doing his mother's bidding. I can see that now.

Then why did he hold my hand while we slept?

No.

No.

No.

Shut it down. Push it away. I started to feel things I never should've felt. I forgot that he was my enemy, and now I get to pay for it. But I can do it. I can be indifferent. I can play this game.

"Tomorrow, we begin lessons." The queen says as I take a tiny bite of my food. Nora wasn't kidding. The food is the most delicious thing I've ever tasted. I resist the urge to shove spoonfuls into my mouth. It seems like the whole table is watching me chew. I look over to find their eyes on mine. Nora is down the line, a small smile on her face as she too watches me. I don't understand what's happening, but I'm not about to ask anyone. Especially not Derek.

"Lessons?" I decide to say. When I glance at the queen, she seems to be studying me again. I take another small bite of meat, waiting for the answer. She shakes herself from whatever trance she's in before replying.

"I have selected tutors to guide you in your magic study. Without the book," she emphasizes the word, but I'm not taking the bait, "we cannot go over specific spells. But you must learn how to harness the gift you have been given. So, we will start slow. At the beginning."

I nod in acknowledgment, as I eat a slice of potatoes. One of the other people present asks the queen a question then, so she turns her attention to the fae beside Derek. There are about ten individuals there, including Nora. Not a huge dinner party, but I would bet my last dollar on the fact that each of these fae is here to watch me like a science project. Every move I make is scrutinized. Yet, somehow, I ignore them. Maybe later I can ask Nora about it. Not that I'm trusting her intel. She said she's related to the queen. I already thought she could be a spy. If nothing else, she's fae. I can't be forgetting that any time soon.

This whole palace is a cage, and I walked into it willingly. But the queen wants to teach me magic, and that is something I need. It's why I'm here. But I have to hold at least some of the cards or this won't work.

"I have a stipulation," I say, my heart pounding loudly in my ears. The whole room falls silent at my outburst.

"A stipulation?"

"My hometown, including my parents, is in danger. I will do your lessons, and I will help you with your war, but you have to promise to protect them. No matter what."

There is no hesitation in my words. They come out strong and I'm proud of myself. Even when I meet the queen's eyes and find hers full of anger, I don't waver.

"You dare to provide stipulations." It's not a question, but I decide to answer it anyway.

"Yes. You need me. There is no doubt about it, or you wouldn't have bothered with all of this." I wave my hand in the direction of Derek, and we all know what I mean. "So, you protect my family, and I work with you. Or this will be an unpleasant experience for all of us."

The bravery I feel comes out of nowhere. But thinking about my parents, my friends, I know this is what needs to be done. I can't cower away from it. I can't cower away from her.

She could probably murder me with a flick of her wrist. But then, she would have no one to read the books, and she can't have that. She wants to win. For that, she needs me.

We're at a standstill.

No one moves.

And then, when I think she's going to throw me into a dungeon and forget about me until I come to my senses, she nods.

"Fine. Your family will be safe."

"Make it a deal." I don't hesitate, and her eyes flash at me. I made myself her enemy, but I don't care. "Deal or no dice."

There's another pause and then, "It's a deal."

CHAPTER 18

"You are out of your mind!" Nora squeals next to me like a thirteen-year-old girl at her first concert. I've seen plenty of movies to know that's a thing. We're back in my room, and I march right to my bed and lay down. "Seriously, you're insane." Nora plops down beside me, her head on her arm as she stares down at me.

"I thought the queen was going to turn you into a tree right then and there."

"Oh, is that one of her powers?" I chuckle, but there's no humor there. I still can't believe I did that either. My parents would be horrified. And proud. But probably mostly horrified.

"Smart of you to make it a deal though. You studied."

"That's my specialty."

I push myself to my elbows, glancing over at Nora. She really is enjoying herself. But even though I'm still terrified this will come to bite me, I'm happy I did it. My parents need my protection. The fae cannot break a promise without it taking an actual physical toll on them. And their powers. That's one of the first few lessons my dad ever taught me about fae. I have to be even more careful about my word use going forward, but this had to be done.

"Also, can I just ask, what it was like to spend all that time with Prince McBroody?"

"McBroody?"

"That's what I call him. As well as McAnnoying and an array of other things."

I try not to remember the way he looked at me when he watched over me in the night, or how his hand felt wrapped around mine. All of that is done. He's not who I thought he was.

"He was... difficult," I finally reply, receiving a snort from Nora. It's such a human thing to do I stare at her for a moment.

"He really is. I wondered how he'd do with you. He's usually sent on all the boring ambassador duties. The only fun part is that he gets to travel and live among humans."

"Is that why you wanted to be an ambassador?" I try to steer the conversation back to her because I definitely don't want to talk about him.

"Yes. He made it sound so exciting. I think we both just wanted a way out of here. But don't tell anyone I said that."

I smile, but it's not like I have anyone to tell. The one individual I thought I'd have here is apparently related to my enemy. So fun stuff for me.

A knock sounds on the door just then. Nora jumps off the bed before I can stop her. Pulling the door open, I can't see who's on the other side, but Nora chuckles again.

"Speak of the devil."

But of course, it's Derek. Because why wouldn't it be? This night is going so well.

"Can we take a walk?" he asks as I continue to sit on the bed.

"I'd rather not." That surprises him. I can see the barely there flicker in his eyes before he masks it. Nora folds her arms, looking between Derek and I as if she's figuring something out.

"Avery, please."

That sends Nora's eyebrows into her hairline, which is why I jump off the bed. I don't feel like dodging her questions right now, and I have to hear him out eventually. I walk past both of them and step out into the hallway. He follows me out, then turns to the left without a word, so I have no choice but follow.

When we reach the courtyard we crossed over into, I instantly head for the trees. There's a cluster of three on one side of the yard, and I want to get a closer look. Derek stays about five feet away from me, but I can feel his eyes on my every move. I keep expecting him to say something, but he stays silent. So then, after a few minutes, I finally turn to face him.

I can't read his expression, but now I wonder if I ever actually could. Or if he just showed me what I wanted to see.

Maybe I could blame him for it, but it doesn't really matter if he's royalty or not. He would've done this if he was just some common fae. I can't hold his title against him.

But I can be mad at the way he's been treating me.

"That's it then? Silence?" I ask, shattering the peace between us. He can't seem to look away from me. I realize I'm still dressed in the dress Nora picked out. It's just another indication of everything that has changed between us.

"I am not going to offer excuses."

"Ah, he speaks." I walk past him, heading toward a bench near the flowers. "And no, I wouldn't expect you to."

I sit, arranging the skirt around me. I've never been much for long dresses, but I do have to admit, there is a charm to this one. If I have to fit in, at least I'll look pretty doing it.

"There are things you do not understand."

At that, I do look at him. He's come to stand near the bench, but he doesn't take a seat. It sounds like there is more to those words than what he's saying, but I can't figure it out. I need more information than what he's giving me.

"I don't understand many things," I reply. "You'll have to be more specific."

He falls silent again, but there's an intensity about him that wasn't present before. He's on the verge of saying something else when someone comes into the courtyard. I don't notice them right away, not until they're standing several feet away. When I do glance over, I don't realize what I'm seeing.

But then, a weight as heavy as a ton of bricks slams into my heart.

"No."

* * *

"THIS IS NOT POSSIBLE," I can barely push the words past my lips as I stare at the person who just walked into the courtyard. My heart hurts, but the rest of me can't feel a thing. My whole body has gone numb from shock.

"Hey, Avery," Julian says, a tentative smile on his face.

He looks exactly how I remember him. Disheveled hair and mischievous eyes. But he was dead. There is no way he could've survived a sword through the heart. He was bleeding everywhere. I remember the sound of his flesh being torn, of the smell of copper in the air. I didn't hallucinate that.

"I guess you have questions," he continues, stopping a few feet in front of me. I stand, automatically taking a step away from him. He freezes. I still haven't taken a full breath. I can't stop staring. That's why, when his eyes flicker over toward Derek, something clicks into place.

I shift my gaze, horror hitting me like a wrecking ball. Derek meets my eyes, and there's no warmth there. He's completely shut down, the impenetrable mask back in place.

"You did this," I whisper, but it seems like I'm shouting. The dull hum fills my ears, my head spinning with the meaning of this. "You know him, and you did this."

"Avery—"

"No!" I put out my hand, stopping whatever excuse Julian was about to offer. "You played me. This whole time. Both of you played me."

I'm backing up, putting some much-needed distance between me and the boys as possibilities race through my head.

"Did you know who I was when you met me?" I direct this at

Julian. Even before he nods, I see the answer in his eyes. It was all a setup.

"And you!" I turn my wrath on Derek, "What was the point of me seeing him die?"

"Answer me!" I snap when it looks like he won't. His eyes flash, but I'm too angry to be afraid. Finding out he's royalty was one thing, but this? It's like he was the one that tore my flesh to shreds. He made me think that I got Julian killed. He even comforted me over the fact. While all along, it was a lie.

And here I thought fae don't lie. I guess they can find a way around anything.

"Why did I have to watch him die?" My voice is once again barely audible. Maybe that's what finally gets him to answer.

"So you would trust me."

Five simple words but they shoot straight to my heart, taking all the wind out of me. He saved me that day. Derek played a part and pretended to help me and save me, all so that I would let down my guard. And I was stupid enough to fall for it. This one is on me.

Way to go, Avery. When you make a mistake, you make one big time.

Stay calm. Stay grounded.

Stay calm. Stay grounded.

Stay calm. Stay grounded.

The flood of emotions I'm experiencing is stirring my magic up. I would like nothing more than to blast both of them across the courtyard and against one of those massive trees. But I have to stay in control. I have to. When I do speak, my voice has found some of that calm.

"I guess your plan worked. I did trust you, and you did get me to Faery. I hope you get an extra special reward for that."

I want to scream. I want to spit in his face. I want to bring this whole building down on top of both of them. Never in my life have I felt so used, so betrayed. I let myself believe that things could be—no. I refuse to let myself go down that path.

No more.

No more self-pity.

No more trusting anyone.

I should've learned my lesson before, but it's too late now. I'll just have to be better from now on.

"I had to come of my own volition, right?" I direct this last question at Derek, and he doesn't hesitate this time.

"Yes."

I'm such a fool. I really, truly am the maker of my own ruined destiny.

"We didn't—"

Julian speaks up again, but I won't listen to it.

"There's nothing you can say that will make up for this," I interrupt, speaking to the air between the two boys. No part of me wants to look at either of them. "I'd like to be taken back to my cell now."

Raising my chin and squaring my shoulders, I wait for Derek to guide me back to my room. He doesn't. We stand like that, him looking at me, me looking out at the outer wall, for a few tense minutes. But I'm not backing down.

Refusing to succumb to begging or any other conversation, I simply pivot and head back out the way we came. At first, I think he'll just let me wander around, but then a shadow falls over me. Immediately I know it's not him. Out of the corner of my eye, I see it's one of the guards who are stationed all over the palace. Good. The less time I send in Derek's company the better.

He used me. He played me. Now I have to find a way to pay him back.

Wondering through the shadows,
Searching for answers.

The questions are asked,
But no one can hear them.

What can compare to the potential you carry?
Look at yourself,
Are you not blooming?
Are you not growing?
Can you not see it?

Magic will show you the way.

I don't remember closing my eyes, but when I open them, I know I'm no longer in my pretty prison with a view. This time, there's no darkness trying to creep in on me at every corner. The area looks bright and inviting.

Glancing down at myself, I find that I'm dressed in a simple green skater dress The color matches my green highlights exactly. On my feet are one of my favorite pair of combat boots, something I left behind at Thunderbird Academy when I ran. The outfit is very me, and it brings a smile to my face. It's really true what they say, a good pair of shoes can make you feel better. Not that I've ever really thought about it before. I never had the time. But now, I'm finding all kinds of interesting tidbits about myself. For example, I'm starting to like fashion. Who would've thought?

Deciding that I can't stand in the middle of this clearing forever, I start to walk. One thing I can never understand is if these visions are dreams or if they're something else. Last time, a dream wraith left marks on my body. The time before that, one of the Ancients threatened everyone I knew. It would be nice to have a simple, pleasant, no doomsday dream one of these nights. But I'm not that lucky.

When I break through the trees, I'm not sure what I'm expecting, but it isn't a small town opening up in front of me. It's one of those picturesque, ready for a postcard places. There's a small town hall on the right and a welcoming park on the left. I say welcoming because it literally has a sign that reads "Welcome to Hawthorne!" on a huge banner over a long table. The table itself is filled with baked goods, and there are children and adults roaming around.

Hawthorne. I know that last name. But for some reason, I can't place it. It's like a fog has come over my memory, associating what I'm seeing with a knowledge I have but not actually accessing it. I know I've never been to this town, but it feels like I would fit right in. I'm not sure what gives me that idea, but I decide I have no other choice but to explore. I can't exactly keep standing at the edge of the woods.

"Have you come to play?" A little girl, maybe five or six, runs up to me, her brown hair braided into two. At first, I don't think she's talking to me, but then she reaches for my hand and tugs on it a few times. "Have you come to play?"

"Oh, I'm not sure," I reply as she grins up at me. She radiates happiness in every part of her being, bouncing up and down as she continues to hold my hand.

"You should be sure!"

She pulls me behind her, and I have no choice but to follow. More children run by me, laughing. My heart swells at the pure happiness of the moment, at the freedom these people are experiencing here and now. But then, is this just my mind's way of dealing with stress? Am I making up charming small towns to help battle the darkness that keeps creeping in? I can't tell anymore.

"Mama, Mama!" the little girl exclaims as we come up to a woman near the outskirts of the park. "Look who I found! A new friend!"

The woman meets my eye and something close to shock goes through her. She's about thirty or so, with long hair that is braided in sections, matching that of the little girl. She's dressed in a floor length dress that swishes around her ankles. An array of necklaces and bracelets adorn her.

"Can she stay and play?" the little girl asks, keeping her hand wrapped tightly around mine. I haven't said a word yet, and I'm not sure why. All I can do is stand and watch the woman study me.

"Bri, can you please come take your sister to the cookie stand?" the woman calls out.

"But Mama! I want to stay with my new friend!" the little girl whines. Just then, another girl comes up, about two years older, her demeanor much calmer than her sister's.

"Of course, Mama," she replies, giving me the same study as her mother. All three are similar, but while the youngest has a little chaotic energy, this sister is much more like I was at her age. Quiet and contemplative. She reaches for her sister's hand. After only a moment of hesitation, the little girl grabs it. She still hasn't let go of my hand.

"I can't go, Mama," the little girl announces. "My friend will disappear."

Glancing between them, I have no idea what she means. But her mother does.

"It's okay, Harper. I have her now. You may let go."

With that, the woman reaches out, placing a small hand on my wrist. Seeing that, the little girl smiles and finally loosens her grip.

"I'll be back!" she announces and then she and her sister leave. I'm still speechless, confused at what is happening, when the woman tugs a little on my hand to grab my attention.

"I think we should have a talk, don't you?"

I nod and allow the woman to guide me away from the crowd and toward a bench on the other side of the park. When we take a seat, she still hasn't let go of my wrist.

"Can you speak?" she asks, completely baffling me. Of course I can speak. I just haven't yet. I go to open my mouth, but no words come out. Panic slams into me as I try again. I don't understand what's wrong with me.

"Shh, it's okay. May I?"

She places her free hand palm out, and I place my own in it almost without hesitation. I don't understand why I trust this woman, but I do. She reminds me of my own mother, for there is a kindness about her that's ever present.

"Close your eyes, child. And concentrate."

I do without hesitation.

"Now, breathe in and breathe out. Focus on the feel of my hand around yours, on the sensation of the breeze in your hair, the sun on your skin. Feel those things."

Up until this moment, I didn't. But then, as she talks, those things come into focus. Suddenly, the breeze is ruffling my hair.

"That's better," she comments with a small smile as I open my eyes. "Now tell me, what brought you here?"

At first, I think I won't be able to speak, but then I do.

"I have no idea."

*　*　*

THE WOMAN STUDIES me quietly for a few tense seconds, and I can't tell if my answer surprised her or not. She has one of those expressions that doesn't change. Yet, she looks approachable. She would be amazing in the Council.

"I take it you've never dream traveled before."

"I'm sorry, what?"

She smiles then, patting my hand a little before finally releasing me. I'm not sure what I'm expecting to happen but nothing does. I'm confused to say the least. This is unlike any dream I've ever had before.

"Dream traveling is very rare, and it's a skill that is learned. However, there are times when dream traveling happens to a witch on a quest without her knowing."

"Well, I definitely don't know what you're talking about. Except for the quest part. I do kind of feel like I'm in in a middle of... something."

She mentions me being a witch, but if I'm honest, that makes me feel slightly uncomfortable. No one can tell I'm a witch just by looking at me, but this woman can. I'm not getting any evil vibes off her, but it's not like I can really sense those things. I have so many questions.

"How can you tell who I am?" I start with the one that's bugging me the most. She smiles at that. Once again, I think of how much she reminds me of my mom. I miss her.

"You aren't exactly dressed as someone from around here. Plus, I know the witches in this town personally. You, my dear, are not one of them."

"Makes sense," I say, glancing around at the people enjoying their time in the park. So carefree. I don't remember if I've ever been that carefree.

"Can you tell me what dream traveling is? I don't think I've ever come across that before. I'm Avery, by the way." I feel extremely rude for not introducing myself right away. Those are my parents' instructions coming out in me.

"I am Meredith." The woman rearranges her skirt around her, making the bracelets jingle. "I am the coven leader in Hawthorne. You met my two little ones."

"Are there many witches are here?"

"More than you can probably imagine. This town is one of the strongest magical hubs in this realm. Many flock here for asylum and knowledge."

"Asylum? I didn't know witches needed that."

"Maybe in your time they don't. But right now, there are those who would hunt us down and have us destroyed. "

"Right now?"

"It is the early 90s, Avery. I assume you are from a later time."

For a moment, I don't think I hear her right. The 90s? Witches can't time travel. Not to my knowledge at least. And if that's what I'm doing, how is that possible? I didn't set out for this.

"Don't fret yourself, Avery. Like I said, dream traveling is a quest manifestation. You needed to come here, so your magic did the work for you."

I nod slowly, giving my mind time to process. There are so many questions twirling in my mind, I have no idea where to start.

"I'm sure you have many questions, Avery. I will do what I can to answer them. But we might not have a lot of time."

"Why is that?"

"Dream traveling is a very powerful magic, and it will cost your body. What is it that you are searching for?"

I go to reply, but then I stop. Can I trust her? Talking about the book and my magic, it's not something that I would do with a stranger. True, she doesn't feel like one. She feels like someone I know and respect already, and we've just met. And if I'm being honest, the whole aspect of the book isn't as much of a secret as I thought it would be. Everyone in Faery seems to know. And so do the Ancients. I just won't tell her anything that's not public knowledge. That would be the smartest thing to do.

She gives me the time I need to process all of my thoughts, sitting beside me patiently. It's something my parents would do, but they understand how my mind works. Maybe Meredith does too, somehow.

"I'm not sure how to answer that, honestly," I finally reply, looking up into her face. "I discovered an ancient book, one that can't be read by anyone in my time. Except for me."

"One of the fae manuscripts."

"You know of them?" I perk up immediately. I haven't had a chance to speak to anyone who was willing to talk about them. And I have so many questions.

"I have seen one myself when I first took the post of the coven leader. We had a little trouble in town that was resolved with some powerful magic. But these books the Ancients left are dangerous to anyone in proximity to them. The fae carefully guard those which have been found. But there are many which have not been discovered."

My right hand makes circles on top of my left as I digest the information. I knew there were other books only because I was told after I found one. Before then, I didn't know they existed. Which is what I ask now.

"We're not taught about these books. We're not taught about the Ancients. But now—"

"Please." Meredith raises her hand, stopping me from continuing.

"You have to be careful with what you tell me about your future. Specifics are dangerous information to me."

Of course. That's one rule of time travel I do know. I learned it from movies, since I didn't actually know it was possible.

"Why are such things kept a secret?" I try again, and Meredith smiles with pride at the attempt.

"The Council has rules. They have them because they believe they are protecting the rest of us."

"But you don't agree?"

"Not always. Knowledge is power, and being ignorant of the dangers out there can be our very downfall."

I understand that, of course. It's why being a Watcher and working for the Council was my life's goal. I knew I couldn't change everything about the way they did things, but I knew I could try. It would've been easier from the inside. That's no longer an option.

"If you can read the books, Avery," Meredith continues, placing a hand over my fidgeting fingers. "It means you hold great power within you. The Ancients will want to harness it. The fae will want to use it. But you must be careful. The extent of such magic will take its toll on you. There are many names for such an occurrence, and each witch is affected differently. But, Avery, when you use your magic, the magic of the book, it takes a little of your soul. You must not give that up for power."

"My soul?" My heart drops, fear rushing through me.

"There is always a cost to magic. Sometimes, it does not manifest until later. Sometimes, it is instantaneous. Be smart about who you give your magic to. If you are to use the book, then be sure you are using it for the right reasons."

I nod as I process everything she's telling me. Queen Svetlana didn't bother to tell me this. Neither did Derek. Or my own parents. Maybe they don't know. Maybe the queen just didn't care.

Of course she doesn't care. She's ready to use me for her own benefit and nothing else.

"Is this why the magic brought me here? To warn me."

"It might be. Only you can figure that part out. Maybe you just needed a safe space for a while. Don't forget that no matter what your magic may be, it is always there to take care of you."

"You truly believe that?"

Meredith doesn't reply right away, glancing over to where her girls are playing. There's a faraway look in her eyes for a moment, as if she's thinking about some other time and place. Then, she turns back to me with a smile.

"I do, Avery. Don't be afraid of your powers. Don't think you're not strong enough to carry them. We are here for a purpose, and each of us has a different path. Whatever yours may be, you are capable of handling it or you wouldn't have been given this quest."

I let that sink in, and a tear escapes, traveling down my cheek. Meredith wipes it away, much like my mom and dad would've done if they were here. I miss them so terribly it almost hurts. It should be them telling me all of this, not a stranger. But then, Meredith doesn't feel like a stranger anymore. We sit like that for a few minutes as I experience whatever emotions I need to experience and then I put them away.

"It's time for you to go, Avery," she says, standing and pulling me to my feet. "I do have one last piece of information for you."

I nod, listening intently.

"When you return to your time, you will not remember any of this."

"What?" I ask in alarm. That makes no sense. How am I supposed to use this information if I don't remember it?

"Dream traveling has its own rules and protection wards. The information will be stored for further use later. It will come to you when you need it most. Until then, it will be a silent reminder in the back of your mind."

"I don't understand."

"Magic does its own thing sometimes, sweet child. But I have full faith in you and what you will do with it."

She reaches over then, taking me by the shoulders and bringing me in for an embrace. She feels solid and comforting, and I give myself a moment to cling to her like a child would. Then, she steps back. In the same moment, everything starts to fade.

"No, Meredith!" I call out, but she's already barely visible.

I blink and then I open my eyes to stare at the ceiling. Glancing around, I forget where I am for a moment. Then the fae palace room comes into focus. My body feels exhausted, as if I haven't been sleeping this whole time. The room is still dark, so I turn over, trying to remember the dream that's at the edges of my mind. But no, I close my eyes again, forcing myself to relax. I have no idea what tomorrow holds, and I'll need to be rested for it. That much I do know.

But before I fall completely asleep, one phrase comes into my mind.

Thank you.

CHAPTER 20

The next morning, Derek is waiting in the hallway when I step out.

"No," I say, raising my hand to prevent him from speaking as I stop and wait to be led wherever they're taking me today. To say I didn't have a restful night would be an understatement. I'm still angry at him, and that won't go away.

He betrayed me.

He lied to me.

He used me.

Apparently, I'm a pawn in everyone's game at this point. Lucky me.

Nora asked me what happened, but I didn't want to talk to her either. I can't trust her, being who she is, but I didn't want to burn all of my bridges at once. I asked her, politely, to let me be and come back in the morning to help me dress. I almost opt out for my jeans and a t-shirt, but I decide it might be better to play the queen's game for now.

Instead, I'm wearing a floor-length burgundy maxi dress. The spaghetti straps leave my shoulders and part of my back bare, reminding me of the dresses my fae instructor wore at Thunderbird Academy. I told her once I could never pull something like that off, and she told me all I had to do was believe. Well, here I am, believing.

Derek decides to follow my one wish and doesn't speak. He pivots silently before leading me down the hallway. They delivered breakfast to my room, so I'm assuming we're going straight to the queen. Or whoever else would like to threaten me into submission.

When the guards open the huge double doors, I see that we have come to see the queen but also some of her advisers. They are all clustered around the table in the middle of the room. They look up when we come in.

"Ah, there you are." The queen greets us, and there is no warmth in her words or her eyes. She eyes me up and down. I can't tell if she approves of my dress or not. Derek leads me farther into the room, stopping near the table.

On it is a map of the Summer and Winter kingdoms. For some reason, the two are right next to each other. I can't see the scale for the map, but even I can see that it's huge. Faery is a large realm, bigger than any other, if I remember my studies correctly. But most of it is uncharted territory. I've heard some very feral creatures live in those parts.

"As you can see, the border has been blocked off at the east end. There seems to be a wall of ice that has grown over the course of the night."

Everyone takes a pause, sneaking glances at me. The queen just watches me expectantly. I nod once before speaking.

"That is unfortunate," I say, receiving a few gasps. But I'm not backing down. "Where are my parents?"

"I gave you my word, Avery Kincade. And I do not break my word."

"Sure. But you also don't keep it in a nice and tight timetable. Just the one that's the most convenient to you."

Her eyes flash at that because of course I'm right. She'd sacrifice my parents in a blink if it means it'll serve her purposes. And if looking for them takes away from this war, she won't do it.

"I have sent out guards and scouts. You will be the first to know when they return with more information." She gives one of the guards a nod. He turns and half runs out of the room. So, I guess she's sending them right this minute. Got it.

"When I have word that they are safe, I'll tell you where I've hidden the pages."

There are more gasps around the room, because of course, they want the book. And they definitely want it intact.

"What did you do, silly girl?" the queen snaps, her voice barely louder than before, but somehow, it echoes all around us.

"Don't worry. The pages heal themselves when placed inside the book. It'll be as good as new."

I found that out the hard way, when one of the people on the street decided to steal it from me because it looked old and valuable. Instead, he ripped two of the pages out. After I kicked him in his nether parts, I sat with the pages in my hands like some failure. When I stuck them inside the book to at least keep them there, they connected back right where they belonged. When it came time to hide the book, I used that to my advantage.

"Foolish girl—"

"Who can read the book while you can't? I'd be careful what you say to me."

"I can always glamour you to obey." There is so much threat in that one statement. If I was smarter, I'd probably keep my mouth shut. But what I am is emotional and angry. The one fae I thought was on my side played me from the very beginning. And I thought we were—no. It doesn't matter.

At this point, I don't feel like I have anything to lose.

So, I lean over the table, keeping my eyes directly on the queen.

"I would like to see you try."

Just like that, I've given her a challenge she can't back down from. But she doesn't know the one secret I've kept for most of my life. I can't be glamoured. I really would like her to try. A part of me wants to know if someone as powerful as her can break through the no glamour rule.

She watches me steadily. To anyone else, it wouldn't look like much. Fae are crafty in their glamour and most can't tell it's happening to them. Last time someone tried, I thought he was flirting poorly. But with her, I can see the power around her, like an aura. She pushes it out toward me, as if looking to envelope me in its influence. But my own magic is there, battling it away without a second thought.

After another few moments, I lean back, crossing my arms in front of me. There's a silence in the room, and maybe in all of Faery. I have challenged their queen, and I have won.

This will cost me greatly.

* * *

AFTER THE FAILED GLAMOUR TRICK, I've been banished to my room. Nora comes to see me. I'm given food but no lessons and no word about my parents. I have two days of this before I'm allowed to leave.

Nora accompanies me everywhere. Then, a week goes by, and I'm still doing nothing. Even the lessons the queen supposedly promised me don't happen. She's trying to make a point, and I get it. But it leaves me restless.

"Can we talk?" Julian asks, coming into the courtyard. I've been avoiding him for days, not ready to face whatever lies he's prepared for me. Or I guess, not lies since apparently, he's fae. But now he's invading the one time I have to myself outside my room, and that makes me even more unhappy.

"We have nothing to say to each other."

"That's not true."

"Do you even know the meaning of that word?"

I can't get over his betrayal. Maybe it's not fair. I barely know him. It's Derek I'm mostly angry at. But it really doesn't change the fact that neither one of them should be allowed in my life.

"I know what I did wasn't fair to you, but I had a good reason."

Fine then. I'll hear him out. Only because I'm curious.

"What could the reason possibly be?"

"The fae, they're not kind to those who have wronged them. My siblings and I have been living in the human world for most of our lives because of what our mother did. We actually don't even know what that is, just that we were not allowed to set foot in this realm. Working for Derek—it gave me a chance to earn that right back."

I can feel his eyes on me, and it's like he's pleading for me to look at him. When I finally do, I find no tricks in his gaze. He's asking me to trust his explanation. While I'm still mad at him, I can't fault him.

"We're not friends, Julian," I finally say, sighing. I could use a friend, but I'm not about to accept him back into my circle just like that.

"But are we enemies?"

I wish there was a way I could answer that question honestly. Because right now, I simply don't know. I thought Derek was—well, it doesn't matter. I thought things would be different when I came here. But nothing is how I expected it to be. But maybe I can offer Julian a nugget of truth.

"I don't want us to be."

The smile he gives me then could make the moon glow in the night sky. There's happiness on his face, as if I've given him the greatest gift. It's hard not to smile back. It makes sense why I never suspected him of being fae. Besides the glamour that made him look human, which now is gone, he acts like a human. Living in the human world will do that to anyone.

"So, any chance not friends and not enemies can hang out?"

The way he asks makes me think he might be as lonely as I am. I'm not sure that's possible, but it makes me hopeful. Because there is one thing that he can help me with.

"How about we spar?"

His face lights up once more, and he doesn't hesitate to come stand in front of me. I'm still dressed in my leggings and t-shirt, which might not last that long. I have a feeling one day, I'll wake up and all of my clothes will be gone. Besides the gowns the queen wants me to wear.

Julian is dressed more formally, how I've seen others dressed in the palace. Derek wears much fancier clothes, but who cares about Derek?

Get a grip on yourself, Avery. Work with what's in front of you.

I take my stance and motion for Julian to attack. He doesn't hesitate, falling easily to our old routine. After all, he's the one that helped me sharpen my fighting skills when I was in Arizona.

It seems so surreal that that life was only three weeks ago. It seems like a lifetime has gone by between now and then. My mind is lost in thought, so when Julian kicks me in the stomach, I don't block it. I stumble back, and he's immediately by my side.

"I didn't mean—"

I don't let him finish. I kick out with my own foot, landing a solid blow to his stomach. Now that I know he's built sturdier, I can practice without holding back. I've gotten stronger, I can tell that already. He punches, and I dodge, delivering my own uppercut.

Our dance continues, a familiar rhythm to our movements. Sweat collects on my forehead. I feel exhilarated for the first time in days.

Punch.

Dodge.

Kick.

Punch.

Dodge.

Punch.

We keep moving, bouncing around each other, both of our muscles working off memory. It finally feels like I'm doing something, instead of sitting in one spot, waiting for the other shoe to drop. It's hard to stay motivated about doing anything when it comes to all of this world destruction when no one has shown me one spell or one book. Like I demanded.

Okay, demand is a harsh word. I asked nicely but firmly. The queen keeps saying she'll get to it, but I'm starting to think she brought me here only to keep me locked up. Easier to control me that way.

When Julian continues to dodge my punches, I throw my whole body at him. We drop together, landing with him beneath me and me straddling him across the middle.

"I still got it," I say, satisfied with myself.

I feel him before I see him. Turning to my left, I find Derek at the edge of the courtyard, watching Julian and me with an unreadable expression. But everything about him has been unreadable. He's become completely the opposite of everything I knew from the moment we stepped foot on this soil.

"The queen is asking for you," he says now, his gaze shifting between Julian and me. I stand, rearranging my clothes a little. When Julian is beside me, he takes one look at Derek and turns to me.

"I'll see you later."

And then he's gone. Derek and I stare at each other, but there's really nothing to say. He pivots to walk back into the palace, and I hurry to follow behind.

CHAPTER 21

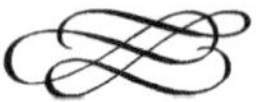

Queen Svetlana is in another room I haven't seen until now. There seems to be a very large number of them. The dress she has on barely covers all of her private bits, and the rest is completely sheer. She lays across one of the love seats, completely unbothered. I try not to show my unease.

"You are wearing your human garb again. Why?"

"I was in the courtyard for exercise. I didn't think you wanted me to get your gowns dirty."

"You could always train naked."

I glare at her, but I don't think she even realizes what she said. She's serious. It's just the way of life for her. So, I don't comment, waiting to hear why I've been summoned. In the short time I've been here, I've learned quickly that she doesn't like to be left waiting. And that's precisely what I continuously do to her.

"Your parents are safe for the time being," she finally announces, as if the words are a bother to say. Keeping my expression in control almost hurts.

"I need proof."

"I figured you would."

She waves her hand, and Derek motions for me to walk over to one of the mirrors hanging in the room. They seem to have more than one, in every area of the palace. He stops me in front of the mirror. I glance at him in question, but he simply inclines his head toward the reflection.

As I watch, the reflection ripples, much like a portal would. Then, my parents are there. They're in the kitchen having a conversation. They both look so good but tired. I've caused that.

"Mom? Dad?"

"They can't hear you," Derek says softly, coming a step closer. "The queen sent one of the wisps to check in on them."

That's why there's a gentle glow around the image. I'm seeing it through the eyes of the wisp. Then, the wisp moves, and I have to stop myself from moving forward to stop it. There's my backyard and then, right beyond the tree line, I see two shadows.

"They'll be nearby if anything happens."

I glance at Derek, too sad for a second to care about hiding my emotions. He stares into my face. In this moment, we're back at the cabin, and he's there for me. Then, everything comes back. I blink, and we're back on our individual sides of the court.

"Satisfied?" Queen Svetlana calls out, and I focus my attention on her.

"Not nearly enough, but it will do for now."

"You drive a hard bargain, Miss Kincaid. You are different than I thought you would be."

"I could say the same thing."

Walking back over to stand in front of the love seat, I place my hands on my hips and stare her down. The less fear I show, the more respect I earn. That's true for every species.

I truly don't understand her. She seems so nonchalant for someone who is apparently fighting a war. When I first met her, she was harsh and determined. Now she looks half drunk at eleven in the morning, as if she couldn't care less about anything. I really don't understand these people.

Just then, the doors open, and a small crowd pours in. Most of them aren't dressed at all. I realize this must be their day off. Slowly, I start backing out of the room, but she's not done with me.

"Now that you have your proof," she comments, sitting up more fully. I notice that her eyes are a lot clearer than they were a second ago. She too is playing a part. "You may start on your lessons. I expect results."

"Great. Show me one of your secret books, and I'll see what I can do."

"No," she says, leaning back once more. "I have something else in mind. Derek will fill you in."

She waves her hand then, dismissing us. I can't wait to get out of the room fast enough. Once the door shuts behind us, I hear bouts of laughter and something else. I move away before I hear too much.

"Glad she has time to host parties," I mumble, as we walk back toward my room.

"She too has a part to play," Derek replies, clearly hearing me.

"Please, I've seen what goes on behind these walls. I'd say doors, but no one ever bothers to close them."

"She has to keep her people happy and her allies happier. It's not an easy task."

"Didn't mean to offend your mother," I say, raising my hands in the air, as if I'm warding off an attack. I'm being a brat, but that's apparently my defense mechanism when it comes to Derek. He stops walking for a moment. I turn to see what's keeping him. He wants to say something, I can see as much. But then, it's like he shakes himself and that stoic mask is back in place. I should ask him how he turns off his feelings so well. I might need a few lessons in that.

"We should get going."

* * *

"You're not trying."

Magic lessons have been going splendidly. It's been three days, and all I want to do is strangle him. The queen thought assigning Derek to train me would work in her favor, but she really forgot the part where

I hate him now. This whole learning how to manage my personal magic before I try messing with the book magic seems more like a ploy to keep my hands occupied while not learning what I want to learn.

"Focus."

All Derek does is bark orders at me. If he was ever kind and considerate, he's the complete opposite now. Every time I actually make eye contact with him, it's like looking at a stranger. That makes it easier for me to do this.

I send a blast of my fire right at him. He sidesteps it while glaring at me.

"Focus on the water."

I'd drown him if I could. I roll my eyes, then turn back to the forest. We're on the outskirts of the palace grounds today. My task is to pull all the water from the ground. The problem, however, is that I can't sense much water at all.

"I am focusing on the water," I finally snap, turning to Derek with my hands on my hips. "There's barely any there."

"There's more than you think."

"Whatever. This is stupid."

I spin on my heels and march off into the forest. Derek calls out, but I ignore him. At this point, getting lost and being eaten by a troll sounds like a better time than spending it with Derek.

Okay, fine, I'm being dramatic. But thus is the life of a teenage witch.

"Avery!" Derek catches up to me in record time. "You cannot be wandering off like this."

"What do you care?" I throw over my shoulder, not pausing for a second. "It would look really bad if I suddenly ended up dead, huh?"

He doesn't reply, only mumbles something under his breath. But I'm not stopping to find out what it is. I need distance from him and from my emotions. Every time I see him, I'm reminded just how stupid I was to trust him. Even an iota.

We continue in silence then, with him a few feet behind me. Close enough for a rescue but far enough that it feels like I'm in the forest alone.

I have to admit, Faery does understand beauty. Even the regular type of trees look more majestic here somehow. The trunks are wider, sturdier. The leaves bigger and brighter. It's as if there's a saturation filter on everything, making the picture the sharpest it can be.

It would be easy to get pulled into its beauty and forget all the ugliness that is right below the surface. I've seen the cruel smiles, the extravagant parties that are nothing but indulgences into every known lust. I've also seen the way those who have wronged them are treated, if the daily executions or torture activities are any indication. Although, I've heard those more than seen. Nora has been keeping me in my room when that happens.

This place may be beautiful on the outside, but it's rotten on the inside. Nothing will change my mind about that.

When the shouting starts, I don't hesitate. Derek calls my name, but it's like my body is prepped for this. I take off toward the noise without a second thought. He's faster than me though, so the moment before I break through the trees, he's on me.

"Let go!"

"Will you shut up for a second?" He wraps his arms around my whole body, pinning my own arms at my sides. My magic flares up, but then his face is right near mine, and his next words are spoken directly into my ear. "Please don't fight me on this."

Instantly, my body relaxes again him. Not by some magic, but because of the way he says the words. There's real emotion there—fear for my safety—and I can't ignore it. This sounds more like the guy I got to know in that cabin. The guy I trusted.

"What's happening?" I ask, this time keeping my voice low as the sound of screaming intensifies around us. We're back near the palace now, but I can't see much through the trees. Derek puts me back on my feet, but he doesn't move away.

"The village is under attack."

"What?"

That seems unreal. The village is farther down. There's a whole lot of plain fields and forest between the palace and the village.

"There's a small collection of houses on the other side of that tower." Derek points, and I can make out the shape of it through the branches. The tower is opposite of where my room is. Because the palace is so huge, I haven't been anywhere near it.

"Those who work in the palace live in the smaller village. The houses are bigger and nicer. It's part of the incentive."

That makes sense. Just then, more screams fill the air, as if the volume was turned up. The ground shakes with magic. Every part of me is itching to get into the fight. I don't understand it, but it's like I need to protect the land I stand on.

"We have to help," I say, turning to look at Derek. "We have to. There are children there."

"You're not ready."

"Don't tell me what I am. If that's the only reason you're standing here and not out there fighting, stop it. I can help. We both can."

I can see he wants to. Just like there's a burning desire inside of me, it's in him as well. Which makes this more confusing, but then he looks into my eyes and he trusts me.

"Come on."

He grabs my hand, pulling me behind him as we take off toward the village.

CHAPTER 22

*W*hen we reach the side of the village, we're met with chaos. Areas are burning, the smoke rising high above the tops of the trees. There's more of it in the air than there should be. I realize the village below is burning too.

"Why didn't they stop them?"

"We had no warning."

Looking at Derek now, I see the horror on his face. He's not trying to hide it from me. He's feeling it all. Maybe he has to be so careful with his emotions because he feels them so much more deeply than others. I squeeze the hand I'm still holding, and he seems to come back to himself.

When I turn back to the scene in front of us, a group of werewolves rush by, chasing a few of the workers. Being this close, I can smell the fire and the burning flesh. And blood, so much blood. I can see it staining the ground near the houses.

"Those things are real," I comment, because for some reason I thought Derek made them up when he and Julian pulled his trick.

"They were back then too." I glance at him sharply, but his eyes are on the scene. "We just used what was available to us in the spur of the moment."

"You know that makes this worse."

He looks at me then. "I know."

"Good. I'll let you make it up to me later."

With that, I rip my hand from his hold and race into the fray. Derek yells, but I'm already halfway there, and the werewolves have seen me. Two rush out to meet me, but my magic is already on my fingertips. One hand forms fire, the other water. Two complete opposites, one incredible power. I thrust my hands in front of me, pushing both at the oncoming werewolves. They're swept straight off their feet, encompassed in the magic.

One drowns while the other burns.

And the sight makes me grin.

The smell of their dying flesh exhilarates me somehow. I have no time to process that information before Derek is there, throwing a blast of his own magic at one of the creatures coming toward me.

"Enjoying yourself?"

"Immensely."

It's strange to feel this excited, but it feels right somehow. As if I'm doing what I'm supposed to be doing.

Back to back, Derek and I move farther into the madness. I wasn't imagining the blood on the ground or the bodies shredded into pieces. These creatures are ruthless and they're here destroying what's mine.

Mine.

Mine.

Mine.

The word keeps ringing in my head, but I don't understand. It means nothing. It should mean nothing. But it feels right. Oh so right.

I send another blast of my magic at a group of creatures, sending them flying in opposite directions. Derek and I don't stop our progress. A part of me wishes I had a sword, so I could have more face to face combat.

What is happening to me?

I don't understand my thoughts. I'm flying high on my magic. Something is happening, and I can't put a name to it.

"Help! Please!" Sobbing reaches my ear, and I pivot toward the sound. Derek is right on my heels as we round the corner, coming face to face with a group of five of these creatures. They're werewolves, yes. But they're also bigger than last time I saw them. Nearing ten feet tall. And more rabid.

"Get away from them!" I shout. I can't see where the wolves end and the innocents begin. If I blast them with my magic, I might hurt one of the very people I'm supposed to be saving. The creatures turn to look at us, and I almost take a step back. Their eyes are red and bloodshot. The rabid part wasn't that far off because they look like they're full of something.

But they're lucid enough that they don't move away, and they don't attack.

"Derek, can you get to them?"

"I don't think so."

Our magic is precise, but if we can't actually see who's who, we might make a mess of things. My mind races with possibilities. The only thing I can come up with is rushing at them. Which probably won't end that well for us, but we have to do something.

And then, I hear it. Over the growling and the screaming in other parts of the village, a tiny sniffle and then,

"Mama?"

That one word goes straight to my heart. I pinpoint all of my focus toward it. The child is somewhere behind this wall of wolves, and he's crying. His little body shakes as he calls to his mom.

Something starts within me, a boiling of sorts. Much like on the highway, I can't tell exactly what's happening, but I don't hesitate to plunge myself right into it.

The magic swirls, rising higher and higher until it is the only part of me that is real. Water and fire dance together as it encompasses me from within. My shoulders snap back. My head falls backward, the power rushing through me. Then, like a butterfly coming out of her cocoon, my magic unfurls all around me.

I bring my head forward, my eyes directly on the group in front of me. And then, there's a smile on my face.

The magic is eager.

The magic is ready.

And so am I.

I blast it forward, zeroing on the wolf creatures, sending a mental block to anyone else in the path who isn't an enemy. It's almost as if I can see it happening. My magic covers the innocents and obliterates the evil. One by one, the werewolf creatures explode.

Dead.

Dead.

Dead.

My power spreads across the whole village, protecting and destroying and still I have more to give.

Then, when the village is clear, the magic snaps back into me. I drop to all fours, breathing heavily. Derek is there, and I see his hand reach for me before he stops. Raising my head, I find his face full of wonder and horror as he stares at me.

"What? That's not one of my bookish powers?" I chuckle, but it turns into a cough. I used so much power, it has drained me. But I also feel more me than I've ever felt before.

"Avery—"

"Don't tell me my hair is all green now."

"No, but you have wings."

I take one look behind me and then everything goes dark.

* * *

I WAKE up in my own bed, or the bed that's been designated for me. Nora is by my side the moment I stir, reaching for a glass of water.

"Here, drink this."

I take it gratefully, my throat completely parched. When the glass is empty, I hand it back. Then, Nora is there helping me sit up more fully.

"What happened?"

"What do you remember?"

"Magic practice. The attack on the village. My powers—" I sit forward, twisting to look at my shoulders but nothing is there. "Did I dream them?"

"No."

This comes from the doorway where Derek has just entered. He looks relieved to see me. Then the queen walks in. Nora stands and curtsies, but I don't even bother. If I wasn't a fan of this woman before, I'm definitely not a fan of her now. She was having orgies within the palace walls while her people were getting slaughtered right beyond them. She will never have my respect now.

"Is there anything you want to tell me?"

"You should really up your security measures in the villages." I don't even hesitate. She's pissed at me, but I'm just as angry at her.

"You think you are so funny. Who are you? What is the meaning of this?"

"Lady, I have no idea what you're shouting about. You're the one who came to find me remember? All I did was read a book."

"Don't sass me!" Her voice rings out all across the room, shaking the walls. It takes her two steps and then she's in my face. "You possess the power of Faery. How?"

She's only a foot away. I can see anger dancing in her eyes. When I met her, I thought her beautiful, and she really is. But she's also hard and ruthless, like the broken pieces of a vase. And ugly on the inside. Maybe that's what makes her such a powerful ruler.

I'm not here to cower at her bullying. Because that's what she's trying to do. My father has raised me around powerful people for this exact reason, so that I could hold my own. So, I lean forward, bringing myself right into her personal space.

"I have no idea what you're talking about."

I don't blink, making sure she understands that I will never yield to her. It might be foolish to keep antagonizing her like this, and it will probably be the end of me one of these days. But I'm not going to be accused of something that's not my fault, and I will not be punished for doing everything I could to save those people.

"You think you are so clever, little girl. But you do not know who you are messing with, child."

"Right back at ya." I smirk, and I'm not prepared for the slap across my face. My head falls back against the pillows, but I don't stay there. Immediately, I'm back, holding her gaze. I can feel the imprint of her palm across my cheek, but I still don't back down. The pain I can nurse later. Right now, I need her out of this room.

"You will learn your place. Count on that, Miss Kincaid."

She doesn't wait for a response and I don't give one. I watch her walk out of the room before my eyes turn to Derek. He watches me with that blank look on his face. When he turns to follow his queen, I notice his hands are clenched. The moment the door closes behind him, I fall back against the pillows.

"Oh, Avery." Nora is by my side immediately as I raise my hand to my cheek.

"Do you think you can get me a cold compress or ice or something?"

"Yes, absolutely."

"Nora?" She stops at the doorway, "Is the little boy okay?"

She knows exactly who I'm asking, the little boy at the village. Nora smiles before replying.

"Not a scratch on him."

She leaves then and I lay there, giving myself a moment to feel it all. Tears leak from my eyes as fear grips my heart. Pulling my knees toward me, I hug them to me, feeling like the loneliest girl in the world. If I give myself the chance, I think I would sob my heart out. But I can't. Wherever this strength is coming from, I have to hold onto it with everything I got. Once the darkness of night comes, maybe I can cry a little more, and maybe I can dream about my family and everything I've left behind. But right now, I have to stay strong.

When the door opens, I wipe at my face quickly, ready for Nora. But it's Derek who steps back in.

"Where's Nora?"

He doesn't reply. He simply walks over to the bed and takes a seat near me. That's when I notice he has a towel in his hands.

"May I?"

I nod, so he reaches for my face and turns it, placing the cold bundle to my cheek. We stare at each other, unblinking. When I reach to take the bundle from him, our hands entwine for a second.

"I can't protect you from her," he whispers, not removing his hand, even though I can hold the bundle now.

"I don't expect you to. She's your mother." Even in this situation, I don't think I can see him going against her to save me. Especially since it would be full-time job.

"No, you don't understand. I can't. I'm physically incapable."

Realization dawns on me. He has shared a real secret with me, something I don't think anyone else knows. She has power over him. I bet she would hurt him if she knew he told me.

"What happened out there?" I ask instead, giving him an out so we don't have to talk about it anymore. And because I want to know.

"You wiped all of them out with your magic. I have never seen anything like it. And then, the most beautiful translucent wings burst out of your back, as if they've been waiting to be free."

His voice is full of awe as he speaks, but I'm shaking my head.

"That makes no sense."

"It would if you had fae blood in you."

"No, I'm part witch, part shifter. My mother is a wolf shifter, and my dad is a witch. I never knew what that made me."

"A little bit of both… and—"

"And what?"

"And you have fae blood in your veins." There are those words again.

"That's not possible."

"Anything is possible."

"I'm already a mutt. That's all there is to it."

"No."

"Yes! I'm nothing special. I'm just a mixture of all the magical leftovers."

"You and I both know you are much more than that."

I glance at him again, at the intensity in his words. He reaches over pushing the hair out of my face and behind my ear. And then, I feel the most amazing tingles work their way from my ear over my neck.

"What are you doing?"

"Looking at your pointed ears."

"What?"

I push past him, dropping the cold compress and getting to my feet. He helps me stand when I sway, but then I retract my hand, heading to the mirror. Moving my hair out of the way I find myself looking at pointed ears, much like those on Derek.

"I don't understand."

"I think I do."

"What are you saying?" I can't seem to take my eyes off the slightly pointed ears.

"That you were glamoured to look a certain way," Derek replies, standing behind me so that I can see his reflection in the mirror. "Your father made a choice, and you had to pay for it."

"By what? Living the life of a lie?"

"If that's the way you want to look at it."

"How do you know it was my father?" I can't get over this.

"If your mother is a wolf shifter, he's the only option."

All of this is too much. I have powers I don't understand. But I guess that's true two times over now. I stare at myself, at the new me, and I can't wrap my mind around it. I thought that it was the magic of the book that was fueling my newfound strength, but what if it's Faery itself? If what Derek is saying is true, then I have finally come home.

The queen summons me the next morning. I've hidden my ears from everyone but Derek so far, but I'm sure that's going to come out soon enough. I asked him what the deal was with my wings, and he said some fae have them as a display of power. Or a conduit. Since they've disappeared after the fight, I'm putting that problem on the back burner for now.

Now, Nora and I are walking toward her war room. I'm once again dressed in one of the dresses Nora picked out for me. This time it's a deep blue, halter top style maxi dress. It's probably the simplest piece of clothing in that closet. Still, it sparkles as I walk, and somehow, that makes me feel better.

When we enter, Queen Svetlana is sitting at the head of the table, her advisers talking around the table as she listens. Nora steps back to stay at the doors as I continue into the room. Everyone stops and stares at me. Honestly, I can't even begin to guess what they're thinking.

"Feeling better, Avery?" It's the first time she's called me by my first name. I have no idea how I feel about it. There's an undercurrent to her words, but I decide to be polite.

"Yes, much better. All the rest has done wonders for me."

She narrows her eyes at my tone but doesn't comment. Instead she stands, then she motions for someone to come over. Derek steps up, coming to stand near me.

"You have finally reached the next level, Avery," the queen says, coming to a stop in front of us. "You wanted more power, and you have it. Now, you have to use it."

"What do you mean?"

"It means that I am sending you on a mission. You and Derek here, since you work oh so well together." She's smiling, but there's no kindness in that expression. I force myself not to look at Derek, but she can tell that too. She's a queen for a reason, I suppose. "I need you to retrieve one of the books."

"They're not at the palace?"

"Of course not. We too know how to hide our treasures. Retrieve it and you may use three passages as practice. But only those I pre-approve."

It's hard not to show my excitement, as I would absolutely love to try out some of those spells. Instead, I just keep my face as impassive as possible, waiting for her to finish this little speech. She moves closer, so that now she's speaking only to me.

"Do not think that you are not a pawn here. My eyes are everywhere and so is my magic. If you cross me, you will pay for it." She steps back, giving me a bright smile. "Now is this not exciting?"

"Absolutely." I reply with my own fake smile in place.

She lets me leave but keeps Derek there. I don't even look at him as I walk out of the room. Nora hurries beside me, chattering about packing and how careful I'll have to be and how dangerous the area she's sending me to is.

"You know where I'm going?"

"The guards talk, Avery. And they especially talk to me. You have to promise to be careful."

The way she's looking at me, I don't think you can fake that kind of emotion. In the time that I've been here, we've become something close to friends. When we reach our room, someone is waiting in front of it.

"Is it true what they're saying?" Julian asks as Nora pushes past us and into the room. I motion for him to follow as well, because at least in the room I can pretend no one is listening.

"To what exactly are you referring?"

"The wings, Avery. You have wings?"

"Do I look like I have wings? You shouldn't believe everything you hear in palace gossip." I give him a small smile, but I'm not fooling him. Even though I apparently don't suffer from the fae rule of no lying. Thankfully, he seems to see through my bluff. But he doesn't push the issue too much.

"What now?"

"Now, she packs because we're leaving as soon as you're ready," Derek announces as he walks into the room.

"Oh look, the whole party is here."

I study each face, the three fae that have become my only companions. I don't have any idea what to think. I can't trust myself to trust them, because clearly, I'm not the best judge of character. But also, how am I supposed to trust anyone when I no longer trust myself?

The only thing I can do is focus on the task at hand.

"Nora says where we're going is dangerous. Is that true?" I direct my question at Derek. He watches me for a moment before nodding.

"It's near the front lines of eastern front. The Ancients seem to be pressing in on us from every side."

"Derek, that's near—" Julian begins, but Derek cuts him off with a look.

"No, please share. It's near what?"

The boys exchange a look, but neither speaks. Nora grunts before turning to me.

"It's near the forbidden forest. The uncharted part of Faery."

"Right. Where all the scary... I mean scarier monsters live." But I'm missing something. All three of them share some other secret I'm not privy to. "What? You all forgot how to speak?"

"You know this errand is a sham, right?" Derek finally speaks up, and I roll my eyes.

"I was hoping not, but I'm not that naïve. I expect her to have something up her sleeve."

"Well, there's a way for you to learn more about your powers. But it would involve going through the forbidden forest."

Of course. Why would I expect anything else?

I turn away, heading to the window to give myself a moment to come to terms with everything that's happening. And it's happening so fast. Every time I think I've found my footing, something knocks me down again. On top of everything else, I now have to figure out this whole who-I-am business. But maybe this explains, at least partially, while I feel so connected to this land and its people. I called them mine before I knew what that meant.

"I heard what she told you." Derek comes up to stand beside me at the window. I still don't understand where he stands. One minute he's my friend, the next, an enemy. Sometimes he looks at me like I matter, and then, I'm nothing to him. Now, he's going to try and help me outwit the queen? It's exhausting trying to guess who he is. It's a ride I don't want to be on.

"I think she meant for you to hear," I reply. I've already decided to keep him at arm's length. Why is it so difficult to keep to my own decisions?

"You're right. Do you still think coming here was the right choice?"

"No. I don't know. A part of me, I guess. I wouldn't have known I have these powers until I stepped foot in Faery, that much I do know. But what does that really make me? I don't even know."

"It doesn't matter."

"Doesn't it?"

"It doesn't matter now, and we both know that. You have a choice to make. Will you let the past rule your present or will you make your own way?" Derek angles himself so he can look me right in the eye. He's right of course, but there's no way I'll admit that any time soon.

"You'd like me to *make my own way* because that would lead me to follow you to whatever battlefield the Summer court is fighting at."

I turn away, frustrated with the fact that there are no good choices.

"No." That one word stops me. I look over my shoulder to find

Derek's whole body one rigid statue. "I would personally never force you to fight. But that is one of your options."

The saddest part of all of this is that I can't trust anything he's saying. How do I know he's not here to make sure I play my part? The Summer Court needs me. I've seen the hunger in Queen Svetlana's eyes. She craves ultimate power, and with me by her side, she'd have an upper hand in every battle.

The Ancients are at her gates. While I don't like her, she is a strong ruler, and she will do what it takes to stay that way. But I now have a chance to become something more than just a pawn, regardless of what she threatens.

When I decided to come to Faery, I decided to give them a chance to teach me about my power. Then, I discovered that I'm made up of even more bits than I thought. It's time to do what I came here to do. Even if I end up all on my own, I have to give it a try. So, I turn to Derek with Julian and Nora standing behind him, and I give them a wide smile.

"Let's go to the forbidden forest."

BLOOD OF THE FAE

THE FAE CHRONICLES #2

The world spins round,
The time flies by.
The day has changed,
The time has come.

The war is here,
As the Ancients rise.
One true hero,
Must take up the fight.

The winds are changing,
As the powers grow.
The night is coming,
But the break of dawn—is not far at all.

CHAPTER 1

I've been staring at the mirror for the last ten minutes, willing the wings to appear once more. Nora is busy packing a bag for me while the guys have disappeared to do their own preparation. I should help or something. But I can't stop staring at myself.

Pulling my hair gently over my ear, I study the upward arch and the pointed end. So far, only Derek has seen this new addition. It's probably wise for me to keep it that way. The wings have stirred enough controversy for now. Queen Svetlana is not happy with my display of power. She was trying to keep me a secret, but that went out the window. That's why she's sending me on this pointless mission.

It's for sure pointless. And dangerous. She's playing with me, but that's fae. I have no choice but to go along. I need answers even more than she needs my power, and this is my only chance. Plus, putting some distance between myself and this palace is an added bonus.

"Are you ready?" Nora comes out of my walk-in closet, and I drop my hair back in place quickly. She holds a cross-body bag in one hand and a jacket in the other. I look down at my dress.

"Let me change."

It takes me five minutes to get into my jeans and t-shirt. The moment the clothes are on, I feel more like myself. Not that I don't love the fancy dresses I've been wearing, but they haven't been mine. Since everything else in my life seems to belong to someone else, I need something of mine right now.

When I step out of the closest, Derek and Julian are back. Both of the guys are in dark pants and dark shirts. Julian is already in a jacket while Derek shrugs his on. They turn to look at me, and no matter how hard I try, I can't read either one of them. Right now, they look more fae than I've ever seen them, even though they're dressed in human clothes. I wonder if that's meant to make me feel better or if the clothes make them more comfortable.

"We need to go. The queen has already inquired about our status." Derek speaks in that detached tone of his. I hate when he sounds like that. It reminds me just how little I can trust him.

"It's been less than an hour," I comment.

"She likes to be obeyed immediately," Nora mumbles, handing over a jacket. I put it on before I pull the strap of the bag on as well.

I grab the hair tie around my wrist and pull half of my hair away from my face, keeping it low enough to hide the ears. Derek doesn't miss the move, his eyes steadily on me.

Once I'm done, I face the guys as we eye each other. If anyone asks, I will lie and say I'm ready. But in reality, my insides are a mess, and I feel like I'm going to throw up. I'm more nervous than I can put into words.

"Avery." Nora's voice breaks through my internal freak out. She steps into my line of sight, forcing my eyes on her. "Trust your instincts above all else. The magic of the forest," she lowers her voice, "it's messy and manipulative. But if you trust yourself, you will get through it."

"That's the problem, isn't it?" I chuckle without any humor. I don't trust myself or my magic. When I found that book at Thunderbird Academy and read the words that haven't been read in centuries, everything I knew about magic went up in flames.

Nora places her hand on my shoulders, meeting my eyes.

"You are stronger than you give yourself credit for. Remember that."

The intensity behind her words doesn't escape me. Fae can't lie, and therefore, she truly believes what she says. It's a good reminder. I just need to get to this level.

"Keep us updated when you can," Derek tells Nora as she steps back. She nods and then it's time.

The queen is sending us to the eastern front, or close to it, to fetch one of the ancient fae books no one but me can read. It seems like so much more than just a simple test though. I'm determined to pass whatever obstacle she throws my way. I'm sure this won't be the only one. She expects me to fail, and I refuse to give her the satisfaction. That thought will have to guide me through what comes next.

"We'll portal into the area and go from there," Derek says. I understand what he's not saying. We have our own mission underneath the one the queen has given us. While I don't trust fae as far as I can throw them, right now, I need them.

"Let's do this then."

* * *

THE PORTAL IS a ripple in the air in front of us. I step through it with no hesitation, much like I did at Thunderbird Academy. Derek leads the way with Julian right behind me. I glance back just in time to watch Nora disappear from view.

When I turn back to the guys, their attention is on the forest around us. I hear it right away, the low hum of activity that surrounds us on every side. The forest is restless.

"We're not too far from the eastern front. There's a base camp to the south, About a two-hour walk or so."

"Why so far?" I ask, facing Derek. He pulls his attention from the forest and looks over at me.

"Since the Ancients are on the borders, magic here is very regulated. The queen doesn't want to unnecessarily fuel something they're doing with her magic. I'm sure you've heard about their syphoning powers."

"Yes."

Everyone knows about what happened in Hawthorne two years ago, and at Thunderbird Academy last school year. The Ancients have a way of getting inside even the most protected areas and then infecting the magical creatures with a disease that steals their magic and kills them slowly. This has happened in many places over the last few years, and it's something the witches are constantly working to prevent. I was going to be on the council to help fight this problem... before my life changed entirely.

"The fae are weaker than anyone would like to admit," Julian says, coming to stand beside me. "We have to take every precaution."

It's one of the few times he's put himself in the same category as the fae, and I take notice. These boys might be different than most of the fae, but they're still here for themselves and their homeland. I can't forget that.

"So, what do we do?"

"We go the other direction."

Derek turns north, squaring his shoulders. He's worried, I think. I can't read his emotions as easily as I could at the cabin. But I do think we're still connected on some level. Despite all the secrets he's keeping, he's been helping me. Or something along those lines. There's tension in his shoulders and determination on his face.

"Anyone going to tell me exactly what awaits us in the forbidden forest?" I ask as we start walking. The trees here are so much bigger than I've ever seen before. At first, I think my eyes are deceiving me. But as I blink a few times, I realize there's a shine around every piece of nature, including individual leaves and blades of grass. Pausing, I reach over to run my fingertips over the closest branch, completely in awe. The magic is in every living thing here. It almost calls to me. It's so beautiful, I think I could stay here forever.

"Avery?" Suddenly, Derek is in front of me, leaning down to catch my eye.

"What?"

"Are you okay? You've been standing frozen for a few minutes."

"I—" I turn back to the leaf, my fingers still touching it gently. Maybe it doesn't *almost* call to me, maybe it *actually* does. And that's dangerous. I remember what Nora said about the pull of the forest. I'll have to be more proactive about keeping myself protected.

"I feel it, Derek," I say, glancing up at him. "I feel the magic in the air and in the leaves and in the ground beneath my feet. It's like... I don't know how to explain it."

But I do. I just don't want to say it out loud. It feels like I belong here, and I have no idea what to do with that.

"Faery is filled with magic, Avery," Derek says, reaching over and tugging gently on the front of my jacket. I step away from the branches, dropping my arm. "There is a lot of it in you. Magic you don't yet understand."

He pauses, as if he's trying to figure out what else to say, but I shrug it off.

"Yes. Let's get going. I'll keep up."

An emotion flashes in Derek's eyes, too quick for me to decipher. He nods and turns away, dropping the front of my jacket back into place. I meet Julian's eye as Derek moves past him. There's something there too, but these fae are good at keeping their emotions under lock and key. I need to take some pointers.

Without a word, I follow Derek as Julian brings up the rear.

CHAPTER 2

The forest grows darker and fuller around us as we walk. The buzz of magic I felt in the air from the beginning has only intensified. There's a film of static over my skin, and I'm hyper-aware of every move we make.

Having fae magic is a new experience, one I don't know what to do with yet. I keep expecting the wings to burst out of my back, but of course, that's just dumb. Or maybe it's not. I have no idea. Not knowing things is very frustrating and not at all pleasant.

"So, how do we know when we've reached the forbidden forest?" I break the silence while still keeping my voice low. I'm smart enough to know there are things hiding in the trees that might not want us here. We have to be careful, but at the same time, I need at least small amounts of information to stay sane.

"We'll know," Derek replies without turning around or slowing down. I roll my eyes at him, even though he can't see it, and I hear Julian chuckle. Glancing over my shoulder, I notice him shake his head before he looks over at me.

"What?"

"Nothing."

I narrow my eyes but don't push further. The intuitive part of me thinks I don't want to know what's going on in Julian's head anyway.

We walk for a few more moments in silence before Julian appears at my side, keeping pace. I wait for him to speak, since he clearly wants to say something. After a few minutes, he finally does.

"The forbidden forest carries magic within in, just like the rest of Faery. The difference is that it's almost dense in a way. The moment we pass the border, it'll feel like we're carrying a physical weight."

I narrow my eyes, mulling over the information. Faery is one of those places that, no matter how much I study about it, I still know next to nothing. I am severely unprepared for the direction my life has turned.

"Is this a well-known fact, or have you been here before?"

"I haven't."

Julian doesn't have to add anything else because I hear the end of that sentence. Derek has. I shift my eyes toward the prince, who's a little way ahead of us now. Once again, I wonder about him. I really should stop, but I'm not going to. It's foolish to pretend I'm not curious about him.

We fall back into silence, the only noise coming from the forest around us. I keep expecting something bad to happen or some attack to come at us from beyond the shadows, but there's nothing. It's almost as if the world around me is also holding its breath, curious to see what will happen next.

The tips of my ears tingle just then, and I reach for them before I can stop myself. It's not an unpleasant feeling, but it's also a very strange sensation. My hair still covers the tips, but when I run my fingers over it, the pointed end is there.

"What is it?" Julian asks, coming up beside me. He fell back behind me, but now he's watching me curiously. He hasn't seen my ears yet, and I drop my hand quickly before replying.

"I'm not sure."

"Avery, are you sensing something?" Derek asks, backtracking to stand in front of me. I send a glare his way because Julian is now ready to ask all the questions.

"What's going on?"

Resigned, I tuck my hair behind my ear as I say, "The wings weren't the only thing to show up with my magic."

When Julian's eyes land on my ear, he takes an automatic step back. Derek does a double take as well, and my heartbeat speeds up at their alarm.

"What?"

Neither one speaks, so I raise my hand and snap my fingers in front of their face. They visibly jerk, as if coming out of a trance, turning their gazes on me.

"You guys need to learn how to voice your concerns. What's happening?"

Julian clears his throat, but it's Derek who finally replies.

"May I?" His hand reaches for my hair, and I have no choice but to nod. He pulls it away from my ear, studying it like he's never seen anything like it before. I try not to fidget under the scrutiny, but both of them are making it very difficult.

"Derek?" I finally prob when his fingers brush gently over the tip of the ear, sending a flood of goosebumps down my arm.

"It's something I haven't seen before."

"What, an earlobe?"

"No," Derek steps back, letting my hair fall back against my scalp. He stays close enough that I have to look up to meet his gaze. "Your skin, it has been…painted."

"What?" Look at that, it's my favorite word.

"There's a sort of design, almost like your veins are full of gold that wraps itself around your ear." He says it gently, but panic comes anyway. My hand flies up to my ear. I rub it and move it around, but I can't feel anything.

"I need to see."

"We're not exactly carrying a mirror with us."

I step over to Derek, push his jacket aside, and yank the blade from the sheath around his waist. He doesn't even react to my proximity as I raise the blade with my right hand and move my hair to see better. It's distorted, but even I can see the golden lines wrapping themselves around my skin. I move to the other side, looking at my right ear, but there's nothing there.

"It's only on my left?"

"It appears so."

"What does it mean?"

I glance from Derek to Julian to Derek again, but they have no answers for me. It's evident that they haven't seen this before, which raises my concern. I can't even demand answers because they don't have any.

My body continues to change in strange ways, and there's nothing anyone can do about it. Not even me.

It's another few hours of walking before Derek decides it's time to stop for the night. We find a small clearing. While Julian is tasked with putting together a fire, Derek disappears into the trees to make sure we're truly alone.

He hasn't said a word to me since the golden design appeared on my ear. He seems to be more concerned than I am. I guess maybe a part of me is getting used to the fact that nothing about me is what I thought.

All my life I just thought I was the normal kind of weird. Half witch, half shifter. Not exactly accepted by the standard magical community, but the blunder my parents created by falling in love is more known than not. Adding to the fact that I have fae blood in me somehow? That's a blunder no one will ever forgive. Maybe not even me.

My parents lied to me. Of that I am sure. The only logical explanation I can come up with is they were waiting to tell me the truth. Maybe once I became a Watcher and would be more protected by the council because of my standing with them, then my parents would be able to be honest with me. Or maybe they were going to keep this from me forever.

The logical side of my brain is working to understand their situation. The emotional side is just hurt they kept such a huge secret from me.

Mad.

Frustrated.

Betrayed.

"Are you okay?" Julian asks, looking up as the fire begins to crackle. The flames dance across Julian's face, and he's not hiding his concern as he studies me.

"I'm working on it," I reply, taking a seat as I shake away the feelings and grab a stick to poke at the fire. It gives me something to do, and Julian doesn't question it. Instead, he takes a seat opposite of me, lapsing into silence.

I have so many things I want to ask him. I've learned a little bit about him since he appeared at the palace, but both he and Derek confuse me so much. I see the way Queen Svetlana is. I watched how the others behave within the palace walls. But these two fae seem nothing like that, and I can't wrap my mind around it.

"So that whole stealing from the Council plan you had back in Arizona, was that just part of the ruse?" I ask Julian, as I tend to the fire. My question clearly takes him by surprise, and he watches me for a second before he replies.

"No." He's silent for a moment, as if he's contemplating how much to tell me. "It was really going to be a way for me to get away. My mission...I didn't have a choice to come find you. But I might've gotten away if we went through with it."

I can't blame him for wanting more out of life than to follow someone else's rules. I guess none of us really have a choice in all of this. But I never thought he wouldn't. I'm learning more and more about the way of the fae, and I have to admit, they're not my favorite people. Or creatures. Or whatever the proper term is because I'm not even sure about that anymore. A lot of good all my education is doing for me now. But I can't really blame the education, just the people who wouldn't teach me what I actually needed to know.

Yes, I'm back to being mad at my parents. Apparently, this will come in waves.

"Why are you and Derek so different from the other fae?" I risk the question, turning my attention to the present. I reach for my bag and pull out some fruit as I wait for Julian to answer. He seems to need a moment to collect his thoughts. When he finally replies, his words are barely a whisper.

"Because we want more for ourselves."

Pausing, I glance over at Julian, but his eyes are on the fire. He seems a hundred miles away. His expression is unguarded, and I realize, it's maybe for the first time since I've met him. There's history there. If Derek was sitting next to him right now, I wonder if his face would carry the same look of wanderlust. But maybe I don't have to wonder. I've seen the way he is with the queen. Regardless of his betrayal toward me, the need for things to be different is real. If nothing else, I can trust that.

"Do you really think I can make that happen?" I ask because I need to know this isn't all in vain. The fear that I'll make things worse is ever present. But before Julian has a chance to reply, another voice speaks up from the shadows.

"We know you will."

Derek steps into the circle of the light, his eyes reflecting the dance of the flames. There's that intensity again, the Derek I'm used to seeing. He truly believes what he's saying, and at this moment, I have no choice but to trust him. Trust both of them. Everyone has something at stake here.

CHAPTER 3

sudden blast of magic jerks me awake. I sit up, panting, as I glance around to see where it came from. But the night is completely quiet. Julian is asleep a few feet to my left on the other side of the fire. The closer we've gotten to the forbidden forest, the less noise the trees around us make. Right now, it's especially unnerving.

I search for Derek and find him a dozen feet away, barely outlined against the tree he's leaning against. His gaze is on me. I don't have to see it to know it's true. My skin prickles with awareness.

Since coming to Faery and finding out the truth about Derek's lineage, we've been in this constant state of suspension. I think if we were still at the cabin, he would come to me. Or maybe I'd go to him. But now, neither one of us knows how to act around the other.

This trip is at least giving us a chance to do something. Whatever it may be. I don't trust Queen Svetlana, but I'm also having a difficult time trusting myself. I hold powers I didn't even know existed. And the land around me is reacting to it.

How I wish for the comfort of books right now. I want my notebooks and big research encyclopedia volumes filled with information. I want a large table where I can sit for hours and pour over the history of Faery and the Ancients. But I don't have any of that. All I have is the memory of a book that I should've never read and the weight of worlds on my shoulders.

I'm not so naive that I don't know what would happen if Faery falls. It would spill into other worlds, other dimensions. There would be no rest for anyone because the Ancients would win.

And they are not kind rulers.

Since waking up, their stories have finally been told, after generations of keeping them secret. I've done all the research I could to learn about them and how they operate, and it's not enough. They want me, and that's a constant fear I carry in my heart.

The same feeling that woke me up returns, magic shaking me from inside. Looking down, I watch as my palm ignites with fire. It's the elemental magic I've carried with me since birth. It's been giving me problems for months now, even before I started at Thunderbird Academy.

But it hasn't acted on its own before.

It makes me feel like I'm a little kid again, just coming into my powers. I've been told my whole life that magic is fueled by emotions, and right now, I have no idea what's going on inside of me.

Just as quickly as the flame ignites, it's extinguished. Only it's not extinguished by my will but by another form of elemental magic. Water pools in my palm. It douses the fire, which dissipates without a sound.

This water magic is a new development and not something I thought was possible. Most elemental witches carry one element within them, while they can respond to others. But to have control over more than one? It's rare and terrifying.

The buzz of magic rushes over my skin as the water spills over onto the ground, as if I've just poured a cup. It's like the land itself is responding to my magic. Leaning down, I watch the water disappear. My palm ignites in fire again, this time, against the dirt. Then, the space around me glows, and I feel my newest additions before I see them.

"Wow."

Turning, I notice Julian sit up. His eyes are on me. Derek has moved closer as well, and they're both staring. I glance over my shoulder. The glow from my wings is the most beautiful light I've ever seen.

The wings are clear with a bluish outline and so shiny, they're blinding. For a moment, I sit mesmerized, but then they move. My heart thuds harshly, as if I've just come through a jump scare, but I don't dare breathe too loudly. The desire to touch them is overwhelming. The moment the thought comes into my head, they move again. This time they open completely, so they're within easy reach.

I raise my left hand, swinging it backwards under the wings before I let my fingers walk over the edges. The sensation is almost indescribable. It's similar to how it felt having Derek touch the tip of my fae ear.

Intimate.

Tingly.

Breathtaking.

Glancing over my right shoulder, I do the same thing, letting my fingers explore. Even though I possess magic and can wield fire, and now water, this still feels surreal somehow. Like it's not me who's experiencing this phenomenon.

Derek and Julian have both moved closer, but they don't reach for my wings.

"I've never seen something so beautiful," Julian whispers. I look over to find him completely mesmerized. He looked surprised by my ears, but he looks in awe at my wings. When my eyes find Derek's, he looks just as amazed as Julian. But his eyes aren't on the wings, they're on me. It's difficult not to let the hundreds of emotions rush into me right then and there.

Wanting.

Needing.

Begging.

"Are there no fae that have wings?" I dare to ask, even though I know it'll break the atmosphere. But I can't let myself be ruled by hormones, or whatever this is. I have to stay on track.

"No," Julian replies. I'm still watching Derek, so I see the moment his jaw twitches.

"Derek?" I prompt.

"There were stories," he replies with a sigh, "of old families with the power of the wings. It used to be common for fae, but it's a magic that has long ago gone dormant."

"Not so dormant, I suppose," I say, reaching for my wings once again. But before I can touch them, they're gone. As if they were never there.

"I don't understand. Where do they go?"

"Back inside of you."

That doesn't answer anything, but when I open my mouth to ask more, Derek turns away.

"We should get some rest," he throws over his shoulder as he stomps away. Okay, maybe stomps is too dramatic, but it feels like he's being dramatic right now. I roll my eyes but don't argue.

However, instead of laying on my back, I turn to my side. Even though they're no longer there, I fear I might squish them. And they're too beautiful for that.

* * *

I SLEEP, but I don't rest. When it's time to move, we have a quick breakfast from the fruit Nora packed for us, and then we're off. Each of us is silent, lost in our own little world. I keep going over what happened last night, the way my magic reacted to the land. And then the wings.

A lost magic. And I have it.

If I'm being honest with myself, I have more than one, and that's scary. I'm trying really hard not to the think about the whole book magic right now because I can only handle so much at a time. So, the wings are where I focus. There is something that's not sitting right with me after last night.

I hurry to catch up with Derek because he's the only one who can provide any kind of answers right now. He's ignoring me extra hard this morning, but I'm relentless.

"What did you mean last night about the families?" I ask, diving right into it. He glances over at me, and I swear there's a spark of amusement in his eyes before he snuffs it out.

"Just like that?"

"Yes, just like that. No reason to beat around the bush." He crunches his eyebrows down in confusion, but I press on. "You have information. I need information. Share. It's that simple."

"Nothing about us is simple, Avery."

The way he says my name sends a plethora of tingles down my back, but I try not to show it. I should not be reacting like this to anything Derek does. Especially the sound of my name on his lips. Yet, my traitorous body has other ideas. It gets all warm and bubbly around him.

What am I even thinking right now? Focus, Avery.

Somehow, I'm afraid Derek can tell what's going on in my mind. So, I put on my best glare and don't let up.

"That may be true, *Derek*, but it doesn't change the fact that you know something. Tell me."

"You're bossy today."

"As opposed to other days? Don't change the subject."

I don't turn around, but I swear I hear Julian chuckle behind us. He's wisely staying out of this. I think Derek is about to argue some more, but then he surprises me.

"There's not much I can tell you, to be honest. The old families, they're not exactly welcomed at court."

"Why is that?"

"Because Queen Svetlana does not like to be one upped in her own palace."

The purely human phrase stumps me for a moment because, even though he usually sounds human, he still surprises me when he says something like that. Then, I realize the other thing I've noticed. He never refers to Queen Svetlana as his mother. Maybe that distance can work in my favor.

"So, who were they? Just other fae who lived in court?"

"From what I understand, the families were all part of a ruling council. Yes, the king sat on the throne, but the council was there to advise and protect. They had the most powerful of Faery magic, and they protected and nourished the land with it."

"Because fae are so connected to the land." It's not a question, but Derek replies anyway.

"Fae need nature, but nature needs the fae. It's a balance of give and take, and it's the most powerful when it's balanced. When Queen Svetlana took the throne, she didn't want balance. She wanted power. So, killing off the council was in her best interest."

"She's that old?" I ask, before I stop to think about it. This time Julian definitely chuckles. Derek manages to mask most of his smile.

"You forget fae live for a long time, Avery." He looks down at me at those words, and there's almost a hint of sadness there. "She is older than she appears, one of the oldest in the land. There's a reason she's held power for this long."

That means she is ruthless, and here we are, disobeying her orders. I'm not sure how I feel about any of this, but I don't have time to mull over it because we're no longer alone.

The feeling comes at once, as if a door has been opened, and we can see beyond it. I'm instantly on alert. A moment later, so are Derek and Julian. I wonder why I sensed it before they did, but I'm not about to question it.

"Avery, you'll need your magic," Derek mumbles as he reaches for his sword. Julian is beside us in a flash, his sword already drawn. We don't stop moving. In the next moment, it feels like a heavy weight has been placed on my shoulders. I glance over at the boys, and I know they feel it too.

We have entered the forbidden forest. And we have company.

CHAPTER 4

$\mathcal{E}$verything is darker here, but somehow, more vivid. It's like the colors aren't bleached out by being in the sun. We move together, keeping our steps sure. I'd be lying if I said I'm not scared. Whatever is out there, it's hunting us now. It was hunting us before we even entered the borders of the forest.

"We need to find high ground or open space," Derek states without missing a beat. Even without giving our surroundings a thorough study, I know that's not possible. We can climb a tree, but I'm not sure that'll do us any good, since we're being watched.

That's the one thing I know for sure. It's like I can feel the extra pressure of their eyes on me. It adds to the heaviness of the forests. After not resting last night, I wonder how I'm going to fight. Because we'll have to. I can feel it coming.

"Derek, on your left."

"I see it."

I shift my eyes in that direction, but I don't see anything. I don't know what I'm looking for, so I can't even pretend to find it at this point. With Derek in front of me and Julian behind me, I'm between two powerful and trained fae. I should feel better, but I can't shake the feeling that whatever is out there doesn't care about them. It's here for me.

Suddenly, a noise like a thousand wolves hounding fills the air, nearly overpowering my eardrums. Grabbing my ears, I look around, trying to figure out where it's coming from. Before we get our bearings, another noise reaches us. Happy yapping scatters all around us.

I glance up. It takes me a second to realize what I'm seeing.

"Are those…" I shout to be heard over the noise.

"Boggarts." Derek and Julian shout together.

I've only ever read about the creatures in books. They don't hang out in the forests around my hometown. They're nasty creatures. Their huge eyes are the size of saucers, and they have lanky limbs. The creatures are about the size of a calf, their skin leather-like. Their arms are so long, they almost reach to the ground. The hair that covers their whole bodies is shaggy and dirty. I can smell them even from a few dozen feet away.

The noise they make is disorienting, their first line of offense. Some can leap up to ten feet in the air and forward, which makes getting away nearly impossible. From what I read, there are dozens of types of these creatures, but none of them are ever nice in the stories. They look like they can rip us limb from limb.

"We need to move. They smelled us even before we stepped into the forbidden part of the forest." It's hard to hear Derek over the noise, but I get the gist of it. The boggarts were lying in wait. Without a moment to spare, we take off running. The boggarts are on our heels.

They're like a swarm of bees, moving together in a swirl of noise. When the first one lands between us, it throws us in opposite directions. I scream. Yanking the knife I carry on my thigh out of the sheathe, I roll to the left as another creature lands in that spot. I'm on my knees in the next moment, grounding myself as I reach for my fire magic.

The creature leans forward, screaming that awful sound into my face. I push my pain away as I swipe at it, swinging, somewhat blindly. My blade connects with his skin, and the creature screams in agony. I don't hesitate to blast a line of fire at it, sending it flying a dozen yards back.

My magic ignites, a rush of power over my whole body as I blast another creature away. It seems the more I use it, the happier my magic is. Maybe it's a strange thought, but I don't push it away. I embrace it.

Another creature reaches me. I swipe at it a few times without landing any blows. Then, suddenly, I'm on the ground as another boggart jumps on my back. The thing is strong, clawing at me with its long arms and even longer nails. Even after all the years of battle training, I am not prepared for this. It takes all my strength to stay upright as I try to shake it off while preventing the other from getting to me.

We drop to the ground. I go to roll out of the way, but now two of them are on top of me, tearing at my hair and my skin. My fire magic ignites, sending a blast all around me. The creatures yelp but don't let up. Their leathery skin is protecting them somehow, and the momentum of the fire is diminished by my position. I have to be smarter.

I kick out, managing to land a blow while I swing my arm out again, still holding onto the knife. I need a protection spell, but my mind is so scrambled, I can't focus long enough to call on my power. In the midst of the battle, I'm useless. The thought almost drags me down faster than the boggart grabbing my leg and pulling me toward him. I end up flat on my back once more, throwing my arms up to protect my face as the creatures descend and scream at me.

My body shakes from the sound, disorienting me once more. That's when I stop thinking.

Instincts take over. The next thing I know, a wall of water rushes up out of the ground, sweeping the monsters away. They scream, this time in agony, as the water slams them against the trees and the ground. It takes me a second to realize what happened, but then I jump to my feet. Julian and Derek are to my left. Both of them are now in the protection of my water circle.

"I thought you were a fire elemental," Julian comments, his face a mixture of confusion and awe. He must not have seen my magic flair up last night before the wings appeared.

"Up until a few months ago, I was." Derek doesn't comment, but he looks a bit proud of me. Or maybe I'm making that up.

"We have to move. We don't know how long the water will keep them at bay," he says. Julian and I move immediately. I have no idea how the water knows what I intend for it to do, but it stays up like a wall as we run farther into the forest.

Magic has always been led by emotion, but now, it's like I have an extra layer of connection between me and it. This is something I'll have to ponder when I have more time. All three of us look like we've been through the ringer, but we have no major injuries as far as I can tell.

It's a few minutes before I feel the magic drop off somewhere behind me. I'm not sure how I can feel it, but I know the water has receded.

"They'll be on us soon," I manage to say as we run. "The magic didn't stay up."

Derek doesn't answer right away as we weave in and out of the trees. Between the fighting and the fact that the forest adds an extra layer of exhaustion to our bones, I'm surprised we're moving this fast. But just when I think we might have a shot at this, something changes.

The air in front of us shimmers like a ripple in the air, coming straight down from the sky. There's no time for us to slow down or change direction.

"Derek, what's happening?" I shout just as the anomaly swallows us whole.

I EXPECT TO FALL THROUGH, but I'm still standing when the lights dissipate. Spinning around, my eyes zero in on Derek and Julian. I breathe a sigh of relief. At least I'm not alone.

When I finally focus on our surroundings, whatever question I had on my lips dies.

We're still in the forest. I think. But everything is different.

The trees surround us just like they did before, except now, they look almost—rotten. Taking a step forward, I reach out to touch the bark, but my hand is snatched back. I look up to find Derek right beside me, his hand on my wrist.

"I wouldn't."

He watches me steadily. The hint of his fingers tingles on my skin, and something passes between us. It feels almost like the comradeship we developed back at the cabin. But then, he drops my hand, and it's gone.

"What is this place?"

Julian comes to stand beside Derek as I ask, and the two exchange a glance. I expect one of them to speak up, but they don't. This whole secrets-keeping shtick they have going on has got to stop. Exhausted, in more ways than one, I place my hands on my hips as I stare them down.

"Both of you need to learn how to speak up. Because if I have to continuously deal with these side glances, I'm going to start throwing punches." There's just enough annoyance in my voice to make it tougher than it usually sounds. I try not to grin. "Well?"

"It's not that we don't want to tell you," Julian begins, as Derek makes the most un-fae snort I've ever heard. Julian and I both stare at him as if he's lost his mind. "Fine, apparently we don't want to tell you," Julian continues. "But having too much information, especially when we have no idea how your magic will react to any of it, is kind of dangerous."

"Good point, but there has to be a way around that. I'm not walking around this... wasteland blindly."

I can smell it now, the potent stink of rotting ground and trees and well, everything. It fills the air with heaviness unlike anything I've ever felt before. If I'm right, I think even the leaves on these trees are spoiled.

"Wasteland is a pretty accurate description," Derek says over his shoulder as he moves forward. Julian and I don't hesitate to follow, even though I'm more than annoyed with him now. Secrets get people killed. I've read enough of our history to know that. I need information.

"Okay cool. Now tell me, where are we?"

"The forbidden forest."

"Is it forbidden because it stinks?" I can't help but ask as we push past some bushes that I try very hard not to touch.

Derek ignores my question, of course.

"It doesn't matter where we are as much as when."

"Wait, what?" I freeze in my tracks, eyebrows raised. Derek and Julian do their whole side glance as I roll my eyes.

"Don't freak out," Julian begins, which makes me a little madder at him than I was a few seconds ago. "Don't let your magic react in any way."

"Stop talking to me like I'm a child, and tell me what's going on!"

"The forbidden forest is full of time loops," Derek says, waving a hand in Julian's direction, as if telling him to stand down.

"Time loops?"

"Yes. The concept is the same as a regular portal, except the destination is another time."

"So what time is this?" I wave my hand around the dying forest.

"A time when the Ancients win."

Whatever snide remark I may have had dies on my lips. I stare at the trees in front of us, cracked and weathered by a storm I haven't yet seen. The sap pours through the cracks, as if the tree itself is crying.

"Does that mean we lose?" I barely get the question past my lips, as the tightness in my chest intensifies. Derek is in front of me in a flash, looking down into my face.

"No, this is just one possibility. There is no future that is set in stone. Every decision changes the outcome."

I look up at him, pushing air into my lungs. I hate to admit it, but his presence is calming. It's been this way since the moment we went into hiding together. No matter how much I wish that wasn't the case.

"What choices lead us here?"

"That's the tricky part. We don't know. And we don't have a way to get out of here unless we find another one of the time loops."

"So, we're stuck here?" I manage to keep my voice from rising. The magic inside of me is twisting every which way, asking if there's a way it can help. But I can't exactly let it free when I have no idea what it actually does anymore.

"Only for a short time," Julian says. But my eyes are still on the fae in front of me. There's emotion in his eyes once more, a reassurance he's trying to show by letting his guard down. I can't look away. I feel his presence in every cell of my body. I feel calm.

"We should get moving though. We don't know what waits in these shadows," Derek finally says. All I can do is nod.

We've been walking for a while when the forest falls away, and suddenly, we find ourselves staring at an open landscape in front of us. It's burning.

The heavy smell in the air comes from the fires that fill the space before our eyes. The forest should keep going, that much I can tell. But it's been cut down by the awfulness of the flames. The sight breaks my heart.

Derek and Julian stand on each side of me. When I glance at them, I see shock and pain on their faces. This is their home in ruins. It's a future that's a clear possibility.

The flames cast colors and shadows across the scorched ground. Seeing no other way around, Derek gives Julian and I a nod, and we step forward. If anyone looks over and see us, we probably look like three avenging angels, walking through the hellfire. The guys stay on constant alert, their eyes darting in every direction. I'm having a difficult time concentrating on anything as I feel a sadness inside of me. It's more overwhelming than ever before.

With each step, it seems to weigh heavier on me. When tears come, I have no power to stop them.

Derek notices right away. In the blink of an eye, he's in front of me, reaching for my upper arms.

"Avery, what is it? What's wrong?"

"I don't know." I hiccup over my words, trying to blink the tears away. As I raise my head, I feel the tips of my ears tingle, then a flash of bright light surrounds us before it's gone again.

"Avery, your wings. It's your magic—" Julian stops abruptly. I feel it. It's not me crying, it's the earth beneath my feet. When my knees give out, Derek is there to catch me.

"She's so sad," I mumble, leaning against Derek as he wraps his arms around me to keep me against his chest. "Can you feel it? She's crying and burning, a thousand degrees of agony."

The space around us lights up once more as my wings shimmer in and out of sight. I can't stop the tears that pour out of me long enough to fight the magic or the pain. It's like my body isn't my own anymore.

"Derek, we have to move." I hear the urgency in Julian's voice, but it seems so far away, as if he's in another world and I'm still stuck here.

"Derek, now! We have to move!"

The urgency in Julian's words seems to reach through the fog. I raise my head just as Derek pulls me up beside him. That's when I hear it. The stomping of feet. Turning my head, I glance behind us, and I see them.

Trolls. Or what used to pass for trolls.

Derek half carries, half drags me along as we try to put more distance between us and them. There are many creatures that I've only ever read about, but these seem like they went through a mutation. With the way the land is around us, maybe I shouldn't be that surprised.

Both boggarts and trolls hunt in packs, and they seem to thrive in this forest.

The movement and the danger at our backs seems to have shaken me from whatever emotional stupor I've fallen into, and I find my footing once more. Derek glances at me as I begin keeping pace with him, flashing me a quick smile.

"They're too fast!" I shout as I risk another glance behind. The worst of it is that we have nowhere to hide. The space in front of us is wide open and mostly on fire. We'll have to go through it to get to the other side. And we have no idea what's waiting out there.

"We need to…" Derek begins, but whatever he was going to say is lost on me as something drops down on my back. It brings me to the ground.

"Avery!"

I hear the shouts, but I'm too focused on the weight on top of me. Twisting, I try to throw it off, and realize, it's one of the trolls. He must've taken a running start and then leaped. He's only about half my size but heavy. It's like he's filled with rocks.

"Get off!" I shout, trying to drag him off me. He won't budge. He scratches at me, and I raise my arms to block him as I try to push him away. It's the weight of him that keeps him solidly planted on top of me, no matter how much I try to wiggle free.

Then, Derek is there, and the troll flies off, landing a few feet away. He's completely enraged as he shouts, spit flying all around him. Derek drags me to my feet once more, and then, we can't run. The trolls are everywhere.

"Here." Derek thrusts a sword into my hands, and I grab it automatically. Here's to hoping the few lessons I've had are enough. Derek is at my back, and so is Julian. We create a small circle as the trolls surround us. Derek tries talking to them, speaking a language I don't understand. It causes them all to scream louder.

"Aim for their feet. Their skin is too thick to cut through easily." Derek shouts to be heard over the noise. "Cut at the ankles or over the toes. It'll slow them down."

There isn't much more to say after that, and even though I have questions, I can't ask them. The trolls jump at us, and all I can do is swing my sword.

For creatures who are stocky and heavy, they seem to be very agile. My movements, and that of the guys, carry us apart as I try to do what Derek said. But it's not easy.

Between the screaming the trolls emit, and the smell all around me, I feel disoriented. And I'm weaker than I've been in a while. The fit of tears and pain I went through hasn't left, it's just diminished. All of this is too much. It's like my every sense is being bombarded.

I swing my sword again, this time connecting with one of the trolls. The scream that leaves his large mouth almost sends me on my back. Instead, I push through and swing again, catching another creature.

But the trolls keep coming. Their large teeth snap close to my skin, as if they want to take a piece of me, which actually makes sense if they're rabid. They do seem to be rabid.

Just then, I hear a yell. I turn to see Julian get taken down by three of trolls. They pin down his arm as one takes a big bite out it. The scream shatters through every emotion I'm experiencing and then my magic is there.

My feet propel me toward Julian. At the same moment, I feel a rush of power. When I swing my sword at the creatures, it's fueled by magic. I manage to get all three of them off before Derek reaches us. We pull Julian to his feet as his arm drips with blood.

The trolls seem to be multiplying. There's no way we're getting out of here. We need one of those ripples to show up and take us back to our time. But then Derek does something that surprises me.

"Hold onto him," he says, pushing Julian toward me. I have just enough time to grab him around the waist. There's not much distance between us and the trolls now. It seems that no matter how many we cut down, three take the place of one. Derek motions me back. I drag Julian with me as I watch Derek take a deep breath.

Then, the fae kneels down, thrusting his hands into the dying earth. I can't see his face, but somehow, I think his eyes are closed. There's a moment of silence, as if the whole world is holding her breath to see what he'll do. And then, there's a roar.

The dirt seems to rise like a wave in front of Derek, rushing up and up and up. He doesn't move; he doesn't speak, and then, the earth falls. The wave of dirt rolls, pushing forward, and I can't see the trolls anymore. All I see is descending dirt.

Derek stands. Without a backward look, he rushes toward us,

grabbing Julian from me. I stare at the fae in awe, but now is not the time for questions. He pulls Julian away, and I rush after him.

When I glance behind us, I see nothing but piles of dirt.

* * *

WE MOVE AS QUICKLY as we can with Derek half carrying Julian. The heaviness of the land is pressing on my heart. The strong emotions I experienced earlier are threatening to rise up again. It takes everything in me not to stop, not to slow down. All I want to do is lay down in the midst of this dirt and weep.

For the loss of the land's magic. For the loss of her beauty.

My beautiful Faery.

My beautiful Faery.

My beautiful Faery.

"Avery!"

I glance up at Derek's tone and the twinge of panic in it.

"What is it?"

"You went somewhere again. We have to keep going."

I didn't even realize we stopped. These random spacing out episodes...I have no explanation for them. I wish there was a way I could control them, especially right now. Derek waits for me to explain, but I just nod and rush off after him.

"Those were unlike any trolls I've ever seen."

"Just like the boggarts," Julian comments. He's covered in sweat, his arm bleeding again. He's still moving as he leans on Derek, but this position compromises us. If we get attacked right now, I'd have to fight them off, and I have no idea if I'm capable.

"What do you mean?"

"There's something wrong with them. That species isn't how they used to be."

The Ancients. That's got to be it. They're messing with the natural order of things, and that includes the creatures that live in these forests.

I'm on a rollercoaster of emotion and magical discovery. No one should be near me right now, especially those in a life or death situation. Taking a deep breath, I try to stay focused. If I let my mind wander, then I'll start feeling everything. If that happens, we're in trouble. Well, more trouble than we've been.

"Do you have any idea where we are?" I ask as I study our surroundings, looking for the next attack. The sight of the trees rotting from the inside out breaks my heart. There are no leaves on them, the branches are bare and fragile.

"None of this looks familiar."

I was hoping that wasn't the case. Wherever the time jumping ripple dropped us, it's not familiar to either fae to be of much use. We're walking around blindly.

"Maybe I can try something," I say, the idea popping into my mind out of nowhere. Derek stops, depositing Julian carefully to the ground. Both of the fae look at me in question, waiting for me to go on.

"Don't ask what made me think of it, but can I feel the ground? And maybe search for something within it? I feel connected to her." A tear slips down my cheek, and I wipe it away quickly. "Maybe I can find something."

"Using your magic could—"

"You just used your magic," I interrupt, because Derek is probably about to deliver another speech on my unstable magical abilities. I still have questions about him being able to use magic, but now is not the time.

"It's not the same."

"No, it's not. I didn't even know you could do that. But something is telling me I can do this, so you know what, I'm not asking for your permission."

I drop down to my knees immediately, thrusting my hands into the ground. Derek is there in a flash, reaching for me. I bat his hand away.

"It's too dangerous."

"You have to stop trying to protect me from everything." I look him dead in the eye. "I can't keep walking around on eggshells, waiting for my magic to do something else I've never seen before. This way, at least I'm trying to learn to control it. You have to trust me to take care of myself."

There is a lot of emotion behind my words, and if asked, I'll blame it on my connection to this broken land. But if I'm honest with myself, right here and right now, I need Derek to believe in me.

He stares into my eyes for a long moment before finally nodding his head.

"I'll be right here."

He moves only a fraction of a foot away, staying on the ground near me. I glance over at Julian, who's watching me steadily, and then, I let my magic dive.

It pours from inside my being into my hands and then into the ground. I close my eyes, pulling on that connection I feel with the land and on the magic that's been brewing inside of me. When the two are called up, I push my intention into the mixture. This is not the way I was taught to do magic, but it feels right somehow. So, I let my instincts guide me.

And then, after I think it won't work, I see it.

I open my eyes slowly, "I know where we need to go."

he fae don't question me. Derek pulls Julian up to a standing position once more and then I'm the one leading the way. The air around us grows heavier. The smoke and ash from the fires is dense enough that it's difficult to see past a few feet in front of us. It's hard not to cough, but we try to do our best. It wouldn't do us any good to give up our position. I'm hoping if we can't see the creatures, they can't see us.

After what seems like forever, I feel it. Pivoting to the left, I pick up speed. The smoke clears, and there it is.

"Avery?" Derek says, looking at the large house in front of us.

"We're going in."

"Are you sure that's a good idea?"

I glance over my shoulder. There's no hesitation in my voice when I reply, "Yes."

I think they'll argue further, but they don't.

The building is a two-story structure with an almost Grecian architecture to it. There are long columns of what was once white marble on each side of the door, as well as imbedded into the front beside the windows. Most of the windows are intact from what I can see, and they are long and narrow.

The door opens without a creak. I step in cautiously. The foyer opens up before me with a large staircase in the middle leading up to the second floor. Doorways are on each side of the foyer, leading to opposite side of the house.

I let my magic out, hoping it will tell me of any danger, but I don't feel anything specific. Granted, this is not something I've tried before, so I could be wrong. But I have to trust that the land lead me here for a reason. Looking over my shoulder, I motion the guys in.

Once inside the building, the air isn't much better. We deposit Julian against the wall in the foyer. I drop down to my knees next to him to assess the damage. He's bleeding pretty profusely, and it's not like I have a first aid kit with me. Wait, maybe I do.

I pull my bag forward. When I rummage through it, there are no antibiotics or bandages inside. I guess that's not something fae pack when they go on a long trip. And of course I didn't think about it either.

"I don't know how to help you," I tell him. He shakes his head looking up at Derek. I glance between the fae, furrowing my brow in confusion. "If you have something to say, gentlemen, then out with it." The number of secrets they keep from me is really astounding.

"It's not something I've done in ages," Derek comments, his full attention on Julian. It's like I'm not even there.

"I'm willing to take that risk."

The fae points to his jacket. The left arm is completely soaked through with his blood. I don't even know what we'll see when we take it off. I realize I need to find a way to at least clean it. Since no one is sharing information with me, I'll do what I can. We do have some water left over.

"Lean forward, Julian," I say, reaching for his jacket. He doesn't hesitate to obey. With his lips right over my shoulder, I hear his sharp intake of breath the moment he starts pulling his jacket off.

"The other side first," I say. Julian shrugs his arm out of the right sleeve, and then I gently move to help tug his left one off. The blood is heavy, making the material stick to his skin.

I have very basic first aid knowledge, just enough that I know it needs to be cleaned and pressure needs to be put on it, or it'll keep bleeding. It would be helpful to have one of the healer witches here now.

Julian jerks from the pain, and I stop pulling. "I'm sorry."

"Not your fault," he replies, his teeth clenched together. He's paler than even ten minutes ago, sweat dripping down the sides of his face. I manage to get the jacket completely off, and thankfully, he has a t-shirt underneath. His upper arm is a complete mess. I have to roll up the sleeve a little, but it looks exactly like what it is. That creature took a chunk out of his skin. The teeth marks are clearly displayed. I can see almost all the way down to his bone. It looks even worse than I imagined.

"Avery—"

"Is your blood...bubbling?" I reach over to touch it, but he catches my hand in his other one.

"Troll bites can be poisonous."

That nearly stops my breath right there.

"I don't think simple pressure is going to fix this," I say, my heart heavy with the idea of losing Julian. Knowing he could bleed out in my arms is almost too much to take.

"Isn't there some magic you fae have that will help fix this? No healing abilities?"

"Not unless you have shifter blood in you too, but even that is rare," Derek replies. That gives me another idea.

"Is there something I can do? I have shifter blood, right?"

"It doesn't work like that, Avery." Julian places a hand over my own, giving it a gentle squeeze.

"Don't do that," I snap, yanking my hand back. "Don't look like you're over here, saying your last goodbye. There has to be some-thing." I don't miss the way his eyes slide over to Derek's for a second, so I jump to my feet. Something passed between them earlier, and they didn't want to go into it. Well, tough luck. We're getting into it now.

"You. There's something you can do. What is it?"

Derek doesn't move away as I march up to him. There are only a few feet between us. He gives me a cold look, which makes him more fae somehow, but I'm not intimidated. Maybe I should be. But I'm already dealing with a lot. I'm not about to deal with this crap either.

"What. Is. It?" I repeat, this time a little slower. "Should I act it out too, or can you understand the three simple words?"

His eyes flash in annoyance or anger, I'm not sure which. And I don't care.

"Your habit of keeping me out of the loop needs to end. Right here and now. Julian is dying. So, whatever it is that you *both*," I turn and glare at Julian, before looking back at Derek, "are keeping to yourself, isn't worth it. Not if it makes him lose his life."

"It's ancient magic, Avery. It's something the royal blood possesses, but it isn't exactly practiced," Derek says, his voice as cold as his eyes. There's more to it, of course. It's like pulling teeth with these two.

"Do you want Julian to die?"

There's a moment of silence where the only sound is our breathing and the drip of Julian's blood on the dark floor.

"I do not."

Three words, but they're the ultimate truth.

"Then, *do* something."

Derek gives me another long look before moving to kneel near Julian.

"Are you sure about this?" he asks, looking the other fae in the eye.

"Yes."

I'm not exactly sure what I'm witnessing, but then, Derek takes Julian's mangled arm into his hands and closes his eyes. For a long time, nothing happens. It's the dormant part of the magic that's reawakening. I've heard of hidden or buried powers. Well, I also have one. So, I wait, even as Julian begins to breathe heavier.

Then a soft glow illuminates Derek. He seems to be glowing from the inside out. I hold my breath as I wait for whatever it is that's going to happen. The glow stays around Derek, and then, it seems to move into Julian. The moment it shifts, Julian screams.

I drop down beside him immediately, but I can't touch him. I don't want to make it worse, whatever is happening.

"Derek, you're hurting him."

"I have to."

Horrified, I watch as Derek pins Julian down. The screams of the fae echo all around us. Then the glow bursts out from inside of Julian's wound, and I fall back away from it. It seems to take forever, but Julian stops screaming, and the light goes out like a candle. He slumps down, completely knocked out as Derek sits back on his heels.

"Derek, is he…"

"He'll be fine. He just needs to rest."

Derek sounds like he's just run a marathon. When he stands, he doesn't meet my eye. He simply walks out of the room. Glancing over at Julian, I watch as his chest rises and falls. The sight of it makes me sigh in relief.

I stand and make sure Julian is laying down comfortably before I go and find Derek.

* * *

I FIND him in one of the rooms down the hall. There's still furniture there, although I don't think I'd want to sit on any of it. It's covered in enough dust and decay that it would crumple under a feather of a touch.

Derek is standing near one of the long, narrow windows, his gaze on something outside. Not that he can see much. The ash and smoke have somehow gotten heavier.

"Are you okay?"

It's not the question I was going to ask, but it's out before I can stop it. I think I surprise him too. He turns to glance at me as I come up to stand beside him. I notice he's a bit sweaty too.

"I'm fine."

"Is that a real fine or a fine that will stop me from asking more questions?"

"Well, clearly the latter isn't working."

I smile a little, despite myself. There's a softness about him right now that I'm not sure what to do about.

The way he is surprises me on a daily basis. He's unlike everything I've ever learned about fae, and I'm not sure what to do with that information.

"It's been a long time since I've done that," Derek finally says, looking back out into the ashy forest.

"Can you tell me what you did?"

At first, I don't think he will.

"I transferred some of my essence into him. Shared a part of me."

"Wait, I don't understand. I've never heard of that before."

"It's from old magic. It's how the rulers gained their power. They had an ability to heal their people. Wouldn't you want a king on the throne who could do that?"

"You sound bitter."

"Maybe I am."

"Your mother." I don't even have to ask because I know that's what this is about. She's been the queen for a very long time, longer than my human brain can comprehend. She doesn't seem like someone who has ever healed anyone.

"She would never and has forbidden me to do so. When a part of the essence is transferred, a part of your time is given away. I feel tired right now, but that will go away with time."

"Wait, you mean, you'll die faster now?" My heart squeezes at the thought, but I try not to show it. I don't need him seeing just how much that distresses me. And I definitely will need to deal with those feelings as well. Anyway.

"No one knows how much time is given away. Fae live for a long time. A little shorter isn't so bad."

There's almost a touch of sadness in his voice, but I don't think he'll appreciate me catching that.

"Is that why you were reluctant to do it?"

There's another long pause before he turns to me and replies.

"No. Anytime I use my magic, the queen can tell. It's a spell—more like a curse—she put on me a long time ago. While I can prevent it when I'm in the human world, here? We're still in Faery. If she senses we're in the forbidden forest...it won't end well for us."

"She's tracking you?" When I think the fae have reached their limit on mind boggling, there's another tier. Derek nods, and I honestly don't even know what to feel about that. I have a hundred questions, but maybe now isn't the best time. I decide to change gears.

"You say we're in Faery, just in a different time."

"Yes."

"Could you explain that a bit better? If we're stuck in a time and place that's a future possibility, does anything we do affect...anything?" I ask, trying to wrap my mind around it all.

"No. It's the future. As long as we don't magically alter anything that can track back to the past, we'll be fine."

"That almost makes sense," I say, sighing. This place is giving me a headache. I'm not sure if it's the weird magic, or if it's just the heaviness of the place, but I'm ready to get out of here.

"So how do we return?"

"We need to find a portal ripple."

"Like the anomaly that swallowed us and brought us here in the first place?" I throw my hands up in the air. "Of course, why wouldn't that be the way to go?"

"It won't be the same one. And..."

"What? Don't stop now."

"The ripples are many, which means, so are the timelines. We might not end up where we need to be right away."

"Cool. This is getting better by the minute."

"We'll get out of here, Avery." Derek's voice is full of conviction, and yes, I do believe him. Especially considering fae can't lie. But I'm still frustrated by the whole thing.

"I need a minute."

He opens his mouth to protest but then doesn't. Smart fae. He's learning.

The emotional weight of this place is really getting to me all of a sudden, so I leave Derek standing near the window and walk back out into the hallway.

I'm restless.

I'm confused.

I'm sad.

That last one is purely because of what I just learned about Derek. I don't want to keep feeling sympathy for the prince. Ever since I've known him, he's done things that are questionable. I'm sure he's done plenty of other things I don't want to know about as well. But somehow, I'm still drawn to him. To this side of him.

The protector.

And that's dangerous. I had to walk away from him, or I would've done something I regretted. I might have reached over to hold him close, somehow thinking my touch could protect him from his monster of a mother. Or maybe I want him to protect me from the reality of this place. I'm all over, up and down, side to side, trying to control all these emotions and thoughts.

It doesn't seem to be working.

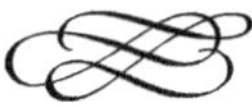

I end up upstairs. After checking to make sure Julian is still resting, I take the grand staircase to the second floor. I'm not really looking for anything specific. I just need a moment to clear my head.

Everything has been happening so fast, and the toll it's taking on me, it's not something I can even describe to myself.

One minute, I'm strong and ready to take on the world.

The next, I want to weep my heart out.

My mother would probably call it hormones. The shifter in me gets those mood swings really bad, especially in the early years. But this seems like more somehow.

I must find a way to keep a lid on the madness going on inside of me. There are creatures all around us that are waiting to pounce. Julian will hopefully wake up soon. Derek is—well, Derek. I need to get a grip on reality, or I'll be even more useless than I was in the forest with the boggarts.

I really do need to learn more fighting skills. Even with what Derek taught me at the cabin, I'm still too rusty to be of much use.

There are a few doorways in front of me, but none of them seem to have doors. I chose one at random, curious about this place, but mostly just needing the space to wander.

The room is in shadows, only one window present on the opposite wall. There's also what seems to be a fog all around me. It reaches for me before I realize what's happening. There's a ripple and then I am through.

When I step out of the fog, my surroundings are completely different. Twisting around, I try to look back, but there's just a sheet of white behind me. The doorway is gone and so is the house.

"Derek! Julian!" I call out, but the only answer I receive is my own echo. I try to reach back through the white, but then even that disappears and now there's a forest there. Seeing no other option, I move forward.

The trees are no longer dying. The ground beneath my feet seems fresher somehow. This place feels just as dangerous as the wasteland I left behind, even though I don't smell the ground burning. It looks serene, but I know better than to trust that. Looks can be, and often are, deceiving.

These time jumps have to have a way out. I can't be stuck in this constant loop. A movement catches my attention, and I swerve in that direction immediately. I'm not about to call out a hello, but I will see if someone other than me is actually here.

The fog dissipates suddenly, and I find myself in a courtyard. It's similar to the one at Queen Svetlana's castle, but also different. The trees here are larger, reaching so high into the sky that I can't see them. Flowers bloom in the darkness, but they grow right out of the tree bark instead of the ground. The space around the trees is lost to the darkness, so I can't see the shape of it.

I move forward, but then stop. My feet are cocooned in something. When I glance down, I find myself in a pink ball gown. My hands roam over my body to see if it's real, and it is. The skirt is full and cinched at the waist. The front is low cut, and my shoulders are bare. My hair is down, falling in soft waves over my back. I'm spotless, as if I didn't just come from a raging fire forest.

"You're here."

The voice snaps my head up, and I squint through the darkness to find the source of it. I know it, even without having to see him.

"Derek!" I pull up my skirt, rushing toward him as he seemingly materializes from the shadows. He's standing near a tree. When I reach him, the glow from the flowers illuminates his face. He's dressed in a dark blue suit, his hair tousled in that sexy way of his. He's just as clean as I am.

"I didn't think you'd show," he says when I stop in front of him. My brows furrow in confusion as I look at him. There's genuine emotion on his face, something that nearly takes my breath away. He is never so upfront about them. That's when I realize this is not the Derek of now. It's the Derek of whatever time this is.

And I'm not me either. I'm whoever he expects me to be, and I can't resist but to play along.

"Why did you think I wouldn't?"

He doesn't answer right away. His eyes do a slow sweep over my face before he glances down at the dress. When his eyes meet mine again, there's real appreciation in them, and it makes my chest hurt. Derek has never looked at me like this in real life. Or *my* real life I suppose. He takes a step forward, reaching for my hands. Taking both of them in his, he peers into my face, his eyes intense on mine.

"I know things haven't worked out how we planned them. But you have to know that everything I've done was to protect you. I would never—" The sadness in his eyes is almost tangible, and his grip on my hands is tight. "Killing them was the only way. You have to know that. They were holding you back. But no more. We can rule now. Their blood is on my hands, but her blood is on yours. We're the perfect match, don't you see? We're—"

"Stop!" I say, yanking my hands back and stepping away. I can't be hearing this. I can't be having this conversation with a future him because I don't know if this is my future or not. What he's saying, it doesn't make sense. And I don't want it to. I don't want to know we've become these evil beings. I can't hear this, because if I hear it and believe it, I will never trust him. And I can't afford to do this without trusting him.

"What is it? I'm sorry, Avery. I'm sorry that I—"

"It's not you." I stop him once more, almost laughing at the absurdity of me using that line. "This, this is all too much, and I have to get out of here."

I turn to flee because that is my only option. This is not my world. This is not my Derek, and I have to get back to both of them. Now.

He calls my name again, but I don't stop. The dress is heavy around my legs, but I keep moving. There's no direction in my mind to go, just away. I hear more movement behind me and turn to see a group of guards rushing after me. I trip over the skirt, falling forward, my hair in my face. Any second now the guards will descend.

But when I glance up, I'm back in the room I was just in. Glancing around quickly, I make sure nothing has come through the ripple with me. Although, I don't even know if that was a ripple. It was so fast and unexpected.

And Derek. He looked so—no, I'm not thinking about that right now.

Push it all down, Avery. You have to find a way to get out of here.

* * *

WE DON'T GO FARTHER into the house than the foyer. When I make it back downstairs, Derek is sitting on the floor, opposite of Julian. His eyes are on me when I walk over to check on Julian, and they are still on me as I settle against the wall near the staircase.

I want to tell him about what happened upstairs, but I also don't. If he decides to go up there, I'll warn him. But for now, I'm going to keep the experience to myself. I'm not even sure it was real. It felt way too disorienting. It wasn't like the ripple we came through to get here. It was more like a waking vision, something the Ancients have done before to talk to me. It didn't feel like them, but I really don't know, do I?

"I'll take the first watch," I say. The way his eyes flash, I know I beat him to it. But he doesn't argue. Maybe it's because he knows his body needs the rest after the transfer. I watch him as he closes his eyes, and then, as his body relaxes.

Thankfully, the whole night goes by without incident. When Derek wakes me up, I feel slightly rested. He kneels over me, his hand gentle on my shoulder. When I look up at him, there's genuine care there.

The flashes of his sad eyes from my vision—or whatever it was—mixed with the reality in front of me, and the desire to hold him, nearly overwhelms me. Instead, I push to a sitting position as he moves back.

"She awakens."

My gaze jerks over to Julian who is sitting up now and looking very peppy. I jump to my feet, rushing over to him.

"You're okay?"

"I'm okay."

I still do a thorough once over and notice that his wound is almost completely scabbed over. Glancing at Derek, I make sure he's fine as well because it must've taken a lot of his magic to make that happen.

We don't linger around after that. Grabbing my bag, we leave through the same door we entered, but we don't go back in the same direction. I let Derek take the lead, with Julian between us, and me bringing up the rear.

I still feel her, the land around me. She's so sad. She's been through so much. Maybe, in some strange way, I relate to her on that level. We've both been put into a situation we didn't chose for ourselves.

Julian calls for a rest mid-morning. We stop, taking a drink and eating some of the fruit from my bag.

"Will I jinx it if I say it's been awfully quiet?" I ask. The fae look at me a little confused. So maybe that's more of a human thing than not.

"It has, but we just might be in an area of the forest that's less populated for some reason," Derek replies. I have to keep myself from smiling. He sounds so serious when I was trying to lighten things up.

"Do you think I can try that magic trick I did to find the house?" I ask, but both of the fae are already shaking their heads.

"It's dangerous to keep doing it. We don't know how it'll affect you or the land around us. This isn't our Faery."

I think part of the side effects was that strange trip I went on, but I'm not about to mention it. It's not like I could replicate what I did anyway. It was all instinct. I'm too much in my head right now to allow my magic to take over.

"Derek, do you actually have any idea where we're going?" I ask, instead of voicing all of my own concerns. He stays quiet for a moment before turning to look over his shoulder at me.

"The only sure thing I know is that no matter where we are in Faery, north is the true direction. So, if we go north here, maybe we'll get somewhere." The *I'm-not-sure* part is silent. We're all just guessing at this point.

"I didn't think the true north nursery rhyme was true," I comment as we begin walking again. Both Derek and Julian glance over at me, but it's Julian who asks.

"Nursery rhyme?"

"Sure. All the kids know the story of the little spider." They continue looking at me like I've lost my mind. I guess fae don't tell the same stories to their children as witches do. I'm not surprised. I can't see someone like Queen Svetlana teaching little Derek about the dangers of walking alone at night.

"There were a few I remember from childhood. Each little rhyme is a story, and it teaches you an important lesson. I always thought the spider one was about resilience and how you can overcome whatever is thrown at you if you only try, but maybe not."

"Can we hear it?" Derek's question is barely above a whisper, as if he wanted to ask but didn't actually want me to hear it. I smile, the fae curiosity is such an interesting thing.

"There once was a spider, who traveled alone.
He lived in the rafters and called darkness his home.
But one day, a storm came, and blew the spider away,
He spun and he spun, then, in a forest he lay.

The spider was scared and lost as can be,
But he knew that true north would guide him, you see.
He followed the signs, and he followed the sun,
And one day he came to his new-found home.

It wasn't the rafters, and he wasn't alone,
For he found his lost family and he no longer had to roam."

The simple words bring another smile to my face because these were the simple days. It reminds me of when I would spend time with my parents and didn't have to worry about some great destiny or powers beyond my imagination. I was still an outcast, half shifter and half witch, but I was loved and protected. I was happy.

"It's an odd rhyme," Julian comments, breaking my trip down memory lane.

"Maybe, but rhymes such as these stick in your mind and are fun as a kid." I shrug because I think this is where I learned to love knowledge. It's why I wanted to become a Watcher, because I wanted to know things.

"It is true though," Derek says from his place in front of us. "True north is a guiding point in Faery. It's interesting that your parents taught you that rhyme."

His words and the way he says them makes me pause. I try to remember if anyone else spoke that rhyme then or in the years since, and I can't think of anyone. There were a bunch of rhymes that my parents made up just for me, and now, it makes sense.

"You think my dad was preparing me." It's not a question, but Derek stops anyway and turns to face me.

"I think he was."

I don't know how to take that, and I don't want their sympathy right now. Pushing past Derek, I continue walking, picking up speed.

Suddenly, the trees in front of me open up. We're in a clearing. The guys come up to stand on each side of me as we take in the scene in front of us.

"It can't be."

CHAPTER 8

e move forward, making sure to hurry across the open space.

"I don't understand," I say as I study our surroundings. My brow is furrowed. "What is this? It looks—it looks like Thunderbird Academy. But—"

"Destroyed"

I glance at Derek at that one word as we stop in front of where the side door used to be. It leads to the now-non-existent gardens.

The school is in ruins. Half of the walls are missing, brick laying in piles, as if an actual bomb went off in there. We step over the rubble, keeping our eyes peeled.

The ever-changing dynamic of this world is dangerous. The air here is clearer, as if the ash and smoke hasn't reached this far. Except, this place looks like it's been right in the middle of a war.

"What do you think happened here?" I can't help but ask.

The guys don't answer right away. I look over to find Derek staring at something on the ground. He seems a million miles away from here and then he snaps back.

"The Ancients got through the wards and destroyed everything in sight. Look at the scorch marks." Derek points to what's left of the wall in from of him, and I can see them now. Black stains of magic curl around the hole that's been created. The grass around the walls is dead as well. It's the aftermath of a powerful magic battle. Nothing will ever grow here again.

"They fought back," I mumble because I know they did. Thunderbird Academy is one of the greatest magical schools in our world. People that I've looked up to my whole life have graced these halls with their presence. They learned here, and they taught here. It was the school that I worked hard to get into to.

Before finding that stupid book changed everything for me.

"This can happen? It's a possible future?" I ask the questions, but in reality, of course it can happen. I know this already. It's why I came to Faery in the first place. I need to learn to use the magic that's been bestowed upon me. The fear that I'll fail is more overpowering here as I stand amidst the ruins of the school I love so much.

"There are many possibilities, Avery," Derek replies, clearly seeing my distress. He comes to stand in front of me, as if he's blocking the ruins from view. I'm forced to look up into his handsome face.

"Nothing you see here is set in stone. This is just one outcome, one out of thousands. Every decision we make in our own time affects what happens here. So, we make a decision not to let this happen."

"It's not that easy, Derek, and you know it," I whisper, all of the emotions creeping up on me at once. "I'm responsible for the outcomes because I'm the one who can read an ancient book no one else can. This will be on me."

"It will be on all of us. If this happens, we failed all of Faery."

I want to believe him, I want to share that responsibility, but the whole land and its people are dependent on me. Just then, something dawns on me.

"Wait, if we're in Faery, how is the school here?" Thunderbird Academy is in the human realm. It's been to Faery before, but Maddie fixed that problem.

"The Ancients must've opened up a rift between the realms with their magic. Everything would be confused if that happened. Or maybe this is a future where the school never made it back to the human realm."

I remember them mentioning before how the Ancients can mess with dimensions and realities, but here's a visual representation of it. I don't like it. I don't like any of this one bit.

The sadness I felt for the land itself is intensified here by my own emotions. I want to take the pieces of this broken school, and put them together, brick by brick. If only fixing everything was as easy as that sounds.

I open my mouth to ask more questions when a noise catches my attention. The fae turn as one, their own focus on whatever it is we're hearing.

"Get down." Derek grabs my arm and pulls me down beside him. We're right on the other side of the wall with the hole blown through it. Julian drops down a few yards away from us. Derek pokes his head up, still staring at the forest right at the edge of the clearing. I'm about to say I don't see anything when a group of the deformed trolls burst out of the trees.

WE STAY AS STILL as possible as the trolls move across the clearing. They're speaking a language I don't understand. I'm almost afraid to breathe lest I get their attention. There's a lot of land around the school, and they seem to be on a mission to get somewhere.

It seems like forever, but it's is only probably a minute before they disappear into the trees on the other side of the school. Yet, we still don't move. I'm back to feeling overwhelmed. And sad. This land is really playing up on the sadness, and I don't blame her. She's been through so much.

"Avery?" Derek's voice reaches out to me, as if through a tunnel. I look up to meet his concerned gaze. He looks blurry.

That's when I realize I'm crying again. I really have no control over the emotions the land evokes in me, or my response to it.

The sobs seem to burst out of me as I try my best to keep the sound down. Sadness overpowers every thought in my mind. I have no control over my reaction to it. I feel it; I feel it all. The torture the land has endured, the terror of the burning fields and the rotting trees, I feel everything. No one is here to sympathize with her, no one is here to comfort her.

The land bleeds, and she feels so alone.

Suddenly, strong arms pull me forward. I fall against Derek's chest as he cocoons me in his embrace. I grab onto his shirt, clinging to him like he's my lifeline, while the waves of sadness try to overwhelm me. One of Derek's hands threads through the hair at the back of my head, pulling me even closer. I breathe him in, surrounded by him on every side.

My body shakes with tears, but he doesn't let go. His other hand makes slow trails up and down my back, soothing my worries away. I give myself over to the feelings. I let the land know that she's not alone. That I'm—we—are doing everything we can to help her. It takes a few moments, but I finally feel the land's power drain out of me, giving me my emotions back. After another minute, I'm in control.

Pulling away, I look up to find Derek staring down at me.

"Avery?" There's so much in just that word and the look on his face.

"I'm really ready to get out of here," I reply, wiping at my tearstained cheeks. Derek nods, but he doesn't take his eyes off me. There's so much emotion there, it's the most earnest I've seen him since we've met. If we weren't us, and if we were in another place and time, I think I could stay in the circle of his arms for forever.

"Guys, we have to move." Julian's voice reaches us, and we both turn to see what causes the alarm in his voice. He's looking out through the torn-up wall. When we follow his gaze, we see them. The trolls have come back.

"They probably heard me—"

"Let's just get out of here."

Derek takes my hands, pulling me up beside him, and then we're running. Julian keeps pace beside us. We have no direction in mind, just away. The trees are in front of us, the ruined Thunderbird Academy behind us, and the trolls coming at us from all directions.

"We can't outrun them!" Julian shouts. I twist my head to glance over my shoulder. They're so much closer and faster than I thought. He's right. They don't leap like other creatures, but they move fast, and we're not moving fast enough.

"Try and lose them in the trees!" Derek commands right as we hit the tree line. Since the air here is cleaner, it's easier to see where we're going. But that means the trolls can see us just as well.

There's nothing I can do. I brought this on us, and now, we're probably going to die in this wasteland before we have a chance to do anything good. The sound of trolls yapping is closing in. I'm out of breath. My only thought is to stop them. Somehow. Someway.

Determination fuels me as I stop running and turn to face them head on. I hear Derek and Julian yell my name the moment they realize I'm not with them, but I have to try this.

Giving myself completely over to my instincts, I don't think. I thrust my hands out in front of me, calling on my magic and the land which I'm so connected to, trusting both of them to guide me.

A burst of fire rushes out of my palms, igniting everything in sight. It sweeps the trolls off their feet. But then, something unusual happens. My left palm becomes a stream of water, enveloping the trolls and drowning them on dry land.

It all happens so fast, I don't have any time to think about it. The wings burst out of my back for a split second, sending the space around me into brightness before they're gone. But I don't give up. I let the magic pour out of me until I have nothing left.

Then, it's done. The fire and water disappear, and the trolls vanish with them. Derek and Julian are beside me, but it's Derek who catches me when I fall. There is no strength left in my body, not an ounce of it enough to hold me up. Derek cradles me against his chest, picking me up off the ground.

No one says a word, as I lean against Derek's strong chest, completely spent. The boys turn, and when they do, a shimmer appears in front of us. I know it's what we've been looking for.

"Thank you," I whisper. The shimmer becomes bigger and then it pulls us in.

CHAPTER 9

The light disappears and then I'm looking at the most beautiful sight I've ever seen. The trees that surround us are fully green. They are big and strong and healthy.

"We're back," Julian says, breathing out a sigh of relief. It's not a question because we all know it's true. The heaviness of being in the forbidden forest is back, but also, this feels like home.

Home.

I never thought of Faery as a place I would ever call home, but in that wasteland, I took ownership of the land and called it mine. I don't think that will ever change now.

"But how?" This time it is a question. Derek lifts me a little higher, to get a better grip on me as I fight to stay awake.

"I think it was me," I mumble, closing my eyes and basking in his body's warmth. I feel safer than I have in a long time now, and it has everything to do with who is holding me.

"I think you're right," Derek says. I know he's looking down at me because his voice sounds closer. A moment later, I feel his breath on my face, and I smile. Or maybe it's only internally, because I don't think I'm strong enough to even manage that right now.

"Rest, Avery. You're safe."

There's nothing else that I can say to that, and a moment later, I'm no longer awake.

The forest is dark around me when I open my eyes. My back is leaning against a tree, and I'm using my arm as a pillow. Sitting up slowly, I look for Derek and Julian, but they're nowhere in sight. Something stops me from calling out to them. I'm not sure what exactly it is that I'm feeling. There's a heaviness around me that has nothing to do with the forest itself.

"You are here and so are we." The voice is sudden, and I jump, as it sounds like it comes from all around me. I get to my feet, spinning in circle as I try to find the source of it, but I don't see anything.

"You are here and so are we, and you will not escape."

The words get louder and louder as they are spoken and then,

"You will not escape. You will not escape. You will not escape."

I jerk into wakefulness, and it's only Derek's arms that keep me from falling. He's still holding me as close as he can. He's visibly concerned when I look up into his handsome face.

"Bad dream," I mumble, unable to look away from him. He's been letting me see these glimpses of vulnerability, and I'd be lying to myself if I said I don't find myself wanting to know more. No matter how much my brain tells me to keep him at arms-length, I can't seem to want to do anything but pull him closer.

"Can I get down?" I ask, even though it's the last thing I want to do. But I seem to have regained my strength, and I don't want to be a burden.

"Are you sure?"

No.

"Yes."

He stops walking, setting me down carefully, keeping his arm around my waist in case I need it. I seem to be steady on my feet. I wonder how long I've been asleep. So, I ask.

"About half a day," Julian replies, coming up to stand beside me.

"What?" I glance between the two fae, completely confused. "It couldn't have been that long."

"It was."

Derek carried me for half a day? And he carried me while in a forest that makes everything heavier and darker? I study his face, but he's back to wearing his princely mask. The frustration at seeing it makes me forget my impulse to thank him. So instead, I only nod.

"We're heading north, I assume?"

"We are," Derek replies, turning on his heels and taking the lead. It's like nothing has even happened between us. He's back to his cold fae self. He's moodier than I can deal with right now, so I ignore the snide remark I want to deliver.

"I'm glad you're better," Julian says, falling into step beside me as we follow Derek. I smile at him, bumping his shoulder with mine. After a few moments, he falls back to bring up the rear, and I veer off to the right a little. I've been with these two for days now, I think maybe my mind is just confused. We've been in life and death situations, it's only natural I feel connected to them.

Nothing else.

"Avery, watch out." Julian doesn't shout, but there's enough alarm in his voice to stop me in my tracks.

"What?" I look around but don't see anything out of the ordinary. The forest is just as heavy around us as it was, the eerie silence a bit more pronounced.

"We're almost there, so we have to tread carefully. There's illusion magic in place."

His explanation does nothing to clarify the confusion, but my magic has other ideas. The moment Julian say illusion, it's like the faery magic inside of me decides to wake up. Immediately, I start to feel things. I can feel the ground beneath my feet, the moisture clinging to the leaves, the sturdiness of the trunks. And then, a dozen yards to the left, I feel something else.

"This way," I announce and shift to the left. The boys exchange a confused look, but I push past them and toward whatever it is in front of me.

"Maybe we should—"

But I'm not listening. Now that I've found the anomaly, my magic is pulling me toward it. When I stop, there's nothing but trees in front of me, but I can feel it. There's a disturbance in the air.

Tentatively, I reach out with my hand, placing my palm against nothing. For a moment, nothing happens. Then the air ripples, and it's like a curtain is opened. I blink, pulling my hand back quickly before I focus on what lies beyond. It's a large house, more like a mansion, with a tree growing out of the south end of it.

The front door is adorned by large columns, and in the next moment, it swings open. My jaw drops as I watch the person step out into the light.

"Well, it's about time," Hannah says, her signature smirk on her lips.

* * *

"Hannah?"

The guys move toward the mansion, but I stay frozen, completely confused. Derek realizes this right away and drops back.

"Avery?"

"I don't understand. This was your big secret? Your way to teach me about my magic? You decided to send me to the person who could've helped me in the beginning and didn't."

"I understand you're angry—"

"I'm furious. I thought I'd finally have some answers, but no. You fae just have to play with me."

Derek's face completely drops at my accusation before he catches himself. His momentary lapse pauses my rant. I hurt him. Somehow, with something that I said, I actually hurt him.

And then it hits me. I called him fae. I threw him in the same category as his mother and everyone else who would like to manipulate me, which, let's be honest, is a huge list at this point.

"Derek—"

"Hannah will help. She will. We wouldn't be here otherwise."

His voice is sure, and when he meets my eye, there's determination there. If nothing else, I can trust that he believes this. So, I will give it a shot.

"You shouldn't be mad at the poor boy, Avery. I wasn't going to help you until I was ready," Hannah says as we reach the front doors. She's wearing another one of her maxi dresses, this one a different shade of red. It covers about as much as a bathing suit, her back, shoulders, and most of her legs bare as she motions us in.

Once inside, I see Julian hugging another guy about a few years older than me. When they pull back, I notice that he looks like a blonder version of Julian.

"Avery, this is Jerome. My brother."

"Nice to meet you," I say, looking from Julian to Jerome. He never mentioned he had a brother. I wonder if that's what drove him to find a better life, or not. Sometimes family is the best motivator.

"You must be tired, and you all could use a shower, that's for sure. You boys know where to go. I'll take Avery with me."

When Derek doesn't move, Hannah levels him with a look.

"I'll take good care of her. Now go."

He gives me a fiery look and then turns and follows Julian and Jerome out of the main hall.

"He's protective of you."

"He knows he's in trouble," I throw back, turning to face the woman in front of me. She's wearing her signature smirk as she looks at me. I try not to squirm under her gaze.

"You really did it, Avery. You made it all that time away from this place, and now, here you are."

"Didn't have much of a choice. It's not like I had anyone to help me."

Hannah's laugh rings out as she pivots and heads in the opposite direction of the boys.

"I've forgotten how clever you can be."

"Wasn't trying to be. Just stating the truth."

"Ah, yes. The truth. Curious that someone with fae blood in her has the ability to...bend it." She stops in front of double doors, giving me another once over before pushing them open.

"I don't know what you want me to say," I begin before I fully see the room we walked into. It's gorgeous. Sure, the room at the palace is too, but this one feels more personable.

The walls are pearl white with a gold trim at the top and the bottom. The bed is on my right, in the middle of the wall, with space on each side. A tulle white canopy hangs over it. When I look closely, it's full of tiny sparkling stars. There's a dresser, a table, a door to what I assume is the bathroom. But what I love most about the room are all the plants.

There are geometrical shelves covering the wall opposite the bed that are filled with various plants. Vining and flowering, they spread out like a work of art. There are vases on every surface and more shelves on the various walls. The room is full of light and oxygen, and it makes me smile.

"I knew you'd like it."

"It's very—modern." I think that's why I love it on sight. True, the room at the palace was straight out of every royalty movie or period drama. But this? It has a different type of a beauty. It reminds me of home.

Hannah doesn't comment on that, but it seems like she's pleased. She motions toward the open door before turning back to me.

"Get cleaned up. There are clothes in the closet or the dresser. Choose anything that strikes your fancy." I glance up at that, and she smiles. "We'll have dinner in a few, shall we?"

She moves toward the door, leaving me still gaping at my surroundings.

"Hannah?" I call out as she pulls the door open. The thank you is on the tip of my tongue, but I swallow it. Instead, I focus on more present issues. "Do you have it?"

"Of course I do."

Once we've all cleaned up, we end up in a large library. Being surrounded by all the books makes me feel better instantly. I took a shower, and my hair is wet and falling down my back. I brushed it out few times, taking my time with it. I didn't think such a small thing could make me feel so much better. The golden veins are still wrapped around my ear, but nothing feels different. The green streaks in my hair haven't gotten more pronounced. I think this is just part of my look now.

Derek is standing at the opposite wall while Julian and Jerome are seated in two of the chairs. I walk over to the love seat as Hannah gives me a quick once over.

"I knew the clothes would fit."

I glance down at the leggings and oversized sweatshirt I found in the dresser. They're so completely opposite of the gorgeous dress she's wearing, but I needed a sense of normalcy in my life right now. This feels cozy enough to let me pretend.

"Let's do this then."

Hannah walks over to the bookshelf, pulling out one of the leather-bound books. I know what she's about to show me, even though the guys don't. She opens the book and pulls out two unattached pieces of paper.

"Is that?" Julian asks, glancing from Hannah to me and back at Hannah.

"It is."

The woman walks over to where I'm sitting and takes the other side of the love seat as she settles beside me. She hands me the two pieces of paper. The moment my hands touch the parchment, a rush of magic goes through me.

Derek, Julian, and Jerome all move forward, fascinated by the papers I'm now holding in my hands. They stare at them like they've never seen anything like them. I smile as I thrust the papers toward them with a little "Boo". The guys jump, and I don't bother to suppress my chuckle.

"It doesn't bite, you know," I say, presenting them with the papers to take them. At first, I don't think they will, but then both Julian and Derek reach for a page. They hold them reverently, and that's expected. The pages are older than they are and the biggest part of their heritage.

"You can really read it?" Julian asks, staring at the page in his hand. The writing is there, but from what I understand, the fae just see gibberish. I'm the only person in generations who has looked at the pages and seen actual words. Sometimes there are also drawings and graphs of sorts.

Before I hid the book, I looked through as much of it as I could. It was difficult to study it, since I couldn't actually read it. Physically, I could. But I didn't want to accidentally start a world war or something if I mumbled a word out loud. Which I have been known to do when I study.

"It looks just like any book to me," I reply honestly. It seems to completely boggle their minds, and it's not like I can explain it any better.

"Boys, could you give me a moment alone with Avery?" Hannah asks, but we all know it's not a request. The guys don't hesitate to obey. Derek stops at the doorway, giving me a long look before glancing over at Hannah. Something seems to pass between them, and then he's gone.

"You're angry with me," Hannah begins, not beating around the bush. I turn to face her. She's seated just a foot away from me on the couch.

"Yes, I am." I don't hesitate to reply. "You left me floundering in the big bad world and for what? Clearly, you could've helped me from the beginning."

"Clearly, I could not."

"I don't believe that. Nothing has changed since I found that book. Well, maybe I have. But you? You're helping now, why?"

She stands, as if she needs distance to orient her thoughts. I don't push, waiting for her to speak up. She rearranges the hair over her shoulder before she finally does.

"This place is a sanctuary for me. Here in Faery, we do not have much say when it comes to what master we serve. If Queen Svetlana found out I was helping you...let's just say it wouldn't end well for me."

"Then why do it?"

"I was honest with you at Thunderbird Academy, Avery. I wanted you to have a choice. Faery is important to me. I want to see it not only survive, but to thrive. There are those in power who wouldn't care about the last one. It should not be so."

The words come out a little more intense than I think she intends for them to, and that's how I know she means it. There's real passion in her. She's not the nonchalant fae tutor that I met at the school. She believes in her homeland, and that, I can understand. That is why I decide to tell her when things changed for me.

"I connected with...her," I say, glancing down at the pages on my lap.

"Faery?"

"Yes. When we were in the other time." I look up to see her nod at me to continue. The guys must've filled her in. "I felt her sadness, her brokenness. I never thought a land could be so alive."

"But she is, and she must be protected," Hannah replies, walking back over to the seat. "Avery, I know you have no reason to trust any of us. Every single person, besides Jerome, has failed or lied to you. But you have to understand that our intentions were true."

"That doesn't make them right."

"No, it doesn't. But I hope you will give us the benefit of the doubt. We're fae…but we're trying."

I stay silent for a full minute, letting that sink in. It's the closest to an apology that I will ever get. I suppose I can continue being angry at her for leaving me alone when I needed someone the most, but that won't do me any good. I need her help. At the least.

"Okay, then keep trying," I say. She flashes a brilliant smile my way.

"Let's go to dinner and see if we can come up with a plan," she says. We both stand to leave. I place the papers on the table, but then I pick them back up again. I don't think I want them out of my sight. Hannah watches me but doesn't say anything, and then she leads the way out of the room.

* * *

THE NEXT FEW days go by in a blur. I learn that this house was setup as a sanctuary many centuries ago, before the forbidden forest was what it is now. Every realm has a version of one of these, something I didn't think about. Hannah was entrusted with the keep of it, but she wouldn't say by whom. It doesn't matter anyway.

What matters is that we are safe here from Queen Svetlana. Even Derek's magic can't be tracked when we're inside of the illusion bubble. That's what I've been calling it. They're not big fans of the name, but oh well. I kind of like it.

I'm not here to please anyone.

I'm here to learn.

That's why Jerome is here, apparently. He's older than Julian, probably around the same age as Nora, and he has a water affinity with magic. Hannah has created a training schedule for me. In other words, they're making a soldier out of me. It's not that I'm protesting, but no one consulted me first. I won't say thank you, even though I'm pretty sure I have to be just that to survive whatever is coming.

I still haven't told anyone about the dream I had. Maybe keeping all these things to myself isn't the best, but it's what I feel is best right now. At least, I keep reminding myself of that daily. I'm trying to learn how to trust the fae, but I cannot give it over completely. No matter what. I'm not sure if it's just my self-preserving instincts or what. But it is what it is right now.

This morning, I'm with Jerome at the back of the house. There's a fountain here, an angel with wings holding out his hands as water pours out of them. Fae are as close to nature as one can get, even more connected than witches. Still, most don't have active powers like elemental witches anymore. From everything I've heard, it's a power play from the royals. Fae can affect nature but don't use the elements in the same way.

Except Derek, of course. He has a lot of tricks up his sleeve.

And Jerome, who is half witch, so it helps him understand the dynamics.

"Can I ask you a personal question?" I begin when it's just the two of us. Hannah came out to give him some instructions, and Derek glared from the doorway. He hasn't been alone with me since we arrived. I'm not sure what caused the change in his behavior, but he does have a tendency to be hot and cold so maybe I should just get used to it by now.

"Ask away." Jerome doesn't hesitate.

"Do many fae have mixed culture parents?" I tried to make it sound as politically correct as possible, and that doesn't escape Jerome. He laughs, a full hearty laugh, before he replies.

"Yes, fae really can't keep it in their pants. And everyone has multiple children."

"Everyone?" I can't help my mind flying to Derek. And even Julian.

"Okay, not everyone," he laughs again, clearly catching my train of thought. "But in my case, my mother is a witch, but Julian's is fae."

"So, he doesn't have the elemental powers you do."

"I'm sure he would if he was taught to use them. Fae are more powerful than they let on. It's a special kind of a tactic."

"Don't I know it," I mumble, and Jerome chuckles. Everything is so calculated here. It's not that I don't appreciate precision, but this is definitely another level. I do like Julian's brother. He's very nonchalant about everything. He reminds me of the fae I met at Thunderbird Academy. I think having a human mother, or father, really makes a difference for these boys.

"Let's get started."

I sober up instantly. I've been able to access my water magic twice in the wasteland and neither time it was something I could control. I need to find a way to call on it, like I do my fire, but the usual ways aren't working for me. Even though Derek and I trained at the cabin, it's like I've forgotten how to do all of it. But it doesn't matter. Derek really has thought of everything.

I overheard him and Hannah talking yesterday, and it really was all him. He planned Hannah and Jerome both coming here and made it happen. He's been the one plotting behind everyone's back. I honestly have no idea how to feel about that. But at the moment, I'm grateful.

"When you access your fire magic," Jerome's voice brings me back to attention, "what do you feel?"

"Feel?"

"Yes. Is there a specific emotion that overwhelms you?"

I think about it, going over the times I have called upon it. Then, I do it in front of Jerome, letting the fire ignite in the palm of my hand before I shake my head.

"Nothing specific. I know this magic. I know the fire will come when call it." He's nodding before I even finish talking.

"I think that's what we focus on today. You getting to know the water magic. Get in."

"I'm sorry, what?"

Jerome points to the fountain again and says, "Get in."

"What do you—"

"Lay down on your back and see if you can float. I want you to be as submerged as you can. Then I need you to feel the water around you and in you because you are connected to it, even if you don't know it."

I stare at him for another moment, before I shrug my jacket, boots, and socks off. Left in my t-shirt and leggings, I step into the water, expecting it to be cool. But it's nice. It's a nice lukewarm, and when I lay down in it, it feels nice.

Following Jerome's instructions, I let myself float as I close my eyes.

"You know that magic responds to emotion, and you and this new magic have no emotional connection besides the few times you've been in danger. So, let yourself relax, let yourself feel, and meet the magic inside of you."

My body doesn't hesitate to follow the flow of his words. I don't think about it, don't think about my fire magic. I just give myself over to the water covering my skin, and I let it in.

I'm not sure how long I float like this until Jerome speaks up again.

"Avery, open your eyes."

When I do, there are droplets of water in the air above me, and I smile.

CHAPTER 11

That night, I leave the fae behind and walk out to the back of the house on my own. The illusion bubble reaches a dozen yards past the fountain, and I'm not really going anywhere farther than that. Slowly, I walk over to a dark spot in the grass, and lay down, giving myself time away from the prying eyes of the fae. I truly feel like they are watching me twenty-four-seven.

My fingers dig into the earth, connecting with it immediately. The connection I felt in the wasteland hasn't gone away. This Faery is just as connected to me as the future one was. But then again, they are one and the same. She welcomes me in. Closing my eyes, I trust this moment in time as I truly relax.

I never feel like I can do that in front of the fae. I always have to have my game face on.

Pretending.

Acting.

Masquerading.

It's becoming second nature to me. If that isn't the most fae thing, I don't know what is. I want to be better than what I know about them. I guess the books I've read only teach the ruthlessness. It's not that my companions haven't done questionable things. But so far, they've mostly been on my side. It's a strange combination of information.

I'm not sure how long I stay like that, just connected to the earth around me, but it refuels me somehow. Finally, I sit up, ready to go inside, when something changes.

The space around me dims, as if someone is turning down the lights, and shadows play against the backdrop. I get to my feet and spin in place, trying to find the source of the sudden change. That's when I notice the house is gone.

"Hello, child."

This time, I turn slowly. When I do, the same robed creature from the previous dream stands but ten feet in front of me. The space round him is even darker, as if he carries his own shadows within him.

"Where am I?"

"Still where you are. Yet, not at all. But we must talk."

Well, that made lots of sense. It's hard not to panic, but I push it down as much as I can. It would do me no good, losing my cool in front of this...creature.

"You have come to Faery. It was unexpected."

"Didn't you want me here?" Maybe I'm braver than I give myself credit for because the question escapes before I can think too much about it.

"We have many plans for you."

I wait for him to continue, but he doesn't.

"That's not cryptic at all," I comment, holding on to every ounce of courage I have in my blood.

"There are forces at play here, much bigger than you can imagine. Your power can open doors that have been shut for generations."

"Yes, I've heard," I mumble.

"There are books hidden within this land that even the queen has no knowledge about."

That perks up my attention. Queen Svetlana really makes it seem like she's all knowing. Granted, there are other queens in faery, but I have a feeling the creature speaks about all of them at once.

"Is that why you're here? You want me to find them?"

"We know where they are."

Then it clicks. They know, but they can't get to them.

"They're inside Faery, somewhere you can't get to."

My voice carries a tone of satisfaction, and it does not go unnoticed. The creature grows in size in front of me, a menacing growl escaping from inside those robes.

"We are unstoppable. Sometime soon, we will be in Faery."

"Then what do you need me for?" My voice shakes just a bit, but it's enough to placate the creature. He shrinks down a little, to appear more...approachable? It's the only reason I see for him to be playing these games. He goes from intimidating to approachable, looking for which one fits more for the situation.

"You can save us time by opening the Faery doors."

It sounds like an afterthought and a command at the same time. It turns my blood cold. The Ancients are more powerful than anything, and I have no doubt they'll break through. But if they're looking to use me, it means they're getting impatient. That never looks good on anyone, least of all a powerful magical entity.

"And if I don't?" I'm terrified of the answer and have every right to be.

"Then we will do whatever it takes to change your mind."

Just like that, he's gone. I'm shaking now, the possibilities endless in my mind. The air around me clears, and I'm once again standing at the back of the house, but this time, I find no calmness here.

Only horror.

* * *

"You're not paying attention," Derek says, his voice low. I glance at him, wiping the sweat from my eyes. We've been outside for about thirty minutes, and I'm already exhausted. Granted, I woke up exhausted because I barely slept. The visit from the Ancients has left me completely unbalanced. Clearly, they appear only to me and don't break any barriers or sound any alarms because no one even noticed.

"I'm doing the best I can."

"Then do better."

I narrow my eyes at him and his tone. He's been standoffish from the moment we got to Hannah's, and I'm sick of it.

"How about you do better? Better at explaining what you want me to do? Better at treating me like a normal human being?"

"You're not normal."

"No duh."

I'm angry, and I'm taking it out on him. Mentally, I know this. But emotionally, I would like to punch him. That's perfect since he's trying to teach me hand to hand combat. Even though we've done this before, I need way more practice than I'd like to admit.

Twice, we've been in a hand-to-hand battle, and I was pretty much useless. Yes, I have my magic...when it works. But that's not going to help if it decides to fritz on me. I absolutely cannot afford that, considering the Ancients are now making indirect threats toward my family. Because of course they are. Why wouldn't they? They will do whatever it takes to reach their goal. I should take some notes on their tenacity.

"Avery."

"What?"

"You're doing it again."

I drop my hands to my hips and face Derek head on. In turn, he folds his arms over his chest, his muscles bulging, but I won't be swayed. We stare at each other for a long moment, and I swear I can hear the air around us electrify. There I go again with my romantic notions. I need to stop thinking anything remotely close to romance when it comes to this fae, but there's just something about him.

Focus, Avery.

Focus.

Focus.

"Doing what exactly?" I finally ask, raising an eyebrow.

"You're a hundred miles away. You have to be present. If you're not, it's easy to sneak up on you."

Just then, Julian appears from seemingly nowhere, grabbing me around the middle. But while I'm not completely present, I'm present enough. I'm ready for him. When his arms come up, I drop my whole body backward, taking him off balance. When we land, I hear a loud whoosh. I deliver another blow to the stomach with my elbow before I roll off him and jump to my feet.

"I think she's good," Julian says from the floor, rubbing a hand over his stomach. I grin down at the fae, pleased with my success.

"Agree to disagree," Derek mumbles. My head jerks up in his direction. The feeling of success evaporates as I narrow my eyes at him.

"Anyone ever tell you positive reinforcement works better than negative?"

"No, actually they haven't." His response is so quick and bitter that it stops me for a moment. I glance at Julian as Derek turns away. The other fae jumps to his feet before giving me a little shrug and leaving. I turn back to Derek, watching the muscles in his back tense under my gaze. He reaches for a cup of water, taking a swig.

Since we left the palace, I feel like Derek has been showing more and more of his true colors. Even going as far as opening up, without actually opening up. Like right now. One sentence, and it tells me so much.

"Let's try something else," I say, because I know he won't take well to me offering any sympathy right now. I'm not supposed to notice his response to my question. That much is true no matter what male I'm talking to. It's a universal character trait.

"Like what?" Derek turns back around, ready to focus on business once again.

"I've been training with Jerome on my water magic. Maybe we can combine the two? I have to learn how to do that eventually."

"I don't think you're ready for that yet. Your magic is still unpredictable, and your fighting skills are basic at best."

"Wow, you sure know how to make a girl swoon," I roll my eyes as he gives me a confused look. Sometimes fae and their honesty is just a little bit too much. But instead of getting offended, I push.

"Maybe so, but I won't learn until you teach me. And you won't teach me until we try it, so it's a vicious circle, and that means we should try it."

"What exactly do you have in mind?" He hasn't agreed, but he's not arguing, so I take that as a good sign.

"I'm thinking Jerome attacks with water, while you attack with a sword, and we'll see if I can keep you both at bay."

"That sounds dangerous."

"Okay, great. Then we're doing it." I don't wait for him to voice any other concerns as I bounce toward the house and yell into the open doorway for Jerome to come outside. He's there a minute later, looking between the two of us.

"What's going on?"

"I need you to attack me with your element, while Derek tries to attack me with a weapon." I announce, grinning.

"Should she look this happy about this? Should you look this happy about this?" Jerome glances between Derek and me.

"Yes, absolutely. I need to know how much I've learned and practice applying it."

When I put it like that, the guys have no reason to argue. Julian and Hannah are now at the back door, watching us curiously, but all my attention is on the guys in front of me. I have absolutely no idea if this will work, but I have to try. The anger I was feeling earlier about the Ancients, and my own lack of progress, fuels me. Granted, I know this isn't how a real battle will go, but I need to know if I can handle the assault from both sides.

Derek picks up his sword, swinging it a couple of times around his body. I glance back at Hannah one more time, but there's no expression on her face. Julian, however, looks a little worried.

The fae don't give me any warning. Suddenly, a wave of water rushes straight out of the ground, sweeping me off my feet. I land hard, but I'm quick to get back up. Derek attacks at the same time, swinging his sword at me. I dodge out of the way, reaching for my magic at the same time.

Another wave comes, but I hold it at bay before grabbing Jerome's water and flinging it at Derek. It slams right into his face, disorienting him enough for me to land a kick. I'm going for the sword, but that doesn't budge. Jerome blasts water at my back, pushing me forward. I'm falling before I can catch myself. I twist around just before I hit the ground, landing on my back. Derek is there, his sword swinging downward. I thrust my hands in front of me, creating a water shield. His sword slams into it and stops.

Happy with myself, I push the whole thing at him as I get to my feet. Jerome sends another water blast at me. I know the moment something goes wrong. My magic shifts, wanting to protect me from the back, slacking on the shield I created at the front. The momentum of Jerome's blast carries me forward instead of back. When I fly through my own water shield, the thing that stops me is Derek's sword.

It rams right into my right arm before either of us can do anything. I scream, dropping to my knees. Derek is instantly beside me.

"I'm—Avery—I'm so sorry." He keeps repeating it over and over, as the pain brings in darkness. I feel myself fading while the fae rush around me. It makes me want to chuckle how human they're acting at this moment. Genuine concern and worry paint their faces.

"Avery, I'm so sorry."

"Wasn't—your—fault," I mumble right before the world goes black.

CHAPTER 12

When I open my eyes, I'm in a bed. It's not the bed in the room Hannah gave me as my own. This one is a little more like what I remember the palace to look like. I turn my head, glancing down at my arm. It's been bandaged from my shoulder to halfway down past my elbow. It's completely stiff, and I can't move it.

"You're awake."

I glance up to find Derek standing at the foot of the bed. At first, I think I'm imagining him, but then he steps toward me and into the light. His face is pale, like a human would look after a bad case of food poisoning. And his face is completely stoic. I realize this must be his room, and that brings a wave of mixed emotions.

"How long was I out?"

"About a day."

That makes me sit up a little farther. Derek is there in a flash to help me sit up. He moves the pillows at my back as I use my left arm to push myself up. His face is only a few inches away, and the desire to touch him almost overwhelms me. Instead, I grip the sheet beneath my fingertip as I settle back against the pillows.

"You cut me. I shouldn't have been out so long."

"I pierced right through your arm with a fae blade. It wouldn't come straight out. We had to...extract it." That means they probably had to cut a bigger hole in me in order to do so. The hesitation in his voice is the only sign of emotion. He's completely shut down. It's much like when I first met him many moons ago in Arizona. Immediately, I miss the fae I've gotten to know since then.

"You could've died."

The words are barely whispered. There he is. He's not meeting my eye now, as if too ashamed to do so. I raise my hand toward him, palm out. Glancing up, he stares at it, as if it's a foreign object, before placing his own in it. I wrap my fingers around his and tug him down on the bed. He sits down carefully, as if he's afraid he's going to hurt me more somehow.

"That wasn't your fault," I say, my words sure and strong. His eyes meet mine. He studies me like he's trying to figure out how much truth is in my statement. I roll my eyes at him, and he furrows his brow in confusion.

"I know I'm not full fae and don't have that whole 'truth only' rule, but I am speaking the truth."

"I should've been able to stop it."

"How? Plus, it wasn't your idea in the first place."

"Exactly." He moves to stand, but I grab onto his arm, keeping him in place. His skin is hot under my touch. He stares at the spot for a moment before looking up again.

"I was bound to get hurt eventually, Derek. I know that's not exactly comforting, but I can't learn if I don't try."

"There has to be another way."

"There isn't. My next lesson with this might very well be an actual fight with actual bad guys and more magic and more weapons. I would be a liability, and I won't be that again."

"You're not."

"But I am." I sigh because even as I'm talking to him, I'm realizing a lot of these things for myself. Maybe I already knew them but saying them out loud is making them more real. "Everything about me is a liability. I can't control my magic, the elemental aspects of it. And now, I can't control the faery magic either. I need to be able to access it and understand it. I can't keep relying on chance, which is what happened in that forest."

"I don't think you give yourself enough credit."

"I think I gave myself too much. Between lessons with Jerome on elemental magic history with Hannah, and you and Julian teaching me fighting, I feel like I don't know anything." I stop, taking a deep breath, because I don't want to cry in front of him.

"My whole life, I prided myself on my education. It's what I did best, learn. Now, I feel like that whole time I've learned nothing. I'm completely blind in this situation, and I have no grounding point to help me find my footing. I can't be babied or protected. I have to do the work."

I'm a little out of breath when I finish my speech, but I'm not sorry. Derek might not understand where I'm coming from, but at least he'll have the information in front of him.

"I don't want to see you hurt."

"It'll hap—"

"No, don't just except this as the outcome. Fight to not make that an option. I need you safe, Avery. I won't be able to live with myself if something happens to you."

His words stun me into silence. It's the most emotion I've ever seen in him. For a second, I have no idea what to do with that. Then, I slide my hand down his arm, taking his hand once again in mine and giving it a small squeeze.

"I know I've failed you," he continues, watching our hands entwined together on top of the covers. "I don't want to be like her, Avery, but sometimes I can't help it." I don't have to ask who he's talking about. I've met his mother. "Spending time in the human world has taught me to be more sympathetic, which is something I was never taught as a child. If the time comes, I might not be able to turn that part of me off. But for you, I want to try."

This time, when tears pool in my eyes, I don't hide them from him. He's opening up to me in a way I never imagined. So vulnerable and so human. For the first time, I actually know for a fact there is no manipulation here. He's speaking from his heart, however far away it may be hidden.

Giving his hand another squeeze, I let the tear slip down my cheek before I whisper, "I forgive you."

* * *

IT TAKES me three full days of staying in bed before I can venture out. According to Hannah, I lost too much blood. On top of my already magic-exhausted body, that means it took me longer than it should've to recover. I also wasn't allowed to practice any of the said magic, but Hannah made sure to bring me plenty of books on Faery to keep me occupied.

The more I learn about this land, the more fascinated and sadder I get. It's beautiful, full of traditions and magical stories that I've never even heard of. But it's also full of cruelty and darkness and madness. It breaks my heart knowing that Derek and Julian, and even Hannah, have had to live in this.

I think of my parents and how angry I've been at them for keeping this secret from me. But at the same time, I miss them so much it hurts. After reading more about this place, I'm also thankful to them for not letting me grow up like that. They have always been there for me, they have played with me and taught me rhymes and song. They made sure we had picnics in the park and mushroom hunts in the forest. They were there, and that presence and their love is what I remember most.

Fae don't exactly operate the same way. Many send their offspring off to be raised by servants or tutors, depending on their standing within the courts. Even when they're left at court, they're looked after by nannies. I can't help but think about Derek and what kind of upbringing he had. He clearly doesn't have a good relationship with the queen, and I'm not surprised. She seems like she'd be the worst at being a mother. I won't pry, no matter how much I want to. But one thing I wish I did know is why she only has the one son. Or maybe I'm missing something.

"How are you today?" Hannah steps into the room without knocking. I have moved back into my room. Still unsure why I ended up in Derek's originally.

"I've been moving around fine. I'm ready to do more."

Hannah studies me carefully, as if trying to find the validity in my words. Today, she's wearing a deep green gown with a long cut all the way up her thigh. The spaghetti straps are barely visible as they hold the dress up. She looks effortlessly beautiful. It reminds me that I'm still in my leggings and t-shirt. I don't know why seeing her dressed up always makes me feel so self-conscious, but it does. I really need to get over it.

"If you're sure," she says, her eyes still narrowed on me. I push my shoulders back to try to appear stronger. She doesn't miss the move. "What do you have in mind then?"

"I want to work on the pages."

She knows exactly what I'm talking about of course. We've been putting off me reading anything from the Ancient's book until I was a bit more stable in my magic. But now it seems that time is running out, and we have no choice but to try. We've been gone long enough that I'm getting nervous about Queen Svetlana showing up and dragging me back, kicking and screaming. After lying in bed for three days, I'm not wasting any more time.

"You seem very determined."

"I think it's time. This land needs me, Hannah. I'm not saying I'm going to save everyone. But I want to do my part. I have to."

She stares at me for another long moment, as if waiting for me to back down, but I won't. Whatever it does to me, I have to try.

"Okay," Hannah finally agrees, turning to head back out of the room. "Do we tell the boys?"

"No."

My quick answer makes her pause, turning to glance over her shoulder at me. I'm not backing down from that either. Derek is too protective right now, and Julian isn't far behind. I think Jerome would understand, but it's not like he needs to know. Hannah doesn't comment. She only leads me back to her rooms.

Once inside, she shuts the double doors, waving her hand over the edges. I'm not sure what kind of magic she possesses. She never displays it all, but she's a powerful fae. I'm not surprised she has a few tricks up her sleeve. Walking over to her nightstand, she opens the top drawer and pulls out the two pieces of paper.

Immediately, the magic inside me wakes up, pulling me toward the bed where she leaves them lying. I walk over, glancing at the words without reading them. I haven't truly read the book since the day in the library when I found it.

"So, I just read the spell?"

"It's not really that simple." Hannah walks over to the opposite side of the bed before facing me. "Just like with any powerful magic, you must carry intention in every word. Since these words are transcribed by fae from thousands of years ago, they already carry with them intention. As you read the words, you must overpower the initial intention and make the words your own."

"Like taking ownership."

Hannah smiles. "Exactly like taking ownership."

I glance back down at the pages. From what I remember before I sent these to Hannah at Thunderbird Academy, they contained at least two spells and some history. The book I found was written almost like a journal. It's like someone was telling a story and then filled in the gaps with spells and diagrams and graphs.

"I'm not sure I can do that."

"You won't know until you try."

"That contradicts the whole part where you were telling me to be careful."

"I will give you guidance from both ends of the spectrum, Avery. You have to be the deciding factor. It's what will fuel your magic."

That makes sense, even though it seems impossible for me to thrust any kind of will on an ancient artifact.

"Okay, I'm ready."

"When you read the words, read them in your mind. They do have to be spoken out loud, in the correct order, which isn't always what is written. That is why you read it in your head first. But don't linger. If something doesn't make sense, keep going. Read the passages as a whole, never individually."

I do have a tendency to get stuck in a word or a sentence and try and figure it out before moving on. Apparently, it's a bad habit. I'll have to keep that in mind.

"Whenever you're ready, Avery."

"Queen Svetlana won't be able to track it?"

"Not here."

I'm going to have to ask more about that later. Right now, I turn to the pages and begin to read.

CHAPTER 13

I don't touch the pages at first. Even though I said I'm ready, the nervous feeling at the pit of my stomach intensifies the closer I get. There really isn't an easy way to do this. I have to stay focused, and I have to dive right in.

Picking up the first page, I flip it over to go to the beginning. There's a drawing of a tree with no leaves in the left corner and some branches at the chapter heading. The number five stands out on its own at the top. Taking another deep, calming breath, I begin to read.

The words don't have to rearrange themselves or jump out at me in any way. They look like any other book I've ever read. And I've read plenty. These pages are a continuation of something I read at Thunderbird Academy, the passage that started it all. Hannah watches silently as I begin to read.

THE TRUE KNIGHT is not only a person but an idea. There are those who believe the power comes from within, and there are those who believe the power comes from the land itself. It never matters where it comes from, as long as the one who wields it, wields it with a pure heart.

. . .

THE STORIES of brave young magicians have been passed down for generations. And yet, they are not to be found hitherto. Ballads and folktales have been created, yet none can truly sing of the grandeur of such a being.

IN THE TIME before time began, they used to say fae came from the heavens above. Angels sent to the land to nourish it and grow it. But the hearts are wicked above all else, and the beautiful creatures lost sight of their mission and became greedy. They created boundaries and warred among themselves, searching for the rush of the ultimate power. They created creatures to serve them as they became their masters, and the land did not grow but withered. Until it could handle no more.

I GLANCE up at Hannah then, as the page comes to another break. She's watching me carefully, waiting for me make my move. The same sadness I felt in the Faery wasteland has entered my heart once more. I didn't think I was still so connected to the land, but maybe that's part of my magic, and it will never go away.

"I don't really understand the pages. Or this book."

"What do you mean?"

"It's written in small paragraphs, and it seems to jump from a journal entry to a bedtime story to actual historical information."

Hannah is silent for a moment, thinking over it.

"When you read it, do you sense the same type of emotions from each passage?"

It's tempting to glance down and read over certain parts, but I restrain myself. Instead, I close my eyes, trying to process what I'm feeling without focusing on the words. It's difficult, since that's not how my mind usually processes information. After a few moments, I shake my head.

"No, they don't seem the same. You're saying multiple authors wrote this?"

"It appears to be so. It's not unheard of. Maybe it was a specific family or a specific court that was entrusted with information."

"So, it's not an Ancient who wrote it."

"I can't answer that, Avery." Hannah shrugs, flipping her long hair over her shoulder. "I don't have more knowledge about them than you do. They are a very taboo subject around these parts."

That part I already knew. Seeing no other choice, I take a second to settle my mind once more before I glance down at the paper.

THERE WERE those who believed the land created the true knights to protect herself. Others thought they were angels sent to replace the ones who became the power-hungry fae. Those with the belief of pure creation would fight to protect the land at any cost. It is why those creatures were the most rewarded. Marks were bestowed on the pure hearted, gifts from the land herself. Some hid such marks, and some wore them proudly.

"MARKS?" I mumble out loud, and the moment I do, my focus shifts.

"Avery!" Hannah's voice is raised in alarm, and I release my fingers to drop the page, but it's too late. The words pour out of me as I read them, the need so overpowering, I can't stop.

"The fae with the purest hearts, with the strongest minds, those with the right intentions. They were meant to rule Faery because Faery wanted to be ruled by them. But the greed was too strong and the fae were too weak to overcome the basis of what was asked of them. To let the land thrive and the pure of heart rule—"

Suddenly, the space around me is thrown into a windstorm. I hold onto the page, afraid it'll be ripped away from me as I stand in the midst of a tunnel. Magic surges through me, rushing through every nerve ending on my body. I can feel it everywhere. I close my eyes, leaning into the rush, wanting more of it.

There's a loud banging somewhere close by and shouting, but I don't care. All I want to do is to stay in the cocoon of this wind and in the ecstasy of this power running through me. The high is almost too much and not enough at the same time.

More shouting reaches me. A huge explosion rocks the floor I stand on, but I don't lose focus of the want that fills me.

I want more.

I want more.

I want more.

The shouting comes again, this time closer. I hear my name called over and over.

I know that voice.

Opening my eyes, I turn to the left to find Derek just on the outside of the wind vortex His face is pale and frantic as he calls out to me. I want to tell him there's nothing to fear. That this magic isn't bad. That I can control it. But then my eyes drop to his mouth, and his lips form a word that breaks through the fog of power in my brain.

"Please."

Just as suddenly as it comes, the wind is gone. I fall forward with Derek there to catch me. The electricity is still running over my skin, and a part of me wants to get back into whatever it was. It's Derek's touch that grounds me. I finally drop the paper back onto the bed.

* * *

"WHAT WERE YOU THINKING?" Derek shouts about an hour later as we're all gathered in the library. Hannah insisted on me eating and drinking after my ordeal before she allowed Derek within shouting distance. I am thankful for small favors.

I'm still a bit disoriented, and I have no idea what I did. I'm not even sure if it was my doing or some Ancient curse put on the pages. Apparently, that can be a thing too. I'm learning so much these days.

If Derek didn't burst through that door with whatever magical dynamite he has up his sleeve, I'm not sure what would've happened. That is why I'm giving him a minute to get the frustration out. It's strange to see him this frazzled, but a part of me likes it. I should really keep that part to myself.

"Those pages are dangerous. What if that vortex killed you? Did you even think about that before you started to read some ancient text for your amusement? You don't think! You don't think what this will do to—if anything happens to you—" He runs his hand through his hair, sending it dancing into disarray. In this moment, he looks so much like just a gorgeous guy I know and not a prince of the Spring Court. Part of me wants to reach out and hold him.

I'm keeping that part buried as well.

"You can't keep taking risks like that, not with your life. It's stupid to—"

That does it. I glance up at him from where he's been standing behind a chair, gripping it tightly.

"Are you done?" I interrupt, shocking him into silence. It takes him less than a second to recover.

"No, I'm not done."

He walks around the chair, marching straight for me. The intensity in his eyes makes my head spin as he stops three feet in front of me.

"You keep taking these risks, and you think you're just going to be fine. Because why? You're not invincible, so stop acting like you are!"

"You have no right to tell me who to be, Derek." I get right in his face. I'm not intimidated, and I need him to know that. "You want me to be strong? You want me to learn my magic and be able to protect myself? Then deal with the consequences of that. There is no growth without growing pains, and I won't be talked to like a child because you don't like the outcome of something."

"I don't like seeing you hurt!" He screams the words, and they shake the glass on the windows around us. I've forgotten that we're not alone. Hannah, Julian, and Jerome have been watching our spitting match in silence. I can't even begin to read what's on their faces. It doesn't matter because all of my attention is on the fae in front of me.

"You can't protect me from everything," I whisper, matching his intensity but with the opposite volume. His full attention is on me, so I know he's forgotten about our audience just like I have.

"What if I want to protect you?"

My heart clenches at the simple question, heavy and hurting as it fills with emotion. Maybe that's dramatic, but it feels like I'm full, and that's a feeling I've never experienced before.

"You can't protect me from this," I reply honestly. We both know it's true. I'm on a path neither one of us understands, and there's only one option for us, to move forward. "But you can help me."

He nods at that, his eyes still on mine. It really does feel like the whole world falls away. Everything between us is more intense, more emotional. I have no idea when I decided to let him into my heart, but here we are.

"Not to interrupt this lovely moment." Hannah's voice penetrates our gaze, and we jerk to attention, glancing at her. "But we have company."

She doesn't say anything else. Standing, she walks out of the library with all of us on her heels. Instead of going outside, she heads for her room.

"Hannah?" Julian calls out, but she doesn't stop. We follow her in as she stops in front of her large standing mirror, placing her palm against it. It ripples like water would and then someone steps through it.

"Hello there!" Nora says, giving each of us a smile.

All I do is stare in return.

"You have a portal in your room?" Julian asks. I'm glad someone decided to ask because I'm a little confused too. We went through all of that forbidden forest drama for nothing?

"Only for very special occasions," Hannah replies as she reaches over to give Nora a hug. I didn't even know the two knew each other. I really don't know anything about these fae.

"It's not a happy occasion, I'm afraid. The queen has sent me to fetch you back. As far as she knows, you are still in the forest looking for her elusive book. So, she allowed me the use of portal magic to bring you back. She just didn't know where I was portaling to." Nora shrugs, giving each of us a once over. "Oh hey, Jerome."

"Hey."

I glance between the two fae. I'm sure I'm not the only one who notices the tone in that one greeting. Curious.

"Why are we needed back?" I decide to concentrate on the issue at hand. I'll have to ask Nora about Jerome later.

"I'm not exactly sure, only that it was urgent."

I glance over at Derek and see him deep in thought. There's something going on, but I can't even begin to guess what it may be.

"How urgent?" he finally asks.

"Urgent enough that we need to leave now."

My only thought is that I'm not ready. I need more time with the pages, I need more time with training. Going back now will be going into the lion's den with no protection. But I also realize I don't have a choice. The internal panic comes anyway. So that's great.

I turn to Hannah, but she beats me to it. "I'll keep them safe. This place is still not on anyone's map." I nod at that. She looks like she's going to say something else, but she moves back away from the mirror instead. Julian and Derek move forward, not even questioning the orders.

"Just like that? We're leaving?"

I'm waiting for the guys to speak up, but they don't. Both of them just look resigned.

"We need to go, Avery, before the queen comes looking herself," Nora urges, holding out her hand to me. I guess we're not even going to grab our stuff or anything. Once again, the choice is taken from me, but this time, at least I expect it. The queen was bound to get restless. Or she decided on a new game.

"If you need us, you know where to find us," Jerome calls out, and I realize this is a goodbye for now. I almost say thank you, but I stop myself, giving them a smile instead. Hannah watches me steadily. I hate that we didn't have time to talk about what happened. I have so many questions.

My skin is still buzzing from the magic, and I'm itching to get back to the book. But there's no way I'm taking the pages with me, and therefore, I'm out of time and out of luck.

The guys step through the portal first and then Nora and I follow. We come out in my room. It feels like I haven't even left, even though it's been over a week now.

I head for the door, but Nora stops me.

"You can't go like that. She'll expect you to look like you've been in a forest for days."

I glance down at my leggings and t-shirt, realizing she's right. I rush into the walk-in closet with Nora right behind me. She pulls a dress out as I tug the shirt over my head. It's a simple flowery dress, barely falling to my knees. The spaghetti straps are a little thicker. When I pull it over my head, I feel like I'm going to a picnic in the park. I tug the leggings off and slip into some flats.

"Well?"

"We'll just say your clothes were too disgusting for her majesty."

"Good plan."

We rush out of the closet where the guys are waiting by the door. Derek gives me a quick once over, his eyes lighting up at the sight of me in this dress. I don't have time to process that because there's a knock on the door. Julian pulls it open to find guards on the other side.

"She is to come with us," the one at the front says, nodding at me. Nora and Derek move to follow, but the guard puts up a hand. "Just her."

We exchange a look, but it's not like we can argue. I give Derek one last look and then I let the guards usher me out of my room and toward the queen.

"Ah, good. You're here. Did you bring it back?" the queen asks the moment we step into the throne room. Her body lounges on the throne like it's a sofa.

"We weren't able to locate it," I reply. The queen doesn't even bother to look disappointed.

"That is truly a shame," she says, and means the complete opposite. Even though I knew this was all a game to her, I'm still mad. She was never going to entrust me with any of her books. And now I'm not even sure she has any. Maybe this was a test to see if I would lead her to the book.

"You have requested my presence urgently. We didn't want to delay," I reply with my best smile. For a queen who's been in power for generations, I'm sure she sees right through it. At least I tried.

"Yes, the urgent matter." She stops then, as if she realizes something. "What are you wearing?"

"My clothes were not presentable to be seen in." I smooth the skirt down over my thighs. The queen narrows her eyes but doesn't comment further.

"Back to the matter at hand, I'm having a ball, and you are to attend. It's time you met the others within the Spring Court. That is all."

Wait, what? She turns away from me, back to the fae sitting at her feet. I don't even want to know what they were doing before I came in, or will continue to do when I leave. I'm dismissed just like that. The guards usher me out before I can make a sound.

A party? In the middle of a war? That sounds great.

* * *

Nora is in my room when I return.

"A ball? She's throwing a party?" I ask, exasperated the moment the door closes behind me. The queen is definitely keeping a close watch on me. My used-to-be shadows are full-on ghosts now, following me whenever I go.

"I can't really explain that to you either," Nora says, standing near my walk-in closet. She seems excited, so I bite.

"Nora, what's in my closet?"

The fae claps her hands together before motioning to follow her. She does a sweeping motion over what hangs there. I can't believe my eyes.

"Is that?"

"Brand new. Just for you."

"You've outdone yourself." And I mean it. I just can't wrap my mind around the fact that the dress is the exact replica of the one I wore in my time leap in the house.

The color is bright magenta, the shoulders open, with a halter top and a deep v-cut in the front. It stitches at my waist before falling out in a flair skirt to the floor. It's elegant and simple, and so me. You'd think the color clashes with the green streaks in my hair, but it compliments them somehow instead.

"You really like it?" Nora asks. There's a strange catch in her voice. Glancing over at her, I find her watching me carefully.

"Why wouldn't I?"

"I'm not sure. I know it's flashier than you like, but once I got the idea in my head, I couldn't let it go."

It really is a beautiful gown, even though the whole situation seems strange. But then again, is it really that strange? If what I saw in the house was truly the future, or one possibility of it, this dress was bound to come around. I guess maybe I didn't want it to be real because I didn't like the way I felt in that garden with Derek. That feeling is what I remember more than what we were talking about.

"You did a lovely job, Nora." It's the closest to a thank you that I will get with her, but it's enough. She beams at me, satisfied. "Do you know anything about this ball?"

Nora sobers up instantly. I knew something was up with this party besides what's on the surface.

"I can't be sure of anything, Avery."

"But?"

"But there has been talk that the queen has a special announcement to make. All the top families are commanded to be there. The preparations have been going on for a few days now."

"And you have no idea what it could be?"

Nora shakes her head as I try to come up with possibilities. She ended our mission before we managed to get anything done. Granted, she didn't exactly know we weren't looking for the queen's books. Still, if she wanted me to have the books, there's a way for her to get them to me. If she wanted to help, she would.

There has to be some devious plan behind this sudden party. The land around her is turmoil, the Ancients are pressing in at the borders, and she wants to host all the high-ranking families in her court? We have to be ready for the worst type of outcome.

"I'll see what I can find out," Nora comments, and I smile in response. The party is in two days, so I have until then to get ready. I'm not exactly sure what I will do, but it feels like having an exit strategy is my best bet. I wonder what Derek thinks about all of this. We've been separated since the moment we returned.

"I'm going to go ahead and wash up," I announce. Nora hurries to grab fresh towels.

It still surprises me sometimes just how modern this place is. The fae have truly adopted the century the world is residing in, even though time really has no meaning to them. I suppose that's what happens when you live for hundreds of years.

I accept the towels from Nora and head to the bathroom. A part of me is tempted to soak in the gorgeous bath, but that would make me a little too vulnerable for my liking. So, shower it is.

The moment I'm under the warm spray, I let my mind focus on creating a to-do list. If I'm to have a way out, I need some supplies. Maybe Nora can find me another one of those handy over-the-shoulder bags I had to leave behind at Hannah's.

The more I think about leaving, the more I think I need to do that anyway. Being in Spring Court has yielded me no help. Maybe there's a way I can go back to Hannah's. Or better yet, I can get out of Faery all together and find a better place to hide. Although, I'm not exactly sure where that would be. The Ancients seem to be able to find me anywhere.

I suppress the shiver that runs down my spine at the thought of the creatures. The last dream, or vision, that I had with them is still sitting heavily on my mind and heart. No matter how mad I might be at my parents, I want them protected at all cost. And that's exactly how far the Ancients are willing to go to get what they want, so it's a no-win situation for me. Unless I can figure something out.

It feels like I'm missing crucial information. Even after reading the page from the fae book, there's so much I don't know. But I do feel more connected to it all. That scares me all in itself. Every single day I think I'm getting closer to losing complete control. I'm a bomb waiting to go off, and someone has already lit the wick.

CHAPTER 15

The next two days go by in a blur of activity. Preparations for the ball continue as if the whole existence of the court depends on the success of it. I can't say that's making me feel any better about anything that's going on.

Derek has been completely missing in action. I saw him once across the courtyard, but he barely just met my eye before disappearing again. I've been training with Julian instead. He's a great sparring partner, but he's no Derek. I try not to let his absence bother me. I have more pressing issues to deal with anyway.

Nora has been great at prepping my to-go pack, if the need arises. I'm not sure when I decided to trust her, but we've become almost like friends. She spends all her time with me, and I know that's partially because she's been assigned to watch me. But there's also an actual friendship forming between us. Just like there is one with Julian.

These fae are so different from anything I've ever imagined, it's hard to reconcile with the image sometimes. I'm still careful, but even so, I've allowed myself to really be present when I'm with them.

"What would you like me to do with your hair?" Nora asks after I've showered and moisturized. The one thing I do enjoy about fae, to a point, is their vanity. Because of it, I have access to the best oils in the world. Since I have to wear such a revealing dress, I want to make sure my skin glows.

It feels very strange having such vain thoughts if I'm being honest.

"I think down and straight will be fine," I reply, sitting down in front of the vanity mirror as Nora takes her position behind me.

"Are you sure about the no curls?"

"Okay, how about waves?" I ask with a smile. Nora really enjoys this part of her job, and I kind of want to give her the chance to do it. She beams at me before taking the damp strands into her hands. She brushes my hair out before using her hands and magic to dry it and give it a slight wave. I have no desire to wear paint on my face like I've seen other fae do. I'm thankful that wasn't a requirement from the queen. Instead, I just dab on two coats of mascara, accenting my already long lashes, and leave it at that.

Since coming to Faery, and especially after my fae powers began emerging, my features have sharpened in a way. My eyes are brighter, my cheeks carry the glow of an artistically applied highlighter. Even my eyebrows don't need any filling in. They're still my features, but more vivid somehow.

The process of applying mascara still calms me in a way, giving me a sense of normalcy I've been so desperately craving. I'm not even sure where such a human object came from, but I'm happy to hold it in my hands.

"What do you think?" Nora asks. I glance into the mirror to see her smiling at me. My hair is shiny, with a barely-there wave that makes it fall gracefully around my shoulders. The green streak that appeared after I used my fae magic for the first time fits me somehow, mixing with my dark brown hair.

"You did a great job," I say, receiving a quick squeeze on my shoulder from the excitement.

"Come, let's get you into this dress."

I stand, dropping my robe from my shoulders as Nora holds out the dress. In the time that I've spent here, I've definitely become more comfortable in my own skin. I think it's a combination of things. The training has definitely helped me to feel more confident. But it's also just my mindset. So much is placed on my shoulders, but if I don't believe in myself, no one else will. Making a plan and making progress has helped me see that I can handle this. I hold on to that ray of sunshine of a thought as hard as I can.

The material is silky against my skin, and it sends a dance of goosebumps down my arms. The back of the dress is lower than I would like, but it also makes me feel good somehow. Once the dress settles over my hips, I run my hands down the sides, enjoying the feel of it. That's when I realize something awesome.

"I didn't know you added pockets."

"Only on the right side. And it's more of a slit than a pocket. I know you'll want to be armed."

Curious, I watch as Nora walks over to my vanity table and pulls out something from the top drawer. It's looks like a leather belt, but when I look closer, I realize exactly what it is.

"Where did you get that?"

"Derek wanted to make sure you had it."

I pull the dress up and slide the leather band over my upper thigh. It sits there comfortably, and when I slip the knife into the sheath, I feel stronger. The dress falls down over my legs and then I place my hand in my pocket. When I do, I feel the knife there. The opening is perfect for me to reach it if I need it.

"This is incredible."

"Glad you think so."

When I turn and look at myself in the long mirror, I'm surprised by how right I look. It's as if I belong here with my hair falling across my naked shoulders, the knife strapped to my thigh. The fact that Derek wanted to make sure I had it warms my heart, but I don't comment on it. I push that away and focus on the task at hand.

Tonight is going to be a long and interesting night. I can feel it.

* * *

When it's time to head to the main hall where the majority of the festivities will be held, Nora leads me out. Even though I've been preparing for this mentally and physically for days, I'm still nervous. It would be very dumb of me not to be. This allows me to stay on my toes. At least, I hope it does.

My increased focus is why I realize we're not heading toward the hall when we leave my room behind.

"Nora?"

"Trust me, Avery."

Since I haven't had a reason not to before, I don't say anything. But my hand is in my pocket, reaching for the knife just in case. When Nora turns, veering off the main hallway, I realize where we're going. The courtyard opens up in front of us, and it looks much like it did in my vision.

The trees are bigger, and the flowers are in full bloom, sending the whole area into an eerie glow. It's beautiful and a bit frightening all at the same time.

"What am I doing here?" I ask Nora, but she doesn't reply. She just nods her head in the direction of the courtyard, so I have no choice but to leave her behind and walk into the garden.

I feel him before I see him. He's standing near one of the trees at the back of the yard, his dark suit accenting his broad shoulders. He turns, even though I'm sure I haven't made a sound, as if he's sensing me as well.

"Avery."

"Derek."

I stop a few feet in front of him, and honestly, I don't know what to say besides his name. He looks incredibly handsome in his suit, which I now can see is dark blue. The light shirt underneath is unbuttoned at the throat. It's such a small detail, but it makes it so much more him. His hair is slicked back at the sides, but even so, he doesn't look quite as polished as he might be trying to be.

"You've been avoiding me," I say, deciding on the direct approach.

"It was necessary."

"How so?"

"The queen commanded it. I could not disobey."

There he goes with his formal speech again. It makes him sound so unapproachable, which is probably what he's going for. Except, he's the one who brought me here.

"So, what about now? You're allowed to talk to me?"

"No."

The one-word answer surprises me. I truly did not think he could go against a direct order from the queen. But then I notice the visible strain on him, and that makes sense. He's breaking her command, and it's costing him. I just don't understand why.

"What's going on, Derek?"

He doesn't answer right away, as if he's trying to find the right words. Or trying to push them past his lips. I really have no idea how faery magic affects this whole situation, but it was important enough for him to try, so I wait him out.

"I want you to be ready, Avery," he finally says, taking the slightest step toward me. "Faery revels are—they are not for the faint of heart. I know—" he hurries on to add, as if he realizes what he just implied, "—I know you can handle yourself, but be on the lookout. Don't...don't eat or drink anything unless Nora or Julian hands it to you."

I notice how he doesn't put himself in that category.

"Where will you be?"

"Near the queen. I am to be beside her the whole evening unless she commands otherwise."

The anger I feel toward that fae is finding new heights. I hate how she manipulates everything and everyone around her. The power she holds over her son breaks my heart. Because she uses it to her own benefit. Someone really needs to teach her a lesson. Or better yet, give her a taste of her own medicine.

"Why can't I eat anything? I've been eating faery food for weeks now."

I know the rules for mortals. If a mortal eats faery fruit, they won't want to leave. Ever. They'll be addicted, and most of the time, they become slaves. But faery food doesn't affect me the same, or I would've felt it by now.

"This is different."

"How so?"

"I can't really explain it, but there are a lot of very powerful fae present. They can do things...things that can have consequences. So be careful."

I close my eyes briefly, taking a deep breath. This whole evening was already making me nervous, and now I'm extra nervous. I need to stay calm and collected.

"I'll be watching over you," Derek says before he pushes past me. I think he's gone, but then his voice reaches out to me. "I'll always be watching over you."

So many thoughts rush over me at those whispered words. It doesn't feel like a hastily spoken phrase. It feels like a promise.

A promise a fae prince just made to me.

The quiet of the night is shattered by my emotions. I wish there was a way I could go after him and tell him that I'll be watching over him as well. The connection I feel toward him intensifies anytime he's near me. He's become that to me, and I have no idea what I will do with that information.

But there's just me and the trees. He's gone.

And I am left all alone.

CHAPTER 16

When Nora and I finally walk into the main hall, it is already filled with fae of every kind. Their clothes are much more elaborate than what I am wearing, but I don't feel out of place. That in itself is very surprising to me. Maybe I'm becoming accustomed to this life. Or maybe I'm still thinking about Derek's words and every little emotion they evoked.

Stay alert.

Stay alert.

Stay alert.

I have to repeat this to myself, because it's way too easy to get lost in a daydream. Now is not the time nor the place. The queen notices me right away. She is seated at the other side of the room in a raised platform. She motions me forward, and I walk across the floor to present myself in front of her throne. Derek is standing right over her right shoulder. It's taking everything in me not to stare at him. I steal a brief glance, but even that isn't missed by Queen Svetlana, so she grins knowingly at me when I stop in front of the throne.

"Welcome, Avery," she says, her voice carrying across the way. Everyone seems to quiet down at once. "You are our honored guest this evening, so I want to start it off with an old tradition." I glance over at Nora, who has moved to stand with the crowd, but she can't help me now. "The first dance."

With those words, the floor at my back clears, as the fae move out of the way and to the sides. I turn, confused as to what exactly is happening when the queen stands.

"The first dance is an old tradition that has not been part of our revels for a while. But tonight, on this special occasion, I would like to ask my son, Prince Derek, to lead our esteemed guest, Avery, in a waltz."

My eyes fly up to meet Derek's immediately. It's only because I've come to know him so well that I see the twinge of shock in his expression before it shuts down. There is no choice here, no way for either of us to say no.

"Go on," The queen urges, and that's when I realize what she's doing. There's a smug smile on her face, and it can only mean one thing. She wants to embarrass me. What teenage girl actually knows how to waltz. Or dance in front of a crowd.

Derek steps down from the platform, offering his arm to me. I have no choice but to take it. He leads me to the middle of the dance floor, sliding his hand down my arm and giving my fingers a quick squeeze.

"Just do the best you can," he murmurs, just loud enough for me to hear. "And don't let them see you sweat."

It's such a human thing to say that I almost smile. Instead, I steel my features, looking up at the prince. He guides one of my hands to his shoulder while he takes the other into his own. When he steps forward and wraps his hand around my waist, I forget to breathe. Our bodies brush just barely. I look up to find his intense gaze on mine.

"Lead the way," I whisper as the music starts.

Derek takes another pause and then he steps forward. My movements are automatic as I trust his leading and fall into rhythm. There's a bit of an audible hush over the crowd, as if they too expected me to stumble.

But one thing the queen or the fae here don't know is that my father taught me how to waltz when I was just a little girl. He continued to dance with me on many occasions. I can see now how it may have been a way to prepare me for this life, if the need ever arose. It's like how those childhood rhymes carried the truth about Faery in them. Our dance lessons were a way to teach me not only self-confidence, but a way to keep myself on the winning side if I ever ended up in court.

When Derek spins me, I see Queen Svetlana's face for the briefest of moments. Her gaze is hard because her plan clearly didn't work. I have no idea why she wants to see me fail in front of all these fae, but she does. Whatever her plan is, I one upped her, and that's going to cost me. I know that for a fact.

But right now, as Derek's hand around my waist pulls me even closer as we spin, I don't want to think about any of that. He moves like someone who is meant to do this with elegance and grace. Even though he's clearly much better at it than I, there is no hesitation in my movements. I think it's simply because I am dancing with *him*.

We have found our footing together, and we glide across the floor as if we've been doing it all of our lives. His skin feels hot under my touch, his shoulders strong and sure under my fingertips. He holds me close but with a gentleness that I have come to expect from him when it comes to me. It's much like when he carried me across the forbidden forest, cradled in his arms.

The whole court falls away as we spin and spin. I think I could dance with him forever, if ever given the chance. It's a dangerous thought and one I shouldn't be having. But as I look into his eyes, I think he might be thinking the exact same thing.

We're a match in every way. Even in this small aspect, even though this dance doesn't feel all that small at all.

It feels more significant than I'd like to admit. I'm not exactly sure what to do with that information.

For now, I let Derek lead me as I hold onto him and forget every terrible thing that has happened to me since I got here.

* * *

WHEN THE MUSIC FINALLY FADES, the court erupts in applause. Derek spins me out, so that I can take a bow, before walking me back over to the queen.

"It seems you are full of surprises," she says, looking down at me. She's unhappy with me. I don't have to be a mind reader to know that. It would be a helpful trait right now because I still have no idea what her intentions are.

"You may go and mingle." The queen looks over at Nora, who hurries over to stand beside me. I incline my head at the queen before I follow Nora to the edge of the room.

"Avery, that was incredible. I didn't know you could dance!" Nora gushes as soon as we're out of earshot of the queen. After that ordeal, I want to slump against the wall and eat some chicken nuggets or something, but I know I have to keep up with appearances. So, I give Nora a quick smile.

"My father was big on educating me in many ways."

"Well, if I ever get to meet him, I'd like to thank him for that myself. The look on her face—"

"Nora." I lower my voice because the last thing I want is for someone to overhear our conversation and get Nora in trouble. But I do give her a bit of a bump with my shoulder, which makes her grin.

"Let's get you something to drink," she says, leading me to one of the tables set up at the edge of the room. Apparently, there will be no official dinner, as this is more of a celebration, which apparently has me as the esteemed guest. But there is food piled on every table, enough to feed these fae, and then some, for days.

I glance over my shoulder. Almost involuntarily, my eyes find Derek. He's back to standing beside the queen as she speaks with a man that has eaten too many donuts in his day. He's shaped like one of them, which is not something I ever thought I'd see in Faery. They have the most perfect complexion, so it looks out of sorts, especially since his face is red and sweaty. I can see the gleam even from over here.

"Who's that?" I ask, nodding at the man.

"Oh, that's one of the human ambassadors. Queen Svetlana has quite a few, and they usually come to these sorts of things."

"A human?" That makes sense then. It's why he seems so dull in color compared to the rest of the people here. I give the crowd another scan, and I realize there are a few humans here. I'm not sure how I feel about that.

"She has been in power for a long time, Avery. There's a reason for that."

Of course. It's smart to make allies, even if they're human ones. I wonder what the man does for a living in the human realm. He has to be someone high up, maybe a politician or a business owner. He looks like he could fit the part.

"Beautiful dancing." Julian appears at my side just as Nora pours me a cup of juice and hands it to me. The fountain that sits in the middle of this table is filled with a pinkish substance, which I assume is faery nectar. It smells sweet and delicious.

"I do have some tricks up my sleeve." I smile at Julian before taking a sip.

"There are no sleeves on your dress, but you do look great in it." He winks, and I roll my eyes at his poor attempt at charm. Sometimes, he really is a lost cause. And at other times, he's as smooth as butter.

"Does that mean you get the next dance?" I ask, which is met by silence. I look up to see Nora and Julian exchange a glance. "What?"

"You're technically not allowed to dance with anyone else. The queen must choose your partner each time."

"Well, that seems strange." Then again, I'm at a revel in Faery while there's a magical war going on. Oh, and I have wings. Everything is strange right now.

"She told me to go mingle. What does that entail?" I ask, taking another sip.

"Just make a circle, be seen," Julian replies. "And keep Nora near you at all times."

Before I can question that any further, someone calls his name, and he's gone. I give the room a thorough study, amazed at just how many fae are here. I guess I should say individual bodies, since not only fae are present. But I'm not actually supposed to talk to any of them? I think I can handle that just fine.

"Let's walk," I say. So, Nora and I do.

It's another hour before the queen calls me to her side. The noise level has truly gone up in the room, fae and humans alike having a little bit too much to drink. There's dancing and groping and a lot of laughter. Nora and I try to stay as much out of the way as possible, but there's really nowhere to go.

When the queen summons me, I'm almost glad. Maybe I can finally know what all of this is about.

"Derek, be a dear, and come stand beside Avery."

The moment queen begins talking, every eye is turned to her.

"Now, my fellow courtesans, I have the best news to share with you all." Derek comes to stand beside me and shifts to be a bit closer at her words. I can feel the tension in him, just like it's in me. I have a feeling I'm not going to like whatever she has to say.

"You are all aware of the awful assault our borders have received in the last year. Faery is holding strong, as we all know she will, but there are steps to be taken to see that she succeeds." She glances over at me before continuing with a smile. "A great power has been given to us, a witch with the Ancient's tongue on her lips. And she is here to help us."

She's spinning a story, trying to show her subjects her strength without giving away too much information. I make my face clean of all emotion as I watch her give her speech.

"This great power needs a home, and I am so pleased to announce that now, it will have one."

The confusion that I feel at that is coupled with dread and rightfully so. Because Queen Svetlana's next words shatter my world.

"May I present to you, Prince Derek and Princess Avery, for they are bound for marriage from here on to the end of times."

There's a hush over the crowd, as if they're waiting for the queen to say she's joking. I'm waiting for her to say that she's joking. Whatever I expected, it wasn't this. It was never this.

Don't panic.

Don't panic.

Don't panic.

I learned about fae betrothals briefly when I was with Hannah. It was in one of the history books. Once an announcement is made, it cannot be unmade. But an announcement by the queen herself? It carries extra weight.

Keeping my expression as neutral as possible, I glance up at Derek. He's completely still, not even his eyes are blinking. What I wouldn't give to know what's going on in that head of his. It's taking all of my self-control not to panic. Not to visibly freak out.

I have to stay calm.

I have to stay calm.

I have to stay calm.

I'm about to be yelling at myself non-stop. What is happening?

When applause erupts this time, I visibly jump, making queen's smile broader. She lets the claps die down, and I know she's relishing in this. No one in this court is happy about this. I can see that by their stares. If the power she's talking about is truly present in me, she just announced to the whole court that she will have control over it.

Because just like she can control Derek with her magic, if Derek and I are married, she gets control of mine.

Don't cry.

Don't cry.

Don't cry.

Angry tears. Sad tears. It doesn't matter. I want to scream. I want to set this whole place on fire. I want to drown Queen Svetlana in one of those faery fountains she loves so much. The panic is turning to rage. I can feel my magic building. My hand is tingling, as if it's ready to set the fire and water at the court.

I feel a slight pressure on my hand when Derek's fingers wrap around it. He gives me a gentle squeeze. It's his only outward reaction to what the queen just announced. I hold onto his hand like it's my lifeline. There's no way he knew about this. No way.

"Let us celebrate!" Queen Svetlana's voice booms out across the crowd. The music starts playing again, and her guests have no choice but to act joyous. Everything is falling apart. I can't seem to find the will to move.

The queen steps down from the podium, coming to stand in front of us.

"Do you like my surprise, Avery?" she asks, grinning. There's so much smugness in that expression. I would like nothing more than to wipe it off with my fist. Derek gives me another squeeze, as if he can tell what I'm thinking.

"You really think Derek and I will be married?" I ask, even though I know the answer. I'm really hoping I remembered the information wrong, but of course, that's not the case.

"You will be. Sooner rather than later. We need to get that power of yours under control and then we need to do some good with it."

"You won't get away with this," I reply, shaking my head. There is no way I will succumb to her control. There must be something I can do. I will figure it out. I promise it right here and right now.

"Oh, but I will. You should have been smarter, Avery. I have been around a long time. I know all the tricks in the book."

Except she doesn't. No matter how powerful she is, she can't read the ancient books. That's why she needs me. That thought will fuel whatever I have to do to get out of it. And I won't fail.

A blast comes unexpectedly, and it's louder than anything I've ever heard before. One moment, there's laughter and shouting in glee, the next, bodies are flying through the air.

I'm thrown backward, losing my grip on Derek as I slam against a wall. Falling forward, I land on my stomach, stunned. Shaking my head, I try to get my bearings, but everything is in chaos. Fae are screaming, there's debris all over the place, and more is falling from the holes blown in the walls.

I get to my feet, pushing the hair out of my face as I search for Derek and Nora, who were the closest to me. The queen is in front of me. A sudden urge to end her rises in me. My hand lights up with a fireball. She sees me a moment before I throw it at her. It catches her on her shoulder. The queen screams, her face full of rage.

Another fireball forms in my hand, but before I can throw it, her guards are there, pulling her to safety. Angry at my missed chance, I snuff out the flame as I look for the others.

I find Nora first. She's to my right, covered by another body. There's blood everywhere.

"Nora!" I fall to my knees beside her, afraid of what I'll find. But then she grunts, and I push the body off her as I reach to help her up. "Are you hurt?"

"No." She shakes her head, running her hands over her body. "What was that?"

"I think that was a bomb."

I glance up at the voice, and the relief I feel is almost tangible. Derek pulls me and then Nora to our feet, giving us a quick once-over. His jacket is gone. His shirt is bloodied, but he also seems to be in one piece.

"Have you seen Julian?" I ask, trying to see past the dust settling over the room. I have to shout to be heard over the screams. Then another blast comes, sending us off our feet.

"We need to get out," Derek says, grabbing my hand and dragging me behind him.

"Not without Julian!"

He stops and groans at me, but I'm not about to leave without our friend. Glancing back at the chaos, I try to see if he's anywhere in sight. But there's too much smoke and dust, and too many bodies.

"Avery, we have to go," Nora urges, right as a group of soldiers I've never seen before rushes into the room through the blown-out walls. "We'll find him. But we can't help him if you're caught."

I glance at her, as this all makes sense. They're here for me. The queen paraded me around the court for weeks, and then tonight, provided them a perfect opportunity to come for me.

"Come on!" Nora rushes to the back. I let Derek pull me with him just as the screams become too much to handle.

* * *

THE CHAOS ISN'T CONFINED to the main hall. There are soldiers fighting everywhere. The palace seems to be overrun. Derek keeps a strong hold on my arm as Nora leads the way. Suddenly, he drops my hand as one of the soldiers jumps on him. Another one grabs me around my waist as I scream. My hands ignite with fire, and I grab onto the arms of my attacker. He screams, dropping me. I twist my body around, slamming my blazing hands into his chest. His chest explodes, a hole burned right through him. Horrified, I step back, glancing at my hands and the amount of power I just displayed.

I don't have time to process. Nora's screams reach my ears, and I turn to see her trying to fight off two soldiers. Without hesitation, I send a blast of fire at them, burning them where they stand. Suddenly, Derek is beside me once more, reaching for my hand. He clearly saw what I did, but he doesn't notice. He just pulls me behind him.

We're almost down the hall when I hear it.

"Stop!" I yell. I turn to see Julian rush at one of the soldiers, his sword in hand. The man meets Julian's attack blow by blow. I watch as he begins to gain an advantage.

"Avery—"

I don't wait to hear what Derek is going to say. The fire ignites again, pushing our hands apart but without burning him. Then I'm racing for Julian. On the move, I call on my magic, blasting it straight at the soldier. The man doesn't see it coming. The fire sweeps him off his feet, dropping him ten feet away. Julian follows the solider with his eyes before turning to me in surprise. The surprise quickly turns into relief and then he's running toward me.

One of the soldiers is suddenly there, grabbing for me. I don't hesitate to slam my elbow into his stomach before dropping my weight and throwing him over my shoulder. Jumping to my feet, I blast a stream of fire straight down, burning through the man. When I look up, I see Derek and Julian completely shocked as they look at what I just did.

"What? I had good teachers." I grin and send another fire blast at the soldiers coming for us. The boys seem to snap out of it and then Derek is reaching for me once more. We take off down the hall, dodging fights as much as possible. When we round the corner, Nora is pressed against the wall. She looks happy the moment she sees us.

"This way," she calls as we reach her before she dives into one of the open doorways. We're right on her heels, and the guys push the doors closed the moment we're inside.

"What are we doing? Can we portal?" I look at Nora, but she's already shaking her head.

"Portal magic is blocked. We have to do this the old-fashioned way." She walks over to a tapestry, pulling it aside. Placing her palm against the wall, she mumbles something I don't quite hear and then the wall moves.

"Secret passages?"

"Absolutely. We hit all the classics." She grins. We move as one, rushing for the passageway and away from the sound of the battle. Derek's hand finds my own again, as if he can't be apart from me for longer than a few seconds. I hold onto him with all I have because I need the comfort too. Everything just spun out of control on us, and we seem to be each other's anchor. Nora presents me with a torch, and I use my fire magic to light it.

"How did they get in?" Julian asks once we're farther down the tunnel, leaving the sounds of battle behind.

"It was planned and executed with perfection. There had to be an inside man," Derek muses out loud. "Someone who knew about the revel, who knew exactly who was the center of attention."

"She played us, Derek," I say, looking up into his handsome face. There's a hard look in his eyes, but it softens when he looks at me.

"She did, but I won't—" He doesn't quite finish that sentence, because right now, we both know he doesn't have a choice. But we'll find a way. We'll figure this out.

"You think it was all about Avery?" Nora asks, and we turn our attention to her.

"Absolutely." Derek doesn't hesitate. "They were looking for something when they arrived, of that I am sure. She's the biggest prize they can find here."

"So, what do we do?" I pull the skirt of my dress a little higher, keeping it from dragging or tripping me. "Can we go back to my room to grab supplies?"

"No, it's too dangerous. There's no direct path to your room from here. Our best bet is the village."

"The servant's village?"

"Yes."

I think back to the last time I was down there, the screams I heard that night. It was the night my wings made their first appearance, and everything changed.

"Who do you think those soldiers work for?" I ask.

"It could be any court," Derek replies slowly, as if he too is mulling over that fact. "The clothes the soldiers wore didn't have any court insignia on them. It was a smart move."

"So, we have no idea who's responsible."

"It doesn't matter who's responsible. Right now, we just need to get you out of here. That's priority number one."

We fall silent after that. The only sound is the distant shouts and the slap of the stone beneath my feet. I shiver at the images those screams evoke, but I don't slow down and I don't stop. There's an urgency to their movements, and Derek's grip on my hand is tight.

This group is determined to protect me, but I'm as determined to protect them as well.

CHAPTER 18

When the passageway slopes upward, we pause. The sounds of the battle seemed to have faded, but we really don't know what awaits us once we step out of this tunnel.

"Nora, do you have any idea where this passageway ends?" I ask, because she seems to be the only one with any knowledge of these in the first place.

"The forest? Maybe? I have only very basic information about the tunnels. My mother shared them with me." I've never heard Nora talk about her mother before, and her tone makes me want to ask a hundred questions. Just not right now.

"It should be right on the outskirts of the village, at least if the distance we walked is to be believed," Derek says. All three of us turn to look at him. He doesn't comment further, only shrugs.

When we finally come to a dead end, Nora once again places her palm against the stone and mumbles a few words.

"How is she doing that?" I whisper.

"It's part of her portal keeper magic," Derek whispers back. That makes sense. I truly do forget that Nora, or any of the fae, has any active magic. They don't use it very often at all.

The stone moves with minimal sound, which makes me feel

slightly better. We come out into the night air slowly, but there's not sudden ambush that awaits us. We are in the woods, and now that we're out, I can hear the screaming and the fighting once again. The sound really carries in these woods.

"Come on, we need to move."

We race off after Derek without a second thought. He weaves in and out of the trees. I'm glad I've been training so much because I wouldn't have been able to handle all this running before now. When we reach the edge of the forest, Derek pauses. The village is surprisingly quiet.

"We can't just walk in there like nothing is happening. If the attacker is smart, there will be soldiers waiting to ambush anyone who escaped the palace," Julian says, studying the houses in front of us.

"So, what do we do? They'll probably be checking the forest soon as well," I comment. Julian's head swivels toward me like he hasn't thought of that. We all wait on Derek to make the decision because I sure don't know what to do.

"We have to brave it. We'll go fast, and we'll go quiet. If we can make it into one of the houses, maybe we can buy us some time."

"Derek—"

"We don't have a choice, Avery." He glances down at me before giving my hand a reassuring squeeze. "Like you said, the forest isn't safe either, and we have to go past the village to get out. It's our only choice."

I don't like it, but he's right. It's not like we can go back. And from what I know about magic, the tunnels are probably not safe either. If they have a way to suppress portal magic, they have a way to track magic. That means, the tunnels might be discovered. We can't take that risk.

"Let's go individually."

"No, we'll go in twos."

I'm not a fan, but I don't have time to argue as Derek pulls me after him. We move together, keeping pace with each other as if we've been doing this forever. It's kind of like the dance. I can anticipate his moves, and he can anticipate mine.

We reach the first building with no problems, and we flatten ourselves against it the best we can. Glancing behind, I see Nora and Julian rush toward us. I hold my breath until they're beside me. It's difficult not to make any noise, considering everything here seems to be standing still. After another moment, Derek guides me to the next building and then the next. It's like we're playing hide and seek, except we have no idea how many people are looking for us.

Just when I think no one is actually at the village, a group of soldiers comes around the corner. Derek and I drop down behind a barrel, and I really hope luck is on our side. I'm not exactly inconspicuous in my bright dress. Neither is Nora in her green one, although hers is a little better.

The soldiers call out to each other in hushed tones, and I realize they're probably going house to house now. A movement catches my attention. I glance over to the house on my left to see the shades move to the side and then a pair of small eyes finds mine. There's a bit of movement and the child gets yanked away from the window, but after a moment, an older pair of eyes replaces the tiny slit. At the sight of us, they grow bigger and then the shades move over more so that I can see the face.

It's the woman whose child I saved last time I was at the village.

She knows exactly who I am. When she motions for us, I don't hesitate. Derek pulls me down when I stand, but I just shake my head, asking him to trust me with my eyes. Thankfully, that's all it takes because he allows me to pull him behind me. We round the corner just as the door at the back of the house opens, and we rush in. The door closes, but I stop the woman.

"My friends," I whisper, and then Julian and Nora are there. The woman shuts the door behind them, bolting it in place. We all crouch close to the floor, afraid to cast any unnecessary shadows around the house. I glance over to see the little boy peeking from around a table. His eyes on me, and I smile. After a second, he smiles back.

"They're looking for you, miss," the woman whispers, getting down to her knees beside us. "You as well, your highness. I heard them shouting before they went quiet. But they didn't leave."

"Is there a way to get out of here without being seen?" I ask, but the woman is already shaking her head.

"They have the road covered, miss. And magic is blocked."

"So, there's nothing we can do?" I glance at Derek, and he's already shaking his head. He's worried, that much I can see. I am too.

"You can stay here till the morning, miss," the woman continues. I really shouldn't be surprised she's talking to me and not Derek. The gratefulness on her face is evident, and I give her a warm smile.

"If you get caught—"

"Oh, but we won't, miss. Here." She motions for us to follow, and we move quickly across the floor to the opposite side of the kitchen. The woman moves a few bags of grain over and then pulls the rug up.

"We have a cellar."

* * *

THE CELLAR IS dark and cooler than the temperature outside, but it's big enough to fit all four of us, and for that I am grateful. The woman waits until we find our places on the ground before she shuts the door and places the rug back over it, cutting off most of the light. A few slivers of light sneak in through the wooden floor, but it's not enough to dissipate the darkness. Nora and Julian are leaning against the wall on my right. Derek and I are sitting right near the ladder. I shiver a little. I'm not sure if it's the adrenaline leaving or if it's the dampness.

"May I?" Derek's words are whispered into my ear. I turn to find his face barely inches from mine. In the near darkness, I still manage to see him somehow, but I don't know what he's asking.

"What?"

"You're shivering. May we share body heat?"

It's such a strange way to ask that I nearly chuckle. But he's serious, and after a moment's hesitation say yes.

He scoots even closer before I feel his arm come around me, and I lean against his broad chest. The feeling of security envelopes me just as his body heat warms me up. I fit against him as if I'm made to be there, and I finally let my mind wander.

I'm betrothed to him. Somehow, someway, I ended up betrothed to the prince of the Spring Court. I have no idea how I'm supposed to feel about that. True, Derek and I—we aren't enemies anymore. At least, not entirely. My feelings toward him have changed. I can't deny that.

But marrying him under the queen's command? It's the worst thing that can happen to me. Not because of him, but because of her. That's surprising all on its own. If this happened even a few months ago, I'd be completely against the idea. But being married to him wouldn't be so bad, I suppose. Except for the part where the queen would control my magic.

I won't allow that.

I won't allow that.

I won't allow that.

"We'll find a way out," Derek whispers against my hair. It's like he knows what I'm thinking about. Maybe he's thinking about it too. I want to ask him about it, but maybe I'm a coward because I don't. I don't know if I want to know his exact thoughts on the situation.

A chorus of voices snaps us to attention. The next thing we know, there's a sound of a door banging open and boots stomping into the house. A deep male voice asks something in a language I don't understand, and the woman answers. There are more questions and more answers as someone continues to walk around the house.

I don't dare to breathe too loudly as we all wait to see what happens. The strange language throws me off a bit, and I make a mental note to ask about it later. It seems like forever, but then finally, the voices and the stomping fades before disappearing entirely.

Yet, still, no one moves, and no one speaks. We're not about to take any chances. And so, we sit like that, in intense silence, until the sun finally comes up.

When the woman pulls back the rug and opens the hatch, I feel like it's been days. I blink at the sudden light before untangling myself from Derek. Neither one of us slept, but he held me tightly all through the night.

"The soldiers have moved down into the forest, miss. Now is your chance."

We rush for the surface. I stop near the woman, reaching to give her shoulder a squeeze. The words 'thank you' are on my tongue, but I stop them before I can utter them. That will never be safe here.

"You have done us a great service," I say instead. She beams at me like I've given her the moon.

"It's the least I could do, miss," she replies, as her little boy pokes his head out from behind his mother's skirt. I give them both a big smile before I join my friends at the door.

"We have to move fast," Derek says, and I shrug.

"What else is new?"

We open the door, and after a quick look around, we run. The houses are still quiet, and the soldiers are nowhere to be seen, but we do the best we can to stay quiet and fast. When the forest is in sight, I almost sigh in relief. But then, I nearly stumble back when I see who steps out of the shadows, right at the edge of the trees.

"Avery, come on."

Derek drags me behind him as we reach Hannah.

"What are you doing here?" I can't help but ask. The other fae rolls her eyes.

"Nice to see you too, Avery. Lovely dress you got on there," she comments. "If you must know, I was looking for you."

"So, you came to the edge of the village forest?"

Even though I don't want to be suspicious, the thought of an insider being behind this attack is at the front of my mind. I definitely don't want Hannah to be the bad guy here, but the coincidence is too much.

"Not quite."

"Hannah."

"Look, don't make a big deal of it, but I spelled you in case I needed to find you. It was a one-time thing."

"What?" I almost forget that we're in hiding as I stare at the fae in front of me.

"It came in handy." She shrugs.

"You people are unbelievable." I throw my hands up in the air, pulling away from Derek. This is all too much, and I'm way too tired.

"Look, don't get all twisted up. I heard of the attack. I came to help. A thanks would be appreciated."

This earns her a roll of the eyes from me, but she isn't deterred.

"You have one shot, darling." She looks at Derek, apparently done dealing with me for the moment. "Where to?"

Derek is silent for a moment, glancing over at me before replying.

"Human realm."

"We're going back?" I immediately forget my grumpiness and walk over to Derek.

"It's the safest bet right now. I need to get you out of Faery."

"But how? Portal magic has been suppressed."

"Only for those within the vicinity. Oh honey, don't look so shocked. I do have some magic up my sleeve," she says, winking at me. "But we better hurry. I don't like being out in the open like this."

Derek doesn't hesitate, giving Hannah a go-ahead nod. Julian and Nora don't offer their opinion. They both look as exhausted as I feel.

"Good luck. To all of you," Hannah says, but her eyes are entirely on me. She waves her hand in the air, saying a few words. Then the space ripples, and I see familiar pine trees on the other side. "Off you go."

Nora and Julian step through first and then Derek takes my hand and pulls me through with him. I turn back around as Hannah raises her hand to close the portal. Something catches her attention off to the side. In the next moment, soldiers are there. They grab her by the arms as one slaps her across the face.

"Hannah!" I yell, ready to jump back through the portal. Derek's arms close around my middle, catching me and keeping me in place. I watch helplessly as Hannah is pushed to her knees. One of the soldiers grabs her face in his hand. There's a look of pure defiance on her face before she spits in his face. The solider backhands her, and she falls out of the grip of the others.

She glances up, her eyes meeting mine through the portal before she yells and swings her arm down. The portal disappears, taking the image of Hannah with it.

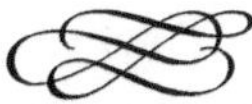

CHAPTER 19

I slump against Derek for a moment before I twist in his arms and slap at his chest.

"I could've helped her!" I yell, completely aware of how emotionally I'm reacting and not caring in the least. Hannah has become important to me. And I feel guilty. I suspected her there for a moment. Maybe that moment is what cost her her freedom, if not her life.

"We couldn't have helped her."

"I could've tried."

"Avery. Avery!" Derek doesn't raise a hand to defend himself. He just takes my smacks, giving me a moment to feel my emotions. I know it's not his fault, not really. So I stop, dropping my forehead against his chest. Breathing heavily, I try to rein in everything I'm feeling. The rational part of me knows I'm exhausted and emotional. But I also feel helpless about the whole situation, and I'm so tired of feeling this way.

"Come on, we need to get going."

"Can they track us?" I ask. Derek gives my waist a quick squeeze before stepping back.

"No. They can't track Hannah's portals, but we shouldn't take the risk."

I nod, turning to go. Julian and Nora have been standing quietly, waiting for me to stop my tantrum. Nora reaches for me, entwining her arm through the crook of my elbow and pulling me close. We offer each other what support we can as we follow Derek down the road.

Hannah opened up a portal right at the edge of the human woods, so it's easy to follow the road. Cars pass us by, but we're far enough from the highway that no one offers us a ride. It's probably better that way. When a gas station comes into sight, I breathe a sigh of relief.

We wait on the side of the road as Julian goes inside to grab us water and information.

"We're in Arizona. Near Flagstaff," he announces, handing over bottles of water. I'm assuming he glamoured the clerk into handing those over, since we have no cash on us. His words surprise me, but Derek seems to expect them.

"We need a car," Derek comments and then walks off toward the parking lot. I'm not even going to comment on what he's about to do because all I want is to be back to the cabin. I assume that's where we're going. The Ancients may have found us there before, but I'm really hoping Derek has a plan for that. I need to get out of this dress, and I need time alone to deal with everything that's happened. This was an exhausting twenty-four hours to say the least.

When a dark green SUV pulls up beside us, I'm not even surprised. We pile in, with me in the passenger seat next to Derek, while Nora and Julian get in the back.

We don't speak the whole way there, as if each of us is lost in our own thoughts. Maybe I should be thinking over everything, but my mind is completely shut down. If I let myself think about it, I'll lose it all over again. I can't do that in front of them. Not again.

To say that I'm embarrassed I did in the first place is an understatement.

No one wants to follow a leader that can't keep their crap together. And that's the level I'm at right now. I think if Derek wasn't here taking care of things, I would've just laid down in the woods and gone to sleep.

Okay, now I'm just being dramatic, and I need to stop.

When we pull up to the cabin, it takes me a second to realize we arrived. Julian and Nora get out first, both heading for the house to give it a check, I'm sure. Derek stays in the driver's seat for a moment, as if waiting me out. I glance over, finding his eyes on me. Somehow, I know what he's thinking.

The last time we were here, things changed between us. Now, things are different again. I have no idea what to do with those thoughts, so I push the door open and get out.

"Welcome back," Derek comments over my shoulder. I don't turn around as I walk into the house.

*   *   *

I RACE for the shower because I know it's the only place I can be alone. Also, I want to wash all the grime off me. The water feels heavenly against my skin. Even though my water magic wants to come out to play, I don't let it. This cabin is our sanctuary for now. Even though the magic is protected and can't be traced, I'm paranoid.

Every time I think that everything is okay, it all goes up in flames.

When tears leak out of my eyes and mingle with the water from the shower, it doesn't even register that I'm crying. I don't even know what I'm crying about. It just seems like the only thing that can release this pressure I'm feeling. So, I let it.

I am entirely different person than I was when I first came here, and even that Avery wasn't who I thought. It seems that my life is spinning out of control, and I'm just trying to hold on to something before I get thrown off the ride. I let the frustration and the exhaustion bubble for so long, and now I'm finally letting it free. Questions press on me from every side. I'm not getting any closer to answers. So far, all that's happened has made my situation worse.

Now, I have to figure out how to fix it.

Once I feel like I can face the group without losing my cool, I turn the water off and get out. Since we left without packing last time, my clothes are still here. I pull on dark leggings as well as an oversized sweatshirt, and I leave my hair down.

When I make it downstairs, Nora and Julian are on the couch. Derek is in the kitchen. The next moment, he comes out, carrying two steaming mugs in his hands, handing one to me. I notice Nora and Julian have mugs in their hands already.

"Green tea?" I ask. Derek nods with a small smile. When I settle on the couch, we each take a sip, none of us sure what to say next.

"So, this has been an interesting revel," Julian finally says. For some reason, I find that funny. The laugh bubbles inside of me, and I don't suppress it. Soon, we're all laughing. In this one moment, everything does seem like it'll be okay. But the feeling doesn't last because that's not our reality right now.

"What do we do now?" Nora asks, voicing the one question on our minds.

"We rest," Derek replies. "And we regroup."

"Do you think Queen Svetlana is alive?"

"She's alive." Derek doesn't hesitate to reply. I wonder if he'd know if she wasn't. "I'm sure she'll have control over her court soon enough and then she'll be coming after us."

By *us* he of course means him, me, and the betrothal she sprung on us.

"How long?"

"There's no way to know. But we'll do what we can. It'll be okay."

"I'm glad you're so optimistic," I reply, not bothering to hide my emotions. "All of this? It's one big freaking mess. Now I'm being hunted by other courts on top of the Ancients? That sounds just swell."

The bitterness in my voice is evident, but I don't care. Apparently, my emotions are coming in waves. So, I'm just riding them at this point.

"We'll figure it out. You know we will. It's the exhaustion speaking. We all need rest."

He's right, of course, not that I'll admit it. I just feel all over right now. The shower didn't seem to help as much as I would've liked it to.

"Are we taking guard duty?" I ask as I stand. I'm ready to rest, but I will do my part as well.

"No. We'll rest. This place is safe."

I take that at face value as I head back up the stairs and toward my old room. I really hope I can turn my mind off long enough to rest.

ossing and turning, I try to find a comfortable position. No matter what I do, I just can't relax enough to sleep. After trying for a few hours, I finally get out of bed and tiptoe downstairs. The cabin is completely still. The rest of the group clearly didn't have the same hiccups I do.

I can't tell where all this pent-up energy is coming from. I'm not sure why my emotions are so unbalanced. I've always worked hard at keeping everything under control. Now I can't seem to keep any of it where it needs to be.

Stepping outside onto the porch, I breathe in the fresh air. I really love this place, even though I probably won't admit it to Derek. The magically created lake opens up in front of me. I feel called to it.

When I reach the edge, I step right into the water, moving my feet around to create little waves. Being near water does wonders to calm me, and I almost let my magic roam free. But not yet.

The space around me darkens suddenly. I spin around, looking for the source. When my eyes land on the creature, I'm not even surprised. He floats a few feet off the ground, his robes moving in the gentle breeze.

"You are back. We knew you would return."

"That just makes you slightly logical. I wouldn't pat myself on the back yet." The words escape me, bitterness dripping off each syllable. This is partially their fault. They could've left me alone. If they did, I never would've gone to Faery in the first place.

"You are growing surer, Avery Kincaid."

I stop whatever retort I had on my tongue as I try to remember if the creature has ever called me by my full name. I honestly can't remember.

"I am growing tireder," I reply, because it's true. I should be treading carefully here, but that doesn't seem to be my response right now.

"You will bring the book to us."

"Why do you want it so much? Don't you already know what's written in there?"

The question seems to honestly baffle the creature because he doesn't respond right away. I can almost see him thinking it through.

"We have been around a long time, young one. Our magic is strong, but our memory is not as long. Centuries have gone by while we slept."

I'm surprised I'm getting any of this information. It's like the creature wants to talk about it. Maybe he was the one who wrote the journal entries in the book I read. Those passages seemed so...human. Maybe that's what the creature is so desperate to reclaim.

"You have read the book."

It's not a question, but I answer anyway. There's doesn't seem to be any reason not to. "Only a few pages."

"The magic is on you."

"On me?"

"We are growing impatient, Avery Kincaid." The tone of voice changes suddenly, as if a switch has turned on. My heart grows cold at the sound, and now I'm back to being afraid. "The book. Bring us the book."

"You no longer want my help to get into Faery?"

"You are there no longer so we have no use for you there. The book is your concern now."

"And if I don't?"

"We have said it once, and we will say it again, we will do whatever it takes." The creature pauses for a moment, as if giving me a chance to prepare myself for its next words. "Your parents are well, Avery Kincaid. They won't be for much longer."

"No!" The word escapes me as the creature begins to fade.

"They will be the first, and then, everyone you hold dear will follow, starting with your fae prince."

"You can't!"

"It is already done."

My heart drops while the horror of that statement fills me. I fall to my knees as the creature disappears and the space around me grows lighter. It's difficult to breathe, but I force air into my lungs.

Derek.

Derek.

My prince.

I gulp air down, concentrating on doing the motions.

My parents are in danger.

My parents are in danger.

My parents are in danger.

I can't seem to think past that statement. I can't seem to stop spinning.

I can't—

I can't—

I can't—

"Avery?" Derek is suddenly in front of me, dropping to his knees in the sand. One look at my face and he stands, spinning around to make sure there is no present danger. Satisfied, he drops back down. This time, he reaches for me. I don't even hesitate.

Falling into his open arms, I cling to him as the air returns to my lungs. I'm a rational individual. I can come up with a plan, and I can execute it. I will not give in to my panic. I will not.

"What happened? Avery?"

"I'm fine. Everything is fine. I think I just had a panic attack, that's all."

"I felt it."

That makes me pull back as I look up into his face.

"You felt it?"

"Yes, I—" He stops, furrowing his brow in confusion. He's not used to this, and I can't blame him. The connection between us has only grown with time. Now, it seems to be at another level. Neither one of us understands it, that much I can tell. But we've become something I never imagined. If this was another time and place, maybe we could explore that further.

I know what I have to do, and Derek will never forgive me for it. None of them will. But I can't let my parents die, I just can't. And I have to protect Derek. And the rest of them. It doesn't matter how I feel about Derek or how he may feel about me.

I guess it's just not meant to be.

He's still trying to figure out what to say when I reach over and place my hand on his cheek. He freezes immediately, his eyes flying over to meet mine. I give him a small smile, rubbing my thumb over his smooth skin. The fae really are so beautiful, but he's even more so. No matter how much everyone tries to make him be a certain type of a prince, he's one with his own mind. And his mind is just as beautiful.

He's going to be so mad.

He probably won't want anything to do with me.

Maybe right here and now is all we will ever have.

So, I do something that I've been wanting do for ages. I close the distance between us, and I catch his lips in a kiss. There's no hesitation on his part.

He's just as hungry for me as I am for him. His arms wrap around my torso, pulling me to him. We both get to our knees while our lips devour each other. He tastes like the most beautiful sunrise and the most relaxing bath. He's all the good things and all the perfect little things, and in this one moment, I give myself completely over to him.

If I could, I would bottle this feeling up and carry it against my heart for an eternity. And then, it still wouldn't be long enough.

When I pull back, I place my forehead against his as we both breathe heavily.

"Avery," he whispers. I put my finger over his mouth because I can't listen to anything he has to say. Instead, I close my eyes, a tear slipping free as I place my other hand at the back of his neck. My lips move but no sound comes and then he slumps against me, completely knocked out.

Placing a soft kiss to his temple, I move him to the ground putting him on his back. Sometimes I forget that I'm a witch above all else. A sleeping spell might not be my best weapon, but it is one I learned a long time ago.

Making sure he's comfortable on the ground, I give him one last look before I jump to my feet and race toward the cabin. The keys to the car are on the counter where Derek had left them.

I put on my shoes, grab a bottle of water and then I'm out the front door.

When he wakes up, he's going to be furious. Nora and Julian will be too. But I have to see my parents, and I have to find a way to protect not only them, but the fae as well.

I was better on my own.

I was less distracted.

I was stronger.

I keep repeating the phrases to myself, willing them to be true. As I drive back into the city, I realize I'm only lying to myself. Yet, it doesn't matter.

I will do whatever it takes to protect those I love. Even if that means doing it all alone.

REVENGE OF THE FAE

THE FAE CHRONICLES #3

There's a story of old,
Where the sky meets the sea,
And a heart grows warm,
With the knowledge it seeks.

Nothing changes at all,
Nothing stays the same.
But a love foretold,
No magic can tame.

When the night comes,
And the demons descend,
Only the pure at heart,
Will have the power to withstand.

CHAPTER 1

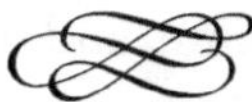

Another day, another bush for me to hide in.

It's been a week since I ran out on Derek and the rest of my friends. Although, are Derek and I really friends? I can't stop thinking about that kiss—and dreaming of it whenever I catch moments of rest. The way his body felt—no, now is not the time and I am not mentally competent enough for a trip down that lane.

I've probably slept about an hour or two a day, and it's catching up with me. Every time I get anywhere near relaxing, I'm afraid the shadows will come, and with them, the Ancients. Granted, they don't need me to be sleeping for that, but I think it's my sheer will keeping them at bay right now. That and a few protection talismans I've put together and now carry on my person.

It won't stop them for long, but it's something. Now I just have to figure out my next move.

While also trying not to think about Derek.

I feel the pain of our separation like a physical ailment.

We started out as enemies, who then became something akin to friends, and now, we're engaged. No one could've predicted that one. Not that it was our choice. What was my choice was leaving him, and a part of me thinks we're back to enemies again. He won't do well with my betrayal. I can't imagine him seeing this as anything but.

What I thought we were, what I think we've become—it's overwhelming and exciting and terrifying. All at the same time. My heart truly yearns to be near him, and for the first time, I'm open to the possibilities. I don't understand it, but a huge part of me wants to. I have no idea what to do with that.

Maybe if this was another time and place.

This is definitely not what I should be thinking about right now.

Stay focused and alert.

Stay focused and alert.

Stop thinking about my prince.

That last thought leaves me slightly stunned but not for long.

A scream splits the night, jerking my attention from my musings. I jump up at the ready, but I have no idea where it's coming from. A glance back at the house tells me my parents heard it too. It seems to have surrounded the whole house somehow. That's when I realize it must've been one of the fae guards the queen sent as part of the bargain I made with her. They wouldn't scream like that unless...

I don't think about it. I jump out of my hiding spot, and I run for them. I'm inside the house in mere seconds.

"Avery. What are you doing here?" My mom's shocked face greets me.

"We have to go. I know that sound, and it's not a good one."

My dad appears by her side, sword in hand.

"Avery?"

"Hi, Daddy." That's all I manage before I'm motioning for them to come. They move toward me without question, but before they can take more than a few steps, the doors burst open at my back. I spin around as a group of soldiers enter, filling up the space around us. They're the same type of soldiers that attacked the Summer Court in Faery, no insignia on them. They're simply dressed in black, wielding magic and weapons.

There's no hesitation on my part. I go straight into battle mode.

The fierce desire to protect my parents rises up inside of me, calling forth my magic. I've got a blade on me, courtesy of Derek, but I'm not using it. My emotions are one hundred percent focused on my magic. That's what I let fly free.

Fire pours out of my hands, slamming like a wall into the soldiers closest to me. It sweeps them off their feet as others try to jump out of the way. The few that get through are stopped by my father, who works the sword like it's an extension of him.

"Avery!" My mother yells out a warning, and I send another blast at the soldier coming at me, knocking him out.

The way has been cleared, but I'm not sure how long that'll keep. I know my magic can only do so much. We need to keep moving. As we race out into the night, there are more of them coming.

"We have to fight!" I shout, just as my mother shifts. It's been years since I've seen her in wolf form, but there's a warmth inside of me at the sight. I've always felt like that, that shifter side of me answering the call, even though I've never been able to shift. She stands tall, coming to the middle of my chest, her fur a deep brown and as shiny as glittering gold.

"We're with you," Dad says as he swings his sword. All of this happens in a matter of seconds, and then the second wave of our attackers is upon us. I reach for my magic once more. The exhaustion of the last week, the worry for everyone's safety, among other things I won't name, hang heavily on my shoulders. The magic is slugging at best, having been spent inside the house.

My mother is effortless in her attacks, grabbing the soldiers by various parts of their body and flinging them against the house or the trees.

But my dad? I'm in awe of my father. Sure, he has trained me in the basics of sword fighting, but this is another level. He spins around, waving his sword as if he's in the middle of a dance. Every movement is fluid and precise. There's a sense of calmness about him it's almost shocking.

I tear my eyes away just as two soldiers reach me. Yanking out the dagger Derek gave me, I move before they have a chance to grab me. One swipe of the blade cuts the closest one on the arm. Blood gushes out. Ducking the other's approach, I spin around with a roundhouse kick. It sends him tumbling. I don't hesitate to push my fire magic out, but there is a heaviness to my limbs, and it's difficult to stay upright.

Dropping down to the ground, I try to catch my breath. More soldiers are coming. If I don't do something soon, we'll be overrun. The soldiers are almost to me when I realize I've been neglecting a part of me during this fight. If my fire magic won't do, maybe my newfound water magic will.

Closing my eyes, I take a deep breath, reaching deep inside of myself. Then I thrust my arms forward. Water and fire pour out of me, blasting our attackers up in the air and away. I'm breathing hard, but I push myself back to my feet and turn to my parents. They're staring at me in complete shock, but now is not the time. We have to move.

"Run now, questions later."

* * *

It's another fifteen minutes until I finally feel like we can stop. Mama is still in her wolf form, running a dozen feet in front of us as a scout. I have no idea how far back the soldiers are, but we have to stop. Dad has blood dripping all over.

"Let me see," I say, halting his movements by stepping in front of him. He moves his hand long enough for me to see the gash. Grabbing my knife, I slice at the bottom of my shirt before I rip it off.

"Avery—"

"I need to bind it." It's the best I can do. He didn't tell me he was hurt, in his typical dad fashion. I know Mama stopped as well, her supernatural hearing alerting her without me having to shout. I can feel her presence at my back. I haven't seen her shift in years, and a part of me just wants to watch her move.

"I'm sorry." I glance up at my dad's words and find him looking at me with all the sorrow in the world. My heart clenches at the sight. and I suddenly want to be the parent and chase his worries away.

"Dad, we don't have to—"

"No, we do. I'm sorry I didn't tell you."

"Why didn't you?"

"It was too complicated. Too much for one kid to handle. Even a strong one, like you." His smile turns into a grimace as I tighten my makeshift bandage. "You already had plenty to deal with being half witch, half shifter. We couldn't risk more."

My mother is back beside us now. I glance over to find her eyes on me as well. Even in wolf form, she's still my mother, and I can read that look. She would do anything to take me away from all this.

"Did you know about my magic?" They haven't seen me use fire and water magic before, since I kept that pretty under wraps until now.

"Not exactly. It was always something that stayed in the back of my mind. But you never exhibited anything but fire magic, and that was your mother's side. Fae have elemental magic, since we're so tied to nature. But you only manifested your mother's bloodline. We thought —well, we thought you were safe."

This is the first time I've heard my father refer to himself as fae.

"Why did you leave Faery?"

"Oh, pumpkin. There are so many reasons. It was too dangerous for us to stay. For myself and your mother. When we found out we were pregnant, I swore to do everything in my power not to have you growing up as one of them."

Since visiting Faery, I can understand what he means. My thoughts involuntarily switch to Derek, but I push those away. He may be different, but he's still fae. And so are Nora and Julian. I can't ever let myself forget that.

"I guess it didn't matter, did it?" I sigh, but I'm not bitter. Only tired.

"We always knew you were special." Dad reaches over to take my hand into his, giving it a gentle squeeze. "We knew you'd do great things. We just didn't want you to carry this kind of burden."

"But we don't get to choose that. I—I wasn't ready for this, but I'm in it now. And I need your help. I need to figure out this magic. I need to find a way out of this engagement. I need—"

The growl beside me stops my rant. I look over to see my mother's full attention on me.

"What engagement?" Dad asks. I shake my head.

"Now is not the time. I need to get you somewhere safe. And then we'll talk."

"Get us to safety?"

"I've been watching you for the last week. You're in danger because of who I am. I've been waiting for them to come for you, and they did."

"Avery, I don't—" But Dad never gets to finish.

Another growl comes from my mother, but this one is different. Dad looks at her, understanding coming over his features.

"It's too late. They're close."

Just then, the shadows move, and I see them. They've used stealth to get close to us. Maybe even some cloaking magic. It doesn't matter. This is on me. I should've simply bound the wound and kept moving. I made a mistake. And now my parents are going to pay for it. There is no way we can hold them off, not when I feel like I've been run over by a truck. Not when my magic is so wonky. It goes between being too much and not enough. I don't know if I can control it when I'm feeling so exhausted.

Turning to face the hoard, I try to find a way out of this, but they're on us before I can think of anything.

CHAPTER 2

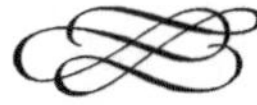

*S*oldiers surround us in the blink of an eye. I have absolutely no time to get my bearings or try and find a way out. Mama gets low to the ground, a growl rumbling her big body as she gets ready to spring. My dad is on the other side of me, and I realize he's weaponless. His sword must've fallen somewhere back at the house.

My emotions and magic are so heightened, I'm praying I don't hurt my parents. It's our only weapon against the assault. It's too volatile, but I have no choice. That will be our only way out of here.

Stay calm. Stay focused.

Stay calm. Stay focused.

Stay calm. Stay focused.

I can feel the sparks at the end of my fingertips, the fire magic I was born with mingled with the water magic I recently discovered. They're both there, both at the ready and begging to be set free. I'm terrified I'm going to make a mistake, but I don't know what else to do.

The mob begins their approach, but then a twinkle of light catches my attention. I glance to the left only to find a portal opening up in midair.

Derek steps through.

My heart plummets and then soars just at the sight of him.

I haven't had a moment to come to terms with my feelings or just how much I missed not being around him, and now he's here.

He's not alone.

"Right on time then," Nora says as the portal closes at her back. Derek and Julian are both armed, a sword in one hand, and in Derek's case, magic in the other. Our eyes meet and hold as chaos explodes around us.

And then we're moving.

The soldiers attack, but now there are six of us against twelve of them. I like those odds a lot better.

I hear a shout and then Julian is throwing a sword overhead. It's my father who catches it. There's no hesitation in the way Dad moves. My mama jumps right into the foray, using her head to butt at one of the attackers. She sends him sprawling across the ground. She then picks up another soldier with her mouth and throws her against the wall.

My battle magic is at my fingertips, and I send it at the man in front of me. He slams against the ground. I send a wave of water at him to push him away, using his body as a bowling ball. Two others go down, but more seem to be coming.

Julian is suddenly at my back. "Fancy meeting you here."

"Julian—" There are a thousand apologies on the tip of my tongue, but he doesn't let me get there.

"Not the time." There's no malice in his words. He sends a wink my way as he swings a sword at his attacker before kicking him a few feet back. My mama is still on the other side of the group, biting people, while my father swings the sword like a professional. I mean, I knew he was good with a weapon, but even I'm surprised. I can't stop watching my parents. I'm seeing them in a whole new light.

The distraction causes me to lose my footing. One of the attackers gets through, and the next thing I know, air rushes out of my lungs as a punch connects with my stomach. I double over, gasping at the pain. Derek shouts my name—I don't have to look to know it's him—as my attacker yanks my head back by my hair. They can't kill me. They need me. But clearly, hurting me is in the cards.

Too bad for him, I don't go down easily. Pushing through the pain, I raise my arms and thrust them right against my attacker's chest. The magic inside of me—the one I know and the one I don't—rushes to the surface. Then the man is flying through the air. Fire pours out of me. Even after all this time, the magic and the way it makes me feel surprises me.

A tightness in my chest alerts me to something, and my head snaps up. Immediately, my eyes zero in on Derek and the men swinging their swords at him from behind.

"Derek, watch out!" I yell as I throw a stream of fire at his attackers. The fire pushes the guy away, slamming him against the opposite wall. Derek turns, sending me a grateful nod as another guy attacks him. The clanging of swords sounds in the air around me as I spin trying to see if I can help any of my friends. The magic inside of me battles, fire or water. Fire or water. I don't know which one to use or how to use either one properly, but both are coming to the rescue.

I rush to Nora, who's holding her own. She's much more skilled with a sword than I could have imagined. But I guess that's just the way of court life, right? Everybody is a warrior in their own sense.

She stabs the guy clean-through and spins around, bringing her sword down on the next one. But she's not fast enough, and two more are on her. That same feeling rushes over me. Instead of fighting it, I channel it. The desire to let it burst free is nearly overwhelming. I push my hands in front of me, pushing magic with it. This time, fire and water comes out, one in each hand. It sweeps the attackers up and down, slamming them against the ground.

I don't even have time to marvel at what my magic is doing. There's no time to waste. We are getting overrun. The twelve against us has turned into twenty, and more are coming. If we don't get out of here now, we won't get out of here at all.

Nora is on one side of me and then Derek is suddenly on the other. Between Nora and him swinging their swords masterfully like they've been doing this all their lives, I can concentrate. My parents are on the other side of the mob. Julian is stuck in the middle.

There are words on the tip of my tongue, words I read in the forbidden book, but now is not the time to test out any kind of theories. The only thing that's left to do is trust the magic I was born with.

As I have done my whole life.

It doesn't matter that now there are conflicting forces inside of me or that my heritage isn't what I thought it was. The magic is still my magic, and I have to trust that. I have to get us out of here.

So, I bring my palms together, and I feel the intensity between them, fire and water.

Two opposites, living inside of me.

When I open my arms, the magic opens up with them. It pours out of me even more intensely than before. When I pushed the soldiers back, I wasn't even using half of the power that's raging inside of me. But right now, looking at my parents and friends, I let it all pour out. No overthinking, no contemplation.

Simply trusting. With complete intention.

My magic sweeps across every attacker. The sight is more terrifying than I'd like to admit. It either burns or drowns. Just like that. I try not to focus on what I've done, because as fast as it starts, it's over. My breathing is labored as I try to slow my heart rate down.

Nora is beside me and then so is a portal. She wraps her arms around me as I sag with exhaustion. No one hesitates as we step through.

* * *

As the portal closes behind us, we find ourselves in a familiar-looking forest. We're back in Arizona near Derek's cabin. I don't need to know the trees to know that. The smell in the air is that freshness I've come to associate with his place. I know I will find the magical lake right behind the building. A part of me wants to go straight there, if only to recapture the safety I felt here before I had to leave.

"Could you?" Nora's voice pulls my attention to her. I glance over to see her watching my dad. My gaze drifts between them, confused. But my dad seems to know exactly what she's asking. After only a moment's hesitation, he nods.

Stepping over to where the portal just closed, my dad crouches to the ground, plunging his hands right into the dirt. Before I can open my mouth to ask, a tree springs up from that spot, growing about a hundred feet into the air. No one else seems to be shocked by this development but me.

"Something you've forgotten to tell me?" I ask, directing my full attention on Dad. He turns, holding my gaze steady.

"There's a lot I haven't told you."

I already knew that but to have him say it is an extra punch to the gut. Magic is still boiling inside of my veins. I murdered or seriously hurt a bunch of people, and my father is apparently some magical...something? I'm flooded with emotion from every side. I'm not even giving myself permission to look at Derek right now.

"Let's start with why you just grew a tree right there?"

"To cover our tracks. Portal energy is disrupted by its living presence."

Nora grins at my father and then launches herself at me. The hug is fast and fierce before she pulls back to look me straight in the eye.

"Don't you ever pull that stunt again. We were worried." I don't miss the way her eyes shift to the right as she says so. I can feel Derek there, even though I'm refusing to look at him.

"We need to move before our combined energy leads them here anyway."

Derek's voice slams into me like a tidal wave. Nora squeezes my hand before turning to follow the fae prince into the woods. I feel a slight pressure on my waist and look over to see my mom's face nuzzling into my side. I run my hand over her silky fur before giving her a smile. I'm sure her "mom intuition" is at an all-time high right now. Even an untrained eye can see the tension between the fae prince and me.

No one speaks as we make our way back to the cabin. I knew I was familiar with these woods, and when we step into the clearing, I almost smile. I've spent so much time here lately; it's become a comfortable reprieve.

Derek doesn't bother with formalities and marches straight for the building with the rest of us following behind. By the time we're inside, he's disappeared.

I glance over at Nora, who shakes her head sadly.

"Okay, let me show you where you can clean up," she says and then motions for my parents to follow her. They each give me a look in turn, but I simply nod. I need a moment to catch my breath.

But no crying.

No crying.

No crying.

The fear I felt back there, for my parents and then for my friends, is what I've been carrying with me for a week now. The sleepless nights, the worry that if I let my guard down for even half a second everything will come crashing down. It's why I left in the first place. To protect the people who have become so important to me. But even so, everything I do seems to backfire.

I left to protect them, and I ended up being the cause of their near demise. I'm so good at this whole thing.

I want to let the tears spill over, if only for a moment, but I know I'm not alone.

Julian leans against the main doorway, his eyes on me. He has only ever allowed me glimpses of his emotions, but right now, they're on full display.

"Don't look at me like that," I whisper, but I know he can hear me even with the distance between us. The tears I'm holding back are threatening to spill over. As tired as I am, I'm not sure how long I can keep it together.

"You really scared us, Avery," Julian says, coming farther into the room. It's just the two of us on the main floor now. I have no idea where Derek is. Nora took my parents upstairs. It's the best time for me to give into emotion because I trust Julian with that part of myself. He's been my friend in all the best ways possible. But even though a part of me wants to break down in front of him, I don't. I'm afraid that if I let myself feel, I won't be able to stop. And then every wall I have put up to protect myself and those I love will be a useless pile of broken stone.

"I had to leave," I say instead, as Julian stops two feet in front of me. "The Ancients...they're too close, Julian. They're in my head, and I can't protect anyone if I..."

"You really scared *him*," Julian says, his voice barely above a whisper. My eyes latch onto his, and my heart squeezes in awareness. Reaching over, I wrap my hand around Julian's arm, giving it a gentle squeeze.

"I'm sorry. Truly."

The words are not something the fae hear very often, if ever. I can see the shock on Julian's face. There's a moment of silence and then he's reaching for me. He hugs me close, cradling me to him like he never thought he'd see me again. I think if I had a brother, he'd be a little bit like this. Or maybe I'd just want him to be exactly like this.

We stand like that for a long moment until a noise catches my attention. I pull back to find Nora coming down the stairs. There's a slight smile on her face as she looks at the two of us. I walk over to meet her at the bottom of the stairs.

"I'm sorry for leaving."

Her face lights up with a brilliant smile before she takes my hand and squeezes it.

"We all do what we think is right," she replies. She glances up the stairs, and the message is received. She's talking about my parents. It's probably time I talked to them instead of hiding in the bushes. I give the room a quick scan before turning to Nora.

"He'll come to you when he's ready."

Of course she knows exactly what I'm doing. I give her hand another quick squeeze and then climb the stairs. It's time for a conversation of all conversations.

CHAPTER 3

I find my parents in the same room I stayed in when I was
last here. Mom is back in her human form, sitting beside
my dad on the bed. She's wrapping his arm in actual gauze, and the
bleeding seems to have stopped. The moment I step through the
doorway, she's on her feet.

"You're hurt."

"What?" Her words take me by surprise. She reaches for my jacket,
and when she does, I realize my arm is sore. When she pulls the jacket
back, I see it's more than that. My upper arm is covered in blood, and
I didn't even notice it. When the material catches on the wound, I hiss
in pain.

"Come here, sweetheart." Mom leads me to the bed as Dad stands
and grabs the first aid kit Nora must've given them.

"I didn't even notice," I say, looking down as Mom cleans the
blood. A large gash opens up from my shoulder down toward my
elbow.

"Adrenaline," Mom replies as she continues to work on the wound.
"Your whole body is running on a different set of rules."

I watch her for a moment, letting myself feel the sadness at how
much I've missed her. I quickly shut that down and turn my attention

to Dad. He's watching Mom work on me, his lips in a tight line. He has kept so many secrets from me, I'm not sure where to even start.

"Dad, are you actually fae?" I ask the one question that's been plaguing me for months. It's the only explanation that would make sense, but I have no idea how that's possible. I know he said he left Faery behind, but that doesn't mean he was fae. He could've been a witch living in their midst. Mom stops cleaning my wound, glancing back at my dad. I know they're about to share something I'm not going to like.

"It's complicated, Avery."

"It's a yes or no question, Dad." I roll my eyes, but barely, just to show my annoyance. My father chuckles.

"You have always been stubborn."

"Yes, wonder who I've learned that from?" I give him a pointed look, and he smiles. For a second, everything feels right in the world and then he sobers up.

"We never thought you'd find out. Your fae magic isn't dominant. We never thought—"

"What? That I'd grow wings? Well, I have."

"I'm sorry, you did what?" My mom's voice is so shocked, my heart rate speeds up immediately.

"I have wings," I reply, looking from one parent to the other. "They're clear and shimmery, and I have no power to choose when they show up, but they've done so a few times. And this..." I pull back my hair so they can see my pointed left ear and the golden design woven around it. If I wasn't already watching my dad for a reaction, I might've missed it. His eyes—just for a moment—seem to glow, full of wonder and light. But then they're back to his regular brown color.

"Dad," I stand as Mom finishes wrapping a bandage around my upper arm. "What is it? Tell me what it means."

"It's not...possible."

"What isn't?"

I'm begging, just a little, but I need to know. This is my life we're talking about here. My magic, my body, my everything. I'm operating on so little information it's laughable. And I might laugh, if this weren't life and death.

"Daddy—"

That one word gets to him. His eyes fill as he walks over and takes a seat on the bed.

"I'm sorry, honey. I never wanted to put this kind of responsibility on you. If I had known—well, I'm not sure what I would've done."

"Tell me."

"The wings and the ear, they're part of the ancient families. Those who were on the council."

"The advisors to the king."

"You've been doing your homework." My father looks very proud of me as he smiles. "The ears were marks of great power. The wings displayed that power, but they also helped equalize it. Magic is all about balance. Once that balance is disturbed, bad things happen."

"Why do fae no longer have wings?"

"Because that magic has been suppressed for hundreds of years, and there is no way Queen Svetlana would allow it to ever return."

"So, you know my mother." Derek's voice catches me by surprise, and I watch as he steps into the room. He's all business, none of the man I got to know underneath, but that's okay for right now. We both need answers.

"She is the reason I was banished from Faery all those years ago. Falling in love with a shifter was unheard of for a council member. I broke her rules, and for that, I was banished."

"So, you are fae, and not just any fae. You're one of the important families from court," I mumble.

You're okay.

You're okay.

You're okay.

I know this is the only explanation that makes sense. I know I should have been expecting this. But at the same time, it feels like I can't get enough breath into my lungs. No wonder my magic is so out of control. I'm the biggest mutt there is. A witch, a shifter, and a fae. The triple threat, some may say. But most would just think I need to be handled. If I felt like I don't belong before, I feel it a hundred times more now.

"Why didn't you tell me?" I ask, looking from one parent to the other. "You didn't think I needed to know?"

"We were going to tell you, sweetheart," my mom says, taking one of my hands in hers and giving me a comforting squeeze. "After you graduated from Thunderbird Academy, we were going to tell you everything. We've been trying to protect you your whole life, and it wasn't enough. For that, we are sorry."

I'm not sure if I should be mad at them or not. But right now, I just need to think. So, without a word, I stand and head out of the door. The lake beckons.

* * *

THE LAKE IS JUST as I remember it. Peaceful and magical. It makes me want to dive right under the surface and stay there until all the worries of the world have passed away. Then I can resurface and simply live instead of being tasked with all these impossible choices.

Because that's all I feel like I'm doing now, making decisions that are leading nowhere. Maybe the magic chose the wrong girl. Maybe I was only ever supposed to be a witch. The words in that book, the rush of that power, none of that matters. But even as I think these things, I know they're a lie. For whatever reason, I was chosen for this. I can't tell if it's because of my heritage, or if that was just a side effect of a prophecy.

For a second, I think I'll give into the tears, but then I feel him behind me.

Derek.

I don't turn. I try not to think about the last time we stood on this tiny beach. Well, maybe standing isn't the right term. Just being here, the memory of that kiss is even more overpowering.

"We should rest," Derek says. He comes into my line of vision but about ten feet away. I turn my head just slightly and see that his eyes are trained on the water. "Tomorrow we can go back to Hannah's safe house. It's the best place for research and your parents will be safe there."

He knows exactly the arguments I would make, it seems. It's like I'm an open book when it comes to him.

"Derek—"

"I heard you apologize to Julian and Nora. You don't need to do the same here. You don't owe me anything."

Isn't that the biggest lie? I try not to let his cold tone get to me, but it's difficult. I'm used to him having his walls down when he's around me. But at the same time, I know I did this. I left him and shattered whatever illusion we were creating. Because it was an illusion. I don't think I have a happy ending at the end of all of this.

And that's what I need to focus on, the end result. The lives of so many are at stake. If he can stay focused on business, then so can I.

"How did you find me?"

He rolls his shoulders, just a tiny bit, which makes me narrow my eyes. It's like he's preparing to offer me half truths.

"Nora was able to pinpoint your location with a portal." There's definitely more to it than that, but he's not sharing. I can almost see him shutting down. I put those questions away for another time.

"What can you tell me about the soldiers?" I ask. There's a slight tick on his jaw, and I wonder what words he's holding back.

"They're highly trained, almost military-like. Only some have magic as far as we can tell. They carry no emblem or name, which makes it difficult to find any information on them."

The words are delivered with no emotion, but I suspect that's an act. There's no way he isn't as unsettled as I am standing so close beside me. Even ten feet apart, I can feel the intensity between us.

"We need more information on them. And on the book," I add. This time, Derek does look at me. There's a slight smirk in his gaze, and that's when I realize the other part of what he said.

"We're going back to Hannah's?"

"Yes. Her house is protected, and Queen Svetlana won't be able to breach it. "

"Derek—"

"We need to talk about the engagement." He's cold, detached, much like the fae I met when he found me in that alley in Phoenix. All the walls we've torn down while traveling together and fighting side by side are back up. And higher. Probably. They seem to be, at least.

Don't get emotional.

Don't get emotional.

Don't get emotional.

Maybe I should start repeating mantras five to ten times instead of three. It might help more. Pulling some air into my lungs, I exhale and turn my focus to the fae prince.

"What about it?" Oh look, that came out with no emotion attached to it. I'm learning. Derek holds my gaze for a moment, and I raise my eyebrows, waiting for him to go on.

"There are magical ways to break the binding. We need to do research, as it has only been done a few times in the past thousand years. Hannah's library should provide some answers."

At the mention of the extravagant fae, my heart squeezes in awareness. We let her get caught. I don't even know if she's alive anymore. She got us out of Faery, and I let her be taken in response. Like I thought earlier, I keep failing. No matter what I do, I keep failing. This whole "chosen one" situation has really shown me how terrible I am at this job.

"Is there a way to know if she's alive?" I ask, stopping whatever other speech Derek has prepared. I can tell I stump him for a second before he recovers.

"What happened to her isn't your fault."

His words and the way he delivers them surprises me. My eyes latch onto his. I can't help but feel the emotions creeping in. He's become so much more to me than I can even name, and I don't know what to do with that. Not when he feels miles away, standing only ten feet down the beach. But that statement—it's as if it bridges the gap. Just a tad.

"Doesn't mean I don't feel like it is."

And that's that. I feel responsible for every little aspect of this whole situation. It's why I had to leave in the first place. But I don't think Derek is ready to listen to any of that. Or maybe it simply doesn't matter. He doesn't say anything further, and I feel the exhaustion seeping into my skin.

"I'm heading to bed. Good night, Derek."

Then, I leave him standing there, staring at the water.

CHAPTER 4

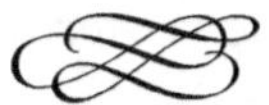

*I*t's been days since I've slept. Even though I'm afraid to let myself relax, I know I have no choice. For a second, I think I'll lay tossing and turning, but then, I'm in dreamland before I know it.

There's a second of peacefulness and my subconsciousness is content before it's ripped away. Suddenly, I'm hurling through mist into oblivion. I scream but no actual sound comes out. The space around me feels disorienting. I don't know which way is up or down. The feeling intensifies. When I think I can take it no longer, it stops.

I find myself on my hands and knees, gasping for breath. Raising my head, I look around and see darkness has descended. The forest opens up around me on every side, and otherworldly mist creeps in slowly. My heart is still beating a mile a second, so I stand slowly, giving my body a chance to adjust. It feels like I might fall over where I'm standing—everything seems to be spinning around me.

Then, he's there.

Don't panic.

Don't panic.

Don't panic.

The creature floats a few feet off the ground, his robes even more majestic than the last time I saw him. He's still dark and velvety but richer somehow. He's also a lot clearer, not the fuzzy outline I remember from before.

"You have tried to escape, Avery Kincaid, and you have failed." The words are also louder somehow. It's as if whatever magic the Ancients have been collecting is powering up this creature.

"I haven't given up yet," I say, raising my chin a little higher. I will not allow this...thing to see me cower. It's been days, and I have kept him at bay. I will do what I need to do now to keep it so.

"It is foolish for you to try," the creature says, moving closer to me, yet staying the same distance away. I don't understand the logistics of this place. But I do know it was my exhaustion that finally allowed him to break through the walls I put up.

"I will continue trying. For as long as there is breath in my lungs." My voice is strong and sure, and I will not waver. Determination fuels my body. The fate of all those I love weighs on my soldiers.

"You think the bond with the fae prince will save you?"

The question comes out of nowhere, and it stumps me. The only reason the creature ever brought up Derek before was as a threat. But now—it's something more. I don't understand the meaning behind his question, but I do know what he means by the bond. It's the engagement that the queen tricked us into in front of the whole of Faery. But I still don't understand how it plays a part in this, in any of this. I can't show my doubts though, not in front of the creature.

"He has no weight in this battle." I keep my voice steady even as my heart threatens to beat out of my chest. I don't understand the response. Except that's a lie. To myself. I know how I feel about Derek, I've just been refusing to admit it. Now is definitely not the time. "This feud is between you and me. You will not win. I hope you know that."

The creature surprises me then—by laughing. The sound is almost melodic and magical and not something I would think he would be able to produce. But then I think back to the last time we talked and how I thought him to be searching to reclaim a piece of his humanity. Is that what this response is?

"You are foolish, Avery Kincaid, yet strong. That strength is admirable but ultimately will be your downfall."

"Are you speaking from personal experience?" Even though I surprise myself with the question, and even though I can't see the creature's eyes, I can feel his glare directed at me.

"You will bring us the book, or we will act upon the promise we have made to you. But we will not stop at your family and your prince. We will take the whole realm with us. Their destruction will be on your shoulders."

The words echo around us, sending goosebumps up my arms. There is no doubt in my mind that the creature will actually go through with his threat. The Ancients are an old magical race, creatures who created the magical world I know today. If they can create, they can destroy.

I open my mouth to speak, but then I hear screaming. Turning my head toward the sound, I'm pulled back, as if by a cord. The next thing I know, I'm sitting up in bed, covered in sweat.

"Avery!" My mom is beside me, holding me by my shoulders, her shocked eyes on me. Confusion mars my expression as I try to figure out why she's there. "You were screaming in your sleep. Thrashing, enough to hurt yourself."

Mom points to my arm, and I see my cut is bleeding again. The screaming I heard in the weird vision thing must've been my own. Just then, Derek appears in the doorway. My eyes meet his. He does a quick once over scan of me to make sure I'm intact before he pivots and leaves once more.

"I have a lot of questions for you, sweetheart," my mom says as she turns away from the doorway and toward me. I want to tell her everything, but I also want to protect her from this. I know she'd say that's her job but not anymore. There comes a time when children do the protecting, and my time has come. But she needs some answers.

"Where's Dad?" I ask, and she smiles.

"Finally resting. It's been a while for him as well."

"He didn't hear my screaming?"

"Not since I used a sleeping spell on him."

My eyes grow round as I stare at my mother. Being a shifter, she doesn't have any witch powers. But I know Dad has prepared a few backup spells for her to use in case of emergency. I didn't think a sleeping one was on the menu.

"He would stay up and worry, and he needs to be at his full strength," Mom continues. "Plus, he gave me permission to do so if I ever deemed it necessary. This was the only time I have ever thought so."

That makes sense. But it also makes me wonder just how much my parents have kept from me. I guess I've been wondering that since I found out about my heritage. One of us needs to be truthful here, so I decide to give my mom the short version of what's been going on. She bandages my arm as I talk, and for just a second, the thoughts of the creature flee. For once, everything I have to do doesn't seem so over-whelming because I am here with my mom and everything will be okay, as long as I have my parents.

* * *

THE NEXT MORNING, I'm more tired than before. Mom and I talked for a while before I climbed back into bed, with her by my side. I actually ended up sleeping, but the two hours didn't do as much for me as they did for her. Wolves truly don't need as much rest. But even after I fell asleep, I was too afraid to actually relax enough to rest. I didn't partic-ularly want another run in with the Ancient.

It's a bit confusing why he waited until I fell asleep, since before he was able to come into my presence whenever. But maybe something changed in his magic. Or mine.

That's a problem for another time, because right now, I need to figure out our next move. And I have no idea what that is. Or even could be.

Nora is in the kitchen with my mom cooking waffles. Julian is at the table, eating the said waffles. I can see my dad on the back porch, coffee cup in hand.

Derek is nowhere to be seen.

Not that I'm surprised. Or looking for him. Mom greets me with a kiss to the temple before handing me a plate.

"Please eat all of it."

I smile and nod, before making my way to the table. Julian grins at me around a mouthful and I chuckle. This whole scene is way too domestic for all the craziness that's been going on.

"I should take a look at that arm after breakfast," Nora says, pointing to my bandage. I look over and see blood has seeped through once more. Maybe those swords were enchanted because this seems to be a bigger issue than I thought. That's something I should probably research, as well as a million other things I have questions about.

Just then Derek comes into the kitchen from outside. Julian is on his feet immediately, taking his plate to the sink. Without a word—or a glance in my direction—Derek walks over to the coffeemaker and picks up a cup. I can't help but watch as he says something to my mom. She smiles at him. After taking a few sips, he walks out of the room with Julian on his heels.

I glance over at mom and Nora and both have their eyes on me. That's that, my appetite is gone. Good thing I finished already. Dropping my plate in the sink and giving mom a kiss on the cheek, Nora and I head to the sitting room.

"I heard you screaming last night," she says, not beating around the bush.

"I had a visitor."

Talking about it makes it worse, but I know I can't keep secrets from them anymore. Their lives are on the line. Giving Nora the shortest version possible, I wince as she takes the bandage off my upper arm.

"It doesn't look good," she says.

"It doesn't feel good either."

It's definitely magically enchanted, so that's another problem to add to the large list of problems. Derek comes back into the room then, his eyes zeroing in on the cut.

"Nora?"

"I think it's magically infected," she replies. He nods, not meeting my eye. He stands at the doorway for about thirty seconds before twisting on his heels and walking back out.

"Think he's ever going to actually talk to me again?" I ask Nora as Derek leaves the room again.

Our conversation last night felt like I was talking to a stranger. I can't blame him for this awkwardness between us, but I miss us talking. I miss him.

Nora is administering aid to my arm, but she stops for a second, watching me.

"Does it matter?"

"Of course it matters," I reply automatically. But there's something in her voice that stops me. I study her eyes as she concentrates on her task. I know I apologized for leaving already, but maybe that wasn't enough.

"You know I had to go. Right? I had no other choice."

She finishes wrapping my arm before she turns her full attention on me.

"We all have choices, Avery. You could have come to him. You could have come to us."

And there it is, the part of this whole situation that we haven't dealt with. Just like Derek, Nora feels like I abandoned her. But more so, like I don't trust her. So wrapped up in my own problems, I didn't even take the time to think about how this would affect them. My friends. Because that's what they are. But maybe even more so—my family. It seems I just keep making mistakes. But I need her to understand as well.

"No, I couldn't have, okay? What's going on with my magic, with the Ancients? This whole thing? It's not your problem. It's mine. And I have to fix it before somebody gets hurt. Because people will get hurt. Everyone in my vicinity is in danger. I can't put that on you. Or Julian. Or Derek."

"And what about you? You don't care if you get hurt?"

This is the first time Nora has ever raised her voice at me, and it makes me pause for a moment. A part of me wants to offer her comfort and reassurance. But I can't do that. I have to be honest with her, without sounding crazy. So I take a deep breath before responding,

"It doesn't matter what happens to me, Nora. I have come to terms with that. If Svetlana gets me, I'm dead anyway. If the Ancients get me, I'm also dead. But first, both sides will use me to destroy Faery, and I can't be the weapon they want me to be. I have to choose my own side and fight."

Nora reaches over to give my hand a squeeze.

"I get it, Avery. I do. But I think you keep forgetting that your side is not just you anymore. You have me. You have your parents. Julian. Yes, Derek. You don't have to fight this fight alone. You can't protect us from wanting to help you."

Passion and determination shines in her eyes as she looks at me, as if willing me to believe her words. The fact that I do is the thing that scares me. Because if I believe it, it must be true. And I don't know what to do with that. It's much better if I'm alone. It's much safer if there is no one relying on me.

But I know I'm only kidding myself when I think that. It's always better to have people on your side, and I have found my people. This ancient power inside of me—it brings with it the weight of many worlds. It's a lot of pressure for one person to carry. But I don't have a choice.

Now that my parents are safe, I have to start making big moves. I can't keep hiding or running. Sooner or later, they'll catch up. The queen will pull some trick or use the engagement to her advantage. I've been trying very hard not to think about it, but it's near impossible. Now, it's even more impossible to talk to him about it without it being just a string of clipped words and barely grazing glances.

"Was he mad?" I ask before I realize what I'm doing. Nora gives me a kind smile before squeezing my hand once more.

"That's a conversation you'll have to have with him."

"That's not helpful." I pout, and Nora simply shakes her head.

"You have to be patient with him. You always have been, so don't stop now. He needs you, just like you need him. Don't forget that."

Before I can respond—or even find a way to process what Nora

CHAPTER 5

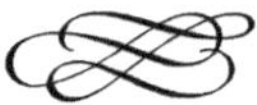

We head to the back porch, taking a seat on the comfortable chairs Derek and I used not so long ago. The lake glistens in front of us, and the guys are nowhere to be seen. Nora stays inside with Mom, cleaning up after breakfast.

"Your mom told me what happened last night. I'm sorry I wasn't there."

"Oh, are we starting off with apologizing already?" The words are out before I can stop them. I'm not typically one to speak so disrespectfully to my father, but I guess there's a time for everything.

"Maybe we should," Dad replies, turning his body toward me. "Because I am sorry. I should've prepared you better."

"You mean like the nursery rhymes?"

If I wasn't watching him already, I would've missed the flash of surprise in his eyes.

"That's right. I figured it out. You were teaching me fae ways, even though you didn't tell me about your heritage."

"You've always been a smart girl, Avery." He smiles, and there's pride shining there. The feeling it ignites inside me is warm and familiar. My parents have always been in my corner. I guess until they weren't. But I can't truly say that anymore. I did the exact same thing when they and my friends became in danger. I protected them by keeping things to myself. I have to understand where my parents were coming from.

"So how did that work then? Did you leave or—"

"No, I was banished. Love between a shifter and a fae was unheard of back at that time. Fae could only be given away to other fae. You heard that right," he says when I raise my eyebrow, "given away. Arranged marriages were all the rage."

My mind briefly shifts toward Derek and our own arranged marriage, but I push those thoughts away and focus on my father. I've been carrying around all these questions, but now I don't even know where to start.

"What made her worth it?" I blurt out the question before I could even think of it. I'm a little surprised but my dad seems to be the opposite. As if he's been expecting that question.

"She's my home in every way possible," Dad replies without hesitation. His eyes look over at the kitchen window, and I turn to watch him watch my mother moving around and talking to Nora. I've watched them love each other with this fierceness my whole life, but I never truly understood what it meant until now. They've given up everything to be together.

"You never regretted it?"

"Never." He turns his attention back to me, his eyes kind. "And after we had you, there was no going back, Avery. I wanted to protect you from that life. I wanted to raise you to have a choice."

I understand that, of course I do. But in the end, I don't really get to have a choice anyway. I was chosen before any of this came about, or maybe not. Maybe it was my parents' love that made it possible in the first place. Because that kind of love, it's magic all on its own.

But of course, I'm not about to say this to my dad. I don't want him to feel any more responsibility for this than he already clearly does.

"Dad." I lean forward, making sure he can see just how serious I am about this. "You have done an incredible job raising me. I am strong enough to handle this because of the kind of parents you are. Don't ever doubt that."

His eyes fill with tears. Then we're reaching for each other. We stand, and he holds me tighter than imaginable, as if he wants to protect me from everything and anything. I hug him back just as tightly because that's my job now. And I don't intend to fail.

* * *

THE REST of the day goes by without a hitch. We decide to wait to go to Hannah's until tomorrow, to give our magic a little more of a break. My arm appears to be healing, finally, and I wonder if some of it was physiological. After my talk with Dad, I feel better. Even though I didn't even ask all the questions I planned, I think I just wanted reassurance, in a way.

Now, I'm by the lake once more, giving myself the time I need to find my center. My magic seems to have replenished itself, but it's restless. I think instead of me channeling it, it's channeling me. So, I really need to chill.

Something shifts in the air. The lake is suddenly as still as a mirror, reflecting the stars above. Glancing around, I try to pinpoint the cause of the uncomfortable feeling, but I see nothing but darkness. The forest seems to be holding its breath as the feeling intensifies.

Everyone else is inside the cabin. I can see them in the kitchen through the large glass doors leading to the back porch. As I scan over everyone, Derek's eyes catch mine and hold. It's like we're attuned to the same wavelength because I can see the same tension I'm feeling in the set of his shoulders.

A silent communication passes between us and then I give him the slightest of nods. He turns to his friends and my parents, speaking urgently. There's no hesitation on their part. They each reach for a weapon while my mom takes a step back from the table so she can shift if need be. I keep my footsteps slow and steady as I turn to head back into the house.

Maybe it's nothing. Maybe I'm just overly aware of every dancing shadow after the creature threatened the wellbeing of my loved ones.

But then I meet Derek's gaze through the glass once more, and I know it's more than paranoia.

I'm reaching for the doorknob when my mom suddenly shifts. There's no time for a reaction. As I pull the door open, I'm yanked backward by a blast of magic. Landing hard on my back, I try to catch my breath as I roll over.

That's when I see them. They're coming out of the water.

The shock of seeing bodies emerge from the lake freezes me for only a moment. Then I'm pushing to my feet, my magic at my fingertips. Fire is what I know, but water is what I'm called to. The constant confusion inside me is frustrating to say the least. But that's when I realize, I should simply stop fighting it.

If there are two sides to me, then I will use them both.

Or I will at least try. I did it in the alley; I can do it now.

Every single time up until now, my magic responded on instinct. Now, let's see how it responds intentionally. I hear shouts coming from behind me as I get to my feet.

Fire and water.

Fire and water.

Fire and water.

I repeat the phrase in my mind, finding my center. Suddenly, Derek is beside me, a sword in hand. Our gaze meets for only a moment and then my magic is set free.

A stream of fire and water pours out of each hand, racing toward the soldiers. The magic sweeps across the open beach, entwining together like two snakes dancing around each other as it attacks the shadowy figures.

The sound of their screams and the smell of their burnt flesh fills the air. More soldiers flank us on both sides, spilling out of the forest. Swords clang around me as my friends and family fight.

Mom is in her wolf form, pouncing on one soldier after the other. Dad is the closest to her, a sword in his hand. He looks like a warrior as he fights off his attacker. I send another blast of magic at our attackers when I realize this looks very much like the attack in the alley. They're flanking almost the same way.

"Derek!" I shout just as the fae prince swings his sword across the closest soldier. "We have to break them apart!"

Derek glances at me, then at the soldiers. A look of understanding comes into his features. He gives me a firm nod and then races toward Nora. I pivot and run toward Julian.

"Come with me!" I shout at him as I send a blast of water battle magic at his attacker. The soldier flies ten feet back, smacking into two others. Julian doesn't hesitate to follow.

My mom must've heard me shouting at Derek and understood as well because she leads Dad in the opposite direction. The three pairs of us disperse, and for just a second, the soldiers stop fighting. Julian and I catch our breath at the edge of the woods as we watch the soldiers. They seem frozen in place before springing into action again.

Separating into three groups, they give chase.

The way they move, the odd way they stand there, something is definitely off about them. But that's a problem for another time. Julian and I take them deeper into the forest. I send blasts of fire and water magic at them as they come. Once we reach a clearing, Julian and I take a stance back-to-back.

"That was weird, right?" Julian asks, his sword firmly in his hand as he watches the trees.

"Extremely weird," I agree as I do the same. It doesn't take long for the soldiers to reach us. Now that there are fewer of them, I think my magic can do extra damage.

"Let me do this," I say softly, but I know Julian can hear me. Once again, he doesn't question. But he also doesn't attack.

Just like back on the beach, I focus on my two magics, putting my intention into them the best way I know how. Closing my eyes, I breathe it all in—the nature around me, the ground beneath my feet, and the power running through my veins. I can feel the soldiers move. Then instead of looking at them, I look up, sending my magic there.

The stream of fire and water rises up out of my palms before it shoots out around us like a sunbeam. There are screams of agony and the smell of charred flesh, and then the soldiers are gone, as if they were never there.

Dropping my arms down, I look around, trying to understand what happened.

"Did I evaporate them?"

"No," Julian replies, also looking at the empty space. "It's something else."

Just then, a scream reaches my ears, and my heart drops. Without a moment's hesitation, I take off toward the cabin.

CHAPTER 6

When we burst through the trees in front of the cabin, my eyes instantly go to my mother. She's on the ground, still in her wolf form, but she's not moving. Dad is beside her, hacking at the soldiers trying to reach her, sweat running down his face.

There's no hesitation in my movements, no thought in my mind. I send a blast of magic out of me, and the soldiers disappear the moment water and fire reach them. My body feels like all my energy has been sucked out of it, but I manage to stay on my feet as I race toward my parents.

Dad is beside mom, cradling her head on his knees.

"What happened? What's wrong with her?"

"She was knocked out by a blast of magic. She'll be okay," he hurries to add. "She just needs rest."

"How do you know though? What can I do?" I can feel panic set in.

I can't lose her.

I can't lose her.

I can't lose her.

"Avery." My dad's voice breaks through my inner chanting, his eyes steadily on me. He knows I do this, understands the need for reassurance. He reaches out, placing his hand over my knee and giving it a tiny squeeze.

"I can feel it through our bond. She's fine."

Bond? Just then Derek and Nora run out of the woods on the other side. Their eyes grow wide at the sight of us on the ground. Derek turns to me immediately, doing the once over he always does. His gaze lingers on the tears holding onto my lower eyelashes. He moves toward me automatically before visibly restraining himself. Instead of rushing to my side, he holds my gaze. The pure confidence he has in me—all his emotions displayed just for me to see—helps me push all the panic away. Right now, I don't need to be held as I cry. I need to be respected as someone who can handle herself and whatever life throws at her. And with that one look, that is exactly what Derek does.

"We need to get out of here," Julian says. I turn to see him standing behind me, his eyes on the woods. "They found us once, they'll be back for more."

"How did they find us?" I ask, glancing from one fae to the other.

"It must be my magic," Derek replies, his features once again as cold as his exterior. "The tracking spell Svetlana has on my magic must be accessible to others, maybe simply because it's not hidden like it usually is."

"So that means this place is no longer safe," I say.

This is Derek's sanctuary. A place he kept away from his fae world so that he could escape. But now, just like everything else in our lives, it seems to have been tainted by the magic of the Ancients. Even though he's keeping his expression neutral, I can see frustration bubbling under the surface. Every rule we know about magic is changing, and we're right in the middle of it.

"If we can be tracked here, we can be tracked anywhere," Nora says. I glance at my friends, one by one, and my heart squeezes at the sight. Tired and dirty, blood and sweat stained, this is not the way the fae live. But they have chosen to be here, by my side, to ensure their world isn't destroyed. I can't thank them out loud, but my heart feels full. So many people have stood by me in this. I have to find a way to make sure they survive.

"No, wait." An idea comes to mind as I stand. Everyone's attention is on me, but I'm only looking at Nora. "There is one place we can go."

She seems to read my mind as she grins. The portal opens, and I glance over at my dad. Mom is back in her human form but still unconscious. I didn't even notice her shifting back. Dad stands with her in his arms. After I give him a firm nod, he walks through the portal without hesitation.

* * *

THE HOUSE FEELS empty without Hannah and quiet somehow, even though I can hear the forest moving around us. It's as restless as I am. My dad cradles Mom in his arms. I don't remember the last time she looked this helpless. My heart squeezes at the sight and at the way my dad looks at her.

Derek and Julian separate, disappearing from view. I can only assume they're checking the house for any dangers.

"You need rest," I say, facing my parents. Yes, I'm the one handing out orders now, but they look worse for wear. The worry that mars their faces is caused by me, which makes me feel like I'm not doing enough to protect them. My mom was in danger because of me. In trying to protect them, I've put them in harm's way. This is becoming a pattern.

"We're okay, Avery," Dad says, but I'm already shaking my head.

"You're not. Julian will show you to a room, and I want you to rest. Please? For me?"

The guy in question just walked into the room, and I look at him as I say the words. He nods his head before motioning for my dad to follow him. Dad gives me a long glance before he follows Julian out of the room. I still have so many questions for him. But right now, we all need a break. And my mom needs to regain consciousness.

She's fine. I have to trust that Dad knows what he's talking about.

Nora and I head to the library, the same room I was in with

Hannah the last time I was here. It's where I finally let my ancient magic out to play. Derek and Julian find us there a few minutes later.

"The house is still protected, but there's no one here," Julian says. I give him a nod.

"Okay, so we regroup. Figure out how they found us, how to prevent that from happening again."

Derek is staying quiet, standing in the corner of the room where he can see both of the entrances. I can feel his eyes on me, and I'm trying not to fidget under the scrutiny. We're in such a weird place. I'm not sure what to do with it.

"We need to figure out what's next."

"What's next is that we need that book," Nora says. Derek looks at her sharply. If I wasn't watching him so closely, I would have missed the glare he sends her way.

But Nora isn't wrong. Everything that's been going on has revolved around this magic, and I need an upper hand here.

"You're right," I say. "We do. The Ancients and the queen, they're not going to stop until they get to me, and I need to be able to protect myself."

"How are you supposed to protect yourself if you're going to use the magic that is meant to destroy you?" Derek's voice is clipped and harsh. He's not looking at me now, but I feel emotion radiating off him. Nora gives me a look and then she leaves the room, grabbing Julian on the way out.

I walk over to Derek slowly, giving him the time he needs if he decides to run for me, but he doesn't. Surprisingly. He's still looking at everything but me, and even though we had a prior conversation, it still feels like there's a vast chasm between us. When I stop beside him, I do the first thing that comes to mine.

I take his hand.

I feel his whole body shudder under the small contact. The skin against skin sends my heart soaring and my soul singing. That pull we've been working against this whole time, it's more intense now than ever before.

There's something between us. I don't understand what it is, but now is not the time to explore it. No matter how much I want to. I have to focus on this.

I have to focus on saving them all and then maybe I can save my heart.

"Derek," I say, keeping my voice soft. "I don't have a choice. In the span of two weeks, my family has been attacked, my friends have been attacked, and a Faery revel was invaded. If things keep up the way they have been going, Faery won't survive long. If Queen Svetlana gets the magic that's inside of me, everything will perish. And everyone."

"I know," he says because he can't actually argue with the truth. But I also need him to understand that it's more than that.

"I know you know, Derek, but you have to understand that it doesn't matter what happens to me. It can't matter. Not if we're going to save Faery," I say, squeezing his hand. He holds on to me just as tightly. His fingers lace with mine and a tingling sensation races up my arm as our palms touch.

When all this started, I ran from the responsibility that came with this magic, but I can't do that anymore. The realms rely on me to choose what's right and to follow through with it. I'm not the first or the last individual who is gifted with such a hard decision, but I want to be one of the ones who makes the right decision. At the end of it all, I want there to be history books written about this time and space, even if I'm not in them. I want there to be a future, and right now, I'm the one responsible for making that happen.

"I can't run from this anymore," I say as Derek finally turns his eyes on me. Now I'm the one looking over his shoulder, at the painting of a forest surrounded by a magical mist. "The last half a year has made me realize that this magic—it's a responsibility that was given to me because I *could* handle it. I should not be afraid of it. And if I'm going to do my part, if I'm going to use this magic to do what I can to stop the Ancients, then I have to risk everything."

There are tears in my eyes when I finally meet Derek's gaze. There is so much emotion in his eyes that I probably would have fallen if I wasn't holding on to him so tightly. But I know that no matter what he says, he can't talk me out of this.

Yet a part of me still wishes he would. I want him to tell me that I don't have to do this, that I can walk away, but we both know it's not true. More than wanting this to be someone else's life, I want him with me.

I want him with me.

I want him with me.

I want him with me.

He takes a step toward me, erasing the distance between our bodies. A part of me thinks he can read the emotion in my eyes or maybe he can just read me.

"Am I going to have to watch you die?" Derek whispers, his voice wavering at that last word. It takes all the wind out of my sails. The tears I've been holding back for what seems like forever slip down my cheeks. I want to say no, I want to make a million promises, but I know I can't keep any of them. It wouldn't be fair for me to bend the truth.

"I don't know, Derek. I don't know. But I know that I can't live with myself if I don't do everything I can to prevent our world from dying."

He takes a deep breath, leaning down so our foreheads touch. His hand is still holding mine and the other curls over my elbow as I place my own on his upper arm. We stand like that for a long moment, connected on an otherworldly level as we breathe the same air. He inclines his head to the side, placing a soft kiss to my cheek, catching my tear with his lips. He moves to my other cheek, his lips only a breath of a touch, but the sensations race through me as he kisses my tears away.

"That means," Derek says, his voice barely above a whisper. "I will be there every step of the way."

Then, he says something I have never heard a fae utter, and I never thought that he would.

"I promise, Avery. I will be there with you every step of the way."

CHAPTER 7

The house is quiet as everyone rests, but I'm too restless to even try. I'm worried, yes. But I'm also high off Derek. I can still feel his gentle kisses on my cheek.

After finding my way back to the library, I spent the last few hours pouring over the books. Research has always been a fun activity for me and a calming one. It's the whole reason being accepted to Thunderbird Academy was such a big deal. I would have access to the greatest magical library. Well, one of them at least. So much knowledge at my fingertips.

But it seems crazy now—that whole life. My plan to graduate from the academy, to go work for the council, to train under my father. All of these are simply dreams that will never come true now.

I remember how excited I was to meet Maddie, the water witch who saved Thunderbird Academy from the Ancients. I thought being in class with her and her wolf shifter boyfriend would be the extent of my excitement at the school. But then before classes even started, I was in possession of an ancient book only I could read.

I chuckle to myself, shaking my head. What a funny thing life is. It never turns out how you want it to. Right now, I can't tell if that's a good thing or a bad thing.

But that's not true either. If I'm to be completely honest with myself, I wouldn't change a thing. My parents have always taught me to live my life without regrets. Each experience is an opportunity to learn and to grow. I've been thrown into the most unbelievable experience and it's my responsibility to learn and to grow. If for nothing else but the fact that I owe it to myself. I also owe it to everyone I love and those who I don't even know. Sometimes destiny chooses you and you have to choose it right back.

It's what I basically decided when I was out on that beach tonight. To allow my magic to be an intentional choice, not just a reaction. That means I need to learn more about it. Surprisingly enough, Hannah's library is stocked with all kinds of books on magic and quite a few on water magic. Those are the books I've been pouring over—no pun intended.

As soon as the thought crosses my mind, I chuckle. Maybe I should go to bed. I seem to be losing my mind.

That's when I feel him.

My eyes go to the doorway and he's there, shrouded in shadows. Even so, his eyes shine somehow through the darkness, and they're on me.

"You couldn't sleep either?" I ask, cocking my head to the side with a small smile. Derek pushes away from the doorframe and slowly makes his way into the room. He's dressed in a dark t-shirt and jeans. It's the most human I've seen him since we met. But of course, he's not. When my eyes meet his, the illusion is shattered, and I can see the fae prince again. It's amazing that I didn't see it right away. His whole being screams royalty.

"I've been researching water magic," I say when he comes to stand in front of the table. He does that thorough study of me that I've come to know as his signature move. When his eyes finally reach mine, there are a lot of conflicting emotions there. Because I've already decided to be intentional about everything else, I'm going to be intentional here too.

"What is it?" I ask, keeping my gaze on his. I know it's something. I see it in the set of his jaw, in the way he's holding his shoulders. I think I surprise him, but at the same time, it's like my question has given him permission. He exhales deeply, as if he's been waiting to breathe.

"I was scared."

Those three little words take both of us by surprise. It's so unlike fae to admit any kind of emotion. Especially to an enemy.

And isn't that what he's been taught I am? From an early age, anyone who was not fae has been the enemy. Which is why our connection has never made any sense to us. Even though I now know I'm part fae, I'm still not worthy in the eyes of the courts. I don't need to be part of that world for a long time to know that. I've read about it in books.

I'm still a half breed, someone who isn't pure fae and doesn't come from a proper family, regardless of my nobility status. They would never accept me in court. I could never have a place there, unless of course, the queen demands it. And that's what she did when she made me Derek's fiancée. Now my magic, regardless of where it comes from, belongs to her and the court will see that.

Derek doesn't see me like that though. And right now, he's being more honest with me than he's ever been.

"Tell me."

His eyes latch onto mine. I think he's going to come around the desk, but he doesn't. He simply stands there, watching me.

"When the soldiers came and you ran into those woods, I didn't think I'd ever see you again. I have no idea what to do with that."

It's an admission worth a hundred admissions in gold.

"Derek," I say, standing up from my spot to go to him. But then, darkness descends. I see him open his mouth, but then he's no longer there. I'm in the strange in between place, still the library but not quite there.

Then, the creature is there.

"What did you do to him?" I scream, pushing away from the desk and moving toward the creature before I can think about it.

"You have disappointed us." The creature ignores my question, his voice louder than I've ever heard it before. "We are done waiting. You have been warned before, and this is no longer a warning."

"Give him back to me now!" I yell. The magic I carry inside of me rises to the top. The feeling stumps me for a moment because I've never been able to use magic in one of these weird out of body experiences before. When fire ignites at my fingertips, time seems to stop. And I with it. Suddenly, I can't move as the creature floats over to me. His attention is on the flame in my hand. I follow him with my eyes as he studies it.

"It should not be possible," he says and then I'm being ripped away. The library falls back into place. Now I'm face to face with Derek.

"Avery!" He grabs me around the waist as I stumble after being frozen, extinguishing my flame. "What happened?"

"The Ancients," I reply. Hannah's place is officially not as safe as we thought it to be.

* * *

"I HAVE TO LEAVE."

My announcement goes about as well as I think it will. Everyone starts talking at once. At least mom is here now, sitting on the couch. She's the only one not freaking out.

Well, she and Derek. I think he's still a little shocked about the whole Ancient being here and not here at the same time. He's known about it, but he's never experienced it. It's different when it's happening to you. The one thing we've learned about the Ancients is that their magic is unlike anything we've ever seen before. It felt different this time, but I'm not sure if it's just my own fears or if something is happening. I mean, something is happening. The Ancient definitely freaked out over the fact that I could pull on my fire magic. But I still need to get away from the people I love. Fast.

"You're not going anywhere by yourself," Nora announces for the tenth time. "I am your lady's maid, and I am to come with you wherever you go."

"Nora, you are my *friend*." I make sure to emphasize the word. "And you are in way too much danger with me beside you."

"Nope, I'm not taking that as an answer, and you can stop arguing. I'm coming."

I glance over at Julian, whose features are set with the same determination as Nora's. I already know Derek is coming. There isn't a force in this realm or the next that would be able to keep him away. Selfishly, I want him by my side. Especially after we sort of told each other some things. And he made a promise. I can't bring myself to force him to break it. Even though I want to protect him.

But Nora and my parents? Them I can try and protect.

"Nora, I need you to stay here and take care of my parents." This time Mom does begin to speak up, but I stop her.

"This isn't a negotiation. You are staying here. Mom, you still need to heal, and Dad will stay by your side. You are directly involved in the threat the Ancients are holding over my head. After I was done freaking out over the Ancients getting into Hannah's place, I realized they didn't actually. They have access to me but not to where I'm at. Therefore, if I'm gone, so is the threat."

"I'm serious about this." I give my parents a stern look. "You're staying and so is Nora. I can't worry about you. Please."

My mom grabs my dad's hand and gives it a squeeze. With that one gesture I know they'll pay heed to what I say. Nora doesn't look happy, but she will also follow my lead. That leaves Julian.

"No, absolutely not," Julian starts before I can even say anything. "I'm not leaving your side. Don't you even try to convince me otherwise."

The look he gives me disputes any arguments I can make. Well, I guess that's that. That's the best half of a plan that we can come up with right now. Once we've put some distance between myself and my parents and Nora, we can come up with a better one.

We say our goodbyes because there is no way I'm giving the Ancients a chance to come back and make good on their threat. Thankfully, Julian has kept his Phoenix apartment.

"I don't like this," Nora announces as she opens a portal to Julian's place.

"I know," I say, stopping in front of her. "But I am grateful you are following my lead." It's the closest I can come to saying thank you, and Nora understands.

"Just make sure you come back in one piece," my friend says, giving me a hug. "And take care of them."

I don't have to ask to clarify. The guys step through first and are already waiting on the other side. My parents both give me a hug, but they don't try to talk me out of anything. I am thankful for that.

"We love you."

"I love you too."

Emotion threatens to choke me, but I swallow it down. They need to see me strong. I have no choice but to be strong.

They will be okay.

They will be okay.

They will be okay.

Giving them one last long look, I step through the portal.

CHAPTER 8

We slept for a few hours. It's all we can manage because we're all a little wired. But we also know we need to unwind. I doubt any of us actually rested. We're going through the motions though, and I think that's the best that we can do right now. It's still dark when I finally can't pretend any longer and make my way to the rooftop.

I walk over to the edge, my hair moving slightly in the wind. The city is restless and so am I. I don't know what to do next, but there is no doubt in my mind that it requires me to get the book.

Nora is right about that. There isn't an option where I won't be using this ancient magic. It runs through me, powering my decisions and my actions. It's part of who I am, even if I don't understand it or truly know how to wield it. The attacks will keep coming, and it's almost like there's a third force out there, hunting our every step. I need to get ahead of this, somehow.

"Running away again?" The question comes from behind me. I'm not even surprised. Without turning, I wait until Derek is standing beside me.

"I'm never running away again," I reply honestly.

"Oh yeah?" The completely human phrase makes me smile. "Is that a promise you're willing to make?"

I glance at him then, as he watches the city below us. His shoulders are tense. There's tiredness in him that I'm not used to seeing in fae. He carries this burden just as fully as I do. I don't think I realized it until this moment. It makes me want to reach out to him.

"Derek—" I begin but then stop because I really don't know what to say to him or how to say it without sounding like a crazy person, or whatever else I am. Because I am so many things right now. Unknown and unfamiliar things.

I feel like I want to apologize again, for leaving. Even though he's clearly forgiven me, there's still tension there. Maybe he's simply worried I'll disappear. Especially after the whole fiasco with the Ancient at Hannah's house.

That's something else I'm trying not to think about—Hannah. I want to go after her, but that's kind of like stepping back into the lion's den right now. Without any way of getting out. Maybe learning more about the magic I possess can give me the option to save her.

One problem at a time.

I have to survive the magic first. In the back of my mind, that has become a big concern.

"We need to go to Thunderbird Academy," I announce, my voice low. This time, he does look at me directly.

"Why is that?"

I don't want to say it out loud, but I know I need to tell him. It's scary to put the words out there because I don't know who's listening. Not when I'm being constantly watched by so many entities. So, I take a step forward, bringing myself right against Derek's side. He doesn't move, keeping completely still as I stand on my tiptoes and bring my lips near his ear.

"I have to get the book," I whisper.

There's a split second where Derek's eyes register the shock before he shuts it down. We have to tread lightly here. He understands that as well as I do.

"You left it there?"

"It's a little more complicated than that."

"What do you mean?"

We're still flush against each other, but now Derek bends down, so I don't have to keep standing on my tiptoes. My body is against his side. His arm comes around my waist to keep me close. If anyone saw us, they'd simply think we're embracing, not discussing matters of grave importance.

"How much do you know about the academy?' I ask.

"There was a witch and a pack of shifters who saved the Spring Court."

I nod, my cheek brushing his shoulder. An array of goosebumps travel up my arm at the small contact. My hand wraps around his upper arm before I can think too much of it. His body is tense but alive at the same time. That sensation mirrors my own.

"I met her friend Liam there, when I was apprenticing with Hannah. When the time came, I sent the pages to her as a backup, but the book itself went back to Maddie."

Derek's eyes light up with understanding. Maddie would be someone who's not directly connected to me, not in any way the queen or the Ancients would really know or think about. After everything that has happened, it's the most protected place I could think of, and the school itself is nearly impossible to breach. After all, that's where I found the book. Or I guess, the book found me. It's been safe there for years.

"That was a smart move," Derek finally says. I look up to find him already looking at me. Our eyes meet and hold, that connection that I still don't understand passing through like we've been holding onto a live wire.

"I do what I can," I reply.

We still haven't moved apart, and I don't think I ever want to. This whole thing, it's crazy. Us getting engaged in front of the whole court as a power move by the queen but also as punishment. Except is it really punishment when it's something I want? And do I want it? I do. I'm coming to terms with that every moment of every day. I honestly don't know what to do about it.

Somehow, we're standing even closer now, our lips just inches apart.

I want to taste him.

I want to kiss him.

I want to hold him close.

The thoughts race through my mind, scaring and exciting me at the same time. This feels so much more than just a crush. It feels like the most important thing in the world. Even that feels wrong to think because there are things so much more important than this.

"Hey." Derek places his forehead against mine, and we both exhale in contentment. "You got this."

The human phrase once again makes me smile, but I don't respond, and I don't move. I just soak in this closeness for a moment longer because I know the battle will come. I'm more than determined to see it through to the end.

* * *

"YOU'RE SURE ABOUT THIS, RIGHT?" Julian asks as we step through the portal. Nora happily provides us with a step-through portal, and I get to look in on my parents. Even though it's only been a few hours, I'm still too nervous about the Ancient's threat to simply ignore it. But I am very tired of simply reacting to the events unfolding around me. I need to be proactive.

It's time I owe up to the expectations this magic has placed on me.

That's why we're in the woods surrounding Thunderbird Academy. We're still some distance away. I didn't want to alert any of the magical wards in place around the school.

"I'm as sure as I'll ever be," I reply.

"Can you explain to me again why we're sneaking into it though?" Julian asks as we move slowly through the forest. "Didn't you go here?"

"Yes. And then I ran away."

"Oh, that's true."

I chuckle at Julian's tone before continuing.

393

"I'm pretty sure the headmaster doesn't want to see me right now. Or ever. Since, you know, I'm bringing doom and gloom to the school again."

"Doom to the school?" Julian rolls his eyes. "That's very dramatic, Avery."

"I can be very dramatic." I shrug.

"Don't I know it."

I smile at him and he at me, and in this moment, I feel a little bit better. Everything has been so off lately. I've been unsure of every move I make, but talking to him like this, while moving through the woods, it feels a little more normal. A little more like us.

Everything I do affects the people around me. I have to remember that.

We're still pretty far away from the academy, even though we've been walking for a few minutes. Shifters patrol the woods, and I'm sure they can probably already sense us. It won't be long until our presence is known. Glancing between Derek and Julian, I'm amazed at how these two fae keep trusting me in my decision making. I just really hope this is the right decision.

"How exactly are we supposed to get into the school?" Julian asks when we come to a stopping point. This is about the area Hannah saw me through a portal, so I know we're close to the school. "Since, you know, you ran away and then basically got banned."

"I'm not sure about the banned part but—" I stop and think. "Okay, yes, I'm probably banned, but I'm going to get in the same way I got out."

"Which is how?"

"With the help of an awesome fae."

The voice comes from behind the trees, and we turn as one, Derek and Julian's weapons at the ready. But I know that voice. Liam steps into our line of vision, leaning against a trunk in his nonchalant way.

"What a warm reception," he says, glancing at the weapons with one eyebrow raised.

"Who is this?" Derek speaks up for the first time since we stepped foot in this forest. He still hasn't lowered his sword.

"This is Liam," I say. "He's going to help us get back into the academy."

"Ah, yes, the famous Liam."

Now, everybody turns and looks at Derek and the bitterness that just came from his tone. That's very unlike Derek and unlike fae. Strong emotions aren't exactly a natural concept to them. Or should I say the portrayal of them to the outside world isn't. I narrow my eyes, studying Derek, but there's nothing there beyond the bitterness I just heard.

"Wow, he really is a charmer," Liam says, giving me a wink. I'm pretty sure that wink was just for Derek's benefit because the fae next to me is about to launch himself at Liam. I'm not exactly sure what's causing that particular response but here we are.

"Okay. Anyway, Liam." I turn to the fae. "What are we doing?"

"We are not doing anything." At first, I don't think I hear him correctly.

"What, what do you mean? You're supposed to help."

"I am helping. Actually, I helped already." This makes no sense.

"How exactly did you do that?" I ask the question, frustration rising to the surface. But before Liam can answer, a noise comes from behind Liam, catching my attention. Liam waives his arm in that direction and says, "This is how."

Just then, three large wolves step through the bushes. As I eye the massive beasts, my own hand conjures up a ball of fire, at the ready.

"Liam, what did you do?"

"He came to me, of course." Maddie is right behind the middle wolf. The moment I see her, I understand. He had to go to Maddie, and Maddie doesn't go anywhere without her shifters. Maybe it's just the suspicious side of me, but I was nervous there for a second that we got betrayed. False alarm.

"Hi there, Avery," Maddie says with a small smile. "You know when I met you, I had a feeling you would be trouble."

"Is that right?" I extinguish the flame on my palm, returning the witch's smile.

"Yep. Saw a little too much of myself in you." We share a smile. I'm still fan-girling a little, on the inside. This witch has really done a lot for the academy and for the fight against the ancients. She knows what's at stake and what it takes to sacrifice in order to protect those she loves. I find a kindred spirit in her. I'm glad I went to Liam for help.

"Do you have it?" I ask. She shakes her head. There's a bit of disappointment in me, but I also understand her not wanting to carry it around.

"It's in a place only I can access," Maddie says. "I didn't want to bring unnecessary attention to myself if I brought it up here, especially since we don't know how the book would react to me."

"That makes sense. Is it far?"

"No, but we're going to have to sneak you in carefully. There have been a few extra security measures put into place since you were last here."

"What do you mean?" I ask.

"The Ancients are knocking on our border doors," Maddie replies, much too calmly. "So, everything is a little more hyped up than before."

She seems comfortable with that knowledge in a way I am not. But I should've guessed. Of course they'd try to come back. Those creatures are relentless. And they want power. Thunderbird Academy is probably one of the most powerful places in the world considering that it houses hundreds of witches and shifters and fae and every other magical being. That's a lot of magic power in one place.

"So, how are we getting back in?"

"First of all, this is something you and I will have to do together," Maddie says. The wolf next to her growls dangerously, and she glances down with a little smile. "You'll be right there, Aiden. As close as ever, watching my back." She reaches over and runs her hand over his fur.

"I'll be fine."

They share a look which kind of pangs at my heart and clutches at my insides. It's the look of pure love, and knowing that the person next to you, or in this case a shifter, is your soulmate. My whole body is hyper aware of Derek standing beside me. It's like both of us are refusing to look at the other. But we're both watching Maddie and Aiden. That kind of connection—it's unbreakable.

"What do we do in the meantime then?" Derek finally says, looking at the shifters and witch in front of us.

"Oh, you get to hang out with me," Liam replies, sending another wink our way.

CHAPTER 9

*L*eaving the guys behind, Maddie and I make our way toward the school. I can feel Derek's gaze on me until he's lost in the trees.

"He's protective," Maddie comments, and I don't have to ask who.

"You know something about that," I reply, nodding toward her shifter boyfriend. Aiden is a few steps in front of us, leading us through the forest. Maddie smiles at my words, her cheeks slightly pink.

"I do. We're protective of each other." Aiden looks back at her, his shifter hearing picking up her words. Even though he's in wolf form, I can see the love shining in his eyes. It makes my heart beat in awareness. To love so fully and to be loved in return, it's a precious gift. My mind goes to Derek, but I don't let it linger there. I don't have time to think about our complicated feelings toward each other. Or how those feelings play into the grand scheme of things.

When we reach the outskirts of the forest, we stop.

"The greenhouse is right over there." Maddie points to the west side of the building where the glass add-on sticks out from the rest of the school's facade. I glance at her in question, and she simply shrugs. "You'll know why when we get there."

There are a few students mulling around on the lawn. It's not like we can do a spell or anything to cloak ourselves, since the academy will be alerted. I wait for Maddie to lead the way, because I have no idea how we're sneaking in.

Just then a pack of wolves burst out of the woods on the opposite side of the field, rushing around the students and howling.

"Let's go!" Maddie grabs my arm, pulling me with her. We take off toward the greenhouse. I spare a glance toward the commotion and see that the wolves are now running circles around the students, pulling all the attention to them. Aiden takes off in that direction as well.

We burst through the greenhouse doors and come face to face with a very tall guy. For a moment, I'm scared we've been caught, but Maddie simply grins at him.

"Thank you, Owen," she says, walking past him. He gives her the tiniest smile. That's when I realize I've seen him before, at orientation when I met Maddie. He must be from Aiden's pack. He looks like a shifter.

Maddie leads me to the corner of the greenhouse where plants are arranged to cover most of it. She begins moving some of them aside before pushing the rug aside and there sits a trap door. She pulls it open, motioning me to go in. I take the ladder, ending up in a tunnel. Maddie drops down beside me before leading me farther down.

We come to an old wooden door, and she opens it with a key. The moment we step inside, Maddie turns to me.

"Sorry for all the secrecy, but the library literally does not allow me to speak of her. I'm physically incapable, so I had to bring you here before I could say anything."

"Maddie, this is incredible. I've never seen anything like it. You can't talk about it?"

"No. There's something preventing me. Only the people who've been here can know about it. Aiden and Liam are both aware it's here, but they can't really be here without me. This place—it has a mind of its own."

That's incredible. A place that responds to the person directly. I guess I'm learning all kinds of new things about magic these days.

"How did you find it?"

"Liam and I found it our first year here. Something called me here; I can't really explain it."

"Wait, so it's a fae creation?" That makes me a little nervous, but Maddie waves my concern away.

"No, actually. I can't explain it, but it's tied to my family." Not that I'm surprised. Hawthorne's are a powerful family of witches.

"So, what happens to it when you graduate?"

Maddie looks around. There's a look of sadness on her face as she studies the books. Her graduation day is right around the corner. Would've been mine too if my life had turned out differently.

"I guess they wait for the next generation of Hawthorne," she replies, smiling to herself.

I'm still amazed that I'm in the presence of a Hawthorne. Maddie's family is one of the biggest and baddest around. They started kind of a revolution when the whole Ancients thing happened. And they keep doing things that help our communities. Maddie's older sister and her husband have been traveling to places all over the world to teach other covens how to withstand the Ancients' assaults. There have been quite a few of those because the Ancients are relentless.

"The next generation?" I ask now because I can't help myself.

Maddie turns and looks at me, her eyes shining. "Yeah. My sister Harper. She and Connor, they're expecting." I can feel the excitement radiating off her.

"That's amazing."

"Thanks, we think so too."

Maddie leads me farther into the library as I continue to stare at everything. I could spend months here reading over every page on these shelves.

"Maddie?" I begin, and she stops to face me. "Is it weird that I sent the book to you? Should I not have put that burden on you? I'm sorry."

"There's no need to apologize. No, it's not weird," Maddie replies. "You felt like you could, right? I think we can find the goodness in people, and those we can trust when the time is necessary. And I think our magic helps us. Sometimes it's not so obvious because we have our own prejudice. But the moment we open up to the possibilities, the moment we trust ourselves to know, then we find those who are on our side."

She grows silent for a moment, and I can't help but ask.

"It's like you speak from personal experience?"

"I do," Maddie nods. "My magic took me on a wild ride. As you know, and in the beginning, I didn't have people beside me that I could trust. I didn't think I could trust anybody. But I opened up my heart, and I was rewarded for that."

"Just like that?"

"No," Maddie laughs. "Of course not just like that. It's a process, and it's a hard one. It's something we all have to learn, but it's not impossible. And those people you're with? They're good people, regardless of where they come from."

For some reason, it feels like Maddie knows about Derek and his lineage. Maybe Liam told her. Maybe she knows after all the experience she's had.

"So me choosing you—"

"Was the most rational choice you could've made. Are you ready to see it?"

Surprisingly, I am thrilled to see it. There's a sort of excitement right under my skin that I can't deny. I nod my head, maybe a little bit too eagerly because Maddie smiles. The pull I've felt toward the book is amplified just by the idea of me holding it again.

But as she turns toward the shelf, a loud siren unlike anything I've heard before, sounds, sending me on full alert.

"Maddie! What is that?" I yell over the noise.

"It's the Ancients alarm," Maddie replies, shouting to be heard over the ringing. "The school is going on lockdown. The Ancients are here."

* * *

MY HEART DROPS at her words. I sprint for the door, but Maddie beats me to it.

"No, we can't leave."

"What do you mean we can't leave? My friends are out there. I have to go."

"We stay here, and we wait. They can't get into the library, even if they got on campus, which they most likely didn't." Maddie's voice is calm, while I feel as if mine is at the pitch of the siren.

"Why can't they?"

"Because the library doesn't quite exist at the school. It's complicated, but we're safe here."

"What about my friends? And yours?"

"Don't worry, Avery. This isn't the first time. The alarms that went off? They're long-range enough to give us time to prepare. The shifters and witches on duty will protect the school. Also, the moment the alarms go off a barrier comes down over the school, kind of like a dome. That's a second wave of protection."

All of that makes sense, but the fact remains that I left my friends in the woods.

"But what about Derek and Julian? Your Liam? We left them in the forest."

"And they're not alone. Aiden is with them. He went back after he did his part in getting us to the greenhouse. Between his pack and Liam, they're going to be just fine. They won't let anyone hurt your friends, even though I think your friends can handle themselves."

"How are you so sure of that?"

Don't panic.

Don't panic.

Don't panic.

"Because I know my people, and they'll protect yours because they said they would." Once again, Maddie's voice is strong and sure, and it has the desired effect. To be honest, I'm a mess still. I'm not sure where this hectic energy is coming from.

My mind is hyper focused on Derek and the fact that I want to be near him right now. To make sure he's safe, to make sure he's going to stay that way. It's very annoying to be having these feelings, especially right now.

"Avery." Maddie's voice penetrates my thoughts. "You need to focus."

"I am focused. I also feel like I'm hyperventilating. I'm not sure what's going on."

"Wait, is it Derek?" That is the last question I expect from her. I look at her sharply, confused.

"What do you mean?" She couldn't possibly know anything about the two of us, so I'm not sure what she could be asking.

"Nothing, I just—you're bonded with him, so I understand that you're concerned, but the best thing you can do is what we came here to do. So let's do that."

Bonded? I don't even know how to unpack that at the moment. She said it so nonchalantly too, like it's just a simple fact. But Maddie is right. This isn't the time to talk about this, and we came here on a mission.

I take a few calming breaths, try to pull my thoughts away from Derek, and follow Maddie to the back of the room.

Then I feel it.

She doesn't even have to pull it out. I feel the book before I see it. It's there, and it's calling to me, just like it always has. The pull is the strongest it's been, as if the distance made it stronger.

"Have you—have you tried reading it?" I ask, approaching Maddie slowly. She pulls the book down off the shelf before turning to me.

"No, it's not my place."

"You're not curious?"

"Of course I am." She smiles. "But I feel like maybe you'll show me what this is all about instead of me trying and hurting my brain."

That I can definitely understand. Being cautious has gotten Maddie this far, why would she change her tactics now?

"I'll show you," I say, placing the book on the table and opening it.

Just like always, the words form on the page immediately, but I don't look at them. I look past them.

"Wow, I can't read any of this," Maddie says.

"I still don't understand it, but nobody can, except me. It's a weird kind of a magic."

"Well, have you heard of story spell casting?" Maddie chuckles. "Because let me tell you, that's a weird kind of magic."

She's right. She carries within herself story spell casting, something else that's been a dormant form of magic for ages. We share a look that I think only the two of us can understand. Neither one of us asked for this special kind of magic, but here we both are, tasked with this job, and we're the only ones who can do anything about it. We've been given a responsibility, and it's our job to see it through.

"So how do you read a book without reading it?" Maddie asks. I shrug.

"That's what we're here to find out."

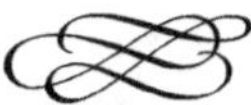

Maddie pulls out more books from the shelf, bringing them over to the table. We decided to do some research on the book itself. Well, in a way. We're looking for any information any of these books might have on who had possession of the book when it was first written. I remember reading a passage that made it seem like it was a personal diary at one time. Maybe if we find more information on the who, I'll figure out the how a little easier.

The alarms have stopped blaring, and it does make me a little nervous. Maddie seems completely at ease, so I don't say anything. Truth be told, both Derek and Julian would probably feel very offended that I'm this worried about them.

"Anything?" I ask after what seems like at least an hour.

"Not really," Maddie says from the other side of the table. "There are mentions of so many various books that it's hard to pinpoint if this is the correct one. The Ancients are notoriously good at not giving up much information. I've been studying the books for a while, trying to learn more about them, but there are only bits and pieces. It's a constant struggle."

"How did you know how to defeat them?" I ask, putting the book

I'm reading down and looking at the witch. She gets a bit of a faraway look in her eyes before answering.

"I trusted my instincts and the people around me. I know that might not seem helpful, but it's the best tip I can give you. Magic is unpredictable, and there's so much we still don't know about the power that runs through our veins. But I have learned that magic won't steer me wrong. Not when I truly trust it."

I nod, mulling over her words. It would be so easy to just act on what I know, instead of giving my magic a bit of a free reign. But this is similar to what I decided already, to be more intentional about both sides of my magic.

"Have you ever heard of a witch developing a different elemental power?"

"What do you mean?"

I raise my hands in front of me, turning so they're not over the table. Concentrating, I create a tiny flame in my right hand before I create a small sphere of water in my left. Maddie gasps, studying the two opposing magics at once.

"How?"

"I have no idea. For a few months now, even before I found the book, I've been experiencing this imbalance with my magic. And then the water came."

"That's a little different than what I'm used to," Maddie replies before making her own sphere of water. It looks the same to me, but maybe Maddie can feel something I can't. "I don't think I've ever seen anyone with double magic. That's incredible."

"And a little weird." I sigh, extinguishing the magic. "Oh, and frustrating. But I'm learning. I wasn't at first, but I am now."

Maddie jumps to her feet suddenly. "I think I've seen something about this in one of the books," she says before weaving her way to the shelves at the back wall. I focus on the book in front of me, my mind still on the magic. The two seem to be related, but I also don't know how that could be. Do I have double magic because of the Ancients or is it because of my parents' lineage? Or even something else. These are questions I wish I had answers to.

"Here." Maddie returns, placing a book in front of me.

"What am I looking at?"

"This is a lineage tree—like a family tree—of the fae courts. Liam and I find it astounding how much we can find out about someone based on who came before them."

The page looks incredible, I'm not going to lie. The tree extends and keeps going with the paper folding out to hold all the information.

"Is this the only book like this?"

"Oh no. There are plenty for each court." Maddie pulls the book closer, pointing at a few entries. "Here and here, do you see that? There was a family that held the possibility of fire and water magic. Fae magic is widely tied to nature, and back when the land was plentiful, more of the fae displayed multiple elemental powers."

I pull the book toward me, looking at the paragraph in the corner of the map. I think of Derek, who does hold some sort of elemental power. The fae now must be royal to have that. It's crazy to think that it used to be a more widespread aspect of their lives.

"What do these mean?" I point to the letters and numbers under the words.

"That's where you can find more on the families. Here." Maddie takes the book back and then flips to a place halfway through the book. She scans a few pages before handing it over to me.

The paragraph starts with the basics about the family, the generations and the lands within Faery. Then it starts on the powers.

"The families of the Sunland were known for their power of the sun. Nurturing and scorching, the magic could heal and destroy. Blessed with the marks of the Ancients, the Sunland was a place of great nobility. When the council was disbanded, the family was lost to the Queen's whims, leaving the land lacking."

"What are the marks of nobility?" I ask, looking up from my reading.

"As far as I know, they were outward representations of inward power. Certain marks on the body, like tattoos. Colorful hair strands or different color eyes..." Maddie's voice fades as she looks at me. I pull the green streak of hair toward me, thinking back to when it first manifested. And then I realize there's something even stronger as a representation. Tucking my hair behind my left ear, I hear Maddie's intense inhale.

"Avery—" she breathes out as she studies the golden veins painted into my skin over my pointed ear.

"My sentiment exactly," I say. I guess my father has kept even more secrets than I thought.

* * *

"You didn't know."

"I'm going to be honest with you, Maddie. I know very little about what's going on." I give her the rundown on the ears and the wings. She sits quietly, listening intensely.

"Wow," is all she says when I'm done. But I guess there's not much more to say.

I'm of noble descent.

I'm of noble descent.

I'm of noble descent.

Even repeating it in my head still doesn't make it any more believable. This makes me want to go have another talk with Dad, but at this point, I'm never going to get all the answers I want from him. He could've told me, but he didn't. All he said was we were a fae family at court. I don't understand why he can't just give me full answers, instead of half-truths.

"Do you think that's why the queen is set on having you marry her son?" Maddie asks, breaking through my thoughts. I'm going to be honest, that didn't even cross my mind, but now, I'm thinking about it.

"I'm not sure. I always assumed she only wanted me for the Ancients' power. I mean, it makes sense that with that kind of magic in her court, she'd be even more unstoppable."

"But if she suspected you're of royal descent...that would be even a bigger power boost."

Maddie is right, of course. I honestly don't know what to think about any of this. With everything that's been going on, it's all I can do to keep it together. Not just with my magic, but mentally and emotionally. It feels like information is being thrown at me at this point, and I don't have the tools to catch all that I need. I want to say that it doesn't matter, that none of this matters, because I am strong and I can handle it. But maybe being strong doesn't mean handling everything. Maybe it's breaking down and maybe it's asking for help, and maybe I simply know nothing of life.

"Hey." Maddie pulls a chair up beside me, taking a seat. She can clearly see the turmoil written all over me. I doubt it's just on my face. "You'll figure it out. It may seem impossible right now, but it's not. That much I know."

"I don't want to be rude when I say this, but just because you handled everything like a boss doesn't mean that I'm made from the same cloth."

The pity party has arrived, and I don't think I have the strength to stop it. All this time I have been holding it together, but I'm not sure how much of that was just a front. I feel comfortable enough with Maddie to show her just how unbalanced I feel. Maybe because I know she's been in my shoes. There's a part of me that's hoping she can offer some nugget of wisdom, to help me see the possibilities at the end of all of this.

"No, you're not made from the same cloth."

The words are spoken with no malice, but they hit me just the same. That is not what I was expecting to hear. I glance at her in shock, and she gives me a gentle smile.

"Avery, you and I are not the same person. We will never be. You cannot compare yourself to me or to anyone else for that matter. You are your own unique design, and trust me, from everything I've seen and heard, you are more than capable. Just because it feels impossible right now, doesn't mean it will always be so. You said it yourself, you have given your magic a chance to grow. You're moving in the right direction."

"Even when it feels like I'm not moving at all?"

"Even then." Maddie reaches over, giving my upper arm a squeeze.

It's a very sisterly gesture, and it nearly brings tears to my eyes. "I didn't choose to be given this gift of story spell casting, and I made every mistake I could with it. But in the end, I trusted myself to do what was right for the ones I love. They were there by my side and together we prevailed. You are never alone in this. There are people cheering you on and holding you up."

"You mean Derek and Julian?"

"Liam told me about Derek." Maddie raises an eyebrow. "And the fae I saw out there with you is unlike anything Liam described. That guy cares for you. Whatever there is between you, it's strong."

I can't help but let my heart hope at her words. Because I've been fighting these emotions for longer than I'd like to admit. Yet, they're always there. When Derek told me he won't leave my side, they became something more. But is it really the time for me to be feeling anything? Of course not. My brain and my heart just want to pile on the stress, apparently.

"It's complicated," I finally say, and this time, Maddie smiles.

"I remember complicated."

She stands then, not giving me a chance to answer. But there's really nothing I can say anyway. I glance down at the book again, reading over the page and the information about the royal family.

It feels like time is running out. The Ancient will keep coming back for me. My family will continue to be in danger. And the queen is going to marry me off for power. So many things are out of my control. I want to defeat the queen and the Ancients. I want to save Hannah. I want to give my parents a chance to explain all these secrets to me in person, with no threat of death hanging over our heads.

And I want to see if what I feel for Derek is real.

But I won't be able to do any of that if I don't start acting instead of simply reacting.

With that thought, I know what I have to do. I've known it all along. I've just been too cautious to do anything about it. Closing the book, I stand, facing the water witch. It's time.

"Maddie, I think I know what I need to do next."

CHAPTER 11

Since the alarm has lifted, we can leave the library behind. The book is in the over-the-shoulder bag Maddie gave me. I feel calm somehow, having it close to me. Maddie leads the way back to the greenhouse before we rush for the trees. The Ancients getting close to the wards has actually given us the perfect cover, since there is so much activity on campus. The guys aren't that far from the outskirts of the forest, and we reach them in no time at all.

Derek's gaze is on me, roaming over every part of my body, as if making sure I'm okay. The look does not go unnoticed. I tear my gaze away before I embarrass myself.

"You know where to find me if you need anything," Maddie says, giving me a quick hug. She glances over at Derek before meeting my eye with a smile. I roll my eyes.

"Thank you, Maddie."

Aiden is beside her in his wolf form. It doesn't matter that he's a shifter, I can see how much he cares for her in his eyes. It makes my heart beat with want, but I refuse to look at Derek.

"Later, gater," Liam calls out with a little salute. I have so many questions for him. He's unlike any fae I have ever met, but now is definitely not the time. Instead, I give them all a little wave and turn toward the guys.

Leaving Thunderbird Academy behind, we head back out into the woods. Maddie wants to help, I can tell. But this isn't her fight, and I won't be putting anyone else in danger. We need to put some distance between the school and myself. I don't want to be reading anything from the book anywhere I could hurt someone. I'm not sure how I would get Julian and Derek away from me, and I don't think I can even try. So that's something I'll have to deal with, I suppose.

But that's exactly what I'm doing—reading from the book. I think it's way past time. I've been doing all this research around the one piece of information that might actually offer me some answers. So, we're about to see how far that'll get me.

"What do you think will happen?" Julian breaks the silence as we make our way through the trees. I told them my plan the moment we met up, and they've been quiet since then. The book is securely tucked away in the over-the-shoulder bag Maddie provided. It seems weird that after all this time running, I'm finally on my way to do something about it. To stop running and take a stand.

"I have no idea," I reply honestly, because I don't. I've only ever had the one experience with the book, and it was under Hannah's guidance. Well, I don't count the very first time I read from the book, since I had no knowledge of its magical powers. But Hannah was there to guide me when I intentionally set out to read the pages. The moment I think about the fae who helped me, guilt and worry return. Not that those two particular emotions are ever that far away. They're mostly just constantly right under the surface.

"We'll set up a protected circle," I say. Maddie and I ran through this together. She likes to be as prepared as I am. "Once the moon is high, I will open the book and read."

"How do you know what to read?" Julian asks. Derek is keeping quiet, his focus on the woods around us. Because of fae's connection to nature, they're more attuned to it. I think maybe that's why I've felt the land at times, especially when we went through that time portal. The connection was the strongest I've ever felt it. I haven't been that connected since. But Derek is always connected, and he's looking for the perfect spot for us. Still, when Julian asks, Derek's eyes turn to me.

"I'm not sure about anything," I say, because I can't lie to them. "The pages I read at Hannah's were the only pages I had, so we had no choice." While I left a few pages at the school, the rest of the book is pretty much an open field.

"The only thing I can think of is to let my magic decide."

"Your magic?" Derek asks.

"It's who I am, right? I've been running from it for so long, but it is my greatest asset. Why wouldn't I use it?"

Even as I say it, it terrifies me. Reading the book, all of it. There is a very good possibility that I will make things worse. That I will bring the Ancients and the queen, right to our front door—or the outer edges of the protection circle. I don't mention my new discovery about my heritage because I simply don't think it matters at the moment. I'd like to keep that under wraps for now and see how far I can go before I have to share any other information about myself. Especially since I can't tell if Derek's beacon of magic also gives the queen an extra in with me. Or if the Ancients may be hanging around, listening in to my conversations. I really have no idea how that works.

"Here." Derek breaks through my thoughts. I glance up to find him pointing to the right. He turns and we follow. It's another few minutes before we come to a clearing.

The trees line up in a circular pattern around a clearing. and I immediately think I'm not the first person to use this spot for magic practice. This seems exactly like what I need.

Pulling out the crystals Maddie gave me, I begin to make my way around the clearing, placing them into the ground at the four corners. Black tourmaline, clear quartz, black jade, and smithsonite. The black tourmaline is larger than the other crystals, since it acts like an anchor. It's often used for grounding your space, and I need it to ground me and my magic. Smithsonite is the second biggest, because it will help me find my calm. Black jade and clear quartz should keep the negative forces away, which is why I've placed them on opposite ends from each other.

"Can you please come stand here and here?" I point to two positions between the crystals where Derek and Julian can still face each other before I take my spot in the middle of the clearing. The moon is just becoming visible, but I know I need to get the space ready before I can truly read from the book. The guys don't question anything. They simply take their positions and wait for me to make my move.

Placing the bag on the ground, I squat down as well. My hands rest on top of the soil. Focusing my energy, I reach for the crystals through the earth, placing intention into them. Water moves underneath the ground, connecting the crystals and where the guys are standing to the middle of the clearing, under my feet. The circle is a simple protection, but it's the best precaution I can take.

Everything else will be up to me.

* * *

THERE IS no other option for me but to dive right in. Once the moon is high in the sky, a soft glow illuminates the clearing around me. I know it's time. I can't pick a page to read because I can't read anything from this book without causing a vast amount of magic offset. I need to trust the magic and my instincts to lead me where I need to go.

Derek is on my right, and Julian is on my left. They're watching me carefully, waiting for me to make my move. It still amazes me that they trust me not to ruin the whole world with my choices. But here we are. I want to say that they put their trust in me, and I won't fail. But I might. I just have to be open to whatever comes my way.

Closing my eyes, I hold the book to my chest, wrapping my arms around it as I breathe in and out. The calming exercise does the trick. My magic comes to the surface. It's right at the tips of my fingers, fire and water, waiting for me to make a decision.

Opening my eyes, I focus on the book in front of me and the intention of what I'd like to accomplish. This is the hardest part about magic, knowing what to ask and how to ask it. Magic is so unpredictable when it's wielded unintentionally. But even when it's a choice, there is so much we don't know about the Ancients' magic.

That's what scares me the most. I don't want to be scared, and I need to find a way not to be.

Focus and breathe.

Focus and breathe.

Focus and breathe.

There's no more time to waste. I have to move forward.

Giving myself the space I need, I sit down on the ground, placing the book in front of me. After another deep breath, I pull the pages open and let the book fall where it may. The immediate desire to look down and start reading is nearly overwhelming. I can't tell if it's curiosity or if it's the magic that calls me to the pages. But I resist it. I need to be more careful than ever.

When I feel like the overwhelming desire has passed, I lean forward and force my eyes to the top of the page. The words look exactly like I remember them from the pages I read with Hannah. There's a bit of comfort in that, and I'm not sure I understand it. It's like a part of me has been waiting for this—a lot more than I would've expected.

Remembering the last time Hannah and I tried this exercise, I make sure to keep my eyes on only one word at a time. I don't give my eyes the freedom to skim. And I try to make sure I don't speak any of the words out loud.

It's hard to not simply read all of the stuff and just become overwhelmed by the magic that's in front of me. I want to be stronger than this urge, which I am sure is coming from the book and the magic it carries.

THE TRUEST KNIGHT knows no bounds. There is not a place, there is not a magic that is too much for it. Summoned by the power of the sun and the moon, there are no secrets between the magic and the power. No one can stop the magic, no one can stop the intention.

THESE WORDS MAKE ABSOLUTELY no sense. I shut my eyes because the desire to keep reading, to skip around until I find a sentence that makes sense, nearly overtakes me. Giving myself a few minutes, I try to level my breathing. And my magic. I can feel it boiling up inside of me, searching for an outlet. And the only outlet it wants right now is the book. Because if I can keep reading, it'll get what it wants.

Or so it thinks.

The guys are completely quiet, letting me deal with this as I see fit. Opening my eyes, I glance to the left and to the right and find them watching me. Giving them a quick smile, I glance down at the page.

THERE IS AN OLD STORY, told through generations, where the fae have come from the sky and where the sky sent the fae. The angels were not the same as those from before, and the magic was bigger than that of now. The sky opened up and the magic poured out, and there was nothing but the sun and the moon working in tandem. That is the truest power of the story. The balance that comes from both sides of the power. Magic is not something to be taken lightly, and power is not something that can be simply given or taken. There is nothing in this world that will show the truest sense of the land, but the one who holds the truest knight's heart.

ONCE AGAIN, I shut my eyes because the words are too much. There is an emotion inside of me as I read them, one I cannot understand, one I cannot put a name to. There is something here, something that is more than magic. It's almost like I'm channeling the writer and experiencing the same emotions he or she did.

That kind of channeling is making it hard for me to stay objective. I want to say that I can be stronger than the urges, but I don't think I can. When I open my eyes a second time, there's a split second when I think I'm fine and then I'm not. Before I can stop myself, my mouth forms the first words I see.

"Mates?"

"Avery!" I hear Derek's shout immediately, but it doesn't matter. I said the word and now I can't stop myself from reading the rest.

. . .

"This balance between two powers is something the world has not seen in a long time. But the truest knight's mate, the other half to the power inside, is the greatest asset one could have in this world. Soulmates of the utmost order, there is strength in giving the other a part of oneself. Nothing is stronger than the bond of the heart. Nothing can withstand that kind of a love."

I can't stop the words or the emotions that pour out with every breath. There is a certain kind of power that races through me, reaching past all the barriers I have put up to protect myself. I drop to all fours, gasping as the magic seems to shoot out of me like a gust of wind. Once again, the world around me spins into chaos. I can hear shouting. I know that it's Derek and Julian, but I can't seem to stop. I hold onto the ground, I hold onto myself, as the magic soars higher and higher and higher.

More.

More.

More.

I can't seem to stop wanting more.

CHAPTER 12

$\mathcal{I}$ force my gaze up, trying to see past the magic. My eyes find Derek and Julian, trying to get to me, but they can't seem to. Then it doesn't matter.

The guys are pulled away, and suddenly, I'm in the forest of nightmares again. There is no hesitation on the Ancient's part this time. He doesn't wait to appear after I'm good and spooked. He's in my face even before I'm fully aware of my surroundings.

"How dare you, Avery Kincaid?"

The voice seems to boom all around me, shaking the very ground I stand on. My body trembles at the magnitude of that one question, of the way my name sounds on his lips. It's a threat of the utmost kind, and it terrifies me.

"You read from the sacred book as if it were nothing. You mock the words written on the pages of history."

My mind races to catch up with the words the Ancient is saying. He's speaking too fast and too loudly to comprehend. But when I realize what he's saying, I can't help but stand up a little taller.

"You've been after me to read from the book for weeks. And now all of a sudden you don't like what I'm reading? It's not like you left an instructional pamphlet! I'm winging it as I go!"

The more I speak, the angrier I get.

The magic has stuck me with this responsibility, and there isn't even a how-to I can refer to. Just a bunch of magical beings—from every side—telling me what to do.

"You do not understand the power you hold."

"No duh!" I snap, entirely forgetting the fact that I'm speaking to an Ancient. But I can't help it. I'm angry. "You and your ancient friends must've forgotten what it means to have common courtesy. You expect all these things of me, and I don't know what I'm doing!"

I can't quite believe I'm yelling all this at the enemy, but maybe he will finally understand. Or maybe I'm not seeking to be understood, I just need to be heard. The feelings I've been dealing with this whole time have literally taken me to my knees. Because the book is so much more than just a gateway to magic, it's a gateway to a life that was lived hundreds of years ago. And I'm feeling all of it.

"You will speak to me with respect."

"Respect is earned and given. You do not demand it like you would an order at a restaurant. I'm tired of constantly trying to hold it together. I can't keep doing this. I can't."

The words leave me in a rush, and I honestly can't believe just how emotional I'm being with the Ancient. He could snap his fingers and take me out of existence, of that I have no doubt. But he doesn't. There's a stillness about him as he listens to me talk, and then, the darkness feels a little less heavy.

"You have been given a great burden, Avery Kincaid. But you have been given the burden because you are capable of carrying it."

That is absolutely the last thing that I would expect the Ancient to say. It sounds almost like something a father would say to me, someone who knows me on a special kind of level. Not a being who's been trying to get me to do his bidding this whole time. I'm missing something.

Again.

"Why would you have chosen me? This doesn't seem like an honor. This is something that I've been tasked with because of...what? What exactly makes me so special?"

The Ancient doesn't respond right away but cocks his head to the side as if he's truly thinking about the answer. After a long tense pause, he seems to flow closer to the ground. It makes him seem less intimidating somehow.

"Long before your kind walked the earth, there was only us," he begins, and I nearly hold my breath. He's talking about his past. He's telling me *his* story. "We were a warring kind, searching for power and needing it like we needed the air and the earth. Before magic was able to be wielded, we held it in the palm of our hands. Some of us wanted to destroy the world. Some of us wanted to save it."

That jolts me in place. Save it? The Ancients wanted to save the world, not destroy it. That's not possible. This sends everything I know into a tailspin.

"We have always known of one way to live and to exist, but some realized there was more to life than power. There was beauty and love." My mind instantly goes to what I just read in the book about mates. "While we slumbered, the world changed. And while some still seek the power and the destruction, not all do."

He stops then, as if taking an emotional pause. I dare to take a step toward him.

"You're saying you want to help me? That's why you've been so pushy about me getting the book? But you have threatened the lives of everyone I love! How could I believe anything you say?"

I can't wrap my mind around what's happening right now. My body is still buzzing from the power, and I'm trying to find my footing when it comes to the emotions I'm feeling. And now, it's so much worse. If what the Ancient is saying is true, then everything I know is wrong. I'm not sure I can reconcile with that, not really.

"My tactics may not have been the best," the Ancient says, and I can hear a tang of apology in his voice. "But it is the only way we know how."

"To threaten and hurt?"

"To utilize the kind of power that requires no questions."

"Sorry to break it to you, but I have done nothing but question. I don't think your tactics are working."

Then the Ancient does something so human, I'm dumbfounded for a second. He sighs. Like an honest, normal individual would when frustrated.

"We are fearful of what will come of Faery if we do not stop the queen of the Summer Court," the Ancient says. At least that is one thing we can agree on.

"Then help me. You've done nothing but hinder, so now, you should help."

He watches me for a long tense moment. I'm not sure what I'm expecting him to do, but then it doesn't matter.

Before I can say anything else, the world around me fades, and I'm on my knees, gasping for air. Derek and Julian are by my side. When I glance up, they look terrified.

"What?"

"You've been gone for hours."

* * *

WE MAKE camp a little farther down from the clearing. I don't want to leave it completely because I know for a fact I need to read from the book again. I think reading from it was a direct gateway to the Ancient, and I have a lot of questions for him. But my body needs rest. So do my mind and emotions if I'm being completely honest.

I scared Derek and Julian, that much I can see. They've been giving me side glances for the last hour. There was nothing left in me to even try and explain what happened. But now, as I'm lying in the grass, my mind races over what the Ancient said.

There's absolutely no way I can trust anything he told me. After all this time, after all the fighting and the threats, he wants me to believe he's been trying to help? No. I don't believe that. Maybe a weaker person would believe it. But if there is one thing the Ancient said that's the absolute truth it's that I can handle this. I am more than capable.

The more this magic throws at me, the more I believe that.

"We should talk about it," I say, sitting up so I can see the guys.

Julian made us a fire, and now the guys sit on the other side of it. The moment I sit up, they move to be closer to me, taking a place near the fire and facing me. "Eager, are we?" I chuckle.

"Avery, I don't think you understand how terrifying it is to see magic explode around you and then have you disappear. We had absolutely no control," Julian says, his words rushing out of him. I can't even imagine what they must've been thinking.

"It was different than the last time," Derek says, his eyes on me. The intensity in his gaze is making my head spin, but I can't look away.

"What do you mean?"

"Last time the Ancient came, you were gone and back before I truly realized what was happening. This time, we could feel the time go by and we could do nothing but stand there, waiting for you to return."

"Like you couldn't move?"

"I think we could've. But not toward you."

That's definitely different than before. I'm not sure why it would be different now. Maybe the Ancient's magic reacted with the book's magic? That's the only thing I can think of, but it seems plausible enough. As much as anything else is I suppose.

"I don't know if you're going to like what I have to tell you," I say, and then give them a rundown of exactly what the Ancient said.

There's a moment of silence after I'm done as the fae process what I told them.

"Do you believe him?" Derek asks.

"Absolutely not," I reply. I don't care if the Ancient is somewhere in the outskirts of the forest, eavesdropping on our conversation. I'm not afraid to stand up to him, not anymore.

"So, what do we do next?" Julian asks. I can see worry in his gaze.

"I need to read from the book again."

"No."

"Absolutely not."

"You guys, I'm not asking for permission," I say, getting to my feet. Maybe I should wait until tomorrow, or until I've rested for more than an hour, but I can't. I can feel the pull toward the magic, and I know that if I don't answer it now, I won't be able to rest anyway.

I won't be able to do anything else.

Plus, the whole mates thing is too curious not to explore.

My eyes find Derek's, almost as if on their own. He gives me a look that might mean he can tell what I'm thinking. But he can't, so I simply just need to stop myself from creating any kind of scenarios in my head and go read the book.

"I'm going back to the clearing. Come with me, or don't. That's up to you."

I don't wait for them to make a decision. Instead, I grab the bag with the book and walk into the forest. Less than ten seconds later, I feel the guys behind me. Smiling to myself, I don't turn around. Let them think what they will.

When we reach the clearing once more, I walk straight to the center and take my seat on the ground. The guys move into their positions, watching me carefully.

This time, when I open the book, I don't hesitate to look down. Trusting my magic and my instincts, I read.

THERE WAS a place in the olden days where the sky met the earth, and the oceans sang the song of nature. It was a place of plentiful bounty and of the kind of love that is only dreamed about. There are places like this in the corners of the sky that hold pockets of magic in them. When the time comes, the pockets open up, the magic falls to the earth, and the earth grows plentiful and the oceans sing.

There was once a power so great that two souls held onto it. The darkness and the light, the night and the day, the broken and the complete. That is the balance of the truest heart, the magic that will save the earth. Time does not change the pull of the heart, and space does not scare the magic away. Two become one when they believe in each other, like the sky believes in the earth. The truest knight and the truest heart have all the possibilities.

· · ·

THERE ARE tears in my eyes as I read the passage. Tearing my gaze away, I glance up to find Derek now directly in my line of sight. He's looking at me with complete awe. I'm confused for a moment, until I realize the space around me has grown brighter.

My wings are back.

They move forward, so I can see the tips of them. I will never get over how beautiful they are. I wipe at my tears with one hand before I give Derek a gentle smile.

"Two halves of a whole." I whisper. Derek's eyes grow bigger and fuller with emotion. He wants to come to me, I can see it in his gaze, but I shake my head just slightly. My whole body is vibrating with the magic. I can feel it now. The words I've been reading, it's like they've been filling up my magic on the inside and that's what brought the wings forward.

It feels like I'm ready to explode, but also, like I can take on everything and everyone.

Before anyone can move, a portal opens up right on the outskirts of the circle, and Nora steps in. She takes one look at me, and her mouth opens in shock. Closing the book, I stand. She stares at me.

"Nora?"

Shaking herself out of the trance, she meets my eye.

"Something happened."

ora doesn't ask questions, but I can tell she wants to. She's never seen my wings before, but whatever has caused her to come find us with such urgency must be more important. When we step through the portal and into Hannah's house, the whole place is dark.

"Nora?"

"It's been like this for hours now," she says, her voice full of worry and something else I can't quite place. "The darkness descended and won't leave. It's as if there is a storm cloud hanging low over the whole building."

"Where are my parents?"

"I left them in the library."

Glancing over at Derek and Julian, I give them a nod and turn in that direction. They follow without hesitation. We only make it two steps before a crash sounds from the opposite side of the house. Without a moment's hesitation, I pivot and take off in that direction. In the back of my mind, I notice that Nora doesn't go with us, but I'm across the foyer before it truly registers.

A blast of magic sweeps me right off my feet, and I land hard on my chest, wind knocked out of me. My head rings from the impact as I push myself to all fours.

"Avery!" Derek calls out. I glance over my shoulder to find him and Julian on the floor as well. Another blast of magic hits, and I twist, landing on my back in agony. Every cell in my body screams in pain. My mind is a blank slate as I try to process. I can't even figure out where the attack is coming from or what to do about it. All I can do is hold on to myself as my body tries to rip itself apart.

I realize the screaming I'm hearing is my own.

My body twists every which way, like a fish out of water. I have absolutely no control over any of it. At the back of my mind, I know I should reach for my magic. I know I should get myself focused but all I feel is pain.

Everything hurts.

Everything hurts.

Everything hurts.

It's a pain much greater than only physical. It's reaching for my magic and agonizing it as well. I can't explain it, but I feel it. The tears that fall from my eyes blind me right along with the pain.

"You said you wouldn't hurt her!" The voice comes through the fog of agony, and I try to force my body to turn in that direction.

"You have become much too human to trust simple words."

I force my body to move, and it's taking all my concentration to do simply that. Finally, after what seems like an impossibly long time, I flop to my side and open my eyes.

Queens Svetlana stands right on the inside of the doorway leading to the foyer. Her bright green gown is adorned with a million jewels. It sparkles in the dim light, as if it carries a light of its own. I wouldn't be surprised. She's that extra. But what does surprise me is the man beside her.

My father.

His eyes are on me. I can tell he wants to go to me, but he can't. He stands frozen, watching me wiggle on the floor. The queen takes a step into my line of vision, blocking out my dad.

"Hello, Avery. It is so nice to see you again."

She glances over my shoulder, presumably at Derek and Julian still on the floor, before she waves a hand in our direction. Her soldiers come for us. I'm picked up off the floor like I weigh nothing. A portal waits on the other side of the doorway, and I see my father being the first one to be pushed into it.

The queen is handed my bag. My body jerks as she takes the book out of it. Everything in me screams to grab and hold it closed. It looks wrong in her hands. But I can't move. I'm being held up by the soldiers.

My feet are placed on the floor, and surprisingly, I stay standing. I can feel the pain receding. I realize it must be a magical ailment, one that the queen can control. Derek and Julian are already on their feet being marched toward the portal. Neither can seem to look at me. They're through the portal before I can even wrap my mind around what's happening.

"You did not really think you would outsmart me, did you?" the queen asks, stepping into my personal space. Her cruel eyes are on me. "Oh, you did. How disappointing for you."

I don't reply as she takes a step away. The guards push me into the portal. Everything seems to be unraveling around me, and I have no idea which way is up or down. I'm dumped on the other side of the portal, falling to my knees.

This is the endgame. I can feel it in my bones. And I'm not ready. I'm not ready at all.

* * *

WE'RE in the throne room when we come through the portal. Derek and Julian stand to one side, Nora in the corner, and my father and mother—in her wolf form—are on the opposite end. I push myself to a standing position, pain still racing through my body. My mother whimpers, but she can't seem to move toward me. One of the guards reaches for her, pulling at her fur. The anger I feel nearly takes me back down to my knees. I want to open my mouth and scream at them to let her go, but I can't. The guard drags my mother out as my heart sinks.

This is too much.

Queen Svetlana takes her position in front of the throne, giving the room a sweep with her eyes. Her arm is wrapped around the book, holding it to her chest. She's gloating before she even opens her mouth again.

"You have done your part well, Kincaid," the queen says. My heart drops. I shift my gaze, staring at my father in horror. None of this makes sense. He opens his mouth, his eyes full of tears, but no sound comes.

"Take him away."

"No!" I scream, managing to push through whatever silence spell the queen has on all of us as I reach for him while the guards grab him. Strong arms encircle my waist, pulling me back. I look up into Derek's stoic face, punching at his grip, but he won't budge.

"Let me go!" I yank at his arms, but he pulls me closer to his body, trapping me.

"It would do you good to control her," the queen snaps, glaring at me. She clearly doesn't like the fact that I spoke out when no one else seems to be able to. I make sure to gloat right in her face. I slump against Derek as my father is nearly carried out of the room, my heart heavy.

"You have also done your part," the queen looks over my shoulder at Derek. I know what she's doing. She's trying to push us apart, but I don't believe for one second that he had any play in this. She's back to her mind games, but I'm not the same girl who was here last time. The queen narrows her eyes at me before looking back at Derek.

"The revel is in a few hours. Be sure to be ready."

The queen gives me one last look before she turns and leaves us there. My mind is still trying to catch up.

The exhaustion in my bones turns to hatred. I'm ready to go after her, but Derek squeezes me against him once more. I turn in his arms, punching him as hard as I can while still being pinned to him.

"What is your problem? You're just going to let her—"

"We have to be smart about this, Avery."

"Don't talk to me like I'm a child." I push at him, and this time he lets me go. Running a hand over my face, I try to calm my racing heart. My father wouldn't betray me like this. He wouldn't. There has to be more to it than that.

"Avery, I would never treat you like a child. But you're emotional, and you cannot let her see that. She will use it against you."

There's sadness in his gaze when I look at him, and my heart clutches for a different reason. He speaks from experience. Fae and their stupid rules and cruelty and a life that is full of hopelessness.

But Derek is right. I can't give into the pain right now. If I'm to get my family out of this, I have to be just as ruthless as the queen. That means that I have to push everything down and take it one step at a time.

"What just happened? I couldn't move or talk. And she's throwing a revel? Doesn't she remember how the last one ended?"

"This is part of her queen magic," Julian says, stepping up to us. The moment he does, the guards move toward him. He lifts his arms in surrender. "I'll find you later," he says before he walks toward Nora and both of them are escorted out. Now it's just Derek and me.

"Julian is right. Her queen magic allows her to control her subjects in small doses. The more powerful she gets, the more control she exhibits. But because you're connected to me, she has an extra in with you."

"Our engagement allows her to control me already?"

"It appears so."

This is becoming a cluster of magical madness, and I have no idea how I'm supposed to unravel all of it. But I can't give in, and I can't give up. More and more, everything seems to depend on me. Now that we're back, I have to play a part.

Starting with this dumb revel.

"I can't believe there's a war going on, and she wants to have a party." My voice comes out cold and unemotional.

Derek's eyes snap to mine, confusion marring his features.

"What?"

"I don't know how you do that. It's a—"

"Fae trick?" I finish for him. Because of course it is. They compartmentalize like pros. But this is definitely not the time nor place to deal with that load of baggage either.

"I can't let myself fall into despair, Derek. I'll give myself time to fall apart when my family is safe and your mother is no longer a threat."

Maybe I shouldn't say it so bluntly in a palace where the walls have ears, but I don't care anymore. Not when every single person I care about is in danger.

"Then we must play our part at the revel."

"Really?"

"Yes. The fae will always choose intimidation and manipulation. This revel is no different. You are her weapon, and she wants to rub that in everyone's face."

I nearly smile. "That's a very human description, Derek."

"You must be rubbing off on me, Avery."

My eyes meet his of their own accord, and that ever present tension between us sizzles to dangerous temperatures. I can't seem to find my footing when I'm around him. Since I decided I no longer hate him, I don't know if I want to. We're two moths drawn to a flame. I'm not sure which one of us will be the first to get burned.

Or maybe we were simply doomed before we even started. Our connection makes this more dangerous in light of the queen being able to control him. We need a plan and one that is more surprising than anything. Thinking logically or like the fae will lead us into another trap.

"Everyone will come to the revel even though the last one wasn't exactly the greatest party ever?" My voice is full of sarcasm now, and I think Derek nearly chuckles.

"They will not disobey the queen. And she will throw as many parties as possible. She will keep inviting everyone in power until she has reached every corner of Faery. Of that, I have no doubt."

"And now she has the book."

That's a sobering thought that I've been trying desperately to push away. I'm here and so is the book and so are all the people I care about. The queen will stop at nothing to make sure she is the only one with power. That means she will use me however she wants. And now, she holds all the cards. I need to find a way to get into the game on my terms.

Except I have no idea how.

CHAPTER 14

There's something to be said about betrayal.

I'm back in my room at the palace, and everything looks exactly like I left it. It seems like no time at all has passed, but so much has happened since the queen sent us on that fool's errand.

Standing in the middle of the room, I try to get my mind wrapped around what has happened. I suppose I kept thinking that maybe this would happen, but I never expected it from my parents and definitely didn't expect it from my father.

But then again, I don't really know them, do I? They have kept so many secrets from me. They have tried so hard to protect me from this world, and yet, they have given me up to it all the same.

But of course, that's not true, is it? There has to be more to it. Rationally, I understand that. Emotionally, I'm angry and ready to burn the whole place down.

I can think of only one way the queen found Hannah's place and that is if Hannah gave it up. But I don't want to think about a way that would be possible. Maybe it's another trick, another power she possesses. Maybe she tracked Derek like she's been tracking his magic this whole time. So many questions and nearly no answers.

This is stupid.

This is frustrating.

This is maddening.

Nora comes in, ready to get me dressed for the dance. She keeps her head down, trying not to meet my eye. Immediately, I know she feels guilty for bringing us back to the house. But I can't fault her for that, not when the queen controlled me as well.

"Nora, please look at me," I say, and thankfully, she does. There's sadness in her gaze. I know she didn't want to give me up the way she did. But there's really no going against the queen, I need her to know I understand that.

"Hey, it's okay. I'm okay. Derek and Julian are okay. My parents are okay, and we'll figure this out." I'm trying to reassure her as much as I'm trying to reassure myself. I'm not sure it's working for either of us.

"Avery, I'm so sorry."

Her words nearly take all the wind out of my sails.

The fae do not apologize. They don't say they're sorry. They don't say they're thankful. They don't give that kind of weakness away verbally. Because that is what it is to them, a weakness. But here is Nora, giving up that kind of power to me.

"Nora, you don't have to—"

"No, I did. I had to say it because I need you to know just how much I did not want to go get you, but I had no choice."

There are tears in her eyes, so I do the only thing I can think of. I take a step forward and reach for her. She doesn't hesitate to hug me, holding me close. I realize this lady's maid has become my best friend through all of this. I can't imagine doing any of this without her.

The way my father reacted didn't seem like he was under the control of the queen. But I really don't know, do I? I have no idea what she's capable of. She has proven that to me.

"Nora, my dad?"

"I don't know, Avery. I didn't see them talk so I have no idea if he was commanded the same way I was."

She knows exactly what I'm asking about. She's been with me long enough that she understands how my brain works.

"Okay, so if he wasn't controlled, then why bring me here? Why give up the book? Why to all of this?"

I ask the questions out loud, but of course, there are no answers. That's what I have to do now. I have to figure it out. I have to make sure I don't make any mistakes when it comes to the queen. She is much more cunning than I could have ever imagined.

It may be that's what the Ancients are afraid of. That she will have the power to overthrow them and take what is theirs.

But I don't want to live in a world where she is the ruler of everything. I don't want to be part of that kind of existence. I know for a fact that she would not be a fair little ruler, and she would not take care of the people that are under her. This land would die because she's greedy and hungry, and all she cares about is herself.

"Nora, tell me about this revel."

"It's much like the last one. The fae love revels. It's a show of power and control."

"The last one ended in a massacre."

"It doesn't matter. The queen calls, and the people answer."

"So, this one is a way to make up for it or to show that the Summer Court is not helpless?"

"Exactly."

"I really do not understand that train of thought," I say. Nora shrugs.

"It's the way of the fae. It's all about showing yourself in the greatest light possible. And Avery? She's going to present you and Derek to the court."

Of course she is. I am nothing but a tool for her. And so is Derek, her own son. She truly will stop at nothing, which makes me want to see her fall in the greatest way possible.

"Okay, I guess this means you need to get me looking presentable."

* * *

A FEW HOURS LATER, I stand inside the main dance hall wearing a bright pink ball gown. The dress is beautiful but only on anyone who is not me. The color really makes my complexion washed out, and the green in my hair clashes with the pink in the dress.

When the guards came to summon me to the revel, I half expect them to bring some magical handcuffs to make sure I don't set the whole place on fire. My magic has been a little restless but muted. It's probably another one of the queen's tricks. She really has too much power.

And she's been walking around, flaunting it.

"She's really playing it up." Derek says, coming up beside me as I stand there watching the queen make her way around the room. This party is much like the last one. There are too many fae, too much food and drink, and everybody is laughing way too hard because, of course, the drink is laced and the spirits are high.

Nobody cares that there's a war going on right outside these walls.

"Of course she is," I reply, not taking my eyes off of her. "She thinks she's won. She has everything. The book, me, you—"

"I haven't been able to locate your parents," Derek says, and that part actually hurts. I want to see my mom and dad, but I know I can't ask for that, not from the queen. She's already using them as leverage. I can't give away any more power to her.

"What about Hannah?" I ask instead. A part of me is still scared that she's dead.

"She's being held in the dungeons as far as I know."

I exhale slowly, my heart feeling a tiny bit lighter at the news.

"Dungeons. That's so medieval."

"Well, it's not around these parts. It's pretty normal actually. The queen likes her torture." That almost makes me look at him.

But we're pretending like there's nothing between us because it's safer that way, especially in front of the queen. She's already played us like a fiddle. I don't want to give anything else to her.

"What's next?" I ask, keeping my voice low.

"Julian is looking into that." I almost smile at that because that boy has become the other part of this team that I could not live without. I haven't seen him since he was escorted out with Nora, but she mentioned he's been around.

"I need to get my hands on that book," I say. It's all I've been able to think about. Even more than getting out of here. The book is my only leverage against her. If I'm to believe what the Ancient told me, they want me to succeed. But I haven't spent nearly enough time with the book to know how to do that.

"She's keeping it safe," Derek replies. Just then, a man walks up to him and starts talking, so he gets pulled away.

I don't leave my spot. Nora stands a few feet behind me to my right, watching over me. Just like she's been assigned to do.

The queen glances over to where I'm standing, and for a second, I think that she knows what we were talking about. But of course she doesn't. She just assumes. At least she can see that I'm doing what I was told. The smile she gives me? It carries all her pride in it. I don't give anything away and keep my face as impassive as possible.

The only move I allow myself is to hold her gaze, letting her know I'm not entirely helpless. Even though I'm feeling terrified. Someone speaks to her then, and she looks away, giving me a chance to breathe a little more freely.

This is a dangerous game I'm playing, and I have no idea what the rules are. But I won't be backing down any time soon.

Nora steps up to me then, gently touching my elbow.

"We should make our rounds," she says. I give her a quick nod. I had to do this last time I was here too, slowly walk around the room, making eye contact with the guests and giving them small nods like I'm the hostess and this is my party.

Nora stays a few steps behind me, ready to jump in if anyone actually decides to talk to me. But I don't need to be afraid of that. Most people don't even make eye contact, which is fine by me. I let my gaze wander over the room, studying the crowd. There are humans here, just like last time. It makes me more unsettled than I'd like to be. But seeing the reach the queen has, even in the mortal world, it shows me just how much I have working against me. She's more powerful and more intimidating than a simple foe. She is the ultimate foe, and I'm against everything she has to offer.

A movement catches my eyes. I turn my head just slightly to the left, wondering what it was that pulled my attention. I give the crowd another scan. At first there's nothing, but then I see it. And my heart drops.

A man in the dark green uniform staff members wear moves near the food tables. He looks much like everyone else around him, dressed similarly and walking much the same way, except for one notable difference. I've seen him before. A bit of panic settles at the pit of my stomach, but I keep it at bay.

There has to be a way for me to talk to Derek without being over-heard. I catch his eye from across the room. It's like he's attuned to me, because he's already moving toward me when I look at him. In a few steps, he's beside me, taking my hand in his.

"Dance with me?"

"I thought you'd never ask."

CHAPTER 15

$\mathcal{H}$e doesn't hesitate to pull me into his arms, and I once again marvel at how perfectly I fit there. His hand holds my own near my shoulder, while his other curls over my waist, pulling me tight against his body. The only space between us is the space taken up by our clothes. Suddenly, I find it very hard to breathe. It has nothing to do with the corset I'm wearing.

"What is it?" Derek whispers into my ear.

"How did you—" I start to ask but decide against it. Not that it matters. Derek reads me like a book.

"I could feel your emotions heighten."

"You could feel them?"

This is news to me and something I'm not sure how to deal with. Clearly, I have felt our bond grow, but it's not exactly something I've read about in my textbooks. I'm not sure what to do with this information, so I'm going to ignore it for now.

"Spin me to the left, about forty-five degrees," I say instead. Derek doesn't hesitate to move our bodies to the position I indicate. My whole front is pressed against him, and I'd be lying if I said I didn't feel him against every part of me. I think I could stay in his arms for a thousand years, and it still wouldn't be enough. Nothing is like what

I've imagined when it comes to him, but he's all the things I would choose for myself if I had the choice. I'm not exactly sure how that works, only that it does. And it's making my head spin.

Focus.

Focus.

Focus.

My emotions are playing me right now. I need to get a grip. It doesn't matter how well I fit in Derek's arms, there are more important matters at hand.

"See the man near the food table and by the outside doors? He wears a green uniform like the others, his hair is a little too long at the sides."

"I see him."

"He was at my house."

The moment I say the words, Derek's body goes rigid beneath my grip. He's coiled like a live wire. I can't allow him to lose it right now. Gently and slowly, I move the hand I've placed on his shoulder down his arm and back up again. The soothing motion seems to calm him. When he glances down and meets my eyes, there's a different kind of fire there. My stomach tightens at the intensity of his gaze, and a part of me wishes we were alone, just so I could see just what that intensity could do to me.

His sharp inhale is the only indication I have that he can read the want in my eyes. We continue moving across the dance floor as one with this battle of wills going on between us. I know we have to get a grip and focus. There might be shifters in the crowd who can smell the range of emotions coming off us right now and then tattle about it to the queen. Queen Svetlana doesn't need any more insights into my life.

So, I inhale through my nose, exhale through my mouth, and find solid ground again.

"You know what this means, right?" I ask, getting us back to the issue at hand. Derek leans down, his cheek to my temple as we sway to the music. His proximity is intoxicating, but his words are sobering.

"She was in control of the massacre."

Derek barely whispers the words to me, but just hearing my suspicions confirmed makes me angry and sad at the same time. Queen Svetlana must've orchestrated the whole thing as a show of power. Or maybe she was trying to paint herself as the savior. Either way, people have returned to her revel, and she has a way to basically do it all over again. We thought a third party had skin in the game, but all this time, it's been Queen Svetlana, playing her twisted games.

Just then, there's a loud noise, and all the music stops. Queen Svetlana takes her place at the front of the room.

"Greetings esteemed guests," she begins, giving the room a quick scan with her eyes as well as a smile. "It pleases me greatly to see so many of you here. Our hearts are heavy with loss, but we have prevailed. We will continue prevailing. You can count on that. The Summer Court has opened up her borders to all those who are searching for refuge. Now eat, drink, and be merry."

There's a flood of applause as she finishes her little speech. I can't take my eyes off her. She has set yet another trap for the residents of Faery. She has named Summer Court a refuge when it is the very place that will destroy them. There's a plan here, but I don't quite understand what it is. Is she looking for support or is there something more to it?

How can I even ask that? Of course there's more to it. She's planning something, but what that may be is beyond me.

"Avery Kincaid." She stops in front of me as she makes her way around the room. "It is time for you to return to your room."

"Am I under guard?" I ask. I don't miss the way her eyes flash at the disrespect. She doesn't answer, only glances behind me and then two guards are beside me.

"Derek, be a darling and come with me."

With that, she turns and walks away. Derek has no option but to follow. He meets my eyes briefly, and I see a promise there. We'll get through this. Somehow and someway.

Turning to the guards, I motion for them to go ahead. Nora keeps up pace with us from behind as we exit the main ballroom. No one spares me a glance, but I'm sure they're all wondering. This was a perfect display of her control over me. She ordered me out, and I had no choice but to obey. It does not go unnoticed by her guests.

I am officially Queen Svetlana's puppet. I just need to figure out how to cut the strings.

* * *

Nora helps me get out of my overly dramatic pink dress before I change into pajamas and get into bed. What I wouldn't give to be able to explore the palace once everyone is asleep. But I know better than to even try.

First, because there will be crowds of people and creatures not sleeping. Faery revels last for days, and what I saw today was only the beginning.

Second, I'm under house arrest, that much is evident. I run over all the information I have in my mind.

Nora is being monitored as well. I wish there was something I could do for her, but I am pretty helpless here. My parents are still somewhere in the palace, and I haven't been able to figure out any of the information to lead me to them. All I'm doing is reacting to my circumstances again. I need to do better.

I still don't understand why I was given this power or how I'm supposed to use it when I have nothing to guide me.

Sitting up in bed, something occurs to me. It's a gamble, a dangerous one at that. But at this point, it might be my only option.

Placing the pillow at my back, I lean against it, situating myself so I'm comfortable. I have no idea if this will work or not, but I have to try. Closing my eyes, I concentrate my mind and my magic. Since being brought back, my magic has been in sleep mode. It's there, but it hasn't been active. I'm not sure if it's the queen's doing or not, but I need my magic now.

It takes a few tries, but I coax it out of its slumber.

With my eyes still closed and my breathing concentrated, I push my magic and intention out. Without having to think about it too much, my mind brings up the words I read in the book. Thoughts mingle with my magic as I breathe through the mix of emotions inside of me. It's risky doing this, since I have no idea what kind of effect it'll have on anything, but I don't stop.

With my mind and my magic, I call out to the Ancient.

I picture his flowing robes, his voice as he speaks. Since he's the only Ancient I've encountered it's easier to not get confused with my intention. But it still takes great concentration, almost as if he has a protection spell placed on him to keep others from finding him.

Just when I think it won't work, I feel the air around me shift. When I open my eyes, I'm in the misty forest.

"You are playing with fire, Avery Kincaid." The voice sounds from my right, and I turn my head to see him floating into view.

"I have no other choice," I reply, shrugging. I wait until he's in the clearing with me before I speak again. "I didn't think you'd be able to reach me here."

"You thought the queen could keep me out with her puny wards?"

I did, actually. From everything I've been told, Queen Svetlana is one of the most powerful queens of Faery. I would think, after she stole all that power, her court would be the most protected from the Ancients.

"If you are here, then why have you ever needed me?" I remember vividly when the Ancients nearly begged me to get them back to Faery. I was the gateway they needed.

"I am not truly in Faery, Avery Kincaid. You are where I am."

"I'm the one who moves?"

"Of course. Manipulating time and space is child's play, but it is not a power you possess."

Okay, that's terrifying. But it does make sense.

"Why is it you have summoned me?" He clearly doesn't like that I'm able to, and that makes me braver.

"You said you wanted to protect your...investment. I need to know how to use the book. There has to be a way for me to control it, instead of it controlling me."

"You have read from it twice. Have you learned nothing?"

"I have not.," I raise my eyebrows at him. "The book is full of emotions and when I read, I tap into them. But that sends me into a tailspin I can't control."

"You can. The gift you have been given is only given to those who possess the power to conquer it."

"It's the most frustrating thing." I roll my eyes, not caring one bit about how childish I may look to this ancient creature. "To speak in riddles when I'm asking for clarification."

The creature is silent for a moment, and for some reason, I think he's trying not to laugh. It feels like I've earned a few points with him, but I'm not sure how that translates to anything.

"The magic of the book is all about connection," he says, surprising me. I thought he'd continue evading the questions. "You have connected with the words, now you must connect with the emotion. You have been pulled toward each other all this time, do not allow outside circumstances and forces pull that away. Trust your instincts. Trust your magic."

As I mull that over, I realize he's fading away.

"No, wait. Come back. I have more questions."

"I will be around when you need me."

And just like that, I'm opening my eyes in the bedroom once more. I can't tell if that was helpful or not, but at least I know I have a direct line to the Ancients. Not that it helped any. Laying back onto the pillow, I mull over his words.

I connected to the words, now I must connect to the emotion. How am I supposed to do that?

CHAPTER 16

It's been days since Queen Svetlana brought us back to the palace. I've mostly been confined to my room. Outside of that first night at the revel, I haven't been able to leave these four walls. Nora brings me food, and I haven't seen Derek or Julian in days.

Surely, by now, I thought she'd make her move. Either she'd take me to the dungeons to torture me or take me to the dungeons and force me to watch my loved ones being tortured. I'm waiting for the other shoe to drop, and it's driving me slightly crazy. That, of course, is just part of her plan. But that knowledge just makes me even more determined to not show any signs of madness. No matter how crazy I'm feeling after being cooped up in here.

In the middle of the day, Nora shows up with food. She's only allowed to stay while I eat, so we try to do as much catching up as we can during that time but in a way where we don't say too much. Except today, she starts the conversation, and her words take me by surprise.

"The queen has begun preparation for your wedding. Derek has been sent away on an urgent matter. We will be having a dress fitting after you have eaten."

I stare at Nora as if she's spoken a foreign language. She gives me a kind smile and a little shrug. The potato I've been chewing suddenly refuses to go down the right pipe.

"You can't be serious."

"It's what I've been told."

Of course Queen Svetlana will want to move that along. The moment I'm married to Derek my power becomes available to her. Maybe married isn't the correct word. Bound would be better, but not the kind of bound Derek and I already are. What we have is something she can't touch. But it doesn't mean she won't try.

She announced our engagement to the court, proclaiming it as truth, so there is no way out of it. But I didn't think she would act on that threat so fast. Then again, that one is on me. She's three steps ahead while I'm still trying to figure out which direction to go.

I finish my food and let Nora lead me into the large walk-in closet in my room. Sitting me down in front of the vanity, she begins brushing out my hair. I give her a confused look, and she smiles.

"Hair is part of wedding preparation, no?"

I understand what she's doing, and I'm grateful. There is no way I'm ready for a parade of dresses, but this is something we can do where we can still talk. And mostly in private. It's harder to hear into the closet from the outside.

"Where is Derek really?" I dare to ask, still keeping my voice low.

"I'm not sure, Avery. She sent him away yesterday, and he hasn't been back."

That actually explains my restless nights. I could feel his absence even though I didn't know he was gone. That's another item to add to my list of items I need to dissect later.

"She's been trying to figure out how to use the book," Nora says. My ears perk up, pushing away the conflicting emotions. "She can't read it, obviously, but she's been trying some rituals—I'm not sure."

"It's okay," I hurry to reassure her. "It's not your job to spy on her."

"It is, and I'm not very good at it," Nora insists. I reach back and place a hand over her own, giving it a little squeeze. Nora gives me a sad smile in return, and I can understand how she's feeling. I'm feeling hopeless as well. It's getting harder each day to keep a positive outlook on things. The Ancients have been quiet, the revel has been loud, and I've been kept in my room like a prisoner.

Because that's exactly what I am.

I open my mouth to say something when a commotion comes from the room. I stand, and Nora and I walk out of my closet only to find a few maids wheeling in wedding dresses. I notice the soldiers right beyond the open doorway. My anger rises up again. These are the same men and women who attacked the court and then my family and me. Queen Svetlana is behind every bad thing that has happened, and I'm in no place to stop her. But I do want to make things more difficult for her.

"What is the meaning of this?" I ask, glancing around the room. One of the maids steps forward, and I immediately know she's the boss. And I'm not going to like her.

"It is time for you to try on these dresses," she announces. I decide to test the waters.

"We've been working on hairstyles. How about we do the dresses later?"

"This isn't a request," the boss maid says, and there it is. The queen is commanding everything about my life. Well, I refuse to give her the satisfaction. I open my mouth to protest when an agonizing pain hits me straight in the stomach. I bend over at the waist, wrapping my arms around the middle.

"She said you might try something like rebellion," the maid continues. "She made sure to take care of that. If you participate, the pain disappears. It's that simple."

That, of course, leaves me no choice. I stand to my full height, pushing the pain away. It doesn't go away completely but enough that I can glare at the maid.

"Bring on the dresses."

* * *

WE SPEND hours trying on stupid dresses that simply don't work. Nothing seems to fit because what Derek and I have is different from what the queen wants. The dresses she brought me all look like way too much. Most have a huge hoop skirt that takes up way too much space and keeps me unbalanced. Although, it's like a tent, so it would keep me upright if I needed it.

Once the servants leave, I lay on the bed, staring at the ceiling. My body feels like I've just had a very tough workout. Every time I went against something the queen wanted, I would get a wave of pain. It makes me angry how powerful she is. She cursed the dresses, and me in the process, just to make sure I stayed in check.

Sitting up, I run my hand over my hair and realize I'm way too restless to simply lay here. I have to do something.

I keep thinking how the queen doesn't even need to be in the room to cast her magic. She's that powerful. If I'm to apply the same concept to my current predicament, maybe I can do something about it. An idea springs to mind, and I jump to my feet immediately.

It's risky, and I have no idea if it'll work or not, but it feels like I need to try. I'm so tired of doing nothing.

Moving to the floor, I sit down cross legged, hands on my knees.

The concept here is that if I can call on the Ancient, maybe I can call on the book. Obviously, I've never tried anything like this, so I have no idea if it'll work or what it'll actually do. But that's better than slowly wasting away in this bedroom while the queen of the Summer Court prepares to destroy everything and everyone I love.

Much like the last time, I close my eyes and concentrate on my breathing. These little inhale and exhale exercises have really helped me stay centered. I've been thinking more about balance, especially since reading about it in the book.

Magic is about balance. It's about equal partnership between the wielder and that which is wielded. It takes discipline and intention, two things I've been learning more about.

I place the back of my hands on my knees as I sit cross legged. My intention is on finding that balance, so when one hand conjures fire and the other conjures water I'm not even surprised. Glancing down, I study the two opposing elements and how they seem to be working in tandem. Keeping that same feeling, I reach for the book.

I have no idea where it's at in the palace, but I know it's here. The pull I feel toward it is still there, and so I tap into that as much as I can. For a second, I feel like nothing is going to happen. But then my body begins to feel lighter. I feel like I'm flying through the hallways, right along with my magic. It weaves in and out of the rooms, checking for the book and its power. My mind fills with random words from the book, things I've read before. I don't say any of the words out loud, but they're there, at the tip of my tongue. It makes me feel more connected to the book.

Just when I think nothing will come of it, the pull becomes stronger. I give my magic the freedom it needs to follow it. However, when I try to feel for the book, I come to a barrier, almost a physical one. I feel like my magic slams into a wall.

Inhaling deeply, I try to push past the barrier. When that doesn't work, I search for a way around it with my mind, but there's nothing.

And then there's pain.

It comes suddenly, and it takes all the breath from my lungs. My magic extinguishes itself as I drop to my side on the floor. Opening my eyes, I see the door to my bedroom open. The queen stands on the other side. Her lips move, but I can't hear what she's saying. Guards are inside my room in the next moment, picking me clean off the floor and following the queen out of the room.

CHAPTER 17

'm dragged into the throne room and deposited onto the floor without ceremony. The queen watches as I push myself to all fours before I feel her magic slam into me. I fly backward, landing hard on my back. The wind is once again knocked out of my lungs. My body feels bruised from the magic, but also like it's being cut open by it. In and out, pain comes in waves as I try to keep myself from crying out. I hate showing that kind of emotion in front of her.

"You really did not think I would notice?" she asks, walking toward me slowly. The echoes of her heels on the marble floor are intensified by my pain. In my hurt brain, the sound seems to be amplified.

"Foolish girl. You will see the book when I deem it necessary. No magic tricks will help you. Do I need to suppress your magic completely?"

The pain makes it hard to hide emotion, and I know she sees the terror on my face at her suggestion. Her lyrical laugh rings out like bells chiming in the wind. She stands from where she leaned down to look at my face and walks slowly back to the throne.

Breath comes back into my lungs again as the pain recedes.

"If you are so keen on reading the book, then let me give it to you." She waves her hand and then one of the guards is there, handing her the book. My magic jumps inside of me, eager and excited at the prospect. I show nothing outwardly. The guard grabs me from behind, yanking me to my feet. I stumble but stay standing.

"Well, Avery, work your magic." She pushes the book toward me. I take it, but I don't open it. There is no way I'm reading the book for her. When I don't automatically do her bidding, she gets in my face. "Isn't this what you wanted?"

"I'm not helping you destroy Faery," I nearly spit out. When her hand slaps me across my face, I'm not surprised. Raising my head back up, I glare at her, making sure to put every part of my hatred for her into my eyes. She stares at me for a second before she laughs.

"No wonder Derek is drawn to you. You are strong. I raised him to look for strength."

I know what she's doing. She wants me to doubt Derek, but she can talk a big game all she wants. I won't believe a word she has to say about him. Not when I know the truth in my heart.

And I do.

Derek is my person—or fae. He's my mate, just like the ancient book spoke about. He's someone who fills up those missing pieces and balances me out. Queen Svetlana can pull every trick in the book, and I still won't back down. Because I know how I feel, and I trust him. Raising my chin, I stare her down. She stares at me for a long moment before she yanks the book out of my hands.

"Fine. Have it your way."

When the blast of her magic reaches me, I drop to my hands and knees, trying to keep myself from screaming. But even as the fire of pain burns through my body, I don't doubt my decision, and I don't doubt my feelings. She can destroy me if that's what she wants, but I'm never doing her bidding.

* * *

THE QUEEN DIDN'T WAIT LONG to dump me back in my room after I refused to read from the book. My whole body still feels like it's been run over by a truck and set on fire. But I'm holding it together. As well as I can. I know I need to rest, but I can't seem to shut off my brain.

I'm laying as still as possible as the door creeps open and a shadow slips in. There's half a second where I want to hurl a fireball at the intruder, but then I realize I'd know that outline anywhere.

"Are you trying to give me a heart attack?" I snap, keeping my voice low. Derek stops near my bed, a huge smile on his face.

"Maybe only a little."

I want to throw something at him or reply with a good comeback, but I can't think straight when he's smiling like that. He's the most beautiful creature I have ever seen. But then his smile is gone as he looks down at me, worry replacing the happiness.

"What happened?"

I push myself to a sitting position. He takes a seat beside me on the bed, his hand reaching for my cheek. I'm sure I'm wearing the imprint of the queen's hand now.

"Avery—"

"The queen happened," I reply with a shrug, even though that hurts. "I did something stupid, and she punished me for it."

Derek's fingers trace my cheek, and I lean into his touch automatically. He cradles one cheek with his hand while his other hand finds mine on the bed. He laces his fingers with mine. I close my eyes at the sensations racing through my body. I give him a quick rundown of what happened, so he can have all the information.

"I wasn't here."

"There is nothing you could've done," I reply, opening my eyes so I can look at him. His are full of sorrow, and once again, I marvel at how different he is from the guy I met many moons ago. That fae was ruthless and on a mission to bring me back here, kicking and screaming. Now, he's the one who wears his heart on his sleeve.

Maybe it's because he feels safe with me. He knows I would never judge his heart.

"She sent me away. There are a few outposts in the woods, scouting for the Ancients or any other kind of danger. She wanted me to check on each one."

"She's giving you busy work." Derek nods at that. I raise my head, so I can look him directly in the eye. "I tried on wedding dresses today." There's a sharp intake of breath on Derek's part, but it's the only indication I have that he's affected. I run my hand over his upper arm before tracing the fingers of his free hand. It's as if, suddenly, I can't stop touching him. I need to feel the way his skin feels.

"I was supposed to get you out of the engagement," Derek whispers.

"We did get a little sidetracked with the end of the world chores," I reply with a small smile. He cocks his head to the side, studying me. I can see the little corner of his mouth moving upward. I take that as a victory.

We stare at each other, as if we've never seen the other before. The electricity we carry sizzles in the space around us. I want to pull him close. I want to wrap my arms around him and never let go.

My prince.

My prince.

My fae prince.

Nearly overwhelmed with the emotions I'm feeling, I try to keep my face as impassive as possible. But that's a futile exercise because Derek can read every emotion like it's his own. He reaches for me at the same time as I reach for him and then the world and worry melt away as our lips come together.

He tastes of the forest and morning dew. I can't keep my hands to myself as I pull him closer. They roam over his shoulders, up his neck, and into his hair. My fingers curl into the strands, pulling on them a little, which elicits a groan deep in his throat.

Suddenly, I'm on his lap, my legs on either side of him as he wraps his arms around my waist and tries to pull me even closer. We're hungry for each other. Hungry and unstoppable. I could kiss him until the whole world burns, and I wouldn't feel guilty at all.

He pulls back slightly before dropping a quick kiss to my lips. Without hesitation, he spins us, so that he's laying down, and I'm on top of him. His arms cradle me to him. I pull him closer as well. I think he knows that if he didn't stop us, we would burn the whole world down together.

"She's going to try to use this against us, isn't she?" I ask, because I need to know. I can feel Derek's heartbeat beneath me. I close my eyes against the sound.

"She won't succeed."

"She might." The words slip out before I can stop them. Derek brings me closer still, exhaling fully before he speaks.

"Avery, there isn't a place or a power in this realm or the next that could keep me from you. Bring on the whole of Faery, every Ancient creature known to the world, it won't stop me. Not when it comes to you."

My heart beats so loudly, it fills the space around us, ready to burst out of my chest. When I place my hand on his chest, his own heart answers my rhythm.

"I'm afraid you keep making promises we won't be able to see through," I whisper. I've come to terms with the fact that if the magic requires it, I will sacrifice myself to save those I love. Not that I have said those words out loud. Derek knows. He knows what the magic can do.

"I'm afraid of losing you," he admits, taking my argument from me. "I will do whatever it takes to make sure that doesn't happen."

I want to tell him that he won't lose me, but I can't. The queen is clearly not afraid to hurt me. I can just see the possibilities of what could happen too clearly to lie to Derek.

So I don't say anything. Instead, I pull him even closer and hold him, until we breathe in sync. Then, only then, do I feel like I can sleep.

CHAPTER 18

The next week goes by in a blur of activity. The queen has decided to go all in on the wedding and is making preparations. The distraction has helped keep her mind occupied, but I've still been summoned multiple times to try and read the book. I've seen my father once, when the queen brought him to the throne room as a bargaining tool. He looked like he hadn't slept in days, and I can understand that. He wasn't allowed to speak, but the look in his eyes gave me the strength I needed to withstand her pushes.

Even beaten down, my father is the strongest man I know, and he believes I can be just as strong.

I've been trying to do my best. But I'm not too sure how much longer I can hold on. The emotional toll all of this is taking on me will break me before the physical will.

Derek has been sneaking into my room every night he's not sent out on some dumb errand. I can't tell if the queen knows about it or not, but we haven't been caught yet. A part of me thinks she's giving us this time so she can use it against us. I wouldn't put it past her.

This morning starts out like all the others. Nora brings me food and stays with me as I eat my breakfast. She looks as tired as I feel, and my heart hurts for her.

"Has Julian come back?" I ask. She told me two days ago Queen Svetlana sent him away. Nora shakes her head no, and I can see the worry in her eyes. It doesn't sit well with me either. I want my friends safe, and there's nothing I can do to make that happen.

I've tried reaching out to the Ancient and haven't been able to get to him. I can't tell if my magic is the hindrance or his. He's probably ignoring me as he prepares for some grand assault.

That's what I feel like is coming next. From the Ancients, from the queen, from a third party I know nothing about. Everything is at a standstill right now, but it won't last long. I can feel it in my bones.

When pain comes this time, it's different. I drop down to the floor, grabbing my stomach. It feels like it's cramping. I try to hold in the tears that instantly come. Nora is beside me in a flash.

"What is it? The queen?"

"No," I gasp. "It's different." I try to force air into my lungs, but the cramps become worse and worse. This feels nothing like Queen Svetlana's torture magic. Suddenly, my arms feel like they're being sliced open. When Nora begins to scream, I realize it's because they are. Glancing down, I watch as cuts appear on my skin, blood leaking through. My own screams come then. Guards enter the room in the blink of an eye. There's a commotion as I drop to the floor. I hold onto my arms, trying to keep the blood and pain at bay.

My vision swims and then everything goes black.

* * *

WHEN I COME TO, the first thing I see is Derek. He's opposite of me, his body attached to a metal pole, hands and feet bound. The image is similar to that of the witches from Salem portrayed when they were sentenced to burning. I try to go to him, but then realize I'm in the same predicament.

"Avery," Derek calls out to me. His voice sounds hoarse, as if he's been saying my name for a while.

"What happened?" I push past my lips, my voice hoarse as well. The last thing I remember was the pain.

"I'm not sure."

Derek looks like he's been through something. His face is marred by cuts and bruises.

"Derek?"

"I'm okay. I was attacked on my way back to the palace and then I woke up here."

Tears fall before I can stop them. This is all my fault. If I was smarter or braver, I could've figured out the book and the magic, and we wouldn't be in this predicament.

"I'm so sorry." I know I shouldn't be saying that to him, I know it's against fae rules, but it's Derek. I don't care. "I'm so sorry, Derek. I should've found a way. I should've done more."

"No, stop, Avery. This is not on you. You have done everything in your power—"

"But it wasn't enough." There are tears coming down my cheeks now. I see no point in holding them back. "I wasn't enough to save you. I wasn't—"

"You are more than enough!" Derek's voice drowns mine out for a moment. His eyes are full of fire, and I can feel the intensity in him. Even from across the room, he's refusing to let me believe I failed, but I did. I failed all of them.

A noise comes from my left. I try to see into the shadows, but I can't quite make out anything. The room appears to be a large square, but the light is dimmed on both my right and my left. But then a voice sounds, and my heart drops even more.

"Mom?"

"Avery, sweetie, are you okay?"

"I'm fine, Mom. Where is dad?"

"Your father is right where he needs to be." The queen is suddenly there, coming forward out of the shadows on my right. She's wearing one of her bright red dresses. The jewels on it sparkle, nearly blinding me.

"I thought you would sleep forever," she continues. I have nothing to say to her.

"You will pay for this!" My mom's voice rings out, and the queen's features harden.

"That is no way to speak to your queen." She waves her hand, and the cries disappear. I can still hear my mom moving and yanking against her restraints, but she no longer seems to be able to talk.

"What did you do?" I ask, surprised Queen Svetlana hasn't rendered me mute either. But I guess she needs me.

"I just wanted a little piece and quiet," the queen replies. She looks much like I'm used to seeing her, except for an extra pinch of madness in her eyes. There's definitely a touch of that in her. It makes me nervous.

"You are such a curious creature, Avery," she says, coming to stand in front of me. "All that raw power with no guidance. You know I could teach you."

"Teach me what? How to steal another's magic and claim it as your own?" I nearly spit at her, my hatred rising. "I'm good."

She's in my face immediately, grabbing my chin to lift it up.

"You will show me respect."

"I will do no such thing." I stare at her unwavering. At first, I think it'll set her off more, but she drops my face roughly before walking back to the shadow filled corner of the room. I push the pain away and concentrate.

"You know nothing, Avery Kincaid. I don't need you as much as you think I do." The voice sounds strange, coming from a place I can see. Then, she steps back into the light with a book in her hands. My heart clenches at the sight of it. I can tell pages are missing. There are rips and cuts on it. She must've been performing rituals on it, trying to extract secrets from the book by any means possible.

My mind goes to the pain I felt and the cuts on my arms. I stare at the book, at the similar patterns, and it becomes clear. My connection to the book is greater than I imagined. When it hurts, I hurt.

"Since you won't read from this, then I will do what I must to get the information I need," Queen Svetlana says, throwing a smile my way. She definitely looks mad now. Hungry on the prospect of power, I suppose.

"Don't do this," Derek calls out. When I look at him, I see fear in his eyes. He knows what she's about to do, and it terrifies him. She places the book at the center of the room on a table before she takes a dagger from beside it. Slowly, she makes her way to Derek. Stopping in front of him, she takes the dagger and runs it across his cheek. It's not hard enough to pierce the skin, but it's enough that I know what she's planning on doing.

"You were supposed to control her. Not the other way around. Now, you will play your part," the queen says. When she grabs Derek's hand, she slices it clean through from wrist to the tip of his finger. He jerks, but she simply wipes her dagger all over the blood, coating it completely before she drops his hand and walks back over to the book. It's open to some page in the middle now. She holds the dagger over it, letting the blood drip onto the page. My chest feels like it's on fire. I can't tell if it's because the book is affecting me or if it's my own anger. I reach for my magic, but I can't access it. Whatever control she has here, it's overpowering all my senses.

All but one.

My eyes meet Derek's from across the room. His gaze holds every promise between us. My mind snaps back to the book and the emotions I felt reading the words. Now, I understand. Whoever wrote those words was in love. The kind of love that builds cities and brings down tyrants and sets the sun in the sky to shine. That's what I feel for Derek.

Not because of a false engagement bond or any other reason, but because he's my perfect half.

"Do not worry, Avery. I will be with you shortly. It seems I need a little more from my son."

The queen sends a wicked smile my way before she walks back over to Derek. This time, she doesn't reach for his hand but for his head. Bringing it to the side to expose his neck, she smiles again and places the dagger there. His eyes meet mine from across the room once more and time stops. In that split second, I see a future in him. A future I desperately want and am not about to let anyone take away from me.

CHAPTER 19

The words I've read in the book come crashing into me, as if they've been circling around and have now found a place to land.

THE TRUE KNIGHT is not only a person but an idea. There are those who believe the power comes from within, and there are those who believe the power comes from the land itself. It never matters where it comes from, as long as the one who wields it, wields it with a pure heart.

AS I REMEMBER THE WORDS, I remember the emotion. Whoever wrote the paragraph must've been greatly overcome as well because I seem to feel everything at once.

The love.

The duty.

The promise.

There are so many ways this story can go. I refuse to let it be anything but a good ending. My magic is brewing inside of me, but I can't reach it. The queen cuts Derek on the neck, not quite the artery but close enough. The scream I hear is my own.

I'm not going to lose him.

I'm not going to lose him.

I'm not going to lose him.

This is my one chance to save the man I love. Pulling on every possible emotion in my body, I send it directly into my magic.

My wings slice through the binding as they flare out around me. The magic I've been carrying inside me all this time suddenly breaks through wherever spells the queen has in place. Queen Svetlana gasps, taking a step back from Derek as she stares at me in awe. I jump down from where she kept me bound, facing her directly.

"Not possible," the queen whispers. "You are not possible."

"Surprise!" I grin.

I can feel my magic grow. I can feel it flourish, even as my wings seem to grow bigger.

I'm not afraid anymore.

I'm not afraid of the responsibility that's been placed on my shoulders. I know that I've been given this power because I can handle it. And even though I've decided to be intentional about everything I do, this is the first time I actually feel like I understand the magic that courses through my veins.

It's love and it's power and it's every mistake and every right decision. It's what makes the world turn. And I hold it in the palm of my hand and in the beating of my heart.

I am my mother's daughter. I am my father's daughter. But I am also the product of the land and the magic that comes with it. My heritage is not just from one line.

I am a shifter.

A witch.

A fae.

All of these make up who I am, and even though I've spent my life being afraid of not being normal, not being normal is the greatest thing that I can be.

The queen moves then, throwing her magic my way, but I'm

prepared. I throw my own shield up, protecting me from her blast. I can see it takes her by surprise. Without giving her a chance to recover, I send my own blast of magic. It paralyzes her in place.

I wouldn't be lying if I said a part of me enjoys the fact that I can make her feel how she has made everybody around her feel, if only for a fraction of the time.

Her magic is powerful, and she is experienced. She breaks through my hold. The next thing I know, she's blasting her magic but not at me. It takes me a second to make sure I stop it before it reaches her intended targets.

She's targeting the people I love.

Without knowing where my father is, I throw a barrier up, but not in front of a specific spot. I throw it around us, kind of like a dome, descending around us. She's trapped in here with me.

Derek is free from his bonds, and he reaches for the dagger she discarded.

"You're not actually going up against me, are you?" the queen asks Derek, but he doesn't even hesitate. Closing the distance between them, he speaks.

"I am standing against you and everything that you have ever tried to do to me and to your people. I will answer to you no longer." There's pain in Derek's words. I want to protect him from it, but I also understand that maybe he needs to exert his own sort of revenge. He's suffered at her hand for so long.

Then, I realize this is not going to be as perfect as I want it to be in my head. The queen screams and then her soldiers spill into the room. They surround the dome of protection I've created, but I have no idea how long that'll last. Derek and I are the only ones standing against the mob. The odds are not stacked in our favor.

Except that's the wrong kind of thinking here. After all, I have a magic no one else has. It's about time I used it.

* * *

THROWING a blast of magic at the queen, I race past her toward the book. It nearly takes me to my knees how destroyed and abused the pages look. I have no time to go through my breathing exercises or to try and find my center. My whole body is buzzing with power, and I can feel danger right on the other side of my barrier. The queen is already getting to her feet, and Derek is beside me, ready to defend me if the need arises.

"Avery."

"Give me a second."

I slam the book shut, placing both hands on it, front and back. My wings move in anticipation. Instead of focusing on what I need, I focus on the emotions.

My need to save my people.

My desire to keep Faery flourishing.

My desire for revenge on the queen.

The book feels all of it and then it begins to shake under my grip. My instinct is to drop it, but instead, I hold on. A bright light spews from the book, encompassing me in its glow. I feel a rush of power through my whole being, and I gasp as it becomes nearly overwhelming. At the back of my mind, I can hear screaming as the barrier comes down and an urgent cry for help from Derek.

"Avery!"

I feel it all, but somehow, I'm also disconnected from my body. And then, I feel the book again, but this time, inside of me. It trusted me to do what needs to be done. I have found my balance.

My magic is old but it's also my own. I hold it all in the palm of my hand. Turning to the hoard of people, I throw a blast of magic at them. I wield both fire and water equally, but there's something more there. The book's magic, it lives inside of me now. I'm not afraid anymore, and a part of me disconnects.

All I feel is vengeance.

All I want to do is destroy everything.

At the back of my mind, I realize those are my emotions, but they're also multiplied by the hatred the Ancient magic feels. Because I now know it's as much alive as anything else. I send another blast of magic at the soldiers when a powerful tug takes me clear off my feet. I land hard. When I glance down, I find nothing there.

Twisting around, I find the queen rising, a smirk on her royal face.

"I can see the power on you," she says, moving closer. "I can almost taste it. I want it. And I know how to take it."

"By bleeding me dry?"

"Well, no, but it's a start."

I feel the same kind of ruthless energy the queen is displaying. I want to take her down and make her pay. When she sends a blast of air at me, I'm nearly lost in my thoughts. But I recover quickly enough, sending my own blast of fire at her. She seems to yank at my magic, pulling me closer.

"You will never defeat me," she says, her voice full of glee. "I will take this land and I will make it mine, just like I will take your magic. You are just a child. You will never be able to stand against me." She laughs then, and I can't believe her. After all this, she thinks she's winning. I'm going to make sure she remembers who beat her.

"My name is Avery Kincaid. I am a daughter of both worlds and a wielder of Ancient magic. You are nothing but a has been. A queen who held onto her throne a little too tightly. I am more than happy to take such a hard burden off your hands."

When I send a stream of fire and water at her, I don't hold back. The fire burns and the water soothes. It's the worst kind of torture. The queen screams, and I laugh, surprising myself and Derek. The need to destroy is nearly overwhelming. I send a wave of my magic at the soldiers. In the next moment, they're all knocked out.

"We are not so different," the queen gasps, blood dripping from her lip. "You have given yourself over to the power. You will be your own downfall."

"You would know something about that," I spit at her as I try to hold onto the magic. I don't want to prove her right. Then, Derek is beside me, his hand reaching for my own. Little by little, the storm inside me calms. Just like that I know exactly what to do.

I make an internal phone call to someone who can handle this magic just fine.

CHAPTER 20

$\mathcal{T}$he Ancient appears in the middle of the room as if he's
always been there.

One look at me, and he seems to know exactly what's happening.
Raw magic radiates off him and then the soldiers who were still
standing are on the floor.

"You have done well, Avery Kincaid," the creature says. "You have
proven yourself worthy of the words of the Ancients."

I glance over at the book, which needs some serious tender love
and care to restore it to its previous glory. For some reason, I'm not
afraid of what I'll find on those pages anymore.

"The wings suit you."

Surprised, I look at the creature, but he's already shifted his attention. He suddenly fills up the majority of the room. He rises above us,
a picture of vengeance and pain. The queen has fallen where I
defeated her, but for some reason, it seems like that's not enough. Not
to the creature.

He's upon her before I can blink and then she screams as he
envelops her in his cloak. The rush of magic nearly takes me off my
feet. Suddenly, the creature and the queen are gone. I don't even have
time to process that before Derek is on top of me.

He nearly body slams me, grabbing me around the waist and pulling me straight into his arms. I wrap my legs around his waist, holding him just as desperately as he's holding me. Our heartbeats begin beating in sync, calming both of us down.

Pulling back so I can look down at his face, I don't even hesitate. My lips crash onto his. He kisses me with the same fervor he does everything. He is my lifeline, and I am in his. In this one kiss he pours his whole being into me. My hands roam over his hair, pulling his head even closer as he cradles me in his arms.

There is no space left between us, yet I'm still not close enough.

I continue to devour him with my mouth, pouring every thought and emotion in the way our lips move together. He pulled me back from the edge. He saved me.

"We saved each other," he murmurs against my lips. I chuckle.

"Stop reading my mind."

"Never."

He places his forehead against mine, and we both exhale. Then he places me back on the floor, and I give him a big smile. Smart guy.

Pushing away from him, I bring the barrier down and race for the corner of the room where my mother's voice was coming from. Dad is also there, strung up on a pole just like we were. I free my parents without a word and then we're hugging.

"We're so sorry, Avery. So sorry." Dad keeps repeating the words over and over, and I simply hold them closer.

Everything will be okay now.

* * *

IT'S BEEN a few weeks since the Ancient took the queen to who knows where. No one has mourned her absence. It actually almost seems like everything was at a standstill, and now, everything is moving so fast.

Derek has reinstated the council. The Sunland family, my family of long forgotten fae, are finally back. My father will be one to guide the council to make the right decisions while Derek rules the Summer Court.

It seems crazy that such an old tradition would be so accepted, but I guess fae have long-lasting memories. When Derek announced he would be taking the throne and the council, Summer Court blew up with excitement. Maybe they have been waiting for Queen Svetlana's downfall as well.

I have forgiven my parents for their secrets, and I'm keeping a few of my own. I suppose that's how the world works, right? We found Hannah in the dungeons. Poor thing had been nearly drained of her magic. Queen Svetlana had been practicing on her. Hannah is back in her house now, recovering. Julian's brother, Jared, is staying there, and Nora opens up a portal for me any time I ask for one.

"Do you remember the first time we met?" I ask without turning around. I'm in the library, a place I didn't even know existed in the palace until I went exploring. Stepping inside this room felt more magical than reading from the Ancient book. So many books and now I have all the time in the world to read them.

"I remember."

I've been waiting for Derek to find me. He always seems to find me.

"I hated you, you know," I say.

"The feeling was mutual."

I turn then, to face him. I don't think I'll ever get over seeing him in his royal garments. The t-shirt and jeans are gone. Instead, his slacks look like they're tailored just for him while his black shirt is unbuttoned at the top and looks like it's made out of the night sky. He still wears his human clothes from time to time. He simply looks like a mafia boss or something. Not that I'm complaining.

"And now you don't hate me at all." I wink and Derek chuckles.

"Ain't that the truth."

I gasp in mock shock and laugh a little.

"Why Derek, that is such a human phrase. Don't let the courts hear you."

"Or what?"

He has come farther into the room, slowly moving toward me like a predator moves toward prey.

"Or they'll task me with punishing you."

That's my position here now. I'm Derek's right-hand woman but also a bit of an enforcer. Our engagement is our own now and we will figure it out with time.

The book's magic lives inside me now. We have found an understanding and a balance, so I can now read from the book without causing destruction. Maybe one day we'll figure out why I was chosen for this, but it doesn't matter. I can't imagine being anyone else.

"A punishment? Could I negotiate some terms?" Derek's teasing voice brings me out of my musings.

"I don't think that's how it works."

"I suppose I'll have to decree something then." He's around the desk and grabbing me in the next second. I try to get away, playfully, but we both know I want to be caught by him. And only him.

He pulls me close, and I jump up, wrapping my legs around his middle. He holds me effortlessly and possessively, and I love him more than words can explain.

"I love you too." He chuckles as he steals a tiny kiss from my lips.

"Stop reading my mind."

"Never."

He captures my lips with his own then, and it's always as if we're kissing for the first time. New and exciting and all the sensations at once. But there's also comfort in his kiss, something that I eat up just as hungrily.

Who would've thought that I would find my soulmate in this grumpy fae prince? I never could've imagined my life going this way, but Maddie was right. I trusted my magic and the right kind of people came along. Speaking of which.

"Did Julian find the t-shirt he's been looking for?"

"That's what you'd like to talk about right now?" Derek pouts a little, pulling back. I grin down at him.

"It's an important question."

Derek sighs. "No. He and Nora are in the room now, going through piles of clothes."

"Perfect. Let's go help them."

I jump down, but Derek doesn't let me move away.

"You're impossible."

"This is true. Better get used to it."

"I already can't live without it." I'm grinning again, as Derek leans down to give me another kiss. I open up to it completely, happy and fulfilled. There are a hundred promises in that one kiss, and I intend on collecting them all.

WANT MORE FROM THE WORLD OF HAWTHORNE?

Get the complete series here:
The Thunderbird Academy trilogy

I'm losing control of my magic... and a wolf shifter has to keep me in check.

An Ancient evil is spreading throughout the land. When it knocks on the door of my school, everyone expects me to fight it.

But I'm hiding a secret….my magic is on the fritz.

Not only that, but the headmaster forces me into combat training lessons with my nemesis.

Aiden Lawson, wolf shifter. Did I mention he's ridiculously gorgeous and impossible to ignore? Our lessons are explosive, and I never seem to come out on top. He won't go easy on me. He's as ruthless as he is loyal.

If I can just get my magic under control, then I can be rid of Aiden for good.

But when the Ancient evil breaks through the school's defenses, Aiden and I have to fight.

Whether we're ready or not.

Welcome to my year at Thunderbird Academy.

Full of magic, adventure, and enemies-to-lovers angsty romance, Thunderbird Academy is an addicting young adult paranormal romance series by USA Today bestselling author Valia Lind that will keep you reading late into the night!

Thunderbird Academy Box Set includes all three books: Of Water and Moonlight, Of Destiny and Illusions, and Of Storms and Triumphs.

CLICK HERE to start reading!

NOTE FROM THE AUTHOR

Thank you for reading my book! If you have enjoyed it, please consider leaving a review. Reviews are like gold to authors and are a huge help!

They help authors get more visibility, and help readers make a decision!

And, if you'd like to stay up to date with all of my shenanigans, sign up for my newsletter today!

CLICK HERE TO SIGN UP!

Thank you!

ABOUT THE AUTHOR

USA Today bestselling author. Photographer. Artist. Born and raised in St. Petersburg, Russia, Valia Lind has always had a love for the written word. She wrote her first published book on the bathroom floor of her dormitory, while procrastinating to study for her college classes. Upon graduation, she has moved her writing to more respectable places, and has found her voice in Young Adult and cozy mysteries.

Sign up to receive updates, behind the scenes, & more!
CLICK HERE

ALSO BY VALIA LIND

The Skazka Fairy Tales

The Scarlet Rose (A Beauty and the Beast Retelling)

The Golden Slipper (A Cinderella Retelling) - coming Autumn 2022!

The Skazka Chronicles

Hardcover Omnibus - 4 books in one

Remembering Majyk (The Skazka Chronicles, #1)

Majyk Reborn (The Skazka Chronicles, #2)

The Faithful Soldier (The Skazka Chronicles, #2.5)

Majyk Reclaimed (The Skazka Chronicles, #3)

Crooked Windows Inn Cozy Mysteries

Once Upon a Witch #1

Two Can Witch the Game #2

Witch's First Zombie - FREE short story

Third Witch's the Charm #3

Witches Four the Win #4 - coming Spring 2022!

Blackwood Supernatural Prison Series

Witch Condemned (#1)

Witch Unchained (#2)

Witch Awakened (#3)

Witch Ascendant (#4)

Hawthorne Chronicles - Each season can be read as standalone!

Season Three

Shadow of the Fae (#1)

Blood of the Fae (#2)

Revenge of the Fae (#3)

Season Two

The Complete Box Set

Of Water and Moonlight (Thunderbird Academy, #1)

Of Destiny and Illusions (Thunderbird Academy, #2)

Of Storms and Triumphs (Thunderbird Academy, #3)

Season One

Guardian Witch (Hawthorne Chronicles, #1)

Witch's Fire (Hawthorne Chronicles, #2)

Witch's Heart (Hawthorne Chronicles, #3)

Tempest Witch (Hawthorne Chronicles, #4)

The Complete Season One Box Set

Havenwood Falls (PNR standalone)

Predestined

The Titanium Trilogy

Pieces of Revenge (Titanium, #1)

Scarred by Vengeance (Titanium, #2)

Ruined in Retribution (Titanium, #3)

Complete Box Set

Falling Duology - YA contemporary romance

Falling by Design

Edge of Falling